ADVANCE PRAISE FOR *ABHAYA*

"An excitingly different take on one of the myriad legends celebrating the light versus darkness matrix that defines Diwali. The sparkling narration adds new facets to the compelling tale of the killing of the demon Narakasur."

—Sangeeta Bahadur, *Ambassador of India to the Republic of Belarus*

"*Abhaya* will inspire you to be who you are, whoever you are. Read it, and get everyone you know to read it too."

—Professor Vamsee Juluri, *Professor of Media Studies at the University of San Francisco and the Author of* Rearming Hinduism: Nature, Hinduphobia, and the Return of Indian Intelligence

ABHAYA

ABHAYA

The Destroyer of Adharma

Saiswaroopa Iyer

BLOOMSBURY
NEW DELHI • LONDON • OXFORD • NEW YORK • SYDNEY

BLOOMSBURY INDIA
Bloomsbury Publishing India Pvt. Ltd
Second Floor, LSC Building No. 4, DDA Complex, Pocket C – 6 & 7,
Vasant Kunj, New Delhi 110070

First published in India 2022
This edition published 2022

ISBN: PB: 978-93-54351-04-4; e-Book: 978-93-54351-10-5
2 4 6 8 10 9 7 5 3 1

Typeset in Fournier MT Std by Manipal Technologies Limited
Printed and bound in India

narayanam nirakaram naraviram narottamam
nrsimham naganatham cha tam vande narakantakam
I Praise him
The essence of mankind; the bravest and best among men;
The lion among men; the saviour of the elephant
(Gajendra);
The annihilator of Naraka

—Hari Namamala Stotram

Map of Jambudvipa or Ancient Vedic India

Notes:

Only those ancient cities where significant events of the story take place are shown in the map.

The map is redrawn based on multiple references and is not to scale. The author is not responsible for inadvertent errors that might have crept in during the process of redrawing.

For a more accurate map of Ancient Bharatavarsha with all the kingdoms, please refer to http://www.mapsofindia.com/history/mahajanapadas.html.

Anagha is a fictional kingdom.

CONTENTS

AUTHOR'S NOTE

My love for Krishna started when I was on the threshold of adolescence. The same love drove me to find him in the literature presented by many learned scholars and the compositions of Indian bards. In my quest, I found my flute holder grow up to become a kingmaker, a philosopher and a yugapurusha. Accordingly, my feelings transformed from infatuation to reverence to continuous enquiry (jignaasa). I revere Krishna today as one of the first architects of a unified India. Yes, I believe he did exist in the obscure history of India.

This story is a manifestation of my fantasies, thoughts and observations around Krishna. It explores the *Narakasura vadha*. This is an episode that has a rich variety of narratives in scriptures like *Srimat Bhagavatam*, *Vishnu Puranam*, *Harivamsham* and even the legends and folklore from Assam.

Narakasura vadha is an important milestone in our scriptures, for it extols the valour of Satyabhama, the wife of Krishna. With Abhaya, I made this audacious attempt to relook at the episode from the point of view of a fictional protagonist and, in this endeavour, I may have shifted the spotlight off Goddess Satyabhama. But the compassionate goddess that she is, Satyabhama, the incarnation of Goddess Bhumi, has given me nothing but her blessings all through. The fact that the story could reach completion itself is an assurance of her compassion.

Though the early drafts of the story sprung from the surge of defence which built up in me when I heard people deny or criticise Krishna, the current version is inspired by my strong belief that everyone can be a Krishna in their own capacity once they find their purpose. For this, I have consciously avoided giving Krishna a superhuman quality. It is not that I deny his divinity. Instead, I maintain that his divinity does not necessarily need magic. Quoting the parable of Sri Ramakrishna Paramahamsa where a group of blind children touch only some specific part of an elephant's body and draw their own conclusions, I seek to explore a minute part of the enigmatic personality that is Krishna.

Creative liberty is not something new to Indic literature. In the medieval period, the aspect of Prabandha became popular in Telugu literature. Prabandha is a literary piece that explores and expounds a Puranic episode, taking generous liberties with the versions in the root scriptures. They explore human angles of thought and often look at Puranic episodes from the perspectives of fictional or obscure characters. They are judged by the depth of the thought and philosophy they churn out than by the so-called authenticity of the events.

It would be audacious of me to say or even think that this attempt of mine is a modern Prabandha. But I would want to thank those Telugu poets in the last millennium who laid strong foundations for taking creative liberties to get closer to the gods and goddesses we worship. As a very humble tribute, I have named some characters in *Abhaya* after the names of protagonists in different Telugu Prabandhas, such as Kalapurnodayam. I hope our prized legacy of creative liberty continues till the end of time.

Talking about the literary giants whose legacy I inherited being a fortunate child of this Bharatavarsha, I remember Sri K.M. Munshi, the founder of the Bharatiya Vidya Bhavan, whose 'Krishnavatara' series was my prime inspiration in feeling and experiencing Krishna from novel angles. In fact, I borrowed some of his concepts about Nagas and Garudas being tribes that worshipped legendary serpents and eagles.

This story—a fictional reimagination of Puranic episodes of the *Srimad Bhagavatam* and other Puranas—explores the *Narakasura vadha* from the perspective of a fictional female protagonist, Abhaya Dhaarmaseni. Be it curiosity, adventure, love or realisation, Abhaya has been my window to explore and experience Krishna Vaasudeva. I hope the readers find her delightful too.

LIST OF CHARACTERS

Krishna Vaasudeva	The eighth avatar of Lord Vishnu in the Dwapara Yuga, Krishna Vaasudeva is the champion of dharma and a Yadava leader in Dwaraka

Anagha

Abhaya Dhaarmaseni	Princess of the city of Anagha
Dharmasena	King of Anagha
Vasumati	Queen of Anagha and wife of Dharmasena, Mother of Abhaya
Vikramasena/ Vikrama	Dharmasena's adopted son
Vajrabahu	Senapati
Katyayana	Priest
Pingala Katyayani	The priest's daughter

Kamarupa

Bhauma	Lord of Kamarupa
Dhatri	Chief yogini at Kamarupa; referred to as Mahadevi
Mura	Senapati of Kamarupa

Others

Subhadra	Sister of Krishna (Indraprastha)
Kadambari	Sister of Naga Chief Varahaka, biological mother of Vikramasena and a Shakta Yogini
Vamanatha	Kadambari's Shakta guru
Anuvinda	Prince of Avanti, which border the state of Anagha
Mitravinda	Sister of Anuvinda, princess of Avanti and wife of Krishna
Vainateya	King of Garudas (Gomantaka)
Shyeni	Sister of Vainateya (Gomantaka)

Chapter One

Borders of Pundra, Eastern Bharatavarsha

Lightning. It seemed like the skies had decided to shred the land to pieces. The horses pulling the lone chariot on the highway to Pragjyotisha neighed in fear and slowed to a trot.

"Just what we needed!" Mura remarked, cracking the whip. "It wasn't a wise idea to come without the guards." His wavy hair fluttered, loosening the cloth he had wound around his head.

"The Supreme Goddess Kamaksha has Her ways, doesn't She, Mura?" said Bhauma, the lord of Kamarupa. He balanced himself against the chariot's flagpole as he tightened his silk headgear.

To Mura, his tone seemed unnaturally calm. He sighed, shaking his head. They were returning from the temple of Goddess Tara in the kingdom of Pundra. For reasons not known to Mura, Bhauma always insisted on going without guards while visiting the Shakta temples. Pundra, at least, was not very far away from Kamarupa and was a sympathetic kingdom.

"But Prabho, in the future if you want to travel to the other temples of Shakti which are farther away, would you still want to travel without a guard?"

Bhauma nodded without a trace of hesitation.

"If you say so, My Lord," Mura shrugged and goaded the horses on, wanting to reach Kamarupa as fast as they could. The skies showed all the signs of an approaching storm.

"No," Bhauma smiled, stretching his arms. Into his forties, he had a physique that could daunt any warrior. "Not because I say so. But, because the Goddess does. Say we are caught in the storm. That, too, is Her will. In time, we shall realise She willed it for the best."

It would have made a good speech for a gathering in the temple, Mura felt.

"I am not capable of that kind of faith," he replied. "Your faith does not surprise me, though, Prabho. Not everybody would have been content with a lordship of a mere temple town over the kingdom of Pragjyotisha."

"Mere temple, Mura?" Bhauma retorted. "It is the temple of the Supreme Goddess Kamaksha who rules the three—heaven, earth and nether—worlds. Lordship over Kamarupa means the lordship over this world."

Is that ambition or mere faith? Mura wondered.

"For now, your nephew has got a larger territory under his control. What did the Supreme Goddess give *you*, Prabho?"

"Is land everything, Mura? The people standing by me are my greater boon," Bhauma said and smiled. Mura stared back at him, touched, as Bhauma's hand rested on his shoulder. "Don't look at me like that! People are more valuable than land, Mura. If someone is ready to stand by me from the shores to the plains of Bharatavarsha, then a part of Bharatavarsha belongs to me as well."

Mura nodded mutely. Bhauma's words always felt inscrutable. But that was the way of men who took to religion, he told himself. The road took a sharp turn and Mura tightened his hold on the reins. His eyes narrowed at the sight of a crowd in the distance. *At this time of night?*

Bhauma did not speak as his eyes too trained on the crowd ahead on the road. "They are moving. Is it a procession for some Goddess?"

He sees the Goddess everywhere. Mura stifled a smile. The smile faded as they rode closer. This was no peaceful procession. It was a mob. "They are chasing someone!"

"Faster!" Bhauma ordered.

"They are armed!" Mura gasped as the moon briefly came out of the cloud cover. "We should be at the borders of Pundra and close to Pragjyotisha." His right hand that held the whip instinctively went to the long sword at his waist. The chariot drew closer to the crowd.

One of the villagers was lagging behind and they heard him shout, "Kill them! This must be a lesson to others!"

Bhauma asked Mura to slow down as they drew level to him. "What is the matter?"

"My nephew's widow, the wretch! She is eloping with that doctor, the son of a whore!"

"We should help them," Mura spoke softly, catching the sight of a man and a woman running from the maddened crowd. "But we will be outnumbered greatly!"

"Just keep going," Bhauma ordered as the horses forced a path through the crowds. He raised his staff at a villager who tried to get into the chariot.

"Catch them for us! Save the honour of our village, please!" someone else shouted.

Mura and Bhauma pretended to take no notice and plunged ahead. The woman was slowing the man down. In a matter of moments, the enraged crowd would be upon them. He felt Bhauma's hand on his shoulder.

"Pull them aboard!" Bhauma shouted as he snatched the whip and reins from Mura. They rode ahead of the couple. "The woman first!"

Mura extended a hand. "Come with us! We want to help you!"

The couple looked at each other in confusion but kept running. A crude knife missed the woman by inches. The man looked shocked as he turned back and saw the crowds catching up. He pushed the woman ahead towards the chariot. Mura caught her and pulled her aboard. The man also extended his hand. The woman fell upon Bhauma.

"Easy!" he shouted, looking back. The frenzied villagers had realised their motive. One of them threw a knife that pierced Mura's shoulder just as he caught the man's hand.

"Amaranatha!" the woman shouted, extending her hand too.

"Careful!" Bhauma pulled her back. A stone hit him. "Quick, Mura!" he shouted.

Mura leaned out, clutching the flagstaff of the chariot for support. "Faster!" He called out to Amaranatha.

The woman screamed something which both the men could not comprehend.

Bhauma suddenly pulled Mura back. "I'll get him. Handle the reins."

"He won't make it!" the woman screamed.

"I've got him!" Bhauma stepped back and bent over. He latched onto the man's hand. "Now!"

Mura cracked the whip and the horses picked up speed. The man placed one foot on the chariot but stumbled before he could put his second.

Another rock hit Bhauma, making him lose his grip on Amaranatha's hand.

"No!" The woman screamed as Amaranatha fell to the ground.

"Prabho!" Mura shouted as Bhauma stumbled back in pain.

"Stop the chariot! Help him!" the woman shouted. Her eyes widened as she saw the villagers pull Amaranatha back.

Mura's despairing glance alternated between the bleeding Bhauma and the fallen Amaranatha who had been already surrounded by the irate villagers.

"Kill them all!" some of the villagers shouted, chasing the chariot. Mura's hand instinctively cracked the whip.

"No! Spare him! I beg you, spare him!" the woman attempted to dismount only to be caught by a weakened Bhauma. "Let me go!"

"They'll kill us all!" he screamed, holding her back.

"I don't care!" she spat, fighting his grip. "Spare him please!" she shouted at the villagers as knives and stones rained upon them.

"Faster, Mura!" Bhauma screamed. Mura cracked the whip again.

As the distance increased, the mob behind them parted and they could see the blood-drenched frame of

Amaranatha on the ground. “You should have saved him and left me to die!”

The woman grabbed his sword and attempted to dismount again. “Demons! I’ll kill them all!” Mura too had to hold her back as he saw Bhauma weaken further. “I’ll drink each one’s blood!” she screamed.

“There are more than fifty of them!” Mura shouted, cracking the whip again.

“Cowards! Both of you!” she spat at Bhauma.

“We tried our best!” Mura protested, seeing Bhauma’s eyes close in shame. “My lord almost lost his life trying to help you!”

“Then just let me die!” the woman screamed and collapsed in hysteric sobs.

The chariot sped towards Kamarupa. When the woman regained consciousness, it was almost dawn. The hills of Kamarupa rose before them.

“He is dead by now, isn’t he?” she asked.

“Forgive us,” Bhauma said.

She sighed in response and banged her head against the flagpole of the chariot.

“No, Devi, no!” Bhauma held her by her shoulders. “A woman’s blood cannot be spilt on this hill of Kamarupa. Goddess Kamaksha will never forgive me!”

“Why didn’t your Goddess save him? If anyone deserves to die, it is me! I was the one who asked him to take me away!”

“No, you don’t deserve to die!” Bhauma replied.

“He didn’t either!” the woman retorted. “My Amaranatha was a vaidya. His whole life was dedicated to helping others, to saving lives.” She pulled out a bundle tucked into her lower garment. “See these herbs? They can save anyone even from the dreadful Shivajvara! My Amara concocted the formula!"

"Those demons in the plains, they didn't deserve him amongst them," Bhauma replied. "But Devi, the Supreme Goddess kept you alive for a reason; trust Her."

"Just shut up!" she snapped.

"Enough now!" Mura shouted. Bhauma held up his hand to silence him but he went on, lowering his voice. "We are as sad about not being able to save him. But my lord does not deserve your anger."

They had reached the gates of Kamarupa, which opened to give them admittance.

"Welcome to Kamarupa," Bhauma said. The woman shrank back as the city guards surrounded the chariot.

"Our honoured guest..." Bhauma turned to the woman, not knowing her name.

"Dhatri," she whispered.

"Devi Dhatri. Treat her as the divine responsibility given by the Goddess herself." Bhauma alighted from the chariot, extending his hand to her. Dhatri pulled her ragged upper garment around herself. "Trust me, you shall not face any trouble in the land of the Supreme Goddess," Bhauma promised her.

Mura followed them inside. In the light of the sun, something about Dhatri intrigued him. For a villager, she possessed the gait of a queen.

The temple of Kamaksha, with its majestic pyramidal tower, ornate pillars and intricately sculpted walls, was designed as a representation of the universal court presided by the Supreme Goddess Kamaksha. The sanctum stood over a high pedestal overlooking a hall large enough to house a gathering of several hundred. The shrine was a sanctified rock and revered as the yoni, the primal womb of the Supreme Goddess.

"It is the very reason behind the sustenance of life and creation. We exist because She wills," Bhauma had explained when Dhatri had first visited the temple.

Dhatri's eyes, however, were fixed on a life-size metallic sculpture of the Goddess beside the main sanctum, whose eyes glowed in the light of the lamps. The lips of the statue suggested a smile. But the eyes carried an inscrutable spark. They continued to hold her gaze every time she visited the temple. The first time she had seen the statue, she had inexplicably broken down into tears. The gaze daunted her. At the same time, Dhatri could not resist staring at the statue for hours. Even after a month at Kamarupa, her fascination for those eyes only seemed to increase. She took no notice of the sprawling temple surroundings or the intricate sculptures that caught the attention of the usual pilgrims. The gaze signalled assurance. It also signalled stern scrutiny.

"Devi Dhatri?"

She turned, startled, and found Mura staring at her.

"Relax," Mura said, holding up his hands reassuringly. Her eyes, he felt, were like that of a doe that had seen a tiger. "You have been standing here for over an hour. Are you alright?"

She blinked and gave a slight nod. Her bosom heaved.

A momentary flutter ran down his body and Mura averted his gaze. "I wanted to apologise for being harsh that day."

Dhatri nodded again. She managed a smile at the plea in Mura's eyes.

"Apologising after a month! Quite a sense of timing," Bhauma said, exiting the sanctum and approaching them. Mura bowed.

Dhatri's hands joined in salutation. "I … I was harsh too. I should be…"

"No!" Bhauma interrupted, making her look up. "You shall not apologise, Devi Dhatri. I have to say that you were looking quite a personification of rage that day." A smile played on his lips. Dhatri's fearful demeanour after coming to Kamarupa, a complete contrast to her hysterical self the day her lover had been killed, had intrigued him.

Dhatri shook her head. Something made her shiver and it was visible to both the men. "I was not myself that day. But I am afraid it was not wise of you to save me. My family is powerful. What if they find me and attack with a force?"

Bhauma wanted to laugh but restrained himself.

"No danger shall befall you here. They can only enter this temple town over my corpse," Mura asserted and bowed, his hand gripping the hilt of his sword.

"She might find it easier to trust you when you are at your post," Bhauma said.

Mura looked at him apologetically and stepped back before he left for the gates. Bhauma smiled and turned to Dhatri. "I would actually agree with him. No danger shall befall you here in this temple town of Kamaksha.

This is a well-fortified place. And, above all, we are under the protection of the Supreme Shakti Kamaksha."

"Prabho..." Dhatri was about to utter a word of gratitude but stopped when she saw Bhauma's outstretched hand.

"Could I show you around the temple?" Bhauma moved a step closer.

Dhatri nodded, swallowing. He reached out and held her hand. She did not resist but avoided his eyes. A mild shiver ran through her frame.

Bhauma waited a moment and loosened his grip. "Maybe some other day," he said.

Dhatri looked up as his hand withdrew. With an inaudible sigh, she turned the other way. The sight that greeted her eyes at the left wing of the sanctum made her gasp and turn around, bumping into Bhauma.

"What's the matter?"

"There! That man and woman!" Dhatri exclaimed. "In the temple!"

Bhauma led her out of the temple by her arm. "Maithuna, the ritual of union," he explained. They descended the stairs of the sanctum towards the lower hall of the temple. "Our ways, Devi, are different from those in the plains. I shall not be surprised if they shock you."

"How is sexual union considered a ritual? Is it not an affront to the Goddess?" Dhatri took a step away from him, smelling wine on Bhauma's breath.

"On the contrary, it is the most exalted of all the rituals." Bhauma pointed to a series of rock sculptures. "We, the worshippers of Shakti, the Supreme Goddess, don't believe in abstinence."

Dhatri moved towards the sculptures, each of which indicated a Shakta ritual. "Are these all rituals? The wine, the meat…" Her hands moved across the rock. The statue of the Goddess having commanded her attention in the past month, her gaze had not fallen on these depictions. "Prabho, I want to know more."

"On one condition," Bhauma said, stepping by her side. "Call me by my name."

He sought an answer to an unasked question and laid his hand on top of the one that was feeling the sculptures. When Dhatri turned to nod, her eyes gave him what he sought.

Chapter Two

Anagha, Western Bharatavarsha

The night was long, even more so for someone whose wife was in labour. Dharmasena moved his seat closer to the couch where Vasumati lay. She was in pain. He put his arm around Vasumati and helped her into an upright position, with her back resting against the headrest of the cot. He pointed at the cradle that was being readied by two maids. In the light of the lamps, the cradle gave new hope. The couple looked at each other and smiled through the apprehension.

The midwife's hurried steps spoke more of her eagerness to deliver the heir to the throne than of concern but one look at Queen Vasumati brought a frown to her face.

Through her pain, the queen clasped Dharmasena's hand and placed it over her womb. "I wish your heir arrives today, Dharma."

"A princess is as welcome, Devi." Dharmasena pressed his hand gently against her belly. The past months had seen bittersweet debates between them, with Vasumati wanting a boy and Dharmasena wishing for a girl.

"No, I shall not last beyond this..." Vasumati gripped his hand tight as another contraction racked her body. She let out a scream.

"Vasumati!"

The midwife took the liberty to lay a hand on Dharmasena's shoulder.

"Prabho, your presence might be of little help."

The sheer concern in her tone made him rise to his feet, his heart beating faster.

He took himself to the corridor, Vasumati's moans piercing through his heart. The priest, Katyayana, was waiting for him.

The tense look on the king's face told Katyayana everything. He smiled and showed the king his astrological charts which he hoped would partially shift Dharmasena's attention.

"The queen's chart shows signs of a girl child, Annadata," Katyayana began, "but yours says you will beget a daughter and a son."

"Twins? No wonder Vasumati is undergoing such pain!" Dharmasena exclaimed, his joy and concern doubling.

Katyayana hesitated at the inconsistency that had struck him ever since he began the astrological calculations. In his vast experience, the priest had seen a lot of ambiguous predictions and had seen how reality sometimes deviated from what was foretold in the stars. That had made him objective about the whole process of calculation and prediction. But he cited this anomaly only when the predictions turned out to be disappointing to the ones seeking it. A scream from the inner chambers made his heart skip a beat. The silence following the scream was excruciating. The two men stood rooted to the spot. Then they heard it. The bawling of an infant. Dharmasena breathed in.

"Jayatu Anagheshwari!" He and the priest called out in unison to the guardian goddess of the fortress after whom the city was named.

The midwife brought the infant out to the corridor. "It is a princess, Prabho!"

"My little queen!" Dharmasena took the infant into his arms and looked at her with wonder and joy. "And the queen?" The king turned anxiously to the midwife.

"She is exhausted beyond the limits, Prabho. "I need to go back to her." Dharmasena's face fell as she retreated into the chambers.

Katyayana felt a momentary shudder pass through his spine, remembering a detail about the queen's horoscope. *The following month is critical!* "Anagheshwari!" he whispered, not wanting to increase Dharmasena's worries by voicing his fears.

Dharmasena cradled the newborn, his heart leaping every time he saw her move in his arms. The infant settled into his warmth and her cries faded into drowsiness. Her half-closed eyes rested on her father.

"Father's pet!" Katyayana exclaimed, touched at the mist in Dharmasena's eyes. "She is going to take after you, Dharma!" Dharmasena was too taken by the infant to notice the personal address. The priest smiled and continued, "She will excel at anything she sets her heart upon! But the planets choose to show me more about her heart. Fearless to the core, she will become the shelter, the refuge, for many. She will travel across the breadth of Bharatavarsha. Her company will comprise royalty, nobility and commoners. In other words, she will take after you, My King."

Fearless, shelter, refuge. The words fell upon Dharmasena's ears the very moment he saw the tiny lips curve into a smile.

"Abhaya," he said. "Abhaya, the daughter of Dharmasena"

"Abhaya Dhaarmaseni!" Katyayana raised both his hands in blessing.

"Prabho!" The voice rang in the corridor. "Has the heir prince arrived?" Senapati Vajrabahu's words greeted them even before he turned the corner into the corridor.

"It is a princess, Senapati," Katyayana corrected him.

"Mahakala has sent his spouse to illuminate Anagha!" Vajrabahu remarked, removing a string of pearls from his neck and making a circular movement with it over the newborn's head. He dropped the string into a large plate placed on the table with some jewels already on it for the palace maids to take as their due.

"Quite the time to come, Vajrabahu!" Dharmasena frowned. "Right after I went through the excruciating wait, all alone. Some friendship this is."

"Forgive me, Dharmasena. My king and lord had placed a responsibility on me to cover his absence during the night and I was just caught up there. I could not be by my friend's side." Vajrabahu alternated his tone between intimacy and formality, making Dharmasena laugh.

"All well, Senapati?"

Vajrabahu nodded. "The city shall wake up to the celebrations now." His face turned serious as he sought Dharmasena's eye. "Prabho. Someone wants to see you."

"At this hour?"

"It is Kadambari, the sister of the Naga chief, Varahaka. The guard would not have entertained anyone else."

Dharmasena became thoughtful. The Naga chief of the small neighbouring settlement was an important friend and he knew Kadambari too.

"She came with her son. I did not have the heart to refuse, looking at her state." Vajrabahu added.

"What state?"

Vajrabahu looked to the corner and clapped. He then turned to the king and whispered, "I noticed welts on her body. Her husband seems to have..."

"What! How dare he..." Dharmasena's eyes widened in disbelief and anger. The sound of anklets made him stop mid-sentence. "Kadambari?" His lips parted as he saw the frail woman approach them. Clad in the usual Naga attire, her shoulders, waist and legs were visible. So were the red marks all over. "Bhagini!"

"Prabho!" Kadambari's voice broke as she bent low. Her eyes fell on the newborn. "Prince ... princess." She began to unfasten a silver bracelet on her left hand, the only jewellery on her.

Dharmasena raised his hand shaking his head. "Who had the bad sense to harm you, Bhagini?"

"Who else?" Kadambari replied. "The man my brother chose to seal my fate with." Fresh tears sprung to her eyes. "I have had enough of this, Bhrata!"

Vajrabahu, seeing the king's joy of becoming a father fade away, intervened and turned to Kadambari. "Stay here in the city, Bhagini, till the ceremonies are complete. You shall be well cared for. We shall then knock some sense into the hard skull of that imbecile who treats you this way."

But Kadambari's eyes were resolute. They remained fixed on the king. "You call me your sister, Prabho, so I ask this favour of you. Care for my ten-year-old. I am leaving this province and that man for good."

Through her apparent weak voice, the three men heard the steely resolve in those words. The solution for a troubled marriage was a social puzzle to which no scripture offered an easy solution. Scriptures had their solutions and their implementation was the prerogative of the rulers, each of them finding his corollaries specific to each case. Dharmasena's eyes sought Katyayana's.

"We cannot stop her, given her claims. Neither by scripture, nor by jurisdiction." Katyayana said, sensing Dharmasena's potential worries. The Naga chief and his brother-in-law would have no justification to blame the king for not stopping her from leaving.

"Where will you go, Kadambari?" Dharmasena asked.

"To the south of Vindhyas, to the ashrama of my guru," Kadambari replied. "He is of the Shakta order," she added, her voice now reduced to the whisper.

Dharmasena's brows rose, as did Vajrabahu's, and the latter whispered, "The Vaamaacharis!"

"Manikandhara!" Kadambari called. A small boy stepped forward. "This is my son. I trust none but you, Prabho! I fear to leave him at the mercy of my husband."

The boy stared at the surroundings, at the unfamiliar people. Dharmasena called him closer and the boy looked at his mother. She nodded. He walked up to the king and felt Vajrabahu's comforting hand on his shoulder.

Dharmasena saw the boy's eyes full of unshed tears. A red welt on the boy's shoulder sent a shudder down his spine. *What kind of a brute would think of hurting a child this young? Kadambari has every right to leave such a husband.*

"I shall take leave, Bhrata." Kadambari bowed. "Stay joyful and live long, Manikandhara," so saying, she hugged the boy and left.

"Amba!" Manikandhara called out. But he remained where he was.

Dharmasena knelt to match the boy's height and smiled. "Welcome to your new home, Vatsa. None shall harm you here." He saw Manikandhara's tearful eyes drift to the newborn Abhaya. Dharmasena felt that the sight of the newborn would distract the boy from breaking into tears. The words came out without conscious thought, "Your younger sister."

"Prabho!" Vajrabahu gasped. "Are you adopting him?"

Dharmasena's eyes conveyed a sense of surprise at his own words. The surprise then gave way to pride and he nodded.

Katyayana's eyes widened in realisation as his calculations made sudden sense to him. Heedless of the reactions of the rest in the room, he strode up to the terrace to catch the movement of the stars as dawn approached. The excitement in his eyes was visible when he returned.

"A daughter and a son," Katyayana said. "Mother Anagheshwari has sent you a son too, Annadata."

Six Years Later

The sight of eastern skies at sunrise made Dharmasena's heart glad, as did the cloud of dust that appeared on the horizon.

"When is bhrata coming?" Abhaya tugged at his arm.

Dharmasena beamed at her and lifted her in his arms, pointing at the cloud of the dust signalling the approaching rider.

"Will he teach me to wield a sword, Janaka?"

Dharmasena nodded. "When you grow this tall." He indicated a height that was more than a foot taller than her current height.

"When will I grow that big?"

Her questions never seemed to end. The spark in Abhaya's eyes brought back vivid memories of his deceased queen, making him swallow. Vasumati had not lived long after Abhaya's birth. But, in Abhaya, Dharmasena felt her virtual presence. Ignoring the question, he kissed her forehead.

"Reserve some love for the boy too, Prabho!" Vajrabahu remarked, playfully ruffling Abhaya's short plait. "I think he needs that."

Dharmasena nodded. Left under Dharmasena's care six years ago, the young Naga boy, Manikandhara, was given the name Vikramasena after the ceremonial adoption. Vasumati and he had seen their joy double. But it had been short-lived. The queen had developed complications and had succumbed barely a couple of months after giving birth to Abhaya. The tragedy had not left Dharmasena with much enthusiasm for bonding with the boy. At Katyayana's suggestion, he had sent Vikrama to the gurukula at Avanti, the place where he had studied. Royal affairs and looking after Abhaya had kept Dharmasena occupied and enabled him to get over Vasumati's death. The mixed account he had received about Vikrama's progress had left him partly guilty and partly concerned. While the boy's progress in martial arts was more than satisfactory, his interest in political education was reportedly low. The boy who displayed utmost agility in duelling with opponents more accomplished than himself lacked the initiative that the other princes in the gurukula had. While his teachers admired his honesty, humility and compassionate outlook, they found him lagging in multiple behavioural aspects required in a king. They opined that his troubled childhood was a probable cause for these limitations and felt that an opportunity to bond with his adopted father would help him gain the confidence he needed. Seeing the sense in this, Dharmasena had summoned Vikrama back from the gurukula, resolving to focus his attentions on his daughter and son alike.

"There!" Abhaya squealed, pointing to the horses that stopped at the gates. "Vikrama is as tall as you!"

"*Bhrata* Vikrama," Dharmasena corrected, letting her jump to the ground. Abhaya leapt down the stairs and ran towards the approaching Vikrama.

The moment left Dharmasena stunned. Had Vikrama been his biological son, he realised to his regret, he would not be standing at the threshold; instead, he would have greeted him at the gates. Abhaya had been a newborn when Vikrama came into their lives and her acceptance of the fraternal bond was natural. Smiling to himself, Dharmasena followed his daughter's lead to see Vikrama lift her into his arms and walk towards him.

The boy, true to what Dharmasena had been told, had everything to make a father proud. His lanky physique spoke of the agility he was capable of on the battlefield, something his teachers had praised effusively. He restrained Vikrama from touching his feet and drew him into an embrace. He was not sure how warm it was but told himself that it would only get better. What he saw in Vikrama's eyes allayed his concerns.

Formal introductions to all the key people in Anagha's affairs were made. Vajrabahu sensed Dharmasena's restlessness and offered to take care of the rest of the day's proceedings, leaving the royal family to bond over their morning meal.

"First, tell us a story, Janaka," Abhaya demanded as they entered the dining hall.

Usually, Dharmasena fed her personally before he ate himself. This was a habit he indulged in religiously as this was the time he got to quench his daughter's never-ending thirst for stories. This was, he had found, as effective a way as any to impart the values and codes of Aryadharma in more inspiring ways. And she was not the only one learning. Abhaya's questions were innocent, yet pertinent, often forcing him to rethink age-old legends and the way they were narrated.

"Vikrama, do you know stories?" She asked, turning to him. Abhaya hated to wait for long once her mind thirsted for a story.

"What did I tell you about addressing your elders?" Dharmasena raised a finger.

Abhaya sighed, "Bhrata Vikrama."

"How would you address Senapati Vajrabahu?"

"Arya Vajrabahu."

"And the priest?"

"Acharya Katyayana." Dharmasena took the opportunity to shove the ball of boiled rice into her mouth. But Abhaya proved to be too agile and dodged. "Story!" she demanded.

Dharmasena shook his head and turned to Vikrama. "Why don't you ask bhrata to tell you one?"

"Tell me a story, Bhrata," she pleaded as she turned to Vikrama, perching herself on a windowsill, beckoning him closer.

Dharmasena could not help noticing her natural way of bonding. A thought struck him as he called Vikrama to sit beside her. "Vikrama, tell us what you learnt about our city and the story of your great-grandfather."

"Virasena," Vikrama started, watching Dharmasena feed Abhaya the first ball of rice. They exchanged smiles, as he continued, "Our great-grandfather was a soldier in the army of Avanti, the neighbouring mahajanapada. He was married to Indusmita, the daughter of a trader."

"Our great-grandmother," Abhaya added. "When they came here, this city was not built. They lived in a forest. Wild animals..."

"Vatse," Dharmasena interrupted, this time successfully feeding her the second ball of rice.

Vikrama smiled to himself and continued. "Great-grandmother's brother was brutally killed by robbers when he was travelling to Saurashtra. The lack of any action on the part of the erstwhile king of Avanti troubled great-grandfather a lot and, with a band of trusted followers, he left the service of the king. The couple came here with their five-year-old son, Vikramasena." Vikrama paused, dwelling on the fact that Dharmasena had given him the name of his father. "They set up a camp that provided a safe haven for traders. The initial years were beset with unpleasant encounters with robbers and wild animals. Great-grandmother died fighting a leopard."

"Grandfather Vikramasena was brave and fought with hyenas at the age of ten. He ate pulses, roots and vegetables without complaining. After he grew up, he built the inner wall." Abhaya pointed outside the window. Dharmasena gave up trying to stop her interruptions. His attention had shifted to Vikrama now. On a whim, he scooped out a bigger ball of rice and pointed it to Vikrama's mouth. The boy's eyes widened as he stared at him for a moment.

"Aaa..." Abhaya prompted him to open his mouth, rejoicing that her eating burden would now be reduced. When Vikrama opened his mouth, Dharmasena knew that he had done the right thing in calling him back. Parenting, he sighed to himself, came with many more lessons than managing kingly affairs.

A new beginning, he told himself as Abhaya and Vikrama took turns in eating and in narrating the story.

"And remember, the kingdom of Avanti is our most important ally," Dharmasena prompted. Vikrama nodded.

"No." Abhaya protested. "When we went there for Maashivaratri, that prince, Anuvinda, called our city an oversized inn."

"I heard the same from him several times in the gurukula!" Vikrama exclaimed as he recounted his first year there, when Anuvinda, the prince of Avanti, graduated.

"They are not our friends," Abhaya concluded.

"And Princess Mitravinda?" Dharmasena asked her.

"She is my friend," Abhaya agreed.

"Then how can you say that they are not our friends?"

Abhaya looked at him for a while and chose not to answer. She instead opened her mouth, asking for more rice, clearly wanting a distraction from the conversation. She then turned to Vikrama. "I shall tell you the story of Queen Vishpala and how she fought the enemy with an injured leg. She lost her leg but then the gods gave her an iron leg and she fought the robbers." She gauged the level of interest in Vikrama's face with the summary before she nodded and started her narration.

Dharmasena smiled to himself. Avanti as a kingdom was too important a neighbour to overlook. Abhaya and even Vikrama were too young to understand the extent to which Anagha depended on the bigger kingdom. Understanding political dynamics aside, he wanted his children to bond together, something he felt he had achieved. The next day, he decided to tell them about the friends of this city, the Nagas, and of Anagheshwari, the spouse of Rishi Dattatreya, who was worshipped as the guardian goddess of the city.

Chapter Three

Four Years Later

"The ritual Friday worship of Anagheshwari!" Abhaya tugged at Dharmasena's arm. "Did you forget, Janaka?"

Dharmasena smiled to himself, knowing that his ten-year-old had her heart set on the games she played with Katyayana's adopted daughter after the worship at the temple. Pursing his lips, he said, "You will have to do it by yourself today. I am tired after patrolling the highway to Prabhasa all night." Keeping the highway secure for the travellers was a task his family had religiously followed. By his time, Dharmasena had sufficient military personnel to carry out the task but he made it a point to personally participate in patrolling the way to Prabhasa every two to three months. The recent reports of robbers waylaying the pilgrims and increased crime required his intervention more frequently.

"Should I?" Abhaya asked, raising her brows. Her father's absence during the worship meant a lot of things, the most disappointing of which was that she would not be able to sneak away in the middle. On the other hand, the act of standing beside Acharya Katyayana and participating in the ritual did make her feel incredibly important. She nodded at him. "And bhrata?"

"He should be coming to the temple directly. He was on highway patrol duty too..." Dharmasena paused, looking at the eastern skies through the window. "He might have returned by now. But you must perform the worship."

Abhaya nodded, tossing her long plait over her shoulder. She took her father's leave and made her way to the king's chariot, her personal maid following with a large brass plate containing vermilion, turmeric and other paraphernalia of worship.

"Take the guards with you."

Abhaya slowed down. Taking the guards meant reduced freedom to play after the puja. She pretended not to hear and darted forward, ignoring the maid's plea. Jumping onto the chariot, Abhaya opened one of the jars that had already been placed on the chariot; the sweet, warm aroma of payasaanna, a dish made by boiling grains in sweetened milk, wafted out.

"This should be sufficient even for the Nagas," she said. The Nagas, especially the younger ones, hiked to Anagha on Fridays to the temple in the latter part of the day. Abhaya had seen her father make sure that there was enough payasaanna to be distributed among all of them. Katyayana too insisted on generous servings of the sweet to everyone. Dharmasena's Friday worship was a ritual he preferred to complete before sunrise so that the everyday visitors to the temple were not inconvenienced.

Abhaya nodded to herself and the maid hid a smile. The maid and other womenfolk who worked in the royal quarters enjoyed seeing the princess inadvertently mimicking her father's mannerisms with comic precision. The chariot rode out of the gates of the inner city so early that Anagha was yet to start its day. It would take a couple of hours more for the markets to open. When they did, they would bustle with activity as traders from the mainland of Bharatavarsha and those who came from the shores of Saurashtra would display their wares to trade in the outer circle of the city. The lone chariot sped towards the outer gates and turned in the north-eastern direction towards the temple of Anagheshwari. They spotted no one on the way to the temple.

The day broke as they finally arrived. Abhaya jumped off the chariot and sprinted towards the temple. As she reached up to ring the bell at the entrance, her eyes fell on a prostrate figure covered with a long yellow cloth. Abhaya could only see his curls as he lay facing the wall of the temple, fast asleep.

Bhrata Vikrama. She desisted from ringing the bell and her lips curved mischievously. The maid and the charioteer were still unloading the jars of payasaanna and Acharya Katyayana was still not at the temple. The life-size idol of Anagheshwari caught her attention and she brought her finger to her lips, winking at the goddess. Noiselessly, she approached the sleeping figure on tiptoe. Stifling the giggles that were about to erupt out of her, Abhaya grabbed the dark curls and tugged them hard. The sleeping figure jerked awake.

"Wha..."

It wasn't Vikrama. Abhaya's grin faded and she backed away. "Who are you?"

The young man's dusky skin and curls had led her to mistake him for Vikrama. But now that his yellow shawl fell from his shoulders, she saw how different he was from her brother. His eyes, despite the rude interruption, had a spark that made him look as impish as a mischievous child. He looked at her with raised brows, displaying three distinct lines across his forehead.

"I am sorry! I ... I saw you from behind and thought you were my brother..." Abhaya stammered. The young man smiled and she instantly felt more at ease. The twinkle in his eye told her that he shared her appetite for pranks. She smiled and was about to say something when, unexpectedly, he grabbed her by the waist and pulled her over him to the other side. Abhaya gasped in surprise. But, before she could react, she noticed a third presence—a stranger just two paces away—behind her.

"Robbers!" she exclaimed. The young man rose to his feet, stepping in front of her, shielding her from the hostile lanky figure who brandished a sickle.

"You seem to be a traveller with nothing valuable. Turn her over to us and we shall not harm you!"

Us? It was then that Abhaya noticed three more dacoits emerge from the shadows. She heard loud bangs on the door of the room where Katyayana lived. The dacoits had locked him in. She then heard a scream from the palace maid outside. The charioteer rushed into the temple only to be overpowered by two of the dacoits while the other two approached the youth menacingly. The young man only chuckled in response, shaking his head.

"Boy, you are new to Saurashtra. Our enmity is not with you, but with her father who needs to be put in his place. Turn her over to us." The other dacoit came forward. His appearance was not too different from the rest. But his manner made it clear that he was the leader.

Abhaya glared at the dacoits. "My father protects the traders. My city is built to safeguard traders and travellers. It is you dacoits who need to be put into place and not he!"

"Shut up!" one of the dacoits snapped. "We will cut you into pieces and feed the vultures, girl. And you too, boy, if you try to act smart with us."

The youth stood his ground, the smile still on his face. The bandit closest to him lifted his sickle. Before anyone could realise he even had a weapon, the young man's sword stopped the sickle midair. The clang of metal on metal echoed in the hall. In the next moment, he had disarmed the bandit with a well-timed swing.

Abhaya gasped in surprise. It was two years since her military training started. She had become skilled at throwing short knives at stationary targets. Her lessons in holding a shield as a defensive weapon had just begun and she was yet to learn to wield a long sword. But she had watched many mock duels on the palace training grounds and she knew a skilled sword fighter when she saw one in action.

The youth's movements were calm and confident, his thrusts deadly in their precision. The bandit, apparently untrained except for his brute strength, was no match for him. The charioteer who had been struggling with two bandits let out a scream, as he was thrown to the ground and Abhaya turned her attention to him, drawing out her knife. The next moment, one of the two robbers was on the ground, clutching at his side in agony, and the charioteer was left with a single opponent. She was ecstatic for a moment—she had finally been able to put her lessons to use.

The youth was facing off with the leader of the gang. The younger robber who had been disarmed made for Abhaya. With her only weapon gone, Abhaya could only back away. Suddenly, the youth's sword came in between them, providing momentary relief. She glanced at the leader who was in a daze and dived in between the clashing men to retrieve the robber's sickle. She did not know how to wield it, though. After a moment's pause, she thrust the weapon into the hand of her unarmed charioteer who now had to contend with his lone adversary. She ran to Katyayana's room and unbolted the door. He emerged from the room and stood stunned at the chaos in the temple. The youth had now engaged all the three remaining bandits at once.

Abhaya watched him mesmerised. There was a curious absence of anger in the youth's eyes. Though he was surrounded, it was clear that he was unperturbed and that he had the upper hand. His movements were easy, even playful. It was almost as if he were toying with his adversaries, not fighting them. Katyayana, gathering his wits, went to the big bell that was hung at the corner of the temple. It was used to alert the soldiers in the city and the sound was different from the other bell that was rung during the usual worship. He rang the bell five times; the number of the rings was the code that would alert the guard at the fortress.

Almost at once, Vikrama came pounding up the steps.

"*Bhrata*!" Abhaya ran to him.

"What's happening here?" Vikrama drew his sword, taking in the scene. But, before he could intervene, two of the robbers fell to the ground and the youth disarmed their leader and held him at the point of his blade.

The soldiers who had arrived with Vikrama rushed to round them up.

"Thank you, Arya!" Vikrama said.

"For a moment, I thought that you are Mahadeva in human form, wielding a blade instead of a trident!" Katyanana exclaimed, clapping the youth on the shoulder.

"Can we know your name?" Abhaya asked, her gaze alternating between his face and his long sword.

He smiled, his eyes twinkling. "Two days back, someone named me Ranachora and, today, you named me Mahadeva." He laughed. "If my identity changes at this rate, I don't see any meaning in having a name."

"Did you say 'ranachora'? A coward? Who called you that?" Vikrama asked, his eyes widening in disbelief. "An expert swordsman like you!"

"What do your dear ones call you?" Abhaya persisted.

"Would you want to be one of them too?" the youth asked, nodding at Abhaya.

Vikrama stepped forward before she could reply. "Our father is Dharmasena, the king of this city Anagha."

"Did you say Anagha, city of the sinless?" His glance alternated between Vikrama and Abhaya. As Abhaya nodded, he continued. "Did a large group of Yadavas stop by here some days ago?"

"So, they are your dear ones," Abhaya said before responding. "Yes, they stopped by. Their leader's daughter, Subhadra, is now my friend. But they all left for the shore city two days ago."

"You are a Yadava then," Vikrama smiled. "Do come into the city and rest for a while, Veeragrani. We shall not press you to tell us your name if you don't want to."

"We shall find it out, though," Abhaya chirped, tossing her plait over her shoulder. "Krishna. Subhadra's brother." She smiled and knitted her brows. "Son of … Lord Vasudeva?"

Vikrama frowned. He remembered that Abhaya had grown friendly with the leading family of the Yadava group and had gathered quite a lot of trivia and insights, which he felt was inappropriate for someone her age.

"Abhaya Dhaarmaseni." Abhaya bowed and added, "And my elder brother, Vikramasena."

"Please," Vikramasena indicated the chariot, inviting Krishna to join them.

"Forgive me, Vikrama. I need to go towards the shores now," Krishna said. Before Vikrama could say anything, his gaze turned towards the robbers. "What awaits them?"

"Death, I think," Vikrama replied.

A gasp escaped the youngest of the robbers.

Krishna's eyes narrowed and put a hand on Vikrama's shoulder. "They were trying to abduct the princess so that they could 'settle scores' with our father for, I assume, fighting off their kind to protect the travellers and traders."

Vikrama looked at Abhaya and she nodded. He drew her close. A bandit attack in broad daylight was abhorrent in itself but an attempt to abduct Abhaya? It made his blood run cold. When he turned to look at Krishna, his eyes were moist.

"Send them to me, Yuvaraja," Krishna said. "Do make a request to the king on my behalf."

"Why? What will you do with them?" Abhaya asked, surprised.

"They shall not rob anyone from today and learn to make a living from hard labour or honest trade, Dhaarmaseni."

"That is not what they are used to, Vaasudeva. You hope to reform them?" Katyayana, who had been listening in silence, spoke.

"They were only afraid to leave what their forefathers did for a living, Acharya. Robbery looked legitimate to their ancestors when prosperity was a captive of brute power. But with the Yadavas settling on the shores of Saurashtra, we hope to usher in an era of trade that releases prosperity. In this new age, they should be given a chance to redeem themselves," Krishna said.

"What if they don't reform and continue in their old ways? What if they harm you or your people like they intended to harm us?" Katyayana argued.

"I hope not." Krishna looked at the crestfallen faces of the robbers. "Who would like to lose lives doing perilous raids when they can instead live with respect?"

Abhaya saw the leader of the robbers drop to his knees and his three comrades followed suit. *He's changed them already.* She exchanged a glance with Vikrama and nodded.

"Why don't you come into our city, Vaasudeva? Our father would want to meet the man who saved his daughter and might also agree to your proposal."

"Another day," Krishna promised, smiling. "And now that we will be neighbours, the frequency of my visits may make you regret having ever invited me."

"No, not at all. But how can we let you go with no token of gratitude?"

"Could you lend me your chariot, then? I could use some speed."

"It is yours," Abhaya said, this time not pausing to confirm with Vikrama.

Chapter Four

Kamarupa

"A Shakta conclave?" Mura stared at Bhauma.

"You heard it right, Senapati," Bhauma said, beaming. "Maybe the first of its kind in our history!"

Mura frowned, thinking about the viability of the idea. Shakta practitioners in the plains of Bharatavarsha chose to remain in secluded places. The job of reaching out to each of the leading practitioners, Mura felt, would be time-consuming. "Prabho, hoping that everything goes according to plan, it might take at least two years."

"Take three." Bhauma's words sounded final. "Also, send a word to Bhagadatta, the king of Pragjyotisha, to request assistance with messengers."

Mura nodded. He doubted the possibility of any kind of help from Bhagadatta. A nephew of Bhauma, Bhagadatta's claim to the throne of Pragjyotisha had fructified only when Bhauma abdicated his claim. Bhagadatta had committed to providing the necessary military support to the temple town of Kamarupa, which remained under the autonomous control of Bhauma. While Bhagadatta had stood by his word in the beginning and supported the three-layered fortifications of the town, of late, Mura had felt his commitment wavering.

"He shall obey us this time," Bhauma said, reading Mura's thoughts. "Remember the untimely monsoon that depleted his granaries after he rejected our request to strengthen our military?"

Mura nodded. The rejection to strengthen Kamarupa's military was the reason why he doubted Bhagadatta.

"The ways of the Supreme Goddess are mysterious, Mura. Bhagadatta would have realised his folly by now."

The conversation was interrupted by the sound of an infant wailing. Mura stood up from his seat involuntarily. Bhauma too rose from his partly reclined position. The wailing then stopped. Mura sat again but his eyes were fixed on the quarters where Dhatri stayed.

"Your daughter is giving Dhatri a difficult time today," Bhauma sighed.

"I am eternally grateful to her … and to you, Prabho." Mura's eyes turned back to Bhauma. "When her mother died barely months after her birth, I was at a loss to…"

"She is *my* child. Not yours." Dhatri emerged from her quarters, carrying Mura's daughter who was now asleep on her shoulder.

Mura smiled with gratitude.

"Come, Dhatri." Bhauma extended his hand. Dhatri took her seat by his side.

Mura's memory went back a decade, remembering the desire that had sprung in his heart, suppressed when he realised their futility. Age had just begun to show in the silvery strands among Dhatri's curled locks though her face retained the flawless hue of her thirties. But her large eyes now looked like the very home of tranquillity. Her voice had a calmness to it, which could settle a mind wrought with restlessness. Mura closed his eyes momentarily, brushing his thoughts aside. He would not let the devotion he nurtured for Dhatri be sullied by memories of unfulfilled fantasies.

"Let me know about Bhagadatta's reaction." Bhauma's words brought Mura back from his thoughts.

Mura bowed and extended his arms to take the infant. Dhatri shook her head. "You will only leave her unattended in her cradle, Senapati. She can stay with me till tonight."

After Mura left, Bhauma inched closer to Dhatri. She returned his smile, shifting the infant to her lap. Bhauma leaned back. "He still loves you, Dhatri."

"Ten years should have been sufficient for someone to overcome that, Bhauma. I don't love him and he has never spoken out his heart to me either," Dhatri said, pensive and unsmiling.

"I am the one standing between you two."

"No, the choice was mine!"

"Calm down, Dhatri," Bhauma said, raising both his hands. "It is just that the two of you are of the same age and…" he trailed off when he saw Dhatri frown. "Besides, we are Shaktas. There is nothing that stops you from gracing him."

"He never sought me. And even if he had, wouldn't my choice also count, Bhauma? I would not have entertained him," Dhatri replied. Glancing at Bhauma, she rose to her feet. "I thought we'd settled this when we had this conversation before and I had expected to hear something important from you. Not the same Mura issue."

She carried the infant back to her quarters without looking back. She was placing the child in the cradle when she felt a tug on her arm. Her heart fluttered—as it always did. Despite reaching fifty springs, Bhauma retained the vigour of his younger years. She faced him, frowning with an effort.

"That made you angry, love."

Dhatri shook her head. She was annoyed but found it impossible to remain angry with him.

"With you by my side, the world will shortly be mine, Dhatri."

"That sounds like something a lovelorn boy half your age would say to his equally juvenile beloved," Dhatri retorted. But gazing into his eyes, she found a keenness beyond all emotional declaration. Bhauma's modulated tone added to his resolve. She reached out to caress his cheek. The wrinkles that had just begun to appear on his face did not make him any less attractive to her. She asked him, "What do you mean?"

Bhauma shook his head. "Never mind. There was something more important that I had to tell you, regarding the next phase of your Shakta practice." He saw Dhatri's eyes widen and smiled. "And it would be the choice of the Supreme Goddess this time."

"I look forward to it, Bhauma." Dhatri's hands pressed upon his shoulders. "To be frank, I am tired of the meat, fish and wine rituals now. I mean, they are fine but the practice should progress beyond them, shouldn't it?"

"I am glad you excluded the other two rituals of meditation and sexual union," Bhauma said and laughed. "But yes, there has to be some progress beyond all this.

The progress is in invoking the Supreme Goddess within you to become her medium in flesh and blood."

"Is that even possible?" Dhatri's jaw dropped. "Within me?"

"It is possible but with great commitment, Dhatri. And you have it in you."

"How, Bhauma?" Dhatri stepped back. "Would I be possessed by the Supreme Goddess? Would I lose all consciousness and let her take over my body and voice?"

"No, Dhatri, that happens only in folk tales that the village patrol guards in the plains make up to stay awake at night. We, the Shaktas, are beyond such conjuring tricks."

Dhatri swallowed and sat on the cot, squirming at the taunt.

Bhauma took his place beside her. "Dhatri, look at me." The sudden return of authority in his tone made her look up. "What do you wish for those who killed your Amaranatha?"

The memory of her murdered beloved had its effect on Dhatri. It was not like he had been forgotten in the last ten years. He was a frequent topic of their conversations in the initial years of her initiation. She also knew that Bhauma's profuse sympathy for her dead lover had endeared him to her. But in his company and through her initiation into the ways of Shaktism, she had overcome the pain in her heart. The same question in the initial years would have seen her thirsting for revenge. But she was past that now.

Bhauma took note of her calm and continued, "There are many Dhatris and Amaranathas persecuted in the plains. Every Dhatri, unfortunately, does not find her way to Kamarupa to find succour at the feet of the Supreme Goddess."

"I seek to end that gore and murder in the name of false honour in the plains. What can we do, Bhauma?"

"That is the Supreme Goddess speaking through you. An ordinary Dhatri would have simply wanted the death of her lover's murderers," Bhauma replied. "At least that is what I feel."

"This is just me growing mature, Bhauma. I shall believe in the Supreme Goddess when I can do something to change the ways of the plains of Bharatavarsha."

"Real change requires them to leave their narrow-minded rituals of abstinence, false beliefs about honour and their irrelevant deities and practices which come in the way of realising the greatness of the Supreme Goddess."

"Can we make them realise that, Bhauma? I want to."

Bhauma saw the resolution appear in her eyes, replacing all traces of doubt. He had waited for this resolution for a long time. Beneath his stoic expression, his heart leapt at what seemed like the fruit of his long-drawn labours. He nodded, looking into her eyes. "That will need sacrifice, Dhatri."

"I am ready to make any sacrifice."

Bhauma sighed deeply and rose to his feet, motioning her to remain seated. He walked towards the portrait of the Supreme Goddess drawn on the wall. Unseen by Dhatri, his face assumed a strange pallor. "We shall show this world its place."

Chapter Five

Two Years Later

"Welcome to the abode of the Supreme Goddess." The voice rang across the temple hall as Bhauma faced the followers of the Shakta order who had convened there from various corners of Bharatavarsha. "In these trying times where lesser gods and their worship has assumed worrying importance, you, the honourable Shaktas, have chosen to stick to the only true path of moksha, the way of the Supreme Goddess."

A cheer erupted in the temple of Kamaksha. The temple hall facing the sanctum of Goddess Kamaksha teemed with hundreds of Shakta practitioners. For a religious community that normally chose a reclusive life, this was a welcome event that brought them all together. Groups had arrived from far and wide, from the secluded hill areas of northern and eastern corners and even from the south of the Vindhyas. The fatigue of travel, though, was forgotten as they listened to the effusive words of praise and reverence from the lord of Kamarupa himself.

Standing a little distance away from the large gathering, a woman stared at the cheering crowd. Perhaps her lack of excitement was due to fatigue. Kadambari had travelled from the southern parts of Bharatavarsha to Kamarupa. She turned to another woman beside her whom she had met at Varanasi on the way to Kamarupa.

"Why does he deem the other gods inferior?" she asked in a whisper. The woman shrugged at the question and turned back to catch Bhauma's words. Another loud cheer erupted. Kadambari looked around. Had she missed something? A male sadhaka sat leaning against a nearby pillar.

"The Mother Goddess will grace us in person!" he said.

In person? Kadambari turned back to the dais where Bhauma stood, facing the sanctum. The door of the small room to the left of the sanctum opened and Kadambari saw three women walk out; all of them were dressed in red. She saw Bhauma's hands rise and come together over his head as he bowed low. People followed suit, saluting the three women as they first faced the crowd, then turned towards the sanctum.

"Supreme Goddess Kamaksha! Your devotees, the Shaktas, have gathered. Bestow your grace. May we bathe in the effulgence that surrounds you. May we drown in the sea of your compassion. May we stay blessed as you grace us in person."

Kadambari watched him prostrate and saw the three women kneel and bow before the shrine of Kamaksha. The shrine that represented the yoni of the Supreme Goddess was decorated with garlands. Kadambari looked around for the members of the group she had arrived with. They were mingling with the rest, making new acquaintances. The most senior among them, her guru Vamanatha who initiated her into the Vamachara Shakta order, sat aloof. The old man's eyes were closed.

When she saw him opening his eyes, Kadambari moved to his side. "Gurudeva."

"I regret coming here." Vamanatha's words were more of a whisper. "This is not the high seat of Shaktism. He is not a true Shakta."

Kadambari held his arm, relieved that he had expressed what she had felt. "Shouldn't we voice our thoughts, Gurudeva?"

"No, just look around you," Vamanatha cautioned. In his tired eyes, there was a disappointment. "The fools get excited at the mere thought of pursuing a 'superior' religion. Practising a religion is a personal sadhana, Kadambari. We don't choose a religion because of claims of superiority. We choose a certain religion not only because its tenets suit our temperament but also because practising those tenets help us to overcome our weaknesses. It is an endeavour to kill false pride and a sense of superiority. It is an endeavour to feel one with the universe." Vamanatha's voice had started to falter.

Kadambari felt a stab of guilt at the thought of her initial enthusiasm about visiting the famed seat of Vamachara Shaktism. Vamanatha had never shown much inclination towards attending the conclave. But he could not deny the enthusiasm of his students.

"Gurudeva, if we don't protest now…" Kadambari stopped when she saw Vamanatha shake his head vigorously.

He glanced around to make sure that none was listening to them. He need not have worried as everyone else was spellbound by the prospect of seeing the "goddess" that Bhauma had promised them in person. "He, this Bhauma, cannot be taken lightly. He seeks to control the Shakta order. I am afraid, it is not just that that he seeks to control. It might be ... it might be…"

Kadambari swallowed nervously, seeing the growing concern on Vamanatha's wrinkled face. His hands sought her support, his discomfort increasing at every word. She stroked his shoulder gently. "I understand, Gurudeva. Who knows, if we are outnumbered, they might even tell these soldiers to harm us."

"We shall leave this place by dawn. This is not the temple of Shakti. This is a tool in the hands of a wayward overlord lusting for power," Vamanatha whispered.

Someone clutched at Kadambari's arm, startling her. She glared at the intrusion. The Shakta looked apologetic. He then pointed towards the sanctum. "Pay attention. Don't miss the spectacle!"

Despite her growing disgust, Kadambari turned back to the sanctum. Bhauma and the three women were seated on the dais. Suddenly, a flower garland fell off the platform onto the shoulders of one of the women. A hush descended on the crowd and then gave way to gasps. Kadambari watched, unsmiling.

"The Supreme Goddess has chosen her medium!" Bhauma announced. His words reverberated across the hall. "You see in front of you the personification of the Goddess—Mahadevi Dhatri!"

Kadambari's eyes narrowed. A cheer much louder than before erupted and the crowds rose to their feet. She glanced at Vamanatha. His eyes remained closed. From what she had learnt about the Vamachara practice, she understood the distinct rituals of mudra, maamsa, madira, meena and maithuna as symbolic of human pleasures. The pinnacle of pleasure, when the mind went beyond physical yearning, was, Vamanatha had taught her, the state of bliss, the state of Shiva.

The Shakta order considered women the embodiment of Shakti, the one who offered that bliss, which made them worthy of worship.

The crowd jostled for a glimpse of the woman declared the mahadevi. Kadambari leaned back against the pillar, rebellion rising in her heart. *Isn't every woman a personification of Shakti, the energy, the very Goddess? What is the need of a mahadevi and how could she become the only voice of the Supreme Mother?*

Kadambari made her way out of the crowds in the outer sanctum to a relatively quieter corner. The day seemed to wane quicker in the eastern part of the land.

The unrest in her heart did not die even by the evening when the other woman from Varanasi came to her side and gave her a leaf bowl filled with a mixture of boiled grains and pulses. It was dark and she did not move from the sheltered corner after eating the meal. Kamarupa—there was something about this place that did not allow her to sleep. She waited for dawn, eager to leave as soon as she could with Vamanatha. Following his advice, she refrained from arguing with anyone.

This place has three layers of fortification. Why, in the name of Amba, does a temple town need such defences? The outermost fortification housed the soldiers and guards. Armed to the teeth, far beyond anything she had seen at Avanti and Prabhasa. The central circle housed the practitioners and the innermost one, the temple and the palaces of Lord Bhauma and his close associates. *Like something is hidden here?*

"You there, it is time to move out of the sanctum." The condescension in the guard's voice irritated her.

"I came here on invitation. Treat your guests with respect!"

The guard looked suitably chastised. "Nobody sleeps in the open. It is an order that the pilgrims vacate this place by sunset. There are rooms made comfortable for you just outside. Where is the rest of your group?"

Kadambari moved towards the nearest exit. The guard took his position there as she left.

"That area over there isn't safe. You might fall off the cliff," he called out and she nodded without turning.

Given a choice, Kadambari wanted to leave the place as soon as she could. Walking around in the central circle, she found the Shakta practitioners chatting. Most of them found the rooms they had been given very comfortable compared to their usual forest residences.

"We don't need to take turns and look out for a wild animal," a woman remarked aloud to no one in particular. "We can all sleep well tonight."

Kadambari sighed. After about an hour of wandering around, she retired to one of the rooms allotted to her. The night was dark outside, and the silence, punctuated only by the noise of crickets, belied the fact that there were so many pilgrims camped there. Kadambari closed her eyes and tried to sleep. She floated between wakefulness and sleep when a sudden scream pierced the night.

She sat up, startled. *Was it a dream?* It seemed likely that she had dreamt it. None of her other companions was wakened by the noise she thought she had heard. Kadambari lay down again but now sleep was beyond her.

It had been a tiring day for Mura. He had foregone sleep for several days, overseeing the necessary arrangements for the Shakta gathering. The guests, weary of travel and unaccustomed to the cold hill weather, would need to be treated with compassion and hospitality. At the same time, it was his responsibility to check everyone who entered the Kamarupa. The entry of everyday pilgrims had been barred for the duration of the conclave. The rooms were filled with guests. The soldiers were made to temporarily vacate their residences in the outer ring of the town to make place for the male guests. The women were housed in the middle ring of the township. He was satisfied that any untoward incident like an attack, however unlikely it was, would still leave him with two layers of fortification protecting the women and the lord of Kamarupa. The soldiers were dissatisfied, of course, but none dared speak up in front of him. They bore the inconvenience, albeit grudgingly, consoling themselves that the guests would leave in a couple of days.

It had been an especially hard task to control the rush of ecstatic Shaktas when Dhatri was declared the mahadevi, the chief yogini of Kamarupa. In their hurry to get closer to the chosen medium of the Supreme Goddess, the guests had caused a stampede that resulted in the weaker among them getting injured. Mura had had to resort to some force to stop a group of aggressive practitioners who might have ended up harming Dhatri in their exultant devotion. Stopping four of them single-handedly, he had pleaded with Bhauma to usher Dhatri inside. Order had been restored after a good deal of effort.

One more day, Mura sighed to himself, striding along the outer ring of the temple town instructing the guards on the night vigil. He longed to catch some sleep before dawn. He came to a halt at the sight of an open door of the quarters reserved for the senior-most practitioner among the guests.

"Where is he?" he asked the guards. They told him that the Shakta guru had been ushered into the inner circle as Bhauma had expressed a wish to meet him.

Isn't it too late for a meeting? Mura wondered, looking at the skies as he made his way into the middle fortress. Before entering the inner circle, Mura glanced at the central circle, wanting to check if the women were all safely inside. A moving shadow made him instinctively clutch his sword. *I wonder who that could be.*

He had only walked a couple of yards in the direction when a distraught woman ran into him, suppressing her screams.

"What is it? Who are you running from?" Mura caught her by the shoulders. Seeing fear and shock in her eyes, he softened and peered beyond her, expecting to see someone coming in pursuit. "Relax, there is nothing here that can harm you. Did you have a nightmare..."

"My guru has been killed!" the woman blurted out, panting.

Mura had hardly comprehended her words when she clamped her hands to her mouth. Her regret of speaking out was obvious. Mura's attention, however, was drawn to an unguarded entrance at the southern corner of the inner circle. He cursed the missing guard under his breath, guessing that the woman had run out from that very entrance. *Why did she even enter the inner circle at this time of the night? And what made her think about her guru being killed?* He then turned to her. "Are you even in your senses?" For all her hysteria, the woman did not seem to mean any harm. Mura started to wonder if she had fallen asleep within the temple premises and had a bad dream.

"I saw him being killed," the woman repeated. "I saw my guru enter the temple at night to meet your lord. I saw Bhauma offering him wine. And then that man killed my guru!"

"You don't even know what garbage spills out of that mouth of yours! Are you accusing Lord Bhauma of murder?" Mura grit his teeth, shaking her by her arms.

"He strangled my guru with his hands!"

"Are you even hearing your own words! You're saying that you saw Lord Bhauma strangle a Shakta guru with his own hands!"

"I saw their shadows!" Kadambari protested, wrenching herself out of Mura's grip.

Something in her eyes made him compose himself. "Come with me." He led her towards the temple.

The woman shrank back. "I am not entering that place again. Just let me go!" He frowned and loosened his hold on her. "I never knew this is what happened at Kamarupa!" she whispered fiercely. "Go on, kill me too!"

"Just wait here. What is your name?"

"Kadambari."

"Where did you come from?"

"From the south of the Vindhyas, towards the western shores."

It could be a lie but Mura was not worried about the details. He settled her on a seat, telling her to wait and entered the inner circle of Kamarupa. He had almost reached the entrance of Bhauma's quarters when he saw the man himself exiting.

"Senapati!" Bhauma's face was pale.

"Prabho?"

"I was about to come to you, Mura." Bhauma's voice, though low, had its usual composure. "The senior-most Shakta guru, Vamanatha, our esteemed guest, breathed his last."

Mura's jaw dropped. Kadambari had been partly right. "How, Prabho?"

"It beats me. I should have curtailed my enthusiasm to meet the great man and should have allowed him to rest."

"But how did he die?" Mura entered Bhauma's quarters and saw Vamanatha's motionless body placed on an ornate couch.

"I have no clue!" Bhauma sighed. "We had hardly begun to talk and he collapsed!"

Mura stared at the corpse and then at Bhauma. He found no marks of strangling on Vamanatha's neck as Kadambari had claimed. "Did he drink something that could have..."

"No, not here at least," Bhauma replied after a moment.

Mura's gaze fell upon a fallen goblet. His finger pointed in the direction. He still could not bring himself to ask the question lurking in his mind.

"That? I was drinking wine when he came in. The goblet slipped from my hands when I saw him collapse."

Mura's unsure glance alternated between Bhauma and Vamanatha's corpse. A strange sense of restlessness came over him. There were neither signs of strangulation nor of poisoning on Vamanatha's body. Yet, Kadambari's and Bhauma's versions differed.

No! She could not have been telling the truth!

Vamanatha's death remained a mystery. Mura rushed back towards the central ring to find Kadambari but found no one. He then spotted the shadow of someone hiding behind a wall. At the same time, he felt Bhauma's hand on his shoulder. He swallowed hard.

"What happened, Mura? Why did you rush out this way?"

"I ... I thought I heard something, Prabho," Mura explained, seeing the shadow disappear. He turned to Bhauma, giving in to his instincts. "I was wrong."

Chapter Six

Two Years Later at Ujjayini, Avanti

The courtroom of Ujjayini, the capital of Avanti, was filled with lords, nobles and neighbouring kings who visited the holy shrine of Mahakala for the annual celebration of Mahashivaratri. Most had spent the day negotiating trade treaties with the kingdom of Avanti, a mahajanapada that enjoyed a measure of economic dominion over its smaller neighbours; this also translated into a tacit political dominion over them.

Dharmasena was seated to the left of the king of Avanti, but one step lower. It made Abhaya's blood boil. Even at the age of twelve, she had a fair idea about her father's dealings with Avanti; she had been exposed to such affairs of the state since she was a toddler.

Why is it taking them so long to discuss one issue? She wondered to herself, gazing down at the court from an enclosed balcony overlooking it. A hand touched her shoulder and she turned.

"Bhagini Mitravinda!" She tried to bring her hands together in salutation but the princess of Avanti restrained her, frowning at the formality.

"Drop the protocols, at least with me." Mitra waved the courtesy aside and held out a plate of a sweet delicacy. "You've been this way right from the temple of Mahakala. You should have come with me instead of watching these boring talks."

"These talks generally interest me, Bhagini, though I quite agree with you that this particular discussion has turned out to be quite boring," Abhaya replied. If there was anything that she liked about visiting Avanti, it was meeting its amicable princess. At sixteen years, Mitravinda was older than her but was easy to get along with. She waved aside formalities and the two always indulged in friendly conversations.

"Have you heard the news?" Mitra chirped as they entered the garden. "The princess of Vidarbha, Rukmini, has eloped with Krishna."

"My father received the invitation to attend the wedding at Dwaraka," Abhaya replied, not surprised. "Good for her. She was being forced into a wedding she did not like, wasn't she?"

"A well-deserved slap on the face of her brother, Rukma! I wish I was at Vidarbha when it happened. Do you know the details?"

Abhaya shook her head. There was a time she could not gauge the importance of such talk and even scorned it as a waste of time. It was then that Mitravinda had explained how marriages came to be looked upon as strategic moves rather than personal ones.

"Rukmini is smart. She planned for Krishna to take her away in his chariot at the temple of Gauri, which was situated outside the city. What an idea!"

"Does that make Vidarbha an ally of Dwaraka now?" Abhaya asked while inwardly reflecting upon the convenience of eloping from the temple as opposed to facing hostilities at the venue of the wedding.

"It's difficult to say anything now," Mitravinda shrugged. "Logic follows that Rukma will not openly antagonise the family his sister now belongs to. But who knows how long blood ties can prevail over bitterness? Krishna anyway does not need an ally in Rukma. But I am wondering ... the non-stop journey from Vidarbha to Dwaraka even with the fastest horses would have taken at least three days. Rukmini would have been..." She stopped midway, biting her tongue. Abhaya's mature questions on other topics had often made Mitravinda forget that she was too young to indulge in the romantic aspects of the news.

Abhaya frowned, her mind still dwelling on the political dimensions of the situation. She remembered that Dharmasena had politely declined to attend the wedding. Anagha could not afford an open friendship with Dwaraka.

"Why does Avanti want to control the friendships of her allies? Why would your family feel insecure if we attend the weddings of our friends?" she asked, looking straight into Mitravinda's eye.

Mitravinda did not have an answer except to pull Abhaya closer. "I admit, we are unfair." She wanted to say much more but stopped herself. She was fond of Abhaya's candour. It showed more curiosity than anything else. Mitra believed in giving honest answers, at least to Abhaya.

I wish we were real siblings. Either I should have been born at your home, or you in mine. But no, you are better off there. Mitra sighed.

"Shall we see what the boys are up to? It is well past midday," Abhaya said, changing the topic.

Mitravinda paused for a moment and then nodded her head, turning towards the quadrangle reserved for her brothers' martial arts practice. "They are probably passing the day in mock duels. Though Mahakala alone knows how they are going to stay up for the Mahashivaratri night vigil if they tire themselves out."

"Mock duels? Why didn't anyone tell me!" Abhaya exclaimed and hastened in her steps.

"Well, I forgot," Mitravinda smiled at her enthusiasm. "You've started training on the long sword, haven't you? Does your brother teach you?"

"Yes, Vikrama used to teach me. But with the recent death of Arya Vajrabahu, the job of heading the army has fallen on his shoulders. Father is busier than ever and I have to stay content with other soldiers training me."

"At least, Vikrama teaches you when he can," Mitra sighed.

"Don't your brothers teach you?"

"You know Anuvinda, don't you?" Mitra remarked, a frown clouding her face.

"But then, how will you ever learn, Bhagini?"

"I shall have to marry someone who thinks it is necessary for women to learn the skill of sword fighting."

The sounds of the clashing steel greeted their ears even before they reached the quadrangle. Mitra saw Abhaya's lips curve as she bolted in. They were just in time to see Vikrama parry Anuvinda's attack on his side by arching his back with amazing flexibility, somehow still retaining his balance. The girls exchanged a smile and Abhaya could not help clapping. Anuvinda stole a glance at the girls and knitted his brows in annoyance. He made his next move. But Vikrama had an advantage with balance and launched into a well-calculated offensive that Anuvinda somehow managed to fend off, thanks in part to his bulk. In the next move, his blade swept towards the unguarded portion of Vikrama's arm that held the shield. Vikrama had to shift his grip on the hilt of the sword to accommodate an upward move to defend his arm as he pulled back the shield to guard his shoulder. The defence worked but the blades locked and it was a matter of raw strength to determine who would throw his opponent off. Abhaya's jaw dropped and beads of sweat appeared on her forehead.

A bell sounded. Anuvinda whirled upon the soldier who was acting as a referee. The soldier backed away under his glare. "The ... princess ... I thought she might have brought a message from the king."

"Need you, son of a Suta, stop the duel for that?!" Anuvinda thundered. He glared at Mitravinda. "So, what's the message?"

Mitravinda shook her head. "No, we just came to watch you duel."

"We can start again," Vikrama offered, brushing the sweat off his forehead and flexing his arms.

"Sure, we can," Anuvinda said and grinned, his mood improving. "The duel was boring without the girls, anyway. How about a stake Vikrama? Your sister if I win..."

Vikrama frowned, his fists and jaws tightening. Mitravinda drew Abhaya closer. "Anuvinda!" She hissed. "Don't shame our family in front of guests!"

"And when did duels stop being about skill and learning and get to be about challenging the honour of your opponents, Yuvaraja?" Vikrama's eyes were narrowed.

"I trust your skill, Bhrata," Abhaya said, loud enough to make the guards exchange a look.

"This is not about skill, Abhaya." Vikrama threw a glance at Mitravinda, hoping that she could take Abhaya away from the quadrangle.

"Relax, Yuvaraja, would I dishonour you or your sister? Besides, you might not have the right to wager her. Being adopted, you know?" Anuvinda smiled, testing the edge of his sword with his finger.

"He is my brother." Abhaya stepped beside Vikrama, defiantly.

"I was only saying a victory deserves a prize even if it's just for laughs. If you lose, don't worry, I'm hardly going to imprison your sister."

"So, how many in your gurukula have won me by that definition?" Mitravinda asked icily.

"Mitra!!"

"I know someone who beat you in every mock duel in the gurukula, Bhrata. Shall I go to him then?" Mitravinda asked in a calculated, docile tone, her lips curled in contempt. Anuvinda strode towards her glaring, his finger raised in warning, but she remained defiant. "In the middle of the duel, Vikrama, just for fun, take the name of Krishna Vaasudeva and see this one's grip falter. You might probably be the third one, after Balarama, to win me as a trophy."

Anuvinda struck her across the face, making the other two cringe. Mitra gasped and took a step back, seeking the support of the pillar behind her.

"Yuvaraja!" Vikrama shouted. The prince of Avanti turned on his heel and left in a huff. Abhaya rushed to Mitra and threw her arms around her.

I'll pay him back for this! Mitra's cheek stung, but she did not allow herself to show the pain.

"It did not have to come to this, Bhagini," Vikrama broke the silence, wringing his hands in embarrassment. But he couldn't hide the admiration in his eyes.

"Never mind, Bhrata. I could not let a dear friend and a sister pay the price of being our guest. My family is much more than Anuvinda's pride and whim."

The trio made their way towards their respective quarters, Vikrama trying to console Abhaya who was at a complete loss for words.

Even as they reached the guest quarters that housed them at Avanti for the festival, she maintained her silence. Vikrama knew her silence stemmed not from shock or fear but sheer disdain over the incident. A thousand questions remained in her eyes but refused to be voiced by her lips.

Vikrama drew her close. "Do you think I would let anything happen to you?"

Abhaya shook her head. "I know you would have won, Bhrata."

"What bothers my sister then? Forget what happened there, Abhaya. We shall not visit this city in the near future, even to worship Mahakala."

"That is not going to stop him from doing horrible things. I ... I feel disgusted thinking about him."

"I shall not let him come anywhere near you. Trust me, Abhaya."

"Bhrata," Abhaya blurted out. "We can tell father and leave this place immediately. But Mitra, she has no one. She needs my help."

"How will you help her?" Vikrama smiled at her. Right from her childhood, Abhaya tended to picture herself in place of the hero of every story she had ever been told.

"We can help her marry a good man and escape this hell. I think I know who she would like to marry. I shall..."

"Enough!" Vikrama exclaimed. "It is not our place to make such decisions."

In his heart, he feared Abhaya was capable of doing something audacious. A single thoughtless action could unleash hell in the region. *Thank Mahakala a wedding is still a couple of years away!*

Chapter Seven

Kamarupa–Two Years after the Shakta Conclave

The number of pilgrims visiting the shrine of Kamarupa had increased steadily. The prasad at the evening prayers was regularly falling short. Demand for the mystic medicine that could cure all diseases had increased, so much so that it was getting scarce, the demand for it far outstripping the rate at which the alchemists of the Shakta order were able to prepare it from the limited available resources. Bhauma looked at the lone pilgrim who was creating a scene at the shortage of the "medicine". *With prosperity come new problems*, he smiled to himself. He rose from the seat which served as his public throne.

"What ails you, Bhrata?" he asked the pilgrim who was being restrained by the guards from advancing to where Bhauma stood in front of the temple.

"You, the lords of temple towns. Why would the likes of you or those high and mighty priests be bothered about what ails people like me? How would you even understand what we go through?" the pilgrim retorted.

Bhauma waved the guard away. He put his hand on the pilgrim's shoulder. "We are indeed unfortunate to hear this, Bhrata. But pray tell me, what I can do so that you don't leave the shrine of the Supreme Mother with a broken heart?"

"All I seek is a remedy for my illness. Look at my leg. It is paralysed!"

Bhauma looked at the skies and sighed. "Why do your children have to go through this, Devi Kamaksha?"

Suddenly, the crowds behind him cleared. Bhauma smiled. "Mahadevi." He bowed low.

"Bhauma," Dhatri acknowledged. The vast crowds of pilgrims held back by the guards reminded her of the day she had entered Kamarupa. The place had indeed become popular in the last couple of years and the reason, according to Bhauma, was Dhatri herself.

"What is the problem?"

"This unfortunate man cannot walk by himself. He came all the way here with sheer devotion towards the Goddess. Have mercy on him, Mahayogini."

Dhatri closed her eyes for a long moment. When they opened, her gaze rested on the pilgrim. Her forehead wrinkled with concentration. Bhauma smiled. The years of practising Shakta ways had only enhanced her beauty.

Dhatri's gaze grew intense. The crowds waited with bated breath. They saw the man moan and groan. On Bhauma's signal, the guards let him free and he stumbled on his unsteady legs before falling onto the ground.

"Arise," Bhauma said. "Arise, taking the name of the Supreme Goddess."

"Amba!!"

"Louder and stronger!" Bhauma shouted.

The man tried again. His groans grew louder.

The mahadevi continued to stand like a statue. She broke her silence and spoke a single command in a clear, loud voice. "Walk!" The word echoed in between the walls of the inner fortress of Kamarupa. None in the crowd dared to bat an eyelid.

The man let out a cry. The crowds gasped as he took a few stumbling steps forward, his confidence increasing with each step until he finally straightened himself and walked. A cheer erupted. He hurried towards the stairs atop which Dhatri stood and fell to the ground.

"Amba! Your compassion is truly the supreme! You never fail your worshippers!" He sobbed out in ecstasy. The cheering by the crowd got louder. They chorused spontaneous slogans in Dhatri's honour.

Dhatri sighed and reached out to Bhauma who hurried to her side. She stared at the pilgrim who had now risen to his feet, still bowing low, tears streaming from his eyes. She felt Bhauma tug at her arm. The guards surrounded them, clearing the way to their residence. The cheers echoed in Dhatri's ears long after they had left the hall.

"How did it happen?" she asked when Bhauma came to her that night.

"You are the mahadevi and you ask me?"

"I really don't know."

"Your will is backed by the Goddess Kamaksha herself," Bhauma responded, opening his arms.

"Why didn't the miracle happen when I wanted the blind child to see last month?"

"Which blind child?"

"Don't you remember the boy who … Prabho!" Dhatri gasped with pleasure as he gripped her waist.

"Devi, you shall not call me that."

Dhatri smiled. "Bhauma, tell me—is all this true? Did the man walk only because of my word?"

"Because of the word of Goddess Kamaksha," Bhauma interjected. "Even after so many years of practice, do you doubt Her, Mahadevi?"

She shook her head. "Not Her. It is myself I doubt, Bhauma."

"Doubting yourself is doubting Her." He held her for a long moment. "Dhatri." The way he said her name made her sigh with pleasure. Bhauma dropped to his knees.

"Do you have to do this every night?"

"Will you, the personification of Shakti, grace your worshipper with the union of your spirit?"

"I am sick of this!" Dhatri exclaimed, backing away.

"As you wish." Bhauma stayed on his knees for a couple of moments, then rose and made for the door.

"Wait, Bhauma! I did not refuse you! I want a break from this routine ritual. I want you to desire me as a lover, not a worshipper."

Bhauma turned back. His eyes narrowed and Dhatri saw him clench his fists as he shook his head. "This is not role-playing, Dhatri. It is a practice, a saadhana. One needs to be true to it."

"I think this is as cruel as the rituals of the plains folk are. There is no value to what the woman desires! There are times where I am tired of being the Goddess, Bhauma! I want your love, not your worship."

She lay down on her bed and turned away. Bhauma looked at her for a long moment, then turned and left the room, his fists still clenched.

Dhatri couldn't keep her tears back. She slammed her fist into the wet pillow. Finally, the tears subsided. Her eyes were swollen and tired but sleep would not come. She tossed from side to side. The lamp glowed as the night grew older and slowly she felt her sorrow grow into a rage. After another hour, she heard footsteps and lay still, facing the wall. She did not turn even when Bhauma's hand clutched her shoulder.

This time, he turned her around with greater force, prevailing over her initial struggle. Dhatri glared at him as she still lay on her back. He came close enough for their lips to touch. She closed her eyes tilting her head backwards but her lips stayed yearning as he slowly rose back. Bhauma saw her lips quiver and her eyes narrow as she pushed him away and attempted to turn. But his hands stayed over hers.

She sighed and then gave up the struggle. The lamp went out and she felt his weight upon her as she undid the knot that bound her garment around her breasts. The night was the most passionate they had shared for quite some time. Bhauma's arms still enveloped her when the ray of the morning sun fell upon her through the latticed screen covering the window. He opened his eyes to find her gazing at him.

"What took you so long to do this?"

Bhauma sighed and rose to a sitting position, draping her garment over her. "Did you want it?"

"Of course! What makes you think I did not?"

"You resisted."

"It was just anger."

"You did not want it then. Technically, what I did was rape."

"Stop being ridiculous, Bhauma!" Dhatri hissed. "I am not a weakling to let anyone touch me without my permission."

Bhauma shook his head and got up. He started to say something but stopped himself. Dhatri frowned.

He smiled. “I’m glad you think so. It is still my sin, though.”

“Your sin? And how exactly?”

“A union isn’t child’s play, Dhatri. It is a sin to force oneself upon a woman who shows even an iota of unwillingness, be it shame or even hesitation. A union is blessed only when the woman is ready. Only then can the Supreme Shakti grant the state of Shiva to a sadhaka.”

Dhatri rose, the frown not leaving her face. Bhauma watched her torso tighten as she raised her hands, gathering her hair into a bun. He felt himself getting aroused again and took a deep breath. “Bhauma … will my whole life be this way?”

“I know it is hard. Harder for those used to the life of Aryas. But, Dhatri, the Goddess made her choice when her garland fell upon you. My love for you gave way to worship. She chose you for a purpose, a purpose higher than you and me. The purpose of bringing the world to her refuge.”

“Bhauma, why would she want me to give up the joy that I have found at last after it eluded me my entire life?”

“This is beyond the burden of rituals, Dhatri. Once you see the purpose and wed yourself to it, you shall not see it giving up your joy.”

“And what will that purpose be, Bhauma? I have been hearing about your bringing the world to the refuge of the Goddess for years now. But how?”

“Start small, Dhatri. You must give others what the Goddess gave you when you needed it. Refuge. There are more women who need to be liberated from the oppressive ways of the Aryas. Six of them just came to our door seeking shelter, Dhatri. The Goddess did not choose you for no reason. Initiate them into the ways approved by the Supreme Goddess."

Bhauma saw Dhatri's gaze shift to the wall that had a depiction of the Supreme Goddess, which she had made herself. There was a striking likeness. The eyes of the Goddess seemed to come alive, especially in the light of the lamps during the night. For some reason, they never failed to disconcert Bhauma. He turned to leave the room.

"I shall do so, Bhauma." Dhatri's tone made him stop in his steps. His smile, unseen by Dhatri, conveyed something other than the nod she saw from behind. Dhatri continued, "I also want to do something else, Bhauma. If the Goddess chose me as the mahayogini, I shall strive to be deserving of that honour. In every walk of life, starting with martial arts. Teach me to fight, Bhauma."

"As you wish, Mahadevi. Senapati Mura would be more than delighted to make himself available to you." Without turning back, Bhauma left the room. His heart had started to beat faster and he found himself unable to meet Dhatri's gaze.

It was less than a couple of hours later that he heard the clang of metal on metal. Through the window, he saw Mura hold Dhatri's hand, showing her how to grip the sword. Bhauma's nails dug into his palm. When the swords clashed again, his eyes remained fixed on the woman who seemed to be applying herself to the art like someone possessed.

This is happening faster than I thought!

Chapter Eight

Prabhasa—Five Years Later

On the western shores of Saurashtra, the turbulent waves were in incessant competition with the bustling activity of the port. The region that had once been a centre for sea trade had faced a period of lull and gloom due to the repeated raids by the pirates of Punyajana. Traders had faced dangers at every step. Those who escaped the attention of the Punyajanas often had to face highway robbers and wild animals on their way to Avanti. The new city of Anagha had, to an extent, helped the traders face the perils on the land. But the troubles on the sea had continued till a confederation of the Yadu tribes from the north came to settle on the western shores. The Yadavas, who had come in search of a new home, were trained warriors who could overcome the pirates. Thus, at last, the seas were safe again, and the last five years had seen an increase in the activity of trade through the western seas.

With the trade, the economy had flourished. Port cities had attracted labour and talent alike. Carpenters were always in demand to make new ships. The young citizens mastered the skill of sailing bigger boats. To a newcomer, the port city of Prabhasa presented a festive picture of a flourishing economy, trade, talent, valour and religion.

A fleet of bigger ships was anchored offshore. Some distance away from the port were ships that needed repairs and reinforcement to their structure after a long journey on the seas. Carpenters set themselves to work enthusiastically and happily, anticipating the generous pay they would receive at the end of the day's labour. Naval architects who worked on the structural aspect sat some distance away, discussing stronger designs for the vessels. Anyone who had known these parts for long could tell the difference that the Yadava cities had made. Apart from the wealth they had created in the last couple of years, they had also fostered hope, faith and aspiration. A day did not pass without the citizens giving mental thanks to the person who had wrought this change.

Krishna Vaasudeva.

The enthusiasm of the labourers working on the ship that belonged to his family was palpable. It wasn't every day that Krishna himself supervised their work and they all bent to their labours with added inspiration. Krishna walked around, examining the structure they were working atop a vessel. A year or two less than thirty springs, he was often mistaken to be far younger. Nothing got past him; he had a way of checking the exact places that could cause structural weaknesses. His attention was drawn to the shelter being built over the deck, wide enough for two people. Aestheticism was not compromised even as robustness remained the top priority. Krishna examined the wooden roof of the small shelter under which workmen were busy honing the surfaces. As his hand touched the wood, his intuition signalled that something was wrong. Amidst the sounds of the tools being used, his ears did not miss the sound of a crack. The roof was about to come crashing down on the two artisans working under it.

It happened just as this realisation struck him. His hands rose automatically to support the roof. But he was in one corner and the roof could collapse on the artisans beneath its other end. Exactly when he expected it to collapse at the opposite corner, he saw two additional hands support it. A momentary smile appeared on his face despite the strain when he saw the lustrous plait of hair falling over the shoulder of the woman who shared the burden. Her strained smile greeted him. Assistance poured in the next minute and the workmen rushed out of the shelter, relieving them.

Relief was writ large on her face as she stepped back, panting for breath. An unimpressed frown knit her brows. "What if I had not reached in time?" Before Krishna could respond, she added, "Well, I know you would have made it to the middle of the structure somehow and taken it upon yourself to save them, never giving a thought to the possibility that the roof might be more than a match to your muscle, Vaasudeva!"

Krishna laughed. "An unforeseen danger often is an eye-opener that makes us realise our true potential, Dhaarmaseni." She saw the twinkle in his eyes and his usual inscrutable smile.

"And which strength of yours did this damned thing make you realise, Krishna?"

"Maybe…" Krishna winked as he continued, "...my destiny of attracting a friend in the moment of need, Abhaya. Are you hurt?" He held her arm, examining a scratch.

"How dare you try to flatter me!" Abhaya pulled her arm back. "When did you last think of this 'friend'?

Not your fault, though, when you have bride after bride keeping you busy. Why would you remember us at all?"

"That's quite an allegation!" Krishna exclaimed in a mock-dramatic tone. "Especially coming from a 'friend' who never cared to grace any wedding of mine."

"As if you don't know why." Abhaya's eyes fell. "Curse the diplomatic compulsions. The twin princes of Avanti, Vinda and Anuvinda, our dear long-time 'friends' or, to be more accurate, overlords. They cannot abide our getting friendly with the Yadavas."

"And why exactly did the princess of Anagha disregard those friends to meet me now?" Krishna turned away, crossing his arms across his breast in mock displeasure.

"Anger doesn't suit you," Abhaya commented with a giggle. She then sighed. "Don't forget, I have a real friend too at Avanti. Princess Mitravinda. Vaasudeva, do you remember her?"

Krishna's brows knitted in concern. "Isn't she going to choose her groom at her swayamvara in two months' time?"

"Swayamvara indeed! A swayamvara where the groom is pre-decided by her brothers, insulting its very spirit! A swayamvara where invitations are sent to only crony supporters and not to the valiant ones who deserve to be considered as suitors. A swayamvara to which the man she loves is not invited." She turned to face him and added softly, "To which you, Vaasudeva, are not invited."

"Dhaarmaseni, did Mitravinda tell you this herself?"

Abhaya nodded. "She also said that she would either consume poison or stab herself if you did not show up at the swayamvara." Krishna sensed her pain as she looked at him, swallowing hard. "Krishna, will you?"

He turned away. His hesitation, she knew, was not unfounded. After all, he was already married to not one but three women—the princesses of Vidarbha, Madra and Kekaya.

Staring into the horizon, Krishna saw a face smile at him. His eyes closed. Air filled his lungs.

"Dhaarmaseni," Krishna spoke suddenly. The decisive tone took her by surprise. "Please tell Mitra not to worry. Assure her that she will not be wedded to anyone against her wishes."

"Krishna!" Abhaya smiled in relief. "I shall be by her side on the big day." Her hands came together in the customary salutation as she took a step back.

Krishna caught her hands, stopping her. "It is now past sunset, Abhaya."

"Yes, I need to get back to patrolling the highway." She smiled. "Remember we made a pact to take turns in keeping the path safe for the travellers. I'll join my soldiers."

"When did you start patrolling?"

"Today," Abhaya laughed. "I had to find a way to get to you without coming to Dwaraka or being spotted by any spy of Avanti!"

Krishna held on to her hands, pulling her a step closer. "You are too young for these intrigues, Abhaya."

"Seventeen was the age when my grandfather killed a tiger," she declared, tossing her plait over her shoulder and grasping the hilt of her sword. "Besides, problems don't ask for our age when they confront us, Vaasudeva." She chuckled and added with a wink, "They instead make us realise how much we've grown."

Krishna smiled in response and let go of her hands. He then pulled out a dagger that was hanging from his belt and handed it to her. "For you."

Abhaya took the weapon. "Well, it has been really long since you last gifted me something!" she exclaimed happily, clasping the stem of the dagger close to her chest. "And now I have something to make all your wives jealous, if and when I get to meet them!"

They exchanged smiles. His glance refused to leave her and it took some willpower to turn away from it.

Who would not welcome an adventure? The courageous are undaunted. Glory favours the dauntless!

Abhaya smiled to herself as she crossed over the wooden plank that connected the ship to the port.

Chapter Nine

Ujjayini, Avanti

The pyramidal tower of the Mahakala Temple was especially splendid when framed by the setting sun. It was the day before Princess Mitravinda's swayamwara. As the pilgrims thronged to the temple for the evening worship, they were stopped at the outer gates and told to wait as the royal and noble guests and suitors were given the privileged darshan.

Abhaya stood a good distance away from the temple, watching the royal parties enter the temple in turn. Shaking her head, she empathised with the common crowd. It was quite contrary to what her father practised. Dharmasena had always taken care to visit the temple of Anagheshwari in her city at such times of the day and week to not inconvenience the common pilgrims and devotees. Even at Prabhasa, she had seen the noble families of Yadavas visit with the commoners. The reserved privileges for the royal and noble to the detriment of the common devotee came as an uneasy reminder of her class.

"What makes the princess of Anagha wait at a distance like a commoner?"

Abhaya, startled by the sudden voice, whirled around. Stifling a sigh, she regarded the imposing figure that approached her.

"Princess or a milkmaid or a daughter of an 'oversized innkeeper', Lord Mahakala is not one to discriminate.

So what difference does it make, Yuvaraja?" She folded her palms but looked him straight in the eye.

Anuvinda had an enviable physique that could intimidate even seasoned warriors. He took a step forward. Abhaya stood her ground and smiled at him. He was not used to rebuttals. The word "innkeeper" was not lost on him, reminding him of a childhood jibe he had made. His smile hid his displeasure and his brows, which almost met at the centre of his forehead, drew closer in scrutiny.

"You don't forget things, do you?"

"Childhood memories are strong, Yuvaraja."

"Let it be. You standing this far from the temple makes me think that you are not really waiting to see Mahakala." He looked around his frown betraying a tinge of suspicion.

"Can Mahakala be restricted to the temple alone?" Abhaya chuckled.

"So, what I've heard is not wrong, Dhaarmaseni—that you have developed a skill of leaving one speechless in a conversation." Anuvinda laughed. "But isn't it time for you to finish the worship and return to the palace? My sister, the bride, would want to spend as much time as she can with her childhood friend before her wedding."

Abhaya wondered how to rid herself of the prince. She hadn't found Krishna yet. Mitravinda had been aghast at Krishna's non-arrival and had declared to Abhaya that she would consume poison if he did not turn up by the end of the day. Abhaya had done her best to reassure her that Krishna would have a plan. But did he? Krishna's cryptic message, which reached her before they had left for Avanti, had suggested that he would meet her in disguise near the temple of Mahakala. The street around the temple had become a noisy marketplace with vendors and devotees. Their meeting would surely go unnoticed amidst the crowds. Their conversation would be lost in the din and, even if someone questioned her, she could always pass it off as a casual enquiry about something she wished to purchase. But, with Anuvinda around, the whole plan was in jeopardy.

Abhaya pretended to look at the wares being sold in the marketplace. "Don't you, as the brother of the bride, have a lot to take care of, Yuvaraja? Do go ahead. I shall come back to the palace soon."

Before Anuvinda could respond, a guard hurried towards them. "Prabho!" he called out and then hesitated when he saw Abhaya.

"I … I shall leave," Abhaya offered. It was the perfect opportunity to get away from the prince.

"Wait! The princess of Anagha is no stranger. Tell me what brings you here."

"The Yadavas were seen at the ashrama of Guru Sandeepani. Every noted maharathi was present … and…"

Abhaya hid her relief. *At least, the Yadavas are here.* Anuvinda's discomfort amused her.

"Has that lowborn cowherd Krishna dared to enter Avanti?" Anuvinda asked and gritted his teeth.

"No, we could not see him but…"

Anuvinda hurriedly dismissed the guard and turned towards Abhaya. She looked him in the eye. Her father's friendship with the Yadavas was frowned upon by Anuvinda. She knew he suspected her father of having something to do with this unwanted arrival of the Yadava host.

"How do you think the Yadavas know about Mitra's swayamvara?" Anuvinda's unsmiling question betrayed his menace.

"Is that such a shameful secret to hide, Yuvaraja?" she retorted. "The merchants trading silk, pearls and gems all come through Dwaraka. It would not take a genius to guess a wedding was around the corner, given the quantities of these things your family has been purchasing."

Anuvinda held her wrist in a firm grip. "That was quite a prompt answer! Should I believe that you or your father did not have a role?" His nails dug into her skin. She tried not to show the pain.

"Let go of my hand, Anuvinda!" she demanded with no visible increase in her tone. Her measured emphasis and stern gaze disconcerted him. His grip loosened and she pulled free.

"You know that such an attempt would amount to sedition, Dhaarmaseni. You may have found prosperity with your new friends but that doesn't mean you can forget old affiliations, does it?"

Abhaya glared at him and, throwing her long plait over her shoulder, she turned to leave the spot.

He stepped in front of her. "You forget that you are on the soil of Avanti, Abhaya," Anuvinda spoke in a soft but menacing tone. "You can't leave without giving me an answer."

"Prince of Avanti! My fortune has smiled upon me, Prabho!" A cheery voice took both of them by surprise. Anuvinda turned to see a bearded merchant dressed in gaudy silks and jewellery that covered him disproportionately. He seemed to be wearing half of his merchandise.

The trader beamed at them. "Pardon, my insolence, Prabho! But, I am afraid, that is not the best way to win a maiden's attention. Try with one of these instead," he said and extended his arm, which was draped with strings of various precious stones.

Abhaya shoved them away. "I need nothing."

"She is angrier than I thought." The trader winked, edging closer to the prince. Maybe you can please her with something more expensive? Like this one?" With a flourish, he displayed another diamond-studded golden wristlet.

Abhaya caught a familiar accent and her eyes widened with realisation.

"It pleases her!" the trader exclaimed. "Now, Prabho, gift her this one and then ask her. See, like this." He took Abhaya's hand and his thumb moved over the welt on her wrist left by Anuvinda's nail. His glance met hers and his poignant blink was followed by a flirtatious smile as he fastened the wristlet. "Why wouldn't she listen to you then?"

"Enough!" Abhaya retorted, trying hard to hide her smile.

The prince of Avanti was more amused than annoyed. "Now bark out your price. And don't dare get too smart here!"

"Would I dare to put a price on the lovely smile that my trinket brought to her lips, Prabho?"

Abhaya chuckled through her displeasure towards Anuvinda. "This is a cunning trader, Yuvaraja. He expects a bigger deal at the cost of this trinket."

"What bigger deal?" Anuvinda frowned.

"Your sister, the light of your land, is going to be wedded tomorrow and you ask what deal a jeweller would want on this occasion, Yuvaraja?"

Abhaya raised her brows. "Perhaps you are too busy doubting your friends to remember the wedding?"

Anuvinda shook his head and shrugged, feeling silly. "I didn't mean to hurt you, Dhaarmaseni."

"Friends again! The gods be pleased! But does this poor merchant get what he seeks?" the trader put in.

"Poor merchant! You are impossible!" Abhaya remarked. "Yuvaraja, he shall not leave you alone until you buy something for the bride."

Anuvinda thought it to be better to get rid of the merchant and nodded. Abhaya volunteered to choose.

"And for the precious princess of Avanti, I have this most prized collection. Each one befits the princess of this prosperous land!" the trader pressed.

"You sure know what suits a bride." Abhaya raised her brows and winked cheekily, adding, "Looks like you have more than one wife."

He blinked then bowed with a laugh. She handed over the selected ornaments to Anuvinda.

Anuvinda threw his signet at the merchant. "Enough now. Show this to the royal treasurer and claim your price." The merchant left with a bow.

Abhaya sighed and turned. "Do you still believe that I intended to spoil Mitra's swayamvara?"

Anuvinda was clearly still in two minds. He suspected she had something up her sleeve but wondered whether a conspirator would linger over wedding jewellery.

Before he could respond, Abhaya walked towards the temple. "The privileged guests, as well as the crowds, have cleared, Yuvaraja. You go on to the palace. I shall be back with Mitra soon after my worship."

Abhaya sighed with relief when Anuvinda went on his way. With all his arrogance, he could still be outwitted. She chuckled to herself as she entered the temple of Mahakala.

God of gods, let Mitra be united with the one she yearns for.

"That was close! But fun nevertheless."

Abhaya shook her head at the voice. "You ... you..." She paused, not finding the right words of rebuke. "You really like trouble. And you drag others into it with you."

The merchant beamed. "Could not have done this without you, Dhaarmaseni."

"What's the plan?" Abhaya asked.

"The honoured prince of Avanti will take care of it!" He smiled.

"How?"

"The jewels, Princess, have a coded message engraved on them. The prince will hand them over to his sister and it shall be taken care of!"

Abhaya stared at him. "You call that a plan? What if he opens the bundle and sees the message?"

"Relax, Abhaya. Do you think someone who did not even care about his sister's consent for the marriage would care about what jewels she wears?"

"But tell me what was written, just in case, and an alternate…"

He shook his head. "No, we cannot entangle you in this more than you already are."

Abhaya looked at him and chuckled. "So it is this simple to be your bride. One has to send a suicide letter and here you come, ready to brave anything and wed her. So easy to claim you, Vaasudeva."

"I *am* a lowborn cowherd after all!" Krishna laughed. "As for your question, should I feel flattered?"

Abhaya grew serious. "Is this the way maidens should be wedded Vaasudeva? The world of Aryas disappoints me with the choices it leaves for a maiden—either of submitting to a contrived alliance forced by greedy kings or eloping against the wishes of her own family. Do maidens not have the right to wed properly?"

"And what would your 'proper' way look like?"

Abhaya fell silent and thoughtfully turned towards the shrine of Mahakala in response. "Uma Haimavati could stand by Mahadeva as he consumed the haalahala. Their togetherness for the sake of universal good touches me, Vaasudeva. Yes, it all might just be a legend. But the message is powerful. When a man and a woman unite for a cause—a cause that is not narrow but one that binds them to itself and together so that they are the same—when the man, the woman and the purpose become one, they are no different from the inseparable Shakti and Shiva. I seek to wed the man who would unite me with such a cause, Vaasudeva."

She expected a well-meaning taunt or a sigh signalling the impracticality of the wish but only silence greeted her. She tore her gaze away from the shrine of Mahakala to look into Krishna's eyes. The expression was neither amused nor concerned, neither indulgent nor discouraging. The wordless communication conveyed a world of understanding. She had shared her views with her father who had told her that she dwelt too much on legends but promised her that she would only wed a man of her choice. Vikrama had promised her the same thing. The only other person with whom she had shared this thought was Mitravinda, who had sighed sadly citing the impossibility of such a wedding in times such as these. But only in Krishna, whose response was just his usual inscrutable gaze, she knew she had found someone who understood the gravity of her wish.

"All lives of the universe are bound with a cause, Dhaarmaseni. Seeking a union for a cause that is not narrow is not unsuitable in any period of time, Abhaya." Abhaya smiled at his words and found that the cheeky spark was back in his eyes.

"Do you want to drown me in philosophical discourse when I have a wedding to plan and a whole host of excited in-laws to face?"

Abhaya beamed in response. Krishna turned to leave and she stopped him by the arm. "I hope that beard of yours is fake. You look atrocious for a groom."

"That jeweller! It was him! Son of a slave!" Anuvinda cried. "Those no-good brutes we employ for guards! Were they drugged when my sister was taken away by that lowborn?" He glared at the guard who brought him the news.

This was an insult beyond anything Anuvinda could brook. The bride eloping the very night before the swayamvara was a shame that sounded the death knell for all his plans for the future. The guests entering the hallway added to his dismay. *How did the news reach them too?*

"What are we hearing, Yuvaraja?"

"This could not have happened without your sister's consent. Was this swayamvara a farce?"

Anuvinda recognised the last speaker as the prince of Kekaya. He chose to not answer and looked at the other guests. "This is an insult to the untarnished pride of Avanti. We shall exact revenge from the lowborn son of the Shooras."

More guests poured in, unsmiling. Anuvinda caught sight of Abhaya entering the hallway along with Dharmasena and walked up to them. His eyes spat fire. "Lord of Anagha, your daughter might have something to say regarding my sister's abduction."

Vikrama, who was behind Dharmasena, stepped in front of Abhaya even as their father put a hand on his arm to restrain him. Abhaya stepped forward, not to be daunted.

"All I can say is that the princess of Avanti went with Vaasudeva on her own accord and was not abducted." In the middle of the sentence, she turned to address the other guests and chose to ignore Anuvinda's piercing gaze.

Dharmasena glanced at her. This was new to him. He controlled his surprise.

"She told me her heart wasn't in the swayamvara as the one she loved was not invited." Abhaya continued, looking at her father.

"Fascinating. Now please enlighten us about why my sister chose to insult her own family and spoke her heart out to the illustrious princess of the neighbourhood kingdom." The word princess and kingdom had a derisive emphasis.

Abhaya chose to ignore the provocation. "And we thought we shared an ancestral friendship."

Dharmasena intervened. "Yuvaraja, you, I am sure, have the wisdom to take corrective actions that would save your pride but blaming your friends is not it."

"Ask your daughter to swear on you that she had no role in ruining my sister's swayamvara!"

"I swear on you, Janaka..." Dharmasena stopped her from saying more. Anuvinda's theatrics had begun to test his patience. He looked at Vikrama, who pulled Abhaya behind them.

"I trust my daughter, Yuvaraja. Another allegation against her, I am afraid, would be an affront to our ancestral friendship." His tone did not carry anger but his eyes signalled the limit of what he could take. "We came to take leave of the king of Avanti."

"And why are we watching this prince blame the failure of his guards on another guest?"

Dharmasena turned in the direction of the speaker; he was not known to him but someone had informed him the day before that the man was the prince of Kekaya. They exchanged a polite nod.

"We did not come to watch a play, Anuvinda. Give us the audience with the king of Avanti. He owes us an explanation."

Anuvinda felt cornered. He took a step back but his angry gaze lingered on Abhaya. "My father is unwell with shock. I am sure that all our esteemed guests realise that paining him further does not help. I promise you all. I am going to get my sister back from that cowherd fool. I shall avenge the hurt pride of Avanti."

"No, you shall not." The voice came from behind him.

Anuvinda whirled around. "Janaka!"

Jayasena, the king of Avanti, entered the hallway. He faced the guests and brought his hands together. "I seek your pardon. But I am happy that Avanti was saved from committing a crime of forcing a daughter into a marriage against her wishes."

Anuvinda's eyes grew wider. He stared at his father and then at the guests in whose eyes he saw rising contempt for him.

"Janaka, he came in a disguise as a merchant trading jewellery and deceived us! Princess Dhaarmaseni saw him too." He turned to her, his eyes almost pleading with her to confirm his claim.

Jayasena continued, undisturbed. "My son-in-law did come in a disguise. With the signet that my son gave him for his 'trades', he sought my audience. My daughter confirmed her heart to me and they left with my blessing."

Abhaya looked away, stifling a smile.

"We wish your daughter a glorious married life, Lord of Avanti," Dharmasena said, breaking the uncomfortable silence. "We are happy she made her choice."

"We would have been saved from this embarrassment if Krishna Vaasudeva had been invited for the swayamvara in the first place. If the princess of Avanti had chosen him, we would have had to accept him as her choice. Please accept my best wishes, too," the prince of Kekaya seconded. Most of the guests chose to agree with them and the others limited their displeasure to stoic silence.

Abhaya met Anuvinda's gaze before she turned to exit and did not miss the threat in them.

In the corner of her eye, she saw the retinue of Kekaya stay close to them. As they waited for their chariots outside the palace of Avanti, she heard Dharmasena thank him.

"Isn't he the other brother-in-law of Vaasudeva?" she whispered to Vikrama.

"Is he?"

"Yes. Bhadra, Krishna's wife is the princess of Kekaya."

She saw Vikrama nod with no excitement but with relief that someone had chosen to stand by them. She smiled to herself. *You did see to it that we were not harmed, Krishna.*

Not long after, they were on the way back to Anagha. Dharmasena's face still spoke of displeasure at the way Anuvinda had spoken to her.

"Wasn't that exciting?" she laughed, trying to break the uneasy silence. "Mitravinda paid him back for the slap from that day so many years ago." She looked at Vikrama, who nodded at the memory. "Will she and Vaasudeva pass by Anagha and stay there for the night?"

"As much as we wish them well, I am not sure how wise it would be to host them," Vikrama remarked, seeing Dharmasena's troubled face.

"That is not a concern," Dharmasena remarked, his gaze steady on the horizon. "Did you both catch the hatred that spewed out of Anuvinda's eyes for his father?"

The thought made all the three shudder.

Chapter Ten

Kamarupa

Bhauma considered the scroll in his hands. He read the message for the third time, throwing sidelong glances at the messenger.

"What would be your response?" the messenger asked. His attire spoke of the prosperity of the kingdom he came from—Magadha. Being a kingdom that controlled a vast part of the plains of Ganga, it boasted of dominion, formal and informal, over a number of other kingdoms across Bharatavarsha. The entire first half of the letter was given to extolling the glory of Magadha.

"Your King Jarasandha remembers the Goddess only when he is in trouble," Bhauma chuckled.

The messenger smiled. "And you know what he can give your Goddess in return."

"The Supreme Goddess needs no gifts. The whole world is an offering at her feet!"

"And my king isn't in any trouble. He only seeks a partnership with you, Prabho. He trusts you, given your devotion to the Supreme Goddess. Not everyone wins his trust so easily."

Bhauma leaned back on his seat, his defences alert at the cautious flattery. "Let us assume what you say is true. From what I understand, your king needs new spies, spies who can spread across the plains. My Shaktas help him—braving Goddess Kamaksha knows what kind of dangers—and he gets to keep his strategic dominion on the region."

"And Kamarupa benefits greatly too," the messenger added with no change in his tone. "And it is negotiable. In fact, I would encourage you to think it over and cite any additional conditions from your side." The messenger saw Bhauma frown in thought. "Is it not worth keeping valuable relationships even at a high cost, Prabho?"

Bhauma sighed, his tone remaining equivocal. "I cannot decide on behalf of the Supreme Goddess. I need to seek Her approval. If She agrees, your king can breathe easy."

The messenger eyed him. "Those with religious commitments have their own constraints."

"Principles, I prefer to call them."

"Very well, Prabho, we shall await the direction from your … I mean, *the* ... Supreme Goddess."

Bhauma rose to his feet. The messenger, understanding that the discussion was at an end, took his leave. Bhauma strode towards Dhatri's chambers. Under his orders, the building had undergone an architectural makeover and now looked just like a temple. Even the pilgrims instinctively bowed before its new tower, for its architectural intricacy was not inferior to that of the main temple. When he entered Dhatri's room, he saw her sitting cross-legged. A smile played on her face. The tranquillity he saw in her made him envious.

"Mahadevi," he said and bowed.

"Bhauma." Dhatri smiled and said, "I was satisfied with the young yoginis. It is extremely fulfilling to teach them about Vamachara worship. It is joyful to see them break social shackles and become one with the Supreme."

Bhauma nodded distractedly.

"Is anything the matter, Bhauma? You seem worried."

"I see a chance to transform the world through the grace of Goddess Kamaksha. But, before that, pardon my insolence, Mahadevi, but what does the Goddess mean to you?"

Dhatri stared at him. Her lips quivered. The few grey locks now threaded in her black tresses only added to her beauty. "Everything, Bhauma. She means everything to me."

Bhauma nodded, solemnly. "Would you like to embark upon a long-term voyage for the Supreme Goddess and spread the message of the Shakta lore in the rest of the world?"

"Yes, Bhauma."

"If an opportunity were to present itself, in the guise of a prayer to the Goddess from a king of the plains..."

"What opportunity?"

"To help him strengthen his spy network by having our Shakta practitioners join their ranks. In return, he promises to make humble offerings to the Goddess."

"This sounds..." Dhatri frowned and closed her eyes.

Bhauma jerked her arm, making her open her eyes. "Disgusting and underhanded," he completed for her. "And you wonder why I come to you with this thought." She nodded. He smiled and leaned back against the chair he had sat in when he entered the chambers. "I felt the same initially, Dhatri. I felt exactly the same. I almost rejected their request with a strong rebuke, when the memory of that night flashed before me. Not in a dream but in a vision. I saw the frenzied villagers, I saw the terrified look on your face and I saw Amaranatha's outstretched hand that I failed to grasp. This seemed like the way to change those barbaric practices in the plains. My fingers shook and I could not seal that letter of rejection. The letter fell from my hands and rolled into the fire. At that moment, the bells rang for the midday worship."

"The bells ring every day, Bhauma," Dhatri protested but he saw confusion in her eyes. "True," he said. "But the signs from the Goddess, the vision during the day, the proposal from the plains ... it just fits so well ... Mahadevi, one word of refusal from you and I will rewrite that letter. I don't want the disobedience of the Goddess on my conscience. So, I seek clarity from you."

Dhatri gasped, feeling the burden of responsibility. Years after she was declared the mahadevi, she had plunged into the Shakta order of worshipping the Supreme Goddess. It felt blissful. Her words were considered those of Goddess Kamaksha herself. It took her hours of sadhana to emerge with clarity from the inner battles with doubt and speculation. Bhauma had been a great companion in this practice and he had helped her arrive at a reasonable decision or advice whenever it was sought. This was considered the "word" of the Goddess.

She cleared her throat. "If our Shaktas help that king, would he care for their safety?"

"Absolutely. And they would get to counsel him over strategic issues. The word from Shakta lore would find its place in the politics of Bharatavarsha, in defining the power structures of the land."

"Why do we need power? We should be content here..."

"Content? Should we allow the order of Shaktas to be limited to the tiny geographical limits of Kamarupa and remote forests? This is our opportunity to transform the land, Dhatri."

"But what if the religious leaders of the Aryas object to this?"

"That is where we need to fight back. Can we let the chosen lore of the Supreme Goddess be relegated to the margins and be dismissed as insignificant?"

Dhatri kept silent. To Bhauma, her eyes showed approval but her lips still quivered in uncertainty. He smiled, running his fingers through her hair.

"I have thought of proposing another condition, Dhatri. The king shall also provide for the teaching of Shaktism and the Vamachara system in particular in the gurukulas."

"But that might not be possible," Dhatri said. "Their gurukulas believe that students should abstain from pleasures and instincts during the period of their education."

"Exactly," Bhauma said. "But if we achieve this even in one gurukula, the others will eventually fall in line."

Dhatri closed her eyes, focussing on the image of the Goddess. Bhauma waited, neither moving nor batting an eyelid.

"Mahadevi, this is only the beginning. Today you have the king of a vast province seeking the help of the Supreme Goddess. This is a Shakta victory. There will be more kings who would seek us out in future. This is the culmination of everything we have been working towards for years. This is the will of the Goddess Herself."

Dhatri nodded, her eyes still closed. She then cleared her throat and said, "Bhauma, I approve."

Chapter Eleven

Prabhasa

The sun was yet to reach its peak but the day was already oppressively hot. The humidity of the seashore made it worse. The only relief Abhaya felt was the warm waves splashing against her feet at regular intervals. The tickling sensation when they tried to snatch the sand beneath her feet made her smile. But her gaze, as she scanned the road every few minutes, was intent. An hour passed before she heard the clatter of horses behind her.

Abhaya turned. The eagle banner fluttered on the approaching chariot, which was closely followed by the guards on horses who had accompanied them to Prabhasa. *Krishna's chariot!* She smiled, recognising the eagle as Krishna's insignia. She had timed her visit to Prabhasa to coincide with Krishna's monthly visit to the shrine of Somanatha. She frowned, spotting Mitravinda with Krishna as the chariot halted at a distance from the shore. Her visits to Prabhasa gave her an exclusive audience with Krishna. She would have preferred it if Krishna had come alone.

Mitravinda jumped down from the chariot, pushing away Krishna's hand when he tried to support her. As her friend, Abhaya noted with satisfaction that Mitravinda had undergone quite a transformation in the months following her wedding to Krishna. Her habitual silence had given way to boisterous chatter.

Gone were the tentative smiles; they were now replaced by unabashed grins and laughter. Abhaya saw her speak animatedly and drag Krishna towards the shore.

Abhaya's eyes misted at the sight of her friend's newfound happiness. She tucked the loose locks of her hair behind her ears. Adjusting the shawl around her shoulders, she walked towards them. Her guards who had carried her message to the couple sensed her signal and stayed behind near the chariot.

Mitra hurried ahead and threw her hands around Abhaya, clasping her face with both hands and kissing her on the forehead. Abhaya's eyes alternated between her and the approaching Krishna. His smile became pronounced by the moment. Abhaya's gaze met his. The expression in his eyes contradicted his smile, giving her the sense that he knew what was on her mind.

She forced her gaze back to Mitravinda. "Seems like you've forgotten the world outside Dwaraka," she teased, trying to sound like her usual self.

"And it seems like Dwaraka does not even exist on your map!" Mitra retorted. "It was you who made me go there. Don't you have the responsibility to ask after my well-being?"

Mitra hardly looked like she needed anyone to ask about her well-being. But her first sentence struck Abhaya.

It was I who made it possible. Then why am I helpless now?

"She has faith," Krishna's words brought her back from her thoughts, "in what she chooses to do."

Faith. If there was anything that had deserted Abhaya in the past days, it was faith. In an unexpected development, her father, King Dharmasena, had received a message from the king of Avanti, seeking her hand in marriage to Anuvinda. It was a moment that Dharmasena had dreaded ever since she was born. No father who knew Anuvinda would give him his daughter. But one could hardly refuse the king of Avanti.

Technically, the city of Anagha bore no formal allegiance to Avanti and was independent, but, in practice, the smaller city was direly dependent on the larger kingdom for its supplies of foodgrains, cattle, labour and even weapons. Travelling traders from the newly developed Yadava confederation had made Anagha prosperous but not independent. Rejecting Anuvinda's proposal might not mean an outright war but Abhaya knew that Anuvinda would do everything in his power to bring her city to its knees.

"My brother's proposal has destroyed your peace, hasn't it?" Mitra's voice was soft when she ventured to broach the topic. Abhaya looked up mutely. "What makes you even think it over, Bhagini? Reject it outright."

"And you know what would follow next," Abhaya replied.

"Would you cast yourself into sure trouble in fear of what would follow next?" Mitra protested. "What happened to the 'determination to find a way out' that you preached to me a year ago?" Mitra looked at Krishna and said, "Why are you silent, Krishna? Tell her." She turned to Abhaya and held her by the shoulders. "Elope ... with someone you trust."

"Surely Mitra, that cannot be the solution to every problem!" Abhaya laughed lightly, as though bantering with her friend was all that was on her mind; the darkness under her eyes, however, indicated something else. "I am not being forced by my father and brother into this alliance, Bhagini."

Abhaya found herself cringing inside, though, outwardly, she remained stoic. "Besides," she added, "if a solution is to be determined, why can't one be determined to cause another to change his heart?"

"What do you even mean?!" Mitra shouted.

"Your little sister has faith in herself, Mitra, the faith that she can 'change' Anuvinda for good," Krishna said. "Do you doubt her capability?"

Abhaya looked up in hope. She clutched Krishna's hands. "Do you believe it is possible, Vaasudeva? Do you believe he can change? Do you believe I can change him?"

"Yes, I believe he can change." He saw her eyes fall before she looked up, trying to absorb his words. The curve on his lips disappeared and his eyes showed a spark of sternness which she had not seen in anyone, not even in her father in any of his harsh moods. "But what are you prepared to lose in this bid to transform him, Dhaarmaseni?"

His tone softened and he extricated his hands from her grip and patted her shoulder. "What if all that you lose is not enough, Abhaya? Your life, the faith that your father and Vikrama have in themselves to protect you, the city that you hold so dear? In this wishful endeavour, Abhaya, do you want to prove Anuvinda right that your duty towards your city can become your weakness? Will you let what is dear to you be your weakness?"

Abhaya shook her head and swallowed hard as Krishna asked, "It is indeed tempting to pass off helplessness as a sacrifice but would you do it, Abhaya?"

"When I stand between my city and what could bleed it to bankruptcy…"

"Strengthen what you hold dear to you, Dhaarmaseni. You don't need me to tell you where to find the strength to keep your faith in what you believe."

"Trade agreements with Dwaraka … and any other friendly neighbour," Abhaya responded as her lips curved. "When Avanti isn't supplying us anything, there is little they can threaten us with unless they want to go in for an open war."

"They can't afford an open war," Mitra intervened. "Not with the uncertainties that are going on in the plains of Ganga. Not when more than a third of their army is elsewhere in a bid to please my brother's so-called 'allies'."

Krishna exchanged a brief smile with Mitra.

"You will hear from me," Abhaya parted, her hands coming together.

"After everything, if you maintain that you love the prince of Avanti so dearly, then … ah!" Krishna grimaced in mock pain and laughed as Abhaya punched him on the arm.

Embracing Mitra again, Abhaya signalled her guards to bring her carriage. The sun had reached the western skies and the shadows had started to lengthen. Abhaya halted, seeing her shadow merge with Krishna's and then climbed into her carriage.

Mitra looked at Krishna's arms which bore the marks of Abhaya's nails where she had held them. As soon as they were alone, she shook her head. "She loves you, Krishna."

"Did she tell you so?" Krishna chuckled.

"You love her, too."

Krishna's brows came together as he looked into her eyes with a plea that made her giggle. "Mitra," He raised his hands, in apparent helplessness. "What in Mahadeva's name can make you believe that my heart can only think of you?"

"Stop right there! You need to come up with a better line." She laughed. "Four brides, Krishna! You can't keep using the same words with all of us!"

"And you still think I dare to love a fifth?"

"Fifth," Mitra sighed, shrugging. *It's better to welcome a fifth and wait a day more rather than have you lost in her* ... Her thoughts were interrupted as Krishna waved his hand in front of her face. She shook her head and walked towards their chariot. "Help her, Krishna. I don't want her to fall into my brother's hands!"

Chapter Twelve

Anagha

"Janaka, what is the status of our granaries?"

Dharmasena looked up. Abhaya's voice lacked her usual restraint. It seemed evident even to the treasurer, who promised to return with the details in a day.

"Should we alert our soldiers to sharpen the war weapons? Or maybe conduct a competition so they keep fit?"

Dharmasena smiled and nodded, keeping aside the leaves containing details about new traders from the western shores who had entered the city.

"Janaka, what is the price we paid Avanti for the swords and javelins?"

"We aren't going to war with Avanti, Vatse," Dharmasena reassured her but he knew it would take more than that to calm Abhaya. It was more difficult to pacify her when she put up a facade of being calm. He rose from his seat and went to her. "You did not tell me everything about your trip to Prabhasa." It was Abhaya's turn to look up as she had, in fact, recounted every single detail of her conversation with Krishna and Mitravinda. Dharmasena waved away his own question, sitting down beside her. "Abhaya, do you trust me?"

"No, I don't."

Dharmasena had to laugh. He was reminded of the many occasions during Abhaya's childhood when she had given unexpected or impudent responses to what she deemed "silly" questions. "Understandable. So, whom do you trust?"

"Anuvinda." The answer earned her a whack on her head and she turned back towards the leaves she was examining with the frown that he felt was an imitation of his. Just as he thought that the mood was returning to normal, he felt the tug on his arm. He had to sit back as she put her hands around him. "I trust him to do something soon that does not bode well for Anagha. You are a king, Janaka. I don't want to become your weakness."

He knew that she was too brave to cry but when her frame shook with a tearless sob, he cleared his throat. "You think I am growing too old to protect those I hold dear? So old that I need to leave one to save the other?" The words, spoken with his characteristic resolve, came out sounding authoritative and final. He sighed. "Maybe I shouldn't have stopped the company of women so early in life."

"Who is stopping you now?" She chuckled and her father joined in.

"Your brother. Who will look at me when he is around in the palace? Here he comes! Vikrama, so you've been to the temple?" he asked, looking at the bowl of payasanna in his hands which made it obvious.

But looking at his face, the father and daughter realised that he was not in a mood to join the banter.

"Some strangers are camping outside the temple of Anagheshwari," he said, extending the bowl towards them. "Shaktas of the Vamachara order."

"I saw them in the past week too," Abhaya said, taking a handful of the sweet. "Anything wrong?"

"What can be right about them, Abhaya?" Vikrama said. "They are the Shaktas."

"Now, Vikrama, I thought you've grown up enough to realise that they aren't some monsters who took your mother away," Dharmasena remarked.

"It is not just me, Janaka. Even the acharya is uncomfortable about them. He said they left pieces of burnt meat scattered in the courtyard of the temple after they were done with their..." Vikrama paused, trying to come up with an appropriate word, "...worship. You would not approve of it if I called their ritual an abomination."

"Certainly not," Abhaya replied, taking note of the disgust in his voice. "Who but the Supreme Goddess or God or whatever can certify whose rituals are right or wrong, Bhrata?"

"Let us not get into a debate about religion, Abhaya. I am neither interested nor qualified," Vikrama said.

Dharmasena smiled at the admission. One endearing fact about Vikrama was that he could never be provoked into arguments over topics he did not know much about, and never hesitated to admit his ignorance. He was open and transparent. But the same thing, Dharmasena sadly noted, could be his undoing if and when Vikrama became the king. Abhaya, on the other hand, was skilled in the nuances of diplomacy. Vikrama's skills lay in swordplay and loyalty to the cause. Such a man, Dharmasena noted, made a fine general but not a fine ruler.

"It is not deniable that Acharya Katyayana would have been shocked seeing the courtyard strewn with pieces of burnt meat," Abhaya conceded.

"The problem is not just that, Bhagini," Vikrama continued and looked at Dharmasena. "Janaka, they have a woman with them and their rituals consist of maithuna too."

"Sometimes, I wonder what stops the world from embracing Vamachara." Abhaya laughed but restrained herself when she caught sight of Dharmasena's disapproving look.

"Katyayana's daughter is of your age, actually a year or two younger than you..." Vikrama pointed out and then cut himself off, not wanting to continue the conversation. "Janaka, let it not be that in being hospitable to the rest of the world, we end up making our own unhappy."

"The foundation of Anagha rests on the principle of hospitability, Vikrama," Dharmasena said, looking from one to the other. "At the same time, Abhaya, we cannot expect a girl of fifteen to stay unperturbed seeing a ritual like maithuna in the open. Send a word to the priest that Pingala Katyayani—isn't that her name?—can stay under your care until the Shaktas leave." Abhaya nodded and Vikrama cast his eyes down. "Vikrama, do take good rest now. I will need you both in the coming weeks when we negotiate new trade agreements with our neighbours. The Shaktas can wait till then."

"No, Janaka, hospitality is meant for guests and for those who mean well. Not for these leeches." Vikrama's eyes signalled a revolt that Dharmasena had never seen.

"I repeat, they cannot be allowed to wander about those premises, not around our home!"

"Vikrama!" Dharmasena rose to his feet, shaking Abhaya's restraining arm off. "You shall not interfere with this!"

"Forgive me, Janaka, I might be forced to disobey you this time." Vikrama turned and left.

Abhaya tried to follow him and was stopped by her father. To her relief, she saw Vikrama moving in the direction of his room.

"Let it go, Abhaya," Dharmasena spoke in a calmer voice.

"That is just not like him!" Abhaya exclaimed.

"When it concerns Shaktas, he is not himself. I never thought that his hatred was so fresh in his heart."

"Why does he hate them, Janaka?"

"Well, I guess it's time for you to know something important, Vatse," Dharmasena replied, motioning her to take her seat. "You know that Vikrama is your adopted brother."

"And I remember you prohibiting me from ever using the word 'adopted' too."

"That was directed more at the women in the palace who were obstructing you two bonding," Dharmasena replied. "He saved you from a cobra when you were three. Let me admit, I lost my senses when I saw the reptile so close to you. He was just a boy of thirteen but, by the grace of Anagheshwari, a Naga by birth. He had learnt the art of controlling serpents as a boy. His mother left him in my care the day you were born. She left him to join these Vamachara Shaktas. His disgust towards them is understandable."

Abhaya's mouth fell open at the revelation. "Janaka, I was told that he was an orphan," she said. Instinctively, she glanced at the door, then turned back. "But why?"

"Kadambari. That was her name. She had an abusive husband. I am not aware of much, to be frank. But the day she came to me, I was shocked at her state. I had a good mind to knock some sense into that man … I forget his name. Does not matter now, anyway. I heard he jumped off a cliff unable to bear the 'insult' of his wife deserting him. Not anyone's loss but I can only imagine what Vikrama must have witnessed in his tender years."

Abhaya nodded, pursing her lips.

"I thought his mother joining the Shaktas was something that he would adjust to and forget about. Well, now you know why he said what he did, so go easy on him when he says extreme things about the Shakta order. He does not mean what he says with even half the intensity. Ideally, I would have been happy for him to just forget everything about this past but we don't have control over one's memory. The least we can do is to not agitate him. Abhaya, I can say with all my heart that a son born of me would not have been more loyal than Vikrama is. You would not have gotten a better brother."

Abhaya smiled and held his hand. "You know that I would not have loved a son born of you more than I love Vikrama, Janaka."

"In addition to Katyayana's daughter, I should ask you to keep a watch on him too. Maybe divert his attention with something else. Mahakala forbid, if he does something rash, I would hate myself for having to…"

"I shall not let it come to that." Abhaya squeezed his arm. "Trust me, Janaka."

"Pingala," Abhaya called out to the absent-minded girl staring out of the window. "Don't you like it here?" It was four days since Pingala had come to stay with her and the girl had remained largely quiet. "Are you missing your father?"

"I do like it here," Pingala replied. "But I am just used to being alone."

"You find it difficult among so many people in the palace?" Abhaya asked, rising from her seat and moving closer to her. She was greeted with a silent shake of the head and an inscrutable expression.

"I found a new friend among those who came to the temple," Pingala said after a long pause. "Father does not like them and that is why he sent me to stay with you. He does not like me talking to them."

Abhaya was at a loss for words. Pingala had been a playmate during her childhood but Abhaya's military training and involvement with royal affairs had led to her drifting away from her childhood friends.

"Am I not your friend, Pingala?" she asked, stroking the younger girl's cheek.

"You are the princess," Pingala replied. "You cannot remain a friend forever."

"Says who?"

"My father."

"Acharya Katyayana is wrong, totally wrong," Abhaya retorted. "When did he tell you this?"

"He's been saying it for many years," Pingala frowned in reply. "Every time I asked about calling you to the temple, he kept saying that you don't waste your time playing games. He used to tell me to study texts and learn the scriptures."

"You don't like to study?"

Pingala shook her head.

"I would have liked to study them all. Tell me about what you read." Abhaya pulled Pingala towards a seat.

"Princess, will you tell my father that those people are nice?" Pingala asked, dodging Abhaya's efforts to start a conversation.

"I will," Abhaya said, with a smile. "But on two conditions. Call me Bhagini, as you used to. And help me perform a vrata."

"Which one?"

Abhaya twisted her curls, thinking. The legends, stories and philosophy of the scriptures had always interested her but never the details of rituals. This was just a ruse to keep Pingala's attention away from the Shakta group till her father could settle matters with them. How was she supposed to know how many vratas even existed or to choose among them?

"I know!" Pingala smiled. "You want to pray to Gauri for a good bridegroom."

Abhaya sank back against her seat. "Is there anything which can help me escape wedding a bad groom, instead?"

Pingala shook her head. "The one I know requires you to survive on a single meal for three days. Can you?"

"Not a problem," Abhaya said, with some hesitation.

"Then how will you train with the sword? If you feel weak, your brother is not going to spare you!" Pingala's eyes were almost misty.

Abhaya laughed. "What do you think he will do to me?"

"I don't know. I saw him scold you so rudely for dropping the shield today morning," Pingala recalled what she had seen in the morning's training session.

"That?" Abhaya chuckled. "Not his fault; my grip on the shield was clumsy."

"Couldn't he have been nicer? Why scold you in front of the other guards for that?"

"Pingala," Abhaya raised Pingala's chin to look at her in the eye. "That is how any weapons' training is done. My hand got cut because I dropped the shield."

"I saw that and he showed no mercy though you were in pain," Pingala frowned. "I could not bear to see it anymore so I just left."

"And that's why you missed seeing how caring Vikrama was when he tended to my wound." Abhaya smiled, showing the bandage around her hand. "Pingala, our people, especially those who teach us, need to be stern at times. And that is because they cannot bear to see us falter. If I had made the same mistake on the battlefield, I would have faced worse consequences than a mere cut."

Pingala nodded and turned away. "You want to perform the Gauri Puja right?"

"Yes, whatever you know."

"I shall check with the kitchen maids if they have everything that is needed." Pingala rose to her feet. "You know, Bhagini, the Shaktas … their rituals will not need you to fast. In fact, they do not need to marry anyone too. They are just so…"

"Interesting," Abhaya completed, forcing a smile.

Pingala nodded and left for the kitchen. Abhaya stared at her retreating figure and fell into a reverie.

She's feeling suffocated with Katyayana's stern regimes and is warming up towards those Shaktas. Restricting her any further would only make her more rebellious.

For the first time, Abhaya did not know what to do.

Chapter Thirteen

Dharmasena stood on the terrace overlooking Anagha. He had a clear view of the heart of the city bustling with trade activity. The royal residence, which was the centre of the city, was flanked by two wings. The left wing of the structure had a partly roofed corridor and led to the entrance to the courtroom. The corridor also served as an informal meeting place for traders from Bharatavarsha and those from across the western seas to meet and greet each other before drawing up plans for long-term trade partnerships. The corridor then extended into the city, serving as a marketplace and ended at the inner fort wall. The right wing was mostly similar in terms of the structure except, that in place of the market, it had guest houses meant for traders and royal emissaries. All this, Dharmasena noted nostalgically, was not achieved in a day. But what was built over two generations could be laid to waste in mere months, sometimes even less.

Dharmasena firmly believed, though, that no threat existed without its solution. Not long before, Anagha had been faced with the threat of a hostile neighbour which commanded a superior army and a treasury ten times richer than hers. But a solution had existed to that problem—a friendship that had started years ago when he had given a night's respite to a tired and weary tribe that had migrated from the northern plains of Bharatavarsha to the shores of Saurashtra. New confederacies sprung up along the shores. Prosperity was galvanised with increased trade activity. Newer neighbours had mutually beneficial trade proposals. Foodgrains from the southern borders of Kunti, weapons and horses from Trigarta and a new trade agreement with Anarta, in addition to a mutual military agreement with Dwaraka—all this had miraculously fallen in place within two months.

The lord of the "city of sinless" sighed with satisfaction, squared his shoulders and read the scroll in his hand one last time before it was to be sent:

To the Esteemed King Jayasena, the Lord of Avanti, the abode of Lord Mahakala

The address to King Jayasena could not have been more ironic; Anuvinda was the true "Lord of Avanti" in all practical sense. Dharmasena shook his head and continued reading:

> *Lord Mahakala has been gracious in bestowing us with your friendship. It was indeed an honour to receive your proposal, asking for my daughter's hand for your illustrious heir, Anuvinda.*

Dharmasena grunted. Illustrious, indeed! It took quite an effort to be diplomatic.

> *But I deeply regret that our princess, Abhaya Dhaarmaseni, has not given her consent to the union. As you well know, a wedding that does not enjoy the consent of the bride is not blessed by the gods. I know that you, the one favoured by the God of the gods, Mahakala, will not let this small matter come in the way of our long*

friendship. I pray to Mahakala that the blessed prince of Avanti finds an illustrious spouse who will become the pride of your holy kingdom.

I know Your Majesty will not consider it below yourself to accept a humble gift from your old friend. As a token of our continued friendship, I send you four horses of the highest breed from Trigarta, a cartload of the new harvest as a sign of prosperity, javelins from the best of forges of Matsya befitting your valour and a trident as my offering to the Lord Mahakala.

With prayers to Mother Anagheshwari for your well-being and that of your empire.

Dharmasena nodded to himself, stamped the letter and handed it to the messenger who had been patiently waiting in the corner.

"Don't be surprised if the letter does not reach the king at all." He smiled at the messenger. "But do ensure that the prince of Avanti receives these gifts."

As he remembered his promise, the king of Anagha sent for his chariot to visit the temple of Anagheshwari at the north-eastern corner of the city. But before he could board the chariot, he saw the priest hurrying towards him.

"Bhudeva Katyayana!"

"Annadata, they have taken my daughter!"

"What! Who?"

Katyayana could not speak. He was out of breath and hysterical with distress. Dharmasena led him inside, sat him down and offered him a glass of water. When the priest had finally calmed down, he said. "Now tell me, Bhudeva. What happened?"

"I had warned you about the Shaktas, Prabho. I had warned the princess. I had warned the prince!" Katyayana's voice broke and his frame shook.

"Send for Abhaya," Dharmasena told the guard without turning and then spoke to the priest. "When did this happen, Acharya?"

Katyayana buried his head in his hands. "Pingala came to me this morning to clarify something about the vrata that your daughter had asked about. Some things needed to be purchased from the market and she never returned! The Shaktas are missing since last night."

"I am sure Pingala is with Abhaya," Dharmasena said, hoping he was true.

"Janaka."

Abhaya faced both men with a question to which she did not have the answer. "Pingala did not return since morning." The sight of shock and displeasure in Dharmasena's eyes froze her limbs.

"Why did she have to go to the market herself to purchase anything? Couldn't you send one of your maids or the guards?" Dharmasena's temper was at its tipping point.

"Nothing was missing in our granary!" Abhaya exclaimed. "When I went to the kitchen, I was told that everything was available. She lied!"

Katyayana's eyes widened in shock. "She lied?"

"Why did she leave the palace by herself?" Dharmasena's angry eyes pierced Abhaya.

"Janaka, I could not have her shadowed that way. It took me more than three days to have her open her mouth!"

She stared at Dharmasena's hand that had risen to forbid any further explanations. His clenched jaw and the vein she could see throbbing in his forehead made her heart miss a beat. It was the first time she had faced her father's wrath this way.

Dharmasena turned to Katyayana. "They should not have gone far. I shall send for the soldiers right away!"

Katyayana shook his head. "I speak with no ill will but the Vamacharis meant no good. Today it was my daughter. God forbid but tomorrow it may be yours." He stood up to leave.

Dharmasena stopped him by his arm. Much to Abhaya's shock, he dropped onto his knees in front of the priest.

Abhaya too sank to the ground, more because the strength in her legs deserted her. Katyayana bent, caught Dharmasena by the shoulder and helped him rise. "You got it wrong, I am not cursing you. I, Katyayana of the Bhargava gotra, am your purohita, the well-wisher of this city and your family. Any ill that befalls the city and your family would have to first pass over my corpse." He sighed, collected his shawl from the seat and left.

"Janaka, Pingala left out of her own accord. I beg you, do not send soldiers to pursue her!" She shrank back, seeing Dharmasena's hand rise violently this time. He stopped himself midway and hit it against the pillar with all his strength, pain erupting on his face.

"Janaka!"

"Later."

She sank to the ground, finding her limbs desert her will. She did not know how long she sat there until Vikrama's comforting arms went around her.

Chapter Fourteen

"This is the first time he thinks you let him down," Vikrama said jokingly, trying to lighten his sister's mood.

Abhaya shook her head. "Bhrata, you know it was beyond my control!" she protested. "Did he have to fall at Katyayana's feet just to show me that I let him down?" She had spent a sleepless night and all of Vikrama's efforts to cheer her went in vain.

"Calm down. Father was just disturbed at Katyayana's state," he reasoned.

"Then he should have heard me out!"

"I told you it is the first time he feels let down by you. And people don't handle things well when that happens." The light humour did not sit well with Abhaya and she turned away. He sighed and sat down by her side. "Bhagini, I have decided to pursue their trail."

Abhaya looked up. "You're joking!" But his face told her he wasn't. "Why Bhrata? If she left by herself, we have no right to pursue her and force her to come back!"

"I am not going to force her to come back." Vikrama glared at her, upset at her assumption. "Abhaya, I have my motive too." He looked away. "You know my mother left my late father before the king adopted me. She too left with some Vamachara Shaktas."

Abhaya continued to look at him and he could read the question in her mind. "I spoke to Katyayana to find more about them. He says they are from the south of the Vindhyas towards the western shores. I remember that my mother went that way too."

"Do you expect to find your mother there now?" Abhaya asked, unimpressed.

"I can at least try."

"Why would you want to find the woman who abandoned you?"

"Don't I have the right to ask her why?" Vikram retorted. "Besides, I think Katyayana is right in saying that those Shaktas mean no good. A true practitioner of any religion does not try to influence a juvenile mind. They did just that in whisking Pingala away. The girl did not know what she was doing."

Abhaya looked unconvinced. He held her shoulders and turned her to face him. "Abhaya, they will come for you. I should stop them before they do that."

"Don't be ridiculous. I shall not go with them if they ever come for me. Are you happy?"

"You refuse to get it, don't you?"

"Have you been taking some hallucinogen? Why on this earth would they come for me?"

Vikrama said nothing. How could he say that he had dreamt about it—that the Shaktas were carrying Abhaya away into the night? He had never told anyone about his dreams, the dreams he had begun seeing when he was just a boy, soon after his mother left him in Dharmasena's care. There was the disturbing recurring dream in which his mother grew wings and flew away, laughing at his inability to follow her. And then there was the dream about Abhaya, who was just an infant then. He had dreamt that a serpent had coiled itself around the toddler Abhaya and, a year later, the dream had come true. In the past month or so, he was tormented by his mother's voice in his dreams, exhorting him to protect his sister. The day Katyayana told him about the Shaktas, he dreamt of his mother pushing Abhaya down a cliff amidst mountains that he did not recognise. In the dream, he remembered running to the edge of the cliff only to find her being carried away by women and men taking the name of the goddess they worshipped. Pingala's disappearance, his instincts told him, was a prelude to something disastrous that would affect Abhaya. But he knew Abhaya would never believe him. He did not know what to believe himself but the beliefs ingrained in him as a child told him that the gods sometimes send warnings about the future in oblique ways. His mother, wherever she was, held the key to understanding what was to come. Of that, he was sure.

"You want to leave us, don't you?" Abhaya said accusingly.

"I am helpless you feel so, Bhagini."

"Janaka shall not let you go!" Abhaya clutched his arm.

"He has already given his permission, this morning." Vikrama smiled as he squeezed her hand.

"Let go of his hand, Vatse," Dharmasena said softly, entering the room.

"Janaka!" Abhaya exclaimed. "How can you let him go?!"

Dharmasena smiled at them and put his hand on Vikrama's shoulder. "Have confidence in the ties that bind us, Abhaya. Don't stop him. This is important to him. And I know he shall come back to us even if his mother tries to stop him."

Abhaya's grip loosened. Her eyes sought Vikrama's and, for a moment, he saw again the five-year-old who had tugged at his hand and heart, years ago, making the bitterness of every other troublesome relationship melt away. "Forgive me if I pained you, Bhrata."

Vikrama shook his head and laughed, running his fingers through her hair, affectionately. "I'm sure you'll enjoy the respite from the 'cruel' training sessions."

"I'll train enough to beat you when you return," Abhaya said. "Let me sharpen your sword for you."

"I have a new one for him," Dharmasena intervened, holding up the shining steel blade, enjoying the momentary gleam in the eyes of both his children on seeing the new weapon. *Children remain children,* he smiled to himself.

They watched him from the terrace, the lone rider leaving the fortress of Anagha behind and disappearing into the horizon.

"Was it wise to let him go, Janaka?" Abhaya asked.

Dharmasena nodded. "I should have done this earlier, Abhaya. This was the first time he took the initiative instead of being a pliant implementer of others' orders."

"You are the first father who complains of his children being too obedient," Abhaya quipped, smiling.

"Not that I would ever accuse *you* of it, Abhaya," Dharmasena said, his eyes twinkling. "You never seek an opinion from either of us when you go ahead and do something."

"What did I do now?" Abhaya looked away, knowing there was truth in his words. "Whatever I did, Janaka, would you not have done the same if you were in my place?"

"That works as an admission more than anything else."

"I am not the one to lie to you. Neither have you been one to make me lie to you, Janaka. Ask me about anything and I'll explain my actions. If I ever did something without your knowledge, it was only to save you a diplomatic dilemma."

"No Abhaya, intentions aren't where I seek to confront you. I did a lot of things without my father's knowledge too, when I was young, Vatse. He was confident about my intentions and he was sure that he could step in if things got out of control. But the intrigues we faced then were much simpler than those we face today."

Abhaya sat down, knowing this conversation would not be short or easy. On the other hand, she also welcomed the lightening of the burden she bore about everything she had done without Dharmasena's knowledge, from helping Mitravinda elope with Krishna to seeking Krishna's help on the recent trade agreements. Finally, she said, "So what bothers you now, Janaka? Let me share those concerns too."

He shook his head. "Watch the people you trust, Vatse. They seem to be too big to have an honest stake in your well-being."

"Who do you mean, Janaka?"

Dharmasena avoided her gaze, debating within himself. As a father, it was a hard choice to make between protecting his daughter and giving her the freedom to make her own decisions and learn her lessons. As long as her fearless honesty remained, he knew that he had little to worry about. "Abhaya, I shall not let my biases affect your judgement. My friendship with the king of Avanti was based on my experience. It cannot continue with you and Anuvinda. You are obviously looking for allies who are worthy of your friendship. I cannot choose these friends for you. I can only tell you to be conscious of whom you trust and what their motives are. An enemy's enemy can be a friend only as long as both enmities stay," he paused and smiled to himself. The conversation was turning into a sermon. Abhaya nodded seriously. "You know the rest, Vatse. All this aside, do talk to Katyayana once. He has been forgiving. But we need to get to the bottom of this abduction. Apart from Vikrama's investigation, we shall send out more soldiers too in search of Pingala."

Chapter Fifteen

Dwaraka

The waves hitting the rocky shore of Dwaraka did little to drown the festive commotion in the mansion that was home to the Shoora household. Festivity was not uncommon in the family but a visit by a newly-wed daughter was extra special. Subhadra's visit to Dwaraka was a short one but tactical too, as those in the know of the correspondence between her brother Krishna Vaasudeva and her marital family understood. The new venture that her brother-in-law, King Yudhishthira of Indraprastha, the eldest of the Pandava brothers, was pondering could potentially redefine the entire political structure of Bharatavarsha. The brothers had sought Krishna's advice at every small and big juncture of their lives. Their rise to power was achieved after successfully overcoming a series of near-fatal problems, which the populace of Bharatavarsha felt had been engineered by their paternal cousins, the Kauravas. This time, Yudhishthira was thinking of conducting a Rajasuya, the ultimate imperial conquest that would unite the disunited janapadas and bind them in a single code of conduct. It would begin with a Digvijaya, a conquest in all four directions. The kings from every kingdom they passed would either have to consent to the overlordship of the one performing the Rajasuya or face war. Finally, it would culminate in an elaborate ceremonial yajna, to which all the subordinate kings would be invited to attend and negotiate the new political structure.

"It is a well-thought-out plan," remarked Krishna, looking up from the map of Bharatavarsha that lay before him, with the campaign strategy marked. Yudhishthira's four brothers would lead the conquest in each of the four directions. The accompanying scroll detailed resources, finances, the counsel of the rishis, the considered speculation about the potential reactions of allies and detractors and so on. This kind of information could not have been entrusted to an ordinary messenger. Nor could one of the Pandavas have come bearing it without attracting unwanted attention. Subhadra's visit to her parental home, on the other hand, would not raise suspicions. It had been a good idea to send the plans through her. Krishna looked across the table at his sister, who sat doing a final scrutiny of the plan. He smiled at her intent expression. Subhadra shared Krishna's dusky complexion and strong jawline. The women of the palace had been teasing her that her skin had paled after her wedding and that she was becoming a northerner now that she was the favoured bride of the famed warrior Arjuna. Even the way she wore her hair had changed; she now wove up her plaited hair into a spiralled bun held in place with ornamental pins and a gem-studded chudamani.

"Are you ready for the journey?" she asked now, interrupting his thoughts.

"Does the journey ever stop, Bhagini?" he said with a smile.

"You seem too thoughtful. Is there something else that needs to be straightened out?"

"How did you guess?"

"Unlike those women you've wedded, I can read your eyes beyond that smile of yours. I can tell when you are preoccupied even when your forehead is placid without a slight frown. I can feel your jaw tightening even when you manage to retain the colour of your cheeks," Subhadra teased. "And let me tell you, Bhrata, even your wives consult me when they are unable to conclude what you feel about something."

"And do you give your brother away?" Krishna asked, letting his jaw drop in mock horror.

Subhadra raised her eyebrows and pretended to consider revealing more. She laughed at his anticipation. "Do you think your little sister will give you away?"

"So you deceive my innocent wives who depend on you?"

Subhadra had expected this trap and was prepared for it. "I do whatever I can to stop them from throwing you out of their beds! Now, let us start early. We can't afford to let the horses gallop." She stroked the gentle bulge of her belly in an unconscious reminder of her early months of pregnancy.

Before long, a chariot set off from the seaside fortress of Dwaraka and took to the highway leading to the northern part of Bharatavarsha; it was followed by a minimal guard. Patrol teams, a collective effort by the different rulers of Saurashtra, had kept the highway safe for travellers, and even royals who traversed this route did not feel the need for an increased guard. Krishna noted with satisfaction that this initiative was also supported by allies like Matsya and Kunti and that their journey to Indraprastha would be safe.

"Can I?" Subhadra reached for the reins. "It has been long since I have held the reins."

Krishna obliged and flexed his arm in relief.

At this pace, we will barely cross Saurashtra before dusk.

"We could stop at Anagha for the night," Subhadra suggested, reading his thoughts.

"We might need to. We need to let the king know of the new developments. The military support we promised them might be hampered for the interim. That is, if everything goes according to the plan. These developments would make Avanti insecure. They would be amongst the first to oppose the Rajasuya. Their next step would be to cut Saurashtra away from the rest of Bharatavarsha, hampering Dwaraka's aid to Indraprastha and likewise. Being the fortress that oversees the junction of three crucial highways, Anagha would be the first target for their defensive expansion."

Subhadra nodded but continued to look at him askance. Adjusting her hold on the reins, she kept the horses at a steady trot. "Is there any other way to alert them without detailing our quest at this juncture?" She added quickly, "Not that I don't trust them. But others have the right to know about the campaign first."

Krishna changed the subject. "So, how does it feel to be the youngest wife of a man whom every maiden across Bharatavarsha dreams about?"

Subhadra looked at Krishna. Behind the twinkle in his eyes and the smile on his lips, she saw concern. She handed back the reins and stretched herself.

"Bhrata, if I were insecure, do you think I would have told you the truth?" Krishna raised a brow. He glanced back at the western horizon and cracked the whip gently. "Polygamy is point-blank unfair, Bhrata. But then, so is pitying women."

"So! My little sister has achieved a new high in her knowledge about social dynamics."

"Stop that," nudged Subhadra. "Let us approach this from the top. When the ones making social constructs, the rulers and the rishis, are too lazy to make proactive changes, the ones implementing them—the commoners and even small-time lords—tend to turn fundamentalist. They tend to think that women are their property and it can't get worse than that. But the ones opposing their fundamentalism make the mistake of feeling that women are abalas and need protection. And they can't go more wrong." She paused, looking for a response in his face. Seeing him nod, she continued, "Each approach has its horrible consequences. In polygamy, if a man favours one wife over the others, the other women pass their frustrations on to the next generation and homes turn into battlefields. Those who think patronisingly about women lose their ability to see women as partners and mistake them for a burden. To change the construct, one needs to see this world as a whole and not from chauvinistic or feministic perspectives. It is this balance that makes us prevail over adversity. Push women to the edge and face the brunt of underhanded scheming, infidelity, rebellion in various shades that marks the end of any balance in society." Laughing to herself on her long speech, she added, "Your wives, by the grace of Goddess Gauri, haven't yet reached that stage."

"Go on, say that I am the last person who should be talking about polygamy and proactive social change."

"If I begin to give in to your baits, I would not be your sister, Bhrata," Subhadra sighed. "But if you run to the rescue of every girl who sends you suicide letters, you will not have it easy." Krishna opened his mouth but, before he could get a word out, Subhadra mimicked him to perfection. "Got it. I shall tell the next maiden who writes to me to go and die. I shall visit her funeral."

"I shall tell the next person who asks my counsel over any sociopolitical issue to instead take your advice. My bhagini surpasses me!" When his smile faded, Subhadra saw a different light in his eyes. "Isn't it like a bunch of entangled threads?"

Subhadra sighed, reaching out to a closet fashioned in the wall of the chariot where she had placed raw mangoes to combat the discomfort of the journey. "Polygamy is just one among innumerable knots. The rot is much deeper, Bhrata." She closed her eyes, savouring the tangy taste. "Bharatavarsha has reached that unfortunate state where every small proposition for change sends ripples of hostility across the classes of people. The ones responsible for bringing about change—the rishis—cannot do it themselves without the cooperation of the rulers. The rulers don't or cannot enforce change if they see it as a threat to their power. The commoners, driven by fear of the unknown, are not open to experimenting with change. The few who rebel are put down in no time ... where do you start unravelling this, Bhrata?"

"The change that you ask for, Subhadra, is not a doctrine or a decree that can be implemented overnight. Change is inspired by the individual's internal will to adapt and not by rebellion spurred by momentary dissent.

And, yes, you got it right. Fear is what stops us from questioning and exploring new shores. Fear was the reason why the idea of our exodus from Mathura to Dwaraka was frowned upon by some of our elders. They preferred to die at the hands of Jarasandha rather than explore a chance to survive. You were too...”

“I remember. I was young but I remember everything. Every single word you had to hear, Bhrata. The very people who called you a god, a deliverer and a boon turned on you and said you were inauspicious, a curse upon the tribe. I was young but my heart burned at the hypocrisy, at the sheer lack of their readiness to take on responsibility. Then I saw you working for their safety, regardless of the unpredictable swing between praise and ridicule.” When Krishna gazed into her eyes, he saw the years of camaraderie and the undying faith she had vested in him. His hand instinctively rose to caress her face. In the glow that appeared in her eyes, Krishna felt renewed vigour himself.

“Hypocrisy, lack of responsibility—these are big words, Subhadra. We only need to accept that everyone is driven by their needs. Once he sees the greater good as his own need and not a favour to the world, the world inevitably becomes a better place. Beliefs are not stagnant, Subhadra. They change. So do the people who rest their faith in those beliefs. Some are guided by their materialistic ends, some driven by the need to secure a better life for their children, some influenced by the sheer logic of the change that is proposed and yet others inspired by the strength of truth. People do welcome change. But then we need to cure their fear and instil faith. Once their fear is dispelled and faith restored, it is they who drive us towards the change and not the other way round."

And they need someone to keep faith in them regardless of how they receive him. Someone like you, Bhrata.

"Can we hope that the new empire of the unified Bharatavarsha will restore people's faith and dispel their fears?"

"We can if we begin by reposing the same faith on someone who trusted us before." Krishna pointed to the fortress which was visible in the distance. Subhadra smiled and nodded.

"I was never against trusting the king of Anagha or his daughter. And the princess, I think, is smart enough to realise the risks when we give her the necessary clues, isn't she?"

With a nod, Krishna turned the chariot in the direction of the fort of Anagha. The momentary twinkle that flashed across his eye made Subhadra wonder if there was more to it than the trust he was talking about.

Chapter Sixteen

Gomantaka

The touch of cold metal on his neck brought Vikrama's weary sleep to an end. His instincts drove his hand to his sword even as he opened his eyes. It wasn't there! The metal drove into the skin of his chin and he realised that his attacker was using his sword against him. The sword prodded him up to a sitting position. He felt the heavy breath of his attacker to his left. He lifted his arms, signalling surrender and attempted to turn left to get a look at his attacker. The tip of the sword immediately pierced his chin deeper, preventing him from turning further.

"Don't I deserve to know who dared to steal my blade and use it against me?"

"Not unless you blurt out who you are and who sent you here!"

Vikrama's brows went up when he heard the voice. *A woman!* A sudden stillness pervaded his chest and he found himself holding his breath. He had to fight the urge to look towards the owner of the voice.

"And if I say that is my own business and concerns none else?"

"If trespassing into our lands is indeed your business…" She stopped as she sensed her captive being unusually still for someone taken by surprise. She let the sword complete the sentence by drawing blood at his chin. She expected a gasp but got a chuckle instead.

"Afraid of strangers, are you?" he asked, provocatively. The question earned him a kick at his side. It was painful but allowed him to gauge her position. The blade on his neck shifted at her momentary loss of balance and, in that instant, he rolled over and kicked her other leg out from under her.

She let out a shrill cry at the unexpected move. She managed to retain her balance, though at a cost of stepping back by a yard or two, and she looked at him warily with renewed respect for his agility. She saw Vikrama rise to his feet and take a step forward in a probable bid to retrieve his weapon. His gaze met hers and the sparkle in his eyes was telling.

Vikrama took another step forward and all thoughts of attack vanished from his mind when he saw her eyes. Her pupils were a shade between that of the bark of the tree and the hue of a cloud about to burst. A voice inside his head told him he was being incredibly foolish to be deliberating on the shade of her eyes when he should be trying to retrieve his weapon but he took another step forward, regardless. What he saw in her eyes made him think that her hostility had dropped. Perhaps she thought that his bid to demand his weapon back was fair. Perhaps she was impressed at his not running away at the first opportunity. He was not a trespasser and he needed to fear no one. Vikrama wished that he could communicate that but words failed him.

A drop of blood dripped from his chin. Her eyes, he thought, showed concern. She threw his sword to the ground and, in the instant that he retrieved it, she had drawn out her blade.

"I don't desire what isn't mine! But..." She brandished her blade, forbidding him from taking any further steps forward.

"I don't desire to duel with ... you either," Vikrama replied, realising in his pause that he had no clue how to address her. "But in our lands, we would welcome a weary traveller with drink, and food and less..." He wanted to say "hostility" but said, "...scepticism." He saw her frown, but her blade descended to her side. "I don't mean any harm. I am here on a quest."

"For diamonds?" she asked, her frown deepening. "Forget about them, unless..."

"I don't seek diamonds. I am looking for someone," Vikrama replied.

She seemed convinced and sheathed her sword, and he followed suit.

"They call me Shyeni."

"The name 'Kalabhashini' would do more justice to your voice," Vikrama said, feeling overpowered again as Shyeni nodded, accepting the compliment with grace. "And they call me..." He was about to blurt out his name when caution stopped him. "Manikandhara," he said, surprising himself. It was the name his mother had given him before he had been adopted by Dharmasena.

"Are you a Naga?" Shyeni asked as the serpent tattoo on his wrists caught her attention.

He nodded briefly. A smile lit her face, making his heart beat faster. She lifted her hand and he saw the eagle tattoo on her wrist.

"Garuda!" Vikrama gasped. He noticed the feathery upholstery over the garment that hung from her shoulders and ran down the length of her frame up to her knees.

"We Garudas eat Nagas for breakfast!" She grinned.

"Well, I might taste better if I am fed first!" Vikrama said, surprised at himself. Humour was not exactly his forte.

Shyeni giggled. Vikrama went weak at the knees. "Follow me." She pointed to the mountain that lay to the west, covered with vegetation which, Vikrama guessed, housed her tribe. "Do you prefer an easier but longer route to my settlement, or a shorter but steeper route?" She regarded him and considered. "Shorter one, then," she decided before he could answer. "Follow me."

Vikrama followed her. The route up the Gomantaka Mountain was as challenging as she had promised.

"So, you did not come for diamonds?" she asked. "Almost every foreigner we encounter comes in search of those."

"I don't desire what is not mine," Vikrama replied, returning the words she had used.

She looked over her shoulder, eyes narrowed. "There is no need to desire what is already yours. And if you don't desire what is not, do you have any desire left?" She chuckled and walked on, her hips swaying gracefully.

They came to a narrow ridge up an almost vertical portion of the mountain. Vikrama stopped short, gaping as Shyeni effortlessly scaled the surface that offered little in the way of footholds. He couldn't help being amazed at her sure-footedness. Noticing his hesitation, she pointed at another ridge hidden by a dried bush.

"Right leg there first. Then hold on to the bush, place your left leg on this other ridge."

Vikrama nodded and followed her instructions. He had almost made it to the top when his foot slipped. He was about to fall but Shyeni caught his arm in a firm grip. Slowly, but surely, she pulled him over. On safe ground, they collapsed, gasping for breath. Vikrama's eyes fell upon her heaving breasts and his heart skipped a beat. He averted his eyes in confusion. When he looked back into her eyes, he saw not an accusation but the reciprocation of his desire. Time seemed to stop and they were lost to the world until the shrill cries of a bird brought their wordless conversation to an abrupt end.

"What sort of a Naga are you? The one who is born in a palace?" Shyeni said, trying to return to casual conversation.

"You can say I was brought up in one."

"Explains your 'expertise' in scaling heights. Thank the Divine Eagle Suparna I could pull you up!" Shyeni rose to her feet. "We'll take the longer route. I doubt you can make it even half the way up on this one. And you can tell me everything about your quest. A story to keep us company on the long trek."

Chapter Seventeen

Anagha

"We had visitors in your absence," Abhaya informed Dharmasena as she sat down for her evening meal with him. "The Yadava leader and his sister ... well, the queen, or should I say, the second queen ... oh, let it be! I can never figure out the hierarchical positions in her marital family."

Dharmasena nodded, raising the first fistful of rice in a mechanical prayer before pushing the rice ball into his mouth. He seemed tired, having just returned from his trip to Anarta and Prabhasa.

"Something is being planned in the north," she added, mulling over the incident that had happened a couple of days ago as she ate. "Strange behaviour on their part. Something was unusual."

"Why? What happened?" Dharmasena looked visibly tired from his travel. But it did not stop him from staying alert and listening.

"I think a conquest. Let me explain. They halted here for the night. As I had almost skipped my evening meal, I sat down with them. And Subhadra, out of nowhere, started to talk about my marriage!"

"For one of her younger brothers-in-law? She probably sees a potential ally in you, another daughter from Saurashtra. Wait, what kind of conquest are we talking about exactly?"

"Janaka!" Abhaya protested. "Yes, she did hint at one of her younger brothers-in-law and..." she hesitated, recalling the scene.

At Subhadra's question, her eyes had instinctively sought Krishna's. She had seen in them the same resistance she felt within herself. It had made her glad. She shook off the memory and continued, "Then, in his usual air, Krish—Vaasudeva only commented that Subhadra was just seeking an ally in me in her conquest of her marital home! Janaka, the way he emphasised the word 'conquest', I felt he was trying to convey something. And then he added in the same flow of jest that a wise princess would consider it a good opportunity to step into the most powerful imperial family of Bharatavarsha and then corrected himself to say the soon-to-be most powerful imperial family. Janaka, at that moment, from the corner of my eye, I saw Subhadra's hand clutch his knee! It's clear she didn't want him to say more. What do you make of it—'the soon-to-be most powerful imperial family'?"

"For the moment, I am inclined to think about the offer if she really meant it. Provided you agree?" Dharmasena replied, a renewed sense of excitement overtaking him.

"I don't think there is any offer." Abhaya shook her head. "Then I changed the topic to Mitravinda and casually asked why Subhadra was taking her brother along to her marital home. I asked if all his brides had come together and decided to throw him out of the home."

"You used those exact words?"

"He did not mind."

"But, Vatse…"

"Janaka, he simply shrugged and said what else could be done if the home turned into a war zone. He added that one might need to flee at least for the time being. Janaka, that was unusual! He is usually very defensive about his wives. Even when confronted with a humorous jibe, he never says a derisive word about them!"

"Abhaya, are we really discussing his marital affairs? What is the matter with you?"

"Listen to me! He again stressed on 'war zone'. After the meal, I offered Subhadra my room. He interrupted and said my room looks like a 'battlefield'. So they insisted on staying in the guest quarters."

"That wasn't very polite," Dharmasena said. "But then, you take inappropriate liberties with Vaasudeva, too."

"Didn't you notice 'war zone' and 'battlefield'?" Abhaya said impatiently. "And one last thing. I accompanied them to the guest house to make sure it was comfortable. Subhadra is with child now. Both Subhadra and I were practically asleep on our feet. And Vaasudeva chose that moment to launch into a sermon on diplomacy."

Thank Mahakala, at least, the conversation turned sensible and civil as against the pointless banter, Dharmasena sighed to himself.

"So this topic was between choosing friends and allies. According to him, there are times where choosing between enemies is more important than choosing between allies." Dharmasena looked up from his food. "At times, when allies cannot be reached out to, or when allies are not in a position to extend help, he said it is advisable to revisit the priorities between rivals instead. A worthy enemy could perhaps save one from a bad ally, he added, and then he stopped abruptly."

Dharmasena was paying attention now. "You know, now that I think of it, I got an odd feeling in Anarta, too. That something was up ... what do you make of Vaasudeva's words?"

"If I'm connecting the dots right..." Abhaya looked intently at her father, "that is, if Subhadra's husband and his brothers, the Pandavas, are planning a conquest, the land might turn into a war zone. Krishna Vaasudeva wanted to alert us about the allies we are banking on coming to our aid if Avanti attacks us. We know it is a distant possibility but a possibility for sure..." she said, then continued thoughtfully, "Now, coming to revisiting our allies and enemies. Our trade allies, the Yadavas, the Trigartas, the Matsyas, the kings of Kunti and Anarta will not be able to honour their pledge of military support if they are called upon to participate in the proposed conquest. Avanti understandably would rally against the Pandavas. That is the time we might need to make a choice. I think he hinted for us to make peace with Avanti for the time being even if it meant a temporary rivalry with him."

"What are you getting at, Abhaya?" Dharmasena's eyes betrayed disappointment.

"I hate to admit this, Janaka, but Avanti, in the interim, would be too powerful for us to take on single-handedly. When the choice comes, I would choose an enemy who would treat us with grace when we are defeated on the battlefield instead of one who would ravage our land and people. At the cost of befriending this 'ally', we would get ourselves an 'enemy' who can free us from the clutches of our 'ally'."

"And what about the clause of your wedding and the numerous insults we would have to face in the process?" Dharmasena's face remained stern.

"Anuvinda has always seen me as a tool to control the highway by expanding into Anagha. He has never really wanted me. Besides, there can be acceptable ways to put off the 'wedding' to sometime later if it came to that."

Dharmasena remained quiet and, in his silence, Abhaya heard disapproval. To her surprise, he pushed his unfinished plate of food away. A hymn he had once taught her when she was young and fussing over her food came unbidden to her mind.

Annam Brahma
Raso Vishnu
Bhokto Maheshwarah

Dharmasena made a point of worshipping food, of not wasting a single morsel. His action told her how upset he was.

"Janaka," she persisted gently, nudging the plate towards him. "I find the idea as repulsive as you do now. But losing one's appetite does not solve anything. Besides, all this might still turn out to be nothing but mere speculation of my bored mind."

Dharmasena resumed eating but remained silent. Going back to Avanti now, with their tail between their legs, would come at a high cost, not to mention personal humiliation. Besides, Dharmasena felt offended that Abhaya thought Anagha would be defeated, either way, no matter whom they supported. He knew that Abhaya's speculation was based on numbers. But Krishna, for all his friendship, had no business to assume Anagha's defeat even if they took on Avanti single-handedly. He was surprised that Abhaya—always quick to anger—had not taken offence at this assumption.

Are she and Krishna growing closer? So close that…?

Dharmasena brushed the thought away, hoping that none of their speculations would ever come to pass. The conversation turned towards trade revenues, palace affairs and onto lighter issues, with each trying to make the other laugh and bring back a sense of normalcy. Vikrama's presence, Abhaya reflected, would have helped. He was the one who was capable of seeing priorities beyond the compulsions of honour.

A time might come when we will need to choose sides, Janaka. Assuring the safety of the citizens of our small kingdom is our true dharma, not what our ego tells us our dharma is.

Chapter Eighteen

Kamarupa

Dhatri collapsed to her knees on the stairs of her residence.

Bhauma hurried to her side and squeezed her arm. "Mahadevi!"

"Nothing has changed in the plains of Bharata! They still kill women just for the 'crime' of pursuing their freedom!" Dhatri groaned.

Bhauma tried to raise her to her feet. Dhatri shook his grip away and rushed down the stairs towards the corpse of a woman that lay before her and screamed, "Arise! Devi Kamaksha says arise to life! You did not deserve this death!"

"Dhatri!" Bhauma dragged her back.

"ARISE!!!"

"She shall not arise, Dhatri! Calm down, Mahadevi."

"Why can't she?" Dhatri demanded, tears now streaming down her cheeks. "It was not her mistake. She came to explore Shaktism. She was not satisfied. She went back home with no idea of what awaited her. What was her crime, Bhauma? Why this death? And why should I remain the mahadevi if I can't bring her back to life?"

"Listen to me, Dhatri, I beg you!" Bhauma pleaded, trying to pull her by her arm. "Mura, see that the unfortunate girl is given an honourable funeral."

Mura had been a mute spectator, too shocked to speak. Some Shakta practitioners, who had left Kamarupa some days before, had brought back the corpse of a girl. She had come to Kamarupa attracted to Shakta lore but later refused to adapt to the Shakta ways. He knew that Dhatri had sent her back home.

Hope had risen in him when Dhatri had called out to the dead girl to rise to life. But, to his disappointment and Dhatri's visible dismay, no miracle happened. He bowed at Bhauma's orders.

But Dhatri hadn't given up on her bid to revive the dead girl. "Where have my miraculous powers gone, Bhauma?" she wailed.

"Mura, you heard me!" Bhauma called out.

"Prabho," Mura bowed again with a lingering gaze on the corpse and then at Dhatri, who had now given up resisting Bhauma's attempts to calm her down. He signalled to the soldiers behind him to take the corpse away for the funeral.

Is the Supreme Goddess so selective? Is she not compassionate? His mind was restless. Even when he was back on the outer fortress wall, uncomfortable questions arose in his mind. The day drew to an end and the gates closed. Mura took a deep breath and went towards the rooms of the Shaktas who had brought the girl's dead body. Something was amiss and he had to find out what.

Dhatri was in deep meditation. It took her quite some time to recognise Mura's presence.

"What can I do for you, Senapati?"

"Are you alright, Mahadevi? I did not want to disturb you yesterday."

"It will take me time to be alright," Dhatri replied, gazing out of the window. It was almost midday and she had lost track of time.

"Why did the compassion of the Supreme Goddess fail the girl, Mahadevi?" Mura asked hesitantly, not wanting to hurt Dhatri further.

"Lord Bhauma and the Goddess, both have graced the wrong woman, Senapati. I am not capable of being the medium of that Supreme Shakti. If I were, I could have succeeded in changing the girl's mind. I could have at least saved her from death. Who am I to now question the grace of the Supreme Goddess?"

The breaking voice made Mura regret coming to her. He had other questions on his mind but Dhatri's state told him that it was not the right time to ask any probing questions. Mura's hands came together and his gaze remained on the ground. He rose to leave when her next words froze him in his tracks.

"Why didn't you seek me out earlier, Mura?"

"Mahadevi!"

"Bhauma deserved a better yogini and this temple of Shakti deserved a better mahadevi. I would have been better off being a quiet yogini of yours rather than betray everyone like this."

It felt as though the ground under Mura's feet had shifted. He needed all the strength to suppress the eruption of what he thought had been buried in the faint memories of a distant past. "Mahadevi!" he managed to say again, resisting the urge to take her name. "You knew?"

"Even the lord knows. It was I who was blind with the ambition to change the world, to save the other Dhatris of the world. I failed bitterly!"

"Not yet!" Mura exclaimed, turning around. "Mahadevi, I do believe you can change the world. I shall stand by you through every moment. I beg you, don't lose your hope due to this tragedy. You shall ultimately win! My heart says that you shall protect the oppressed women in the plains. You shall not fail, not when I am alive." He regretted his outburst almost at once. He could not bear to look at Dhatri in the eye. He dragged himself out of Dhatri's residence.

"Mura, is everything alright?" Bhauma met him on the steps outside Dhatri's residence. In Mura's nod, Bhauma sensed restlessness.

"Prabho," Mura called out after a couple of moments. "It's about my daughter Mauri, Kamakanthika … her uncle and grandparents want her to stay with them for a while."

Bhauma descended the steps. "What did you say?"

"Nothing as yet. It might also be unfair of me to deny their wish."

"No, Mura." Bhauma caught his arm. "I don't have the courage to send her or any girl or woman out of Kamarupa now. Her mother's family is still Arya."

"How is that an issue, Prabho? They all know that we follow the Shakta lore and have never had a problem with that. They only want to see their granddaughter and that…" Mura stopped as he felt Bhauma's grip over his shoulder tighten.

"You have seen how yesterday's unfortunate incident has disturbed Dhatri. Your daughter is the only one who can cheer her up. I cannot say much beyond that."

Mura nodded. Something about Bhauma's reaction gave him the answers that he had sought; they left a bitter taste in his mouth.

"What had the senapati come here for?" Bhauma asked in a soft tone.

"He is as disappointed with the absence of compassion in the Goddess, as am I," Dhatri replied, fresh tears springing to her eyes.

"It is time to face new challenges, Mahadevi." Bhauma reached out to wipe her wet cheeks. "The Goddess has chosen to test us. Jarasandha, the king of Magadha, was killed." He saw that the news did not have much to affect Dhatri. "The Arya forces are consolidating in the plains, Dhatri. This does not bode well."

Dhatri saw the frown on his forehead and sighed. "What was the use of that political friendship anyway, Bhauma? Your king of Magadha helped change little down in the plains of Bharata."

"But he was an important ally down there." Bhauma sank into a seat. "I am convinced that trying times await us."

"How was he killed?"

"By treachery. There is this king of Indraprastha who has sought to become the emperor of Bharatavarsha. His brother killed Jarasandha by deceit. I am also informed that Jarasandha's son has joined the killers of his father."

Dhatri responded with a wry smile. "Does that affect us badly, Bhauma?"

"Not really," Bhauma spoke in a low voice. "He did have some allies who could help us out. But that is still not my concern, Mahadevi."

"Stop calling me that, Bhauma. I don't deserve to be…"

Bhauma put his hand over her mouth. "Will you let one tragedy undo all the work we have done in the past years, Dhatri? This event is a lesson for us to relook at what we do. It is a signal from the Supreme Goddess again."

Dhatri looked at him. Her eyes were eloquent with her helplessness and anger. She craved to do something to correct the death of the maiden and spent a sleepless night thinking. Everything was in vain. Even the rituals failed to console her heart.

Bhauma's eyes signalled a new resolve. They narrowed and then closed. "We need to think about what we can do going forward, Mahadevi."

After a long pause, Dhatri nodded, curling her fingers into a tight fist. "Bitter medicine at times is unavoidable, Bhauma. We need to steel our hearts for now." She missed the gleam that passed across Bhauma's face.

"What did you tell Mura about sending his daughter to her grandparents at Pragjyotisha?"

Dhatri frowned at the abrupt change of topic. "Nothing yet, because he never bothered to ask me. And tell him I shall not send her anywhere outside the gates of Kamarupa."

"Of course." Bhauma did not say anything else and left. *Mura, you don't know what is in store for you.*

Chapter Nineteen

Anagha

It was a new moon night, dark and cloudy. Abhaya watched the palace staff go about their work as usual. She stopped pacing and went to the end of the corridor, to the room which Dharmasena used as a study and for private council with trusted friends. She saw him studying some parchments, presumably trade proposals. The traders often carried these requisitions and pacts from the royals of the kingdoms they came from.

Dharmasena sensed her presence and, without turning, he waved her in. A sudden gust of wind threatened to blow the lamps out. Abhaya instinctively cupped her palms over the lamp nearest to her. She heard a sigh from her father and turned. He hadn't saved his lamp in time. She carried the lamp that was still burning towards him, shielding it from the wind. Dharmasena smiled and went back to his parchments.

"It would be better to move the lamps to the other corner, Janaka," she said, lighting the other lamp from the lone flame. "You can read in peace."

"That would require moving my seat too," Dharmasena replied, glancing at her. "Not that it is not possible. It would just feel..."

"Different?"

"Very much. Anyway, I can resume work in the morning." Dharmasena stood up, winding the thread around the parchments after separating the ones yet to be read.

"Giving in to the gale, Janaka?"

"Can we afford to take on the god of winds?" he chuckled.

"Just choose not to be in his path," Abhaya said, laughing.

All of a sudden, the night was pierced with a shrill ringing.

"The eastern tower bell!" Abhaya rushed to the window. It was too dark to see anything but the continuous ringing of the bell meant only one thing—a breach.

Dharmasena went for the swords that hung on the wall. Abhaya reached out for the armours. They saw a soldier rush in. "Prabho! They are the soldiers of Avanti! We are attacked!"

"Avanti!" Dharmasena exclaimed. "How, by the trident of Anagheshwari, did they..." The sentence remained incomplete. Abhaya was already donning her armour. The ringing stopped abruptly. In the sudden calm, the long-drawn-out cry of someone falling to his death from the eastern tower was clear and ominous.

"Guards!" Abhaya called out, her voice conveying calm authority. "Sound the alert! Gather around the inner walls. Make sure all civilians are inside the inner walls. Whomever the enemy is, let him taste the edge of our swords and tips of our spears!"

"Let them realise that they have awoken a hungry lion!" Dharmasena growled. The guards who had collected in front of the room immediately fell into a two-line formation. More bells started to ring. As the father and daughter ran down the stairs leading to the exit of the palace, they met the anxious soldiers.

"Prabho, they managed to breach in and open the gates. They have come in hundreds! But we have managed to insulate the western wing of the city."

"How about the distress fire at the western towers?"

The soldier bowed his head. "All the soldiers rushed here and…"

"Follow me!" Dharmasena ordered, knowing the futility of berating anyone at this point. Had Vikrama been here, such a vital thing would not have been omitted. Dharmasena caught Abhaya by her arm and paused by the penultimate gate, letting a battalion of guards go before them.

"Janaka?!"

"We shall not last..."

"No, Janaka, don't..."

"...if we don't get help by morning. You should rush to the western tower and light the fire atop. Keep it burning high and bright!"

"Yes, I'll send someone," Abhaya said.

"No, you should do it yourself. The Nagas, the highway patrol groups from Dwaraka and Anarta. At least, they should know the danger that has befallen us!"

He lowered his voice. "You should escape if you can."

"No!"

"It will make it easier for me. You know it. Mahakala forbid, if they get you, it will be all over. Abhaya, don't be my weakness!"

"It cannot come to this!" Abhaya protested as Dharmasena led her firmly by the arm to the corridor leading to the western towers of the fortress.

"You think fast on your feet. Trust your instincts. I do." Dharmasena nudged her on her way and turned back.

Abhaya stood rooted to the spot, a few guards surrounding her. Soldiers rushed past them on the way to the western tower defences. When the last of them crossed, she heard the words that pierced her sharper than any weapon she had known.

"If I die, let it not go waste. Escape, Vatse!"

Dharmasena turned a wheel that brought the portcullis down, its metal teeth biting firmly into the ground, blocking the entrance to the western wing of the palace. The gates to the western side of the city had already been closed. Dharmasena was striding towards the eastern fort walls. He turned back to give her a final smile before disappearing into the ranks of running soldiers. Would she ever see him again? With a deep breath, she turned and darted towards the western towers.

The corridor in which she had pranced about as a child stood in grim silence. It suddenly brought back old memories. She remembered the games of hide-and-seek she had played with the daughters of the palace maids, she heard the childish orders she used to pass to the guards in an attempt to imitate her father.

This shall remain, Janaka. I shall not let you down!

It was not long before Abhaya raced up the spiral stairs of the north-western tower, instructing the soldiers with her to take positions.

The flames went up, consuming the logs and inflammable material. She turned to look at the western landscape. The tower was twice as high as the tallest tree one could find in the vegetation that lay to the west of the city. She hurried between the fireplace and a small shelter where the wooden logs and oil were stored. The growing warmth of the flames soothed the numbness that had built up in her limbs. An old soldier called out to her.

"The king told you to escape, Vatse!"

"No! I am not leaving this soon!" Abhaya shouted, throwing a fistful of the inflammable mixture into the fire. The mixture contained camphor, oil and other inflammable material, and the flames immediately leapt to a height of several metres. The soldier stared at her, unsure about her decision to not escape.

Her eyes closed. *This is just a nightmare. When I open my eyes, everything will be alright.*

Screams coming from below the tower startled her to alertness. Abhaya was instantly on her feet, her hand gripping her sword. The soldier hurried down the steps before her. Abhaya heard another scream and could wait no longer. She rushed down the first flight of stairs. She froze at the sight of the scene before her.

"Aren't you surprised, Dhaarmaseni?" Anuvinda's cold voice greeted her and the prince of Avanti emerged around the curve of the spiral stairs of the tower. "I am afraid, insulating the western wing happened a bit too late!"

Abhaya froze, though standing her ground, and looked over his shoulder.

"No, My Princess, all of them are safely pinned to the ground by my soldiers. No, wait! No, I'm wrong, not all. My condolences for two of them."

"Not surprising, Anuvinda, the likes of you can murder your father if he came in your way."

"Pardon me for proving you wrong," Anuvinda bowed in mock humility. His stare turned cold again, "but if you come with me, you will find your future father-in-law alive."

"Stay there!" Abhaya warned, raising her sword.

Anuvinda laughed aloud in response. The laugh confirmed Abhaya's worst fears. Her jaw trembled but she stood her ground. She saw him grin before his sword changed its course and drove at her soldier held immobile by three of Avanti's soldiers.

"No!" Abhaya roared, and, in a flash, her sword stopped his from stabbing the helpless soldier.

"Such concern for those who are meant to die saving their kings and queens, Abhaya! I forgot you are not really of royal birth. Luck could bring you prosperity, not royalty. Now stop pretending and put your toy away. And put off this fire. We don't want anyone intruding on our private moment, do we?" He winked meaningfully and made a sudden thrust with his sword in a bid to make her lose her balance and fall to the ground. To his disappointment, Abhaya stood unflinching.

She raised her brows. "Royalty does not always bring valour, does it, Yuvaraja?" She smiled as she saw annoyance flash across his face. "Nor does it promise nobility or chivalry, or any of those qualities with which one rules hearts instead of mere mud and rocks." She had barely finished the sentence when he thrust his sword again, this time with the intent to harm, and she jumped back, barely avoiding its point. She launched into an offensive, bringing her sword upon his shoulder at a speed he could not calculate. He reeled back with the force of the blow which, but for his arm plates, would have severed his arm. With a low grunt, he dived, landing his fist upon her side. Her sword still caught in its midair trajectory, Abhaya backed away to escape but her left arm took the hit. She couldn't prevent a cry of agony from escaping her lips and what she had feared, happened.

"Let us play it this way—one attack by you and a soldier of your 'inn' loses his head."

"No, Anuvinda, spare them."

Anuvinda curved his lips further, hearing the break in her voice. "...if you throw that wretched sword of yours to me."

She knew she had to comply to save her soldiers. She threw her sword at his feet and kept her eyes on Anuvinda as he approached her, a triumphant grin on his face. He held his sword to her chin but she made no move to push the blade away.

"This bloodshed helps nobody, Abhaya. Come with me. And a lot of unnecessary bloodshed can be avoided."

Abhaya could feel a trickle of blood flowing down her neck from her chin. She shook her head defiantly and stepped back climbing the spiral stairs. "Your target was only to control the highways by taking over my humble, 'oversized inn', Yuvaraja. Am I not just a pawn?"

"In all honesty, I cannot disagree but, given your wisdom, I could always have second thoughts about your utility being more than a means to dominate this highway. Probably you could make a great wife and a greater lover, Dhaarmaseni!" Anuvinda smirked and advanced further. "If that flatters you enough, make haste now!"

They had reached the top of the stairs by now. Abhaya realised that a delay from her could cause the death of her soldiers. Dharmasena's words rang in her ears: *Escape, Vatse. Don't let them get you. Don't be my weakness.*

She could not see her soldiers being slaughtered for a show of her valour. Neither could she let down her father by surrendering to Anuvinda.

What if I…? She knew that the solution had a huge risk where death was a greater probability and survival could happen only by a miracle.

The tip of Anuvinda's sword passed along her chin and left cheek. "Now, my love, bear some humiliation for the night. I promise you'll reap more than it's worth for the rest of your life."

The sword cut the threads that bound her armour. Abhaya needed all her forbearance to keep her limbs from viciously attacking. The thought of having a soldier's head roll only because he served her made her swallow the humiliation of being disarmed without a fair duel. She turned in the direction of the edge of the tower. If she died in the process, it saved her from a life of humiliation and servitude. If she survived, she could keep up hope.

"Let me admit, it takes more courage to stand this than showing off your juvenile valour with the sword, Abhaya. I am impressed."

Through her gritted jaw, Abhaya smiled at Anuvinda. "You should also be impressed with this Anuvinda. Remember this?" She showed her diamond-embossed bracelet on her wrist.

It had the desired effect on Anuvinda, refreshing his memories of Mitravinda's elopement with Krishna. His eyes narrowed and the sword shook.

"A gift from your dear brother-in-law, the Yadava leader Krishna Vaasudeva for helping him." She laughed. Another memory flashed before her mind as she said these words. Another gift from the very same Krishna—the dagger that was hidden in the pleats of her garment, a weapon she seldom used but which had become more like a part of her dress.

At the very instant, Anuvinda grabbed her wrist in the bid to crush the jewel and even her wrist if he could. It happened. The golden outer sheath of the bracelet collapsed under his strength but the diamonds were sharper. They pierced his palm at multiple places and he withdrew his hand as though he had been stung by a scorpion.

Abhaya took the opportunity to take out her dagger and drove it into his side. He yelped at the sudden pain. If she took the prince of Avanti himself as a prisoner, Abhaya knew that she could save the lives of her soldiers as well as save herself from further ignominy.

Anuvinda's defences, however, were quicker than she expected. His mounting rage had made his jeer and sneer disappear. He held her hand as she pulled out the dagger and his knee hit her in the belly.

Abhaya did not give him the joy of hearing her cry out in pain but her steps stumbled. Neither of them had noticed that even as they scuffled, she was right over the edge of the tower. When her foot lost its hold, even Anuvinda's grip over her hand was not strong enough to stop her from falling from the tower, straight into the moat.

Chapter Twenty

The crocodiles had sensed the action at the city walls. The moat that was their home was, after all, the first line of defence around the city. The ferocious reptiles were tended to by skilled workmen who ensured that they were always hungry enough to serve the city when it was in danger. Not that the crocodiles differentiated between defender and attacker. Whoever was unfortunate enough to fall into the moat was a legitimate prey.

Death.

One part of Abhaya marvelled at the calmness she felt even as death approached in the form of the open jaws of a crocodile. Abhaya got back to her feet, standing waist-deep in the muddy waters, despite the numbness in her body. Even with the unexpected fall, her hand had not let go of the dagger that was still red with Anuvinda's blood. Her lips curved into an ironic smile as she realised that it would all boil down to how she faced the reptiles that were reared to guard her city. A crocodile swam towards her with its characteristic placidness. She sensed another approach her from the side. The first one was bigger. Abhaya held her breath and bided for the right moment. Wading backwards, she saw the reptile open its jaws to grab at her outheld left hand. Abhaya arched right, frustrating the crocodile which leapt at her. Arching further, she gouged the right eye of the reptile which turned in pain violently swishing its tail at her. Holding on to the reptile's back, Abhaya stabbed blindly hoping to catch the other eye of the crocodile. In the meantime, the second crocodile, much smaller in size, had approached and almost caught Abhaya's leg. The princess of Anagha, still struggling with the first one, kicked back at this smaller one. The bigger reptile seemed to weaken but another violent turn of its tail threw Abhaya into the waters, almost face to face with the second. At this point, she suddenly remembered something Vikrama had once told her about crocodiles—their lower jaw was its weakest point, and, without stopping to think, she dove under the reptile and cut open its lower jaw with the dagger but the weapon got caught in the body of the reptile. Not pausing to check the damage done, or retrieve the weapon, Abhaya furiously waded towards a corner of the moat where a tree stood in search of temporary respite.

Her way, however, was blocked by two more crocodiles. Abhaya steeled herself. She had neither the strength nor the will left to fight. She thought she heard a creaking sound from the tree and it seemed to bend towards the water. But she had no time to pay heed to this. She felt the ripples of water behind her as more crocodiles approached. Abhaya did not have the courage to turn around and instead faced the two reptiles before her, wondering if she could somehow slip between them to safety. It seemed like a slim chance but it was still worth taking. She remembered her father's words. She could not fail him. But would she have the strength to fight? *If only Vikrama were here.* Despite the danger she was in, she felt a moment of anger that he had left when he was so sorely needed. The tree was about twelve to fifteen feet away from her and, if she managed to run past, she could scale up the tree and wait for rescue, though the chances of that remained bleak. Nodding to herself, Abhaya closed her eyes, summoning whatever strength her limbs could muster. A smile filled her vision.

Yes, that is a smile worth dying for. Suddenly, as though the vision were speaking, she heard, "Dhaarmaseni!"

Her eyes shot open and she stopped. Were her ears deceiving her? The tree creaked violently and, suddenly, inexplicably, crashed across the moat right beside her, blocking the rest of the reptile host. As if guided by some external force, she turned, hauled herself on a sturdy branch that hung low, still dazed at the fortuitous crash.

"Dhaarmaseni!"

There was no mistaking it now. Abhaya got to her feet and, struggling to maintain her balance, started to make her way across the tree branch which had formed a bridge across the moat. The moon emerged from the clouds and she saw him.

"Come on! Cross over!"

Her gaze locked with his, she moved forward. The branch creaked a couple of times under her weight but held. The branch thinned as she approached the other end and threatened to break any moment. But the authority in his voice and the assurance in his eyes gave her the strength to keep going. With only a couple of feet remaining, she stretched her hands to his. The branch broke as she still was two feet away but his hands gripped Abhaya by her arms and pulled her to safety. She let out the breath she had been holding and threw her arms around him. "Vaasudeva!"

Krishna held her tight as her frame shook with suppressed sobs, wordlessly letting him know what she had gone through. His eyes glanced up and caught sight of a retreating figure.

Slowly, her breathing returned to normal.

Gently, he pried her away so he could get a look at her. "Are you hurt?"

"Just a little."

He led her towards his chariot. She saw the rope he had tied to the tree and marvelled at his ingenuity.

"I thought you were at Indraprastha."

"We were returning. I had actually gone to Prabhasa first."

Krishna cracked the whip and the horses cantered away from the fort. Abhaya opened her mouth to say something but stopped, sensing they were not alone. Then she spotted the horsemen who had stationed themselves in the cover of the woods. She saw the Yadavas, the foot soldiers and the Nagas too. Her father had been right in raising the alarm.

"Soldiers of Avanti led by Anuvinda himself attacked in the night! I am yet to find out how they broke in!"

Krishna frowned as she filled him in on whatever details she knew. "I expected this kind of surprise. The additional patrol teams on the highway proved handy."

"How many?"

"Over a hundred, counting you and me."

"I am not sure if the number can suffice!" Abhaya blurted out, the fatigue of what she had faced weighing her down.

"It does not matter, Abhaya," Krishna turned her face to look at him. "I know that he is going to retreat now."

He saw her brows come together, unconvinced. "Anuvinda planned to keep this takeover a secret so that he could surprise the kingdoms of Saurashtra with his control over the highways. He would have been successful if this night had gone unnoticed by Dwaraka or Anarta. He is not fully equipped to hold the fort if all of us attacked even with our limited reserve forces in the morning. He is retreating right now."

Abhaya nodded in relief.

"But how can we go in, Abhaya?"

"A few of my soldiers are there, held by his soldiers, they can open the gates for us." Abhaya looked in the direction of the gates. And the realisation struck her that Anuvinda's men would have mostly killed all of them.

Krishna looked at her and shook his head. Abhaya cringed. All the risk taken to save the soldiers had gone in vain. But fate did not give her the luxury to grieve. She thought fast. There were two secret entrances into Anagha from outside. One from the eastern side was through the temple of Anagheshwari and the one from the western side was through another well-hidden tunnel that opened into the Naga graveyard to the southwest of Anagha. This was a secret known only to very few people. She swallowed, making her decision to reveal it. Getting into the fort was a priority.

"I am trusting you with a secret, Krishna." She pointed in the direction of the graveyard.

Krishna turned the chariot in the direction she indicated. "This will not be the last of the surprises you might face. You will need to think about what needs to be done next."

"What about the campaign for Rajasuya?"

"It can start any time," Krishna replied, holding the reins as they gained pace.

"How long before Avanti is suppressed?"

"A good three months. Could be longer if the monsoon doesn't favour us."

She leaned against the side of the chariot. "Your forces would join the campaign." She thought aloud. "That would leave us without access to help from you if we came under attack again."

"I am afraid the luxury of 'if' is unaffordable, Abhaya. It is a matter of 'when'."

Abhaya could not help but smile. Krishna was not the one to deal out false hopes. He was speaking of doom, and yet, surprisingly, she felt at peace.

Is this the power of truth?

Chapter Twenty-One

The metal tip of the javelin pierced Dharmasena's belly right below the armour but the king of Anagha would not allow his opponent the pleasure of seeing his pain. Holding two other soldiers of Avanti at bay with his javelin, he whirled and kicked strongly at the third opponent's stomach. The impact made him go down on his right knee, giving the other opponent the chance to bring his sword dangerously close to his neck. Sacrificing his right flank, Dharmasena sank further to the ground, holding off both the blades before swinging around and upsetting the opponent on his right with another measured kick with his injured left leg. The move released him from the deadlock while stunning both his opponents, who fell in a tangled heap. Before they could untangle themselves and get to their feet, Dharmasena's blade cut them down ruthlessly.

"For the honour of Mother Anagheshwari!" Dharmasena roared, pushing their bodies down the terrace of the inner fort. He turned around at a cry from one of his bodyguards who had been cornered against the wall by four enemy soldiers. Dharmasena rushed over, ignoring the pain that shot up his left leg, and took on two of them. An unexpected blow behind his right shoulder left him stunned for a moment and the other soldier took this opportunity to try to drive his javelin into his side. Dharmasena ducked in the nick of time, using his weight to upset one of the opponents.

The other opponent aimed at his throat but the injured bodyguard threw himself in the way. His headless body crashed onto Dharmasena's lap, who could only murmur a prayer as his strength began to desert him with every passing moment.

"Retreat!"

The cry was followed by chaos and confusion amongst the invading soldiers. Dharmasena's eyes widened and, with renewed energy, he gripped his sword and lifted himself to his feet. "Anuvinda, you curse to the womb of the woman who bore you!"

"Retreat!"

The stunned soldiers of Avanti ran helter-skelter. Dharmasena engaged two of them and, with the help of another guard who came to his side, cut them down. Whatever resolve remained with the soldiers of Avanti disappeared at the sight of Anuvinda racing his horse out of the gates, as though intending to sacrifice them to the anger of the soldiers of Anagha in his attempt to escape.

"Kill each one of them!" Dharmasena shouted to his soldiers who fought with renewed courage at the sudden turn of events. They did not know what had spurred the retreat but all they wanted for the moment was revenge on the intruders who had broken into their city in the dead of the night and wreaked such havoc, violating all codes.

Another piercing cry from the inner chambers reached Dharmasena's ears and he raced towards the sound, directing the rest of his guard to pursue the intruders till they could kill as many as they could. The cry, he recognised, was that of Kamalakshi, one of the girls who helped around in the palace. Weren't the inner chambers guarded well?

Each scream felt like a blow to Dharmasena. The blood oozing from his wounds left a trail behind him but he ran like one possessed and stormed into the hall of what served as his public court. Two intruders were holding the girl down while another was attempting to pry her legs open. Dharmasena's blood boiled. He drove his dagger into the back of the nearest man and, before the others could react, he picked up a heavy bronze lamp and hurled it at them. One of the intruders drew a dagger only to have it wrested out of his hand and stuck in his throat by the enraged king.

Dharmasena went to her side. He noticed for the first time that she had been stabbed. Or she might have done it herself when she thought no one would come to her aid. Tears blinded him for a moment before they fell upon her chest and he drew out the knife, not flinching even when she let out another painful scream and thrust it at the lone intruding soldier who by now was too scared to even run.

"Prabho!"

The tone was feeble, shattering any remnants of his hope that she would survive this ordeal. He checked her pulse and felt it petering out under his thumb. Dharmasena held her head in his hands, unable to stop his tears. The dead girl lay before him, a telling example of his inability to protect those who depended on him. A part of him wanted to tear every soldier of Avanti to pieces. A part of him railed at himself for being unfit to rule anymore. He had not cared for the unfortunate girl as he had worried about his daughter. The thought rent his heart and soul. In her lifeless face, he saw Abhaya.

The guards who rushed in had no courage to approach him. People filled into the hall and a hush descended over them as the horror of the scene sunk in. After a while, an older woman, who worked in the palace kitchen, approached in silence and gently closed the girl's eyes and covered her with a garment. But no one could make the king recover from his daze.

"Abhaya!" he called out to the corpse to everyone's shock.

"Abhaya, open your eyes." He prodded the body, just as he used to do to wake his sleeping daughter in her younger years.

"Janaka!"

"Janakaaa!" It wasn't until Abhaya strained her voice to the limit that Dharmasena looked up. If Abhaya had felt any triumph in driving the intruders away, it faded when she saw his blank stare. "Prabho!" She hoped the formal address would stir him into action. "The intruders are gone. But our people need you!"

Dharmasena continued to stare at her and then pointed at the girl's corpse.

"Janaka, worse things happened out in the city!" Her heart by now had numbed and hardened to such ghastly sights.

"What?"

Abhaya turned to face the guards who stood by, not knowing what to do. "We have work to do. Go to the streets and reassure the people that Anagha is safe. Assess the damage and report back. The king shall address the citizens by midday." On her way to the fort, she had seen a granary that had been set on fire. She had seen houses that had been looted. People—soldiers and civilians alike—needed medical care. She turned to the two women who had stood behind her in mute sorrow. "Tell the vaidyas to get their supplies ready and be prepared for a long day. Gather every man and woman in the palace who knows to treat wounds and get to work."

The older woman who had been her nurse in her childhood had a spark in her eye, the same kind that lights up a parent's eye when she realises that the child who played in her lap has grown up. The authority in her tone served to calm those who had gathered in the hall and they dispersed without a word to attend to their allotted tasks.

Abhaya strode over to Dharmasena, who still sat with a vacant look on his face. She held him by the shoulders and helped him up. That's when she noticed the blood that had drenched his lower garments and the carpet where he had been sitting. Helping him to the nearby seat, she tied a cloth around his wound, trying not to think of how much blood he had already lost.

"Devi!" A Yadava soldier rushed in, reminding Abhaya that the soldiers who had come to their rescue needed to be thanked. "Arya Vaasudeva wants to see you. We have discovered how the soldiers of Avanti broke in. It was from the temple."

Katyayana's motionless body lay in a pool of blood, his head in the lap of a young Naga who was tending to him.

Abhaya turned to Krishna, fresh tears filling her eyes. "They did not even spare him! He used to say that ill could befall this city only over his corpse."

Krishna knelt by Katyayana's side to feel the priest's pulse. Abhaya saw his eyes close for a moment before he stopped the Naga boy from applying the primitive medicine on the priest's wounds and shook his head. "Get the fire logs, Bhrata."

"His was a life spent in worship," Abhaya said.

"Did he know about the secret tunnel opening?"

"Yes, but he would not have given it away." *Pingala.* The name of the priest's daughter rang in her mind.

"He resisted them as best as he could," Krishna told her, extricating a piece of clothing from Katyayana's grip. "The colour worn by the soldiers of Avanti," he said, holding it up.

But Abhaya was not looking at him or Katyayana.

Were those Shaktas from Avanti?

She looked at the statue of Anagheshwari, presiding dispassionately over the site of the carnage.

Do you exist, Goddess? If you do, do you have the heart of a mother? That is what we thought you were. And you are but a statue. A statue with no life, no heart—only a product of a sculptor's imagination. You do not exist, Anagheshwari. If you did, your smile would have vanished when this priest was attacked. Your trident would have sprung to action when the enemy's feet stepped upon your land, the land that worshipped you! We trusted you in vain!

She got to her feet and was about to storm out in a rage when Krishna held her back. He resisted her efforts to push him away and turned her around to face him.

Abhaya's eyes met his gaze and her heart slowed like a horse being reined in.

"Dhaarmaseni, rage is a luxury you cannot afford."

"Those innocent soldiers, citizens, even he, Katyayana, everyone who stood by us, Krishna..."

"It is those who survived you should be thinking about, Abhaya. This fort is vulnerable. They will return. And when they do, it will be with a bigger force."

"If they dare to return..." Her jaws tightened as she scanned the entrance of the temple.

"*When* they dare to return, which they will," Krishna corrected, "you do not have the strength and numbers to defend the fort."

The vulnerability of the fort struck her with full force when she heard him say these words. A second attack would not bode well for her demoralised soldiers. Besides, the soldiers of Avanti now had a clear idea of the inner defences of Anagha. Her father was in no shape to lead another defence. As for Vikrama, she didn't even know where he was. Anagha was at its most vulnerable state.

"Surrendering tactically is not an option anymore," Krishna went on. He looked at her, his grip on both her arms tightening. "Abhaya, flee."

"Flee." She stared at him. "And go where?"

"Indraprastha."

"Indraprastha?"

"The safest place I can think of. Till the conquest is done, even Dwaraka is not safe. Which is why the traders, women, children and elderly of Dwaraka are also moving to Indraprastha. Our soldiers are joining the campaign."

Abhaya stared at him, her eyes conveying the struggle that raged within her bosom about admitting defeat and fleeing elsewhere to seek refuge.

"Can you convince your father about this?"

Abhaya nodded, meeting his gaze again.

"Your people will be well cared for. You can take my word for it on behalf of the ruler of Indraprastha."

The Naga boy interrupted the conversation. The pyre was ready. When Katyayana's body was placed on it, Abhaya handed the flaming torch to the boy, who looked puzzled.

"You were the son who tended to him in his last moments," she told him. "He died in your lap."

The boy's eyes welled with tears. He took the torch from Abhaya and lit the pyre. The logs caught fire and flames enveloped the body of the priest and counsellor of Anagha.

Chapter Twenty-Two

The city square of Anagha was a picture of woe and anxiety. In the light of the day, the ravage it had undergone was clear to see. Amidst the blood and gore and burnt houses, the weary citizens waited for the king to address and assure them. Fear was writ large on many faces. The suffering of her people surrounded her as Abhaya approached the square.

She had seen houses ransacked. The soldiers of Avanti had not missed a single opportunity to loot or rape. Wails and groans rent the air. Dead bodies of guards and civilians lay in the streets, waiting to be claimed. A woman with an infant suckling at her breast sat on the stairs of her ransacked house, calling out to her lost husband. Abhaya felt her soul tear apart, each sight proving itself to be worse than the previous one. The assuaging by the guards and the limited doctors was clearly to no avail. Someone cursed the soldiers who could not fight for them. But Abhaya knew they were unprepared and the attack was deceitful. Then she heard someone curse the king. Swallowing her emotion, she hurried towards the square. She passed by a groaning woman with injuries to both legs, waiting for someone to tend her wounds. She passed by a wailing toddler who was bewildered at not finding his parents in the crowds. She swallowed hard, hearing a scream from a guard as a doctor pulled out a dagger stuck in his chest.

A hush fell on the assembled crowd as she ascended the steps of the dais. She scanned the crowd.

Their hope depends on what I am going to say.

"Beloved sisters and brothers," she began only to see anticipation rise in every pair of eyes her gaze met. "The fort was breached last night by the soldiers of Avanti, a kingdom which we had wrongly considered an ancestral friend and ally. Greed and envy of the prosperity that you all have generated in the past few years made them stoop this low."

Abhaya paused for breath, fighting to keep emotion from her voice. "What they did once, they can do again. And the next time, they will come better prepared. Uncertainty has gripped all of Bharatavarsha and the worst is yet to come." Her people had been expecting hope and reassurance from her but she had only harsh reality to offer. Her heart broke as she spoke but there was no other way to say those words. "We need to abandon this city to protect whatever is left of all that we hold dear."

Ripples of shock went through the crowd. She waited for them to quieten down before she continued. "We have been extended a welcome by the young queen of Indraprastha, the new imperial city on the banks of the Yamuna. Our children, our elders and our dependents will be well-protected there. We have the word of the Yadava lord, Vaasudeva, who assisted us in fighting off the enemy last night." Her eyes went to where Krishna stood, by the shelter of the main entrance to her father's court. He nodded in encouragement.

Resolve entered her voice when she spoke again. "This does not mean we are abandoning the land that has sustained us for so long. We shall come back to reclaim our land. Once the imperial conquest is done, we shall not rest in peace until we return our beloved city to its past glory. We shall make our enemies pay for their sins. We shall announce the plan of our departure in a couple of days. But if even one of you wants to stay back, your injured king will not leave the city."

She did not avoid making eye contact with her people as she descended the steps of the square dais. Loyalty, pity, contempt, pain, disdain—she saw it all in their eyes. A voice in the crowd hissed, "It's all her fault. She was the one who rejected the wedding proposal from Avanti."

Abhaya, knowing the futility of anger or explanation at the moment, chose to ignore the comment and walked towards the arch of the entrance where Krishna stood with the Yadava soldiers and the Naga warriors. She brought her hands together in gratitude, giving them her heartfelt thanks for their timely help.

"Are you sure, Dhaarmaseni? You have made the announcement without consulting the king."

She shook her head. "This will disappoint him, I know, Vaasudeva. But I can take his disapproval. I will not risk any more lives by giving the people false assurances."

Krishna gave her a long look, then covered her folded hands with his own. "I heard those angry words blaming you for what happened, Abhaya," he said. "Steel yourself, because you will hear worse and even be cursed in the course of this long journey."

Abhaya could not help but smile. Krishna always knew what she was thinking. His hand caressed her cheek as their eyes locked. For a long moment, the rest of the world ceased to exist. Then, Krishna pulled back and the spell broke. He took her leave and led the Yadava soldiers out of the city gates. Abhaya looked after him for a long time before turning back to her brutalised city. She made a mental map of the activity needed to move the citizens. The traders from other lands, she knew, would start before midday and the families of resident traders would need a couple of days to deliberate over what to carry.

"What is this I hear, Vatse? Did you tell the people we are abandoning the city?" Dharmasena's voice remained weak but his eyes blazed.

"I saw no other way out, Janaka. Our fortress is damaged. We can't protect our people in the event of another attack." Abhaya sat at his feet and started undoing his bandage which was soaked through with blood again.

"So, you told them their king is no longer capable of protecting them."

The disappointment in his eyes was terrible. Abhaya swallowed hard.

"Janaka, you know we cannot withstand another attack," Abhaya said quietly. She held Dharmasena's hand but, with an effort, he shook it off.

"Did you consider consulting me, Abhaya? No, you didn't. Not now, nor when you helped the princess of Avanti elope with Vaasudeva. That is what marked the beginning of their hostility. And now you want us to leave the very..." His words faded away as he paused to catch his breath.

"I failed to prevent Pingala from leaving the city. That resulted in our enemy breaching our fortress. Even in the middle of the attack, I could have surrendered to Anuvinda and begged him to stop the bloodshed. But I chose not to. Janaka, I know I am the root cause of all this trouble, and that is why I'm asking you to let me set it right. By admitting to the people that we are incapable of protecting them from further attacks, I know I have dented our reputation. But isn't that better than watching them die before our eyes? Now they accuse me of not marrying that prince of Avanti. I can take that. But I will not let them accuse you of failing them, Janaka."

"I am prepared to die protecting them and you, Vatse. Who cares what they accuse me of after my death?"

"Death is not an escape from our obligations, Janaka. We are not running away to avoid facing the enemy. We are only facing the truth of our present weakness and fulfilling our responsibility to our people."

Dharmasena pulled himself to a sitting position with difficulty. He could see the pain in Abhaya's eyes, and part of him took pride in her courage for speaking hard truths. But the truth was too hard to bear. "So, you would have me fall at the feet of the king of Indraprastha and your friend Vaasudeva, begging for their favour?"

Abhaya fell to her knees beside the cot. She spoke as a supplicant but her words were that of a queen. "Prabho, I beg you, this is not the time for pride. Follow the path of your dharma, King Dharmasena. You have been a mother and a father to me, and it is you who taught me that the safety of the dwellers of this city is paramount. You taught me that we live and die for them. I am just doing that, Janaka. If I have let you down, let me face the consequences of my actions, may the worst miseries befall me in life and death. Let me…" His hand locked her lips from speaking any further.

"Say no more, Abhaya. I am your father and I have never wished anything but the best for you." He gestured for her to sit by his side, and she put her head on his chest and wept. He stroked her hair. "Vatse, you have not let me down. You make me proud even in the moment of defeat." He felt her sobbing silently and held her as tightly as his strength allowed him. He knew he had reached his end and the last thing he wanted was for her to carry an undeserved burden of guilt all her life. "Your courage in facing the truth is greater than mine in facing the enemy on the battlefield," he reiterated. "You make me proud, Vatse." Her sobs gradually stopped and her breathing evened out. He sensed her falling asleep and smiled to himself. He put his hands around her and watched her sleep as she had done as an infant, secure in the cradle of his arms.

"My little queen, you were born to be the refuge and shelter of many. How can I see you seeking refuge elsewhere? How can I see you falling at anyone else's feet for my sake? By Mahakala, not when I am alive!"

The night passed slowly. His thoughts drifted to Vikrama. *Where was he?* He sent a prayer up to Anagheshwari for the boy's safety. He drifted in and out of consciousness, alternating between this world and the next—a bright place of luminous truth—and, finally, he felt drawn inexorably into the latter. When Abhaya awoke, his body was limp.

The doctor checked his pulse. He replaced Dharmasena's hand gently on his chest and stood, unable to meet Abhaya's eyes.

"My Princess…"

To his surprise, she rose to her feet and stopped him from speaking further. "Go back home, Vaidya, and get ready for the journey ahead. We shall leave by midday, after the king's final rites."

Chapter Twenty-Three

Gomantaka

The stillness of the night was undisturbed except for the sound of waves that came from a distance far enough from Gomantaka to be soothing rather than intrusive. It was the kind of night conducive to sound sleep. But Vikrama's eyes shot open even before the moon had begun its descent from the zenith. The vision he had seen in his dreams left a bitter taste in his mouth and his body was slick with sweat. Relief washed over him when he realised it was only a dream but there was still the lingering sense of unease. It was a nightmare that repeated time and again in different versions after Pingala's disappearance.

He had seen vague images of vultures hovering above the fortress of Anagha, tearing its flag to bits with their talons. He had seen the city burning. He had tried to run towards it but the distance between him and the fortress only seemed to increase. He could not recall the details of the dream. He had not seen Abhaya in danger. He had not seen her at all. He closed his eyes again but sleep evaded him. The thought that Pingala's disappearance would have something to do with the safety of his sister had not stopped gnawing at him though he could find no logical reason.

It was only when he shifted in the feather bed that he felt someone beside him. Shyeni! He sat up in shock as the memory of the previous evening came to him in a flash. It was the seventh night he had spent with the Garudas on his quest for the Shakta group. The hospitality of the Garuda king, Vainateya, had left nothing to be desired.

That afternoon, the Garuda king had sent for him having heard from another young Garuda about a group of ascetics who had camped two yojanas away from the shore to the south-east of Gomantaka. He had sought to leave immediately but Shyeni, the sister of Lord Vainateya, had insisted him to stay the night. One look in her eyes and Vikrama could not refuse. He promised himself he would return to Gomantaka as soon as the Pingala issue was sorted out. He had not eaten much during the meal but he knew he had gone overboard drinking the wine as she filled pitcher after pitcher. When he could take no more, she had helped him to his hut. Vikrama could not remember anything beyond that and the sight of Shyeni lying in his bed, her clothes barely covering her frame, came as a shock.

By Mahakala! What came over me!

He sat up, pulling the rug over Shyeni. She sensed his movement and opened her eyes, the effect of wine still evident.

"Manikandhara!" Her lips curved into a lazy smile. She reached out to pull him back under the covers.

"Shyeni!" Vikrama leaned over her, brushing the hair out of her face. He didn't know what to say.

"You will leave by dawn, won't you?" Shyeni asked, still languorous with sleep and lovemaking.

Vikrama felt his throat go dry. *I cannot leave Shyeni; not after crossing the line.* "I don't want to ever leave your side Shyeni. But I am on a mission."

"Fine, leave if you have to." Shyeni yawned and turned to her side. A baffled Vikrama shook her awake.

"Do you even remember what we did, Eagle Princess?"

Shyeni sat up, sensing his discomfort, and smiled, putting her arms around him. Vikrama's hands went around her, his heart at a loss to understand how he could protect her from the consequences of the night. "I want to ask you to stay for another night. But that would hold you back from finding your mother and investigate whatever threatens your family. So, I shall not. I shall remember you, Mani, forever."

"Come with me!" Vikrama said suddenly. "I shall go right now to Lord Vainateya to seek your hand. We shall leave together."

"Wait!" Shyeni said, pulling him back. "Why would I leave my home and come with you?"

It took some moments before Vikrama fully comprehended what she was saying. He swallowed hard, hoping that it was the wine that was making her speak in this manner. He gently replied, "My home is yours too, love. My father and sister will welcome you."

Shyeni smiled again, running her fingers through his hair. "I would love to visit you, Manikandhara. Just that your city seems so far from my home..." She stopped as she saw his shoulders droop and his hands fall to his side. "Manikandhara..."

"Vikramasena. That is the name with which people at my home call me."

"Well, that is new! What do you want me to call you?"

His eyes narrowed, his gaze no longer tender. "It does not look like it makes much difference."

"Come on Mani, or Vikrama, or whatever your name is. I love you. Nothing would delight me more if you could stay here with us forever. But did you expect me to be one of those women who leave their homes to live with one man for the rest of their lives?" He turned away from her and got out of bed, adjusting his garments.

"Don't you ignore me this way!" she screamed, jumping out of the bed in a resolve that startled him.

"Listen, Manikandhara ... Vikramasena, my home is to me as yours is to you. The social norms of your world don't bind me. You came here seeking your mother and want to return to your family. I want to stay here, ensuring the well-being of my family. Do you still want to make it look like I am cheating you? No! I do love you ... but I won't leave all that is dear to me behind to prove that. And if you truly loved me, you would not ask it of me!"

Vikrama shook his head. But, looking into Shyeni's indignant eyes, he found nothing but sincerity.

His eyes softened. "I shall never ask you to do anything that pains you, Shyeni. But will you be fine after I leave?"

Shyeni shrugged. "What makes you think that I shall not be fine, Vikrama, if I can call you that?"

The question made him smile. He knelt before her and held her hand. "Can I ask you something, Shyeni? Don't refuse me this, I beg of you."

"Arise, Vikrama! I understand this is hard for you. I shall not refuse you anything that is within my power."

"If you discover that you are pregnant with my child, will you let me know? You know where to seek me out." Shyeni nodded. She knew she had the right and the power to decide about any child that she might bear. But if the divine eagle Suparna willed, destiny would fall in line and Vikrama would return to Gomantaka. Vikrama's relief showed on his face. He got to his feet and collected his sword and upper garment.

Shyeni approached him and held his arm. "I shall walk with you till the foot of the mountain, Vikrama." Vikrama agreed, hoping against hope that she might still change her mind. But when they reached the bottom of the mountain, she turned to head back. She turned around again to give him one last smile and wave and he felt a lightness in his heart, knowing he couldn't expect more.

Duty and destiny. Strange are their ways indeed! If Shyeni's duty towards her home and family came first, I have to respect her choice. But if we love each other, may Mahakala unite us when one needs the other.

Chapter Twenty-Four

Kamarupa

It was past sunset and Kamarupa's gates had long been shut for the day. Mura walked across the terrace of the fortress wall. Most of the guards had retired to their rooms except for those scheduled to keep the night vigil.

Where did that imbecile disappear to now! he exclaimed to himself. He was waiting for the arrival of the head of one of the guard divisions who had left for Pragjyotisha a couple of days ago. Mura had expected him to return long before sunset and he wondered what had kept him this long. With each passing minute, Mura's heartbeat quickened.

Several events had occurred in the past months that had robbed Mura of his peace. A maiden from the Pundra kingdom who had rejected to accept Shakta religion had left Kamarupa and her corpse was found by two strange Shakta practitioners who had mysteriously left Kamarupa the same night. Despite Mura's best efforts to brush away his worries, the memories of the Shakta conclave that took place years ago haunted him. He had brushed aside the death of the Shakta guru, Vamanatha, as a natural one and disbelieved the yogini who claimed that Bhauma had killed him.

Kadambari. Her name echoed in Mura's ears in the wake of these events. The only satisfaction he could derive from the incident was that he had trusted his instincts and let the woman escape before her claims were heard by anyone else. Back then, he had suffered from pangs of guilt at allowing someone who dared to blame his lord of a heinous crime to leave. But, as Mura pieced together the mysterious facts around the girl's death, he felt increasingly uncomfortable about Bhauma's intentions. Before he took any step further, Mura wanted to secure the safety of his daughter and Dhatri.

Sowing doubt about Bhauma in Dhatri's mind, Mura knew, was an impossible task. It was all the more impossible as Mura only had theories and no proof. Bhauma's objection to sending Mura's daughter to her mother's family only strengthened Mura's doubts. As a consequence of his disturbing thoughts, he had sent messages to the family at Pragjyotisha to come to Kamarupa and take the girl away to safety. But he had received no response. Further dismayed, Mura had bid the head of the guards to carry his message personally.

A bang at the gates caught Mura's attention. His messenger had returned!

"What did they say?" Mura asked as soon as the guard was ushered inside.

"Forgive me, Senapati. I found the house of your relatives locked. The neighbours told me that they had left for a long pilgrimage and shall not be back for at least a year."

Mura's heart sank at the news. His disappointment was visible.

"What disappoints you, Senapati? I thought your message was a casual one."

Mura shook his head, calming his thoughts. "It is just that I find my daughter disturbs Mahadevi too much. She is becoming impossible to manage."

"The fact that you waited for me this long in the night for such a trivial issue intrigues me," the guard remarked.

Mura managed a laugh. "I am just developing sleeplessness." He then turned solemn. "They could have informed me about their pilgrimage. I was just concerned when I did not hear from them for so long." He waved, dismissing the guard, whose remarks made him feel even more uncomfortable. He spent another hour walking the fortress wall, offering explanations to his troubled self.

Maybe it is just me. They say that doubt, once it is sown in one's mind, becomes an overgrown banyan tree, leaving no opportunity for other thoughts to survive.

In a bid to calm himself, he decided to patrol the outer ring of Kamarupa one last time before turning in for the night. Everything seemed to be in order. He walked towards a quiet corner of the outer fort wall which overlooked the expanse below and stood there for long, wanting to be alone with his thoughts. The cool breeze helped, to some extent, to calm his mind. He told himself to let the issue rest, to not pursue a path that would lead him to the sin of blaming a devout lord like Bhauma. Just as he was about to retire to the warmth of his home, Mura heard a groan from the very stairs of his house.

Rushing there, he found a woman in a pool of blood. Mura frantically called out to the guards on vigil. Coming closer, he was shocked to find her gagged and stabbed in several places, her clothes torn at places suggesting even worse things had happened to her. He undid the gag and lifted the woman to a sitting position. She groaned, partly recovering from her swoon.

"Who did this?!"

"Bhau…"

"What?" Mura saw the guards approaching and shouted at them to hurry. "Who did this to you?"

"Bhauma. He is the one … Save me, Senapati!" The woman fell limp in his arms.

Several things happened then. The guards gathered around him. Mura lay her on the porch of his house. Before he could order anyone to get medical help, Mura saw Bhauma rush in from the gate.

"What, by the Supreme Goddess!" Bhauma exclaimed. "Senapati!"

Mura glared at him, too shocked and too angry to speak. A guard checked the woman's pulse.

"She is dead."

"What!"

"She is dead, Prabho."

"No!" Mura cried, feeling for her pulse himself.

"Will someone tell me what happened?" Bhauma growled.

"Prabho!" A guard said, trembling. "The woman left her room sometime after sunset saying that the senapati had sent for her. I saw her exit the middle fortress. Then, then…"

"I never sent for anyone!" Mura spat.

"Then what?" Bhauma shouted, glaring at the guards. "Speak out, imbeciles! What were you doing when she was being…? Speak out!" He slapped the nearest guard hard.

"I only came here hearing the shouts of Senapati Mura!" the guard cried. "We all were on our night vigil near the gates, Prabho! We came hearing his calls. We only saw her screaming 'senapati' before she died."

"Were you all lying drunk at the gates in the name of the night vigil? You good-for-nothing brutes! Mura, you tell me the truth!"

Mura had a good mind to fly at Bhauma but he could do nothing at the moment. Bhauma's cold hand held his arm.

"Senapati, tell me you did not do this!"

Mura thought he saw a momentary smile on Bhauma's lips. He was about to raise his hands when he saw Dhatri behind Bhauma. Mura closed his eyes, unable to see her shock, and sank to his knees.

Conversations went on above him. The guards reported to her what they had told Bhauma.

"I was around the southern end of the outer fort wall till now, Mahadevi!" Mura exclaimed, struggling with the sudden turn of events. "Surely someone of you must have seen me there!" He glared at the guards and they looked at each other and then back at Bhauma fearfully shaking their heads.

"I was … by the southern corner, Lord." A guard stuttered. "But you passed us quite a while back, Senapati!"

"No! How dare you! No, Mahadevi! I was by myself for a long while! There must…" Mura saw Bhauma smirk to himself again. A chill went down his spine. If Bhauma had planned to frame him for the crime, he could have managed the guards too! Mura turned to Dhatri, steeling his heart to expose Bhauma. But words failed him at the sight of the shocked reproach in her eyes. He saw Bhauma hold her by the arm and instruct the guards. His limbs felt like they were not his own when the guards hauled him inside his own home and blocked the exit.

"You are lucky, Mura. After that heinous crime, you get to live and continue being the senapati."

"Bhauma!" Mura finally found the strength to reach out and grab hold of Bhauma's neck in a bid to strangle him.

"Now, now, my dear Mura, you don't want to kill the only friend you have in this fortress."

"I will give you the most painful of deaths, you demon!"

"What a clumsy way of showing gratitude to the one who can protect your daughter!"

Mura's hands fell back.

"And she will be safe, I promise you," Bhauma whispered with a wink.

In the light of the flickering lamp, Mura saw the monster that Bhauma was.

"You have quite a list of things to do to atone for that heinous, brutal and inhuman act of yours, Senapati. But quite a small price to pay for the safety of your precious child, isn't it? I would hate to lose a warrior like you and that is what saved you! I spent the whole night convincing the mahadevi that a crime of passion does not warrant death but an atonement and that letting you live and binding you to the services of Kamarupa was a well-deserved punishment, better than death."

Mura stared at him, desperately trying to calm the rage that boiled within. He would have preferred to die rather than serve Bhauma anymore. *What kind of a coward is Bhauma, who lacks the resolve to kill me? No, he just wants to use me till he can find someone else to replace me. Of all things, did my valour have to prove my weakness now? Had I not been a warrior, nobody would have asked me to defend Kamarupa while heinous crimes are committed right in the presence of the Goddess Herself! My daughter would have been safer ...* His hands ached to kill Bhauma and end the matter for good. But if he killed Bhauma then and there, Mura would have to bear Dhatri's hatred forever. He couldn't bear the thought of that.

"Have you ever thought what she will do the day she discovers the fiend that you are, Bhauma?" Mura's broken voice sounded like that of an apparition.

Bhauma's laughter told Mura everything. He sadly realised what Bhauma was capable of doing to Dhatri the moment she found out the truth. He realised the daunting task he had before him; he had to ensure Dhatri's safety and, for that, he needed to stay alive.

No, he would not leave Kamarupa, not until he could prove his innocence to Dhatri and save his daughter.

When the gates of the inner fortress closed on Mura the next day, he steeled his heart further.

Wake up from your slumber, Supreme Goddess Kamaksha! See for yourself who pollutes the air he breathes, taking your very name. See how innocent women are killed, or worse, violated. Wake up to punish the demon who has turned this temple into a hell! Wake up to end this naraka, this hell on earth! Wake up!

Chapter Twenty-Five

Indraprastha

She awoke at the deep sound of a conch being blown in the distance. The rhythmic sound of drumbeats took up the conch's call, followed by a voice raised in song:

The jingle of anklets of the fair Uma
The arrow from the bow of Kama
Stirred the king of dance, the Shiva
Could he remain a recluse, the Bhava?

The song had become familiar by now. It was heard from the nartanashala every morning, punctuated by the sound of musical instruments and the accompanying tinkle of anklets. The sessions of music and dance started with the first rays of the sun falling on the placid waters of the Yamuna. The lines evoked smiles from those in the neighbourhood, despite the interruption to their sleep; the legendary story of Girija Kalyanam was dear to artists and commoners alike.

Abhaya, though, did not smile. She lay staring at the ceiling. Nothing seemed capable of penetrating the gloom that had enveloped her. She had reached Indraprastha the previous evening. Some of the citizens of Anagha had gone to live with their relatives in the neighbouring cities of Saurashtra but most had accompanied her to Indraprastha, where Subhadra had received them with open arms. For Abhaya, she had reserved quarters at her residence.

What struck Abhaya the most about Indraprastha was the whole different scale of things here. Subhadra's mansion was almost as huge as the royal palace at Anagha. Given the large family of the five Pandava brothers and their multiple wives, the royal residences of Indraprastha in themselves could have easily housed the entire population of Anagha. The wide streets, the jostling masses, the hustle and noise had made Abhaya feel lost the moment they entered the city. As she had passed through the streets that housed the nobles and counsellors, Abhaya couldn't help but notice the lavishness of their homes. Prosperity was at its peak in Indraprastha. But despite the air of luxury and abundance, Abhaya had felt intimidated and unwanted. Gathering herself, she had blamed her mood on her bereavement and tried to clear all traces of envy from her mind. Her heart broke, though, to see her people stopping to admire each home on the street with longing.

Abhaya lifted herself from the bed and went to the mirror. The turn of events and the fatigue of the long journey had taken their toll on her. Her hair had lost its lustre, her skin was dull, there were dark circles around her eyes but, most of all, it was her restrained demeanour that rendered her practically unrecognisable from her usual ebullient self.

"Devi, let me wash your hair today." Abhaya looked up and saw the female attendant Subhadra had assigned to attend to her. The woman was in her fifties and looked familiar. Abhaya recognised her as one of the older maids at Dwaraka who had accompanied Subhadra to Indraprastha. The woman introduced herself as Mrinalini. Abhaya was about to follow her to the adjoining bath when another voice caught her attention.

Speak not, words of empty love, Dark God
Play your flute, cure my fatigue, Dark God

Like one enchanted, Abhaya moved to the window. A woman was milking cows in the backyard. She sang as she worked, occasionally caressing and kissing the calf that waited its turn for the milk.

You now move, in the attire of a prince,
Don't you remember the grove, even once?

She sang of longing and separation but her tone, as she went about her work, tapping her foot to keep the rhythm, was far from sorrowful.

Your smile, not Spring, makes flowers bloom
Your gaze, not the sun melts the gloom
What of your words of unending Joy and Love?
Won't you return to me in your Vrinda Grove?

"Now what?" she said to the cow. "I can't sing new songs for you every day!"

Abhaya found herself smiling involuntarily. "Who is that?"

"That woman? She is a gopika, a milkmaid from the village across the Yamuna," replied the maid who had made herself busy making the bed and removing the flowers on the bedside table that had withered overnight. "These cows were also brought from the village. Devi Subhadra was so particular about them. That gopika comes from the village to milk them every day. She has a way with them."

"Yes, my love, my queen! A little more milk, Amba, for your children. We are all your children, like this calf," the gopika went on, negotiating with the cow. Abhaya could not help chuckling. "Alright, this is the last one. I shall not sing further."

Did you see him, the dark-hued one?
Did you see him, the Lotus eyed one
The one from whom grace and beauty flow;
The one for whom the plumes of peacock glow
Smile bewitching never leaves his face;
To the call of his flute, our hearts race
Bushes of the Vrinda Grove, Speak well;
Is that one hiding among you? Do tell

"Sunanda!" The maid called out to the gopika.

Sunanda turned towards the window. She smiled and waved to indicate she was coming. Before long, Abhaya heard the tinkle of anklets in the passage outside.

"Is Govinda here?" Sunanda entered the room, the pot balanced on her waist. The beaded jewellery around her neck swayed to and fro as she walked.

"No," Mrinalini replied, unplaiting Abhaya's hair. "This is..."

"His wife?" Sunanda interrupted as she came closer to pat Abhaya on the cheek.

Irreverent, but charming. Abhaya looked up at Mrinalini.

Mrinalini frowned at Sunanda. "Where are your manners? She is Abhaya … Dhaarmaseni, a princess from our Saurashtra. A friend of Devi Subhadra."

Sunanda's lips flattened. "I thought he had come. I had brought the piyusha for him. My queen, Saurabhaa, gave birth to a calf."

"They call Vaasudeva Govinda. He was brought up in their village, Vrindavan," Mrinalini explained.

Sunanda, her disappointment visible, turned to leave.

Abhaya chuckled. "Will you not give me the piyusha? Is it reserved for your Govinda?"

Sunanda stopped and turned around. "You like it?"

"Keep the pot there," Mrinalini signalled.

Sunanda was about to place the pot on a wooden stool. She then looked at Abhaya. "My Saurabhaa's piyusha is only for those who have never slaughtered a cow."

"Sunanda!" Mrinalini exclaimed, throwing an unsure glance at Abhaya.

"That is alright. I have never slaughtered a cow, by Mahakala," Abhaya said. She was not sure what in Sunanda was more endearing, her boisterous chatter or her complete disregard for protocol.

Sunanda nodded, her eyes twinkling. She put the pot of piyusha down on the stool and left, promising to bring more the next day.

"Someone needs to teach her how to behave," Mrinalini said, apologetically. "But I'm sure you'll like her. Devi Subhadra has a special affection for that village. Their sacrifice, of course, is something that can't be forgotten."

Abhaya looked up. Mrinalini collected the bath oils and led Abhaya into the adjoining bath chamber.

"The Vaasudeva we know … his birth was full of intrigues. Let me just say that death chased him even before he was born. His father and mother were kept prisoners by his uncle Kamsa. He, Kamsa, the paranoid tyrant, wanted to kill Vaasudeva as soon as he was born. This was when the head of the gopas, the cowherds, stepped in."

Abhaya nodded as Mrinalini paused. "I did hear in detail about what happened after Vaasudeva killed Kamsa from Subhadra herself." The fragrance of the sandalwood paste that Mrinalini was applying to her arms and shoulders soothed her and, feeling lighter, she closed her eyes to rest.

"Devi Subhadra reveres these gopas, and not without a reason. To ensure Vaasudeva's safety, the gopa headman left his newborn daughter in Krishna's place."

"And?" Abhaya looked up at Mrinalini in horror.

The maid shook her head, dipping a bronze pot into the large container of warm water. "I hear many stories. They say she turned into a goddess. They say she disappeared into the air. The truth is, she is…"

Water drenched Abhaya's frame and, in the sound, she could not hear the rest of the sentence.

"What?"

Mrinalini shook her head. "We will never know the truth. But the sacrifice of Nanda and Yashoda…" The maid brought her hands together in devotion.

Abhaya nodded, rubbing the sandalwood paste off her limbs. The rest of the bath happened in companionable silence.

"I'm sorry for causing you such melancholy, Princess. Cheer up! Anyway, all that is in the past," Mrinalini concluded in a more cheerful tone, covering her with a long dry shawl.

"But a burden enough for life," Abhaya murmured. She shook her head when Mrinalini returned with clothes and jewellery.

"No, I don't want the jewels."

"But my mistress insisted you should wear these, Devi. Your mourning period concluded a fortnight ago."

"They aren't mine, Mrinalini. I cannot wear them."

"I heard from my mistress, Devi, that you gave up all your jewellery to secure provisions for your people during the journey. Devi Subhadra has made it clear that the expenses throughout the journey were the responsibility of Indraprastha. These jewels now belong to you."

The words annoyed Abhaya. But she knew that Mrinalini was not the right target for her anger. "I shall talk to Subhadra, Mrinalini. Don't worry, I shall make sure that she does not chastise you for not wearing any jewellery."

Mrinalini sighed. "You are a princess. But do heed my advice, Devi. Given all that you have faced, I know jewels and such are of least interest to you. You might even scorn and spurn them as luxuries. But this is Indraprastha, the capital of western Kuru, and not our Saurashtra. The royal family might be friendly and even humble. But the zillions of people who work in the palace are used to seeing royalty in a certain way. Your attire will bring you immediate authority and respect.

It will give you unquestioned access to every part of the palace and the city. I hope you understand, Devi."

Abhaya heard her words with a neutral expression. "I understand, Mrinalini. I shall send for you if I want to leave these chambers and go anywhere. But, for now, I beg of you, don't force me. I shall speak to Subhadra myself and sort this out." Mrinalini bowed. She turned to the task of tying Abhaya's hair and, once finished, turned to leave. "Wait." Abhaya held her hand. "Why did Sunanda come here and ask for Krishna ... Vaasudeva?"

"These chambers are usually where he resides when he is at Indraprastha. For now, he is staying in the emperor's mansion. Some of his belongings are still here. When you came yesterday, Devi Subhadra sensed you seemed to be at peace here and decided to give you this room." She smiled at Abhaya's consternation and hurriedly reassured her. "Please don't worry! I am sure it was no trouble."

As she left, another maid walked in carrying the morning meal. She informed Abhaya that Subhadra would come to her later in the day.

When Subhadra arrived in her chambers, she gave her a scroll detailing the housing arrangements that had been made for the citizens of Anagha and the facilities that had been provided to them.

Abhaya accepted the scroll, forcing a smile.

"Don't hide your sorrow, Abhaya, not from me," Subhadra implored.

Abhaya shook her head. "Subhadra, I accepted your brother's assurance that we would receive asylum here and did not even think of asking you or the king of

Indraprastha even once. Are we being a burden? I ... I don't want to..." The lump in her throat did not allow her to speak further.

Subhadra shook her by the arm. "Firstly, take that word 'asylum' out of your head. Secondly, if coming to the aid of a friend is considered a burden, then what is the use of such friends? Didn't your city receive us with open arms that night when we were en route to the shores of Saurashtra?"

The memory did affect Abhaya and her frown evened out.

"Take your time and go easy on yourself." Subhadra smiled. "The scrolls will convince you that neither you nor the citizens of Anagha are a burden on Indraprastha."

Abhaya nodded and Subhadra left, informing her that she could meet the Pandava royal family the next day once she had recovered from the fatigue of travel.

Abhaya turned to examine the details in the scrolls. The soldiers were invited to join the army of Indraprastha once they were ready. Abhaya signed her consent as that would provide them and their families a legitimate livelihood and they would not remain dependent. It was the same with the artists, performers and the women who had worked in the palace of Anagha. It was a matter of time before one of her own would start attending to her. She went through the details, deliberating where to cast her seal and where not to. Uncertainty was faced mainly by the traders who were left with little wealth to start a trade of their choice. The guild of traders at Indraprastha had proposed a discussion with them. Abhaya knew she would have to preside over the meeting to see that her people were treated fairly. She mulled over the terms till she was interrupted by a polite query by another maid. Abhaya nodded and gazed out of the window. To her surprise, it was twilight.

Abhaya's eyes fell on the closet in which Mrinalini had said Krishna's belongings were kept.

Should I have them sent to him? she wondered and walked to the closet. It contained mostly weapons and garments. Abhaya's eyes fell on the sharpening stone. She took it and began to sharpen her sword. After she was done, she leaned against the backrest of the luxurious cot and closed her eyes. It seemed like only a short while but when she awoke, it was dark. There was no sound of activity from the corridors and Abhaya wondered what time it was. A sound of breathing behind her made her whirl around.

"Krishna!"

Abhaya's sight blurred as his hands cupped her cheeks. She had thought that her suppressed sorrow would break its bounds when she met him. But, on the contrary, she felt it melt away in a single teardrop that fell upon Krishna's palm.

"You made it, fearless Princess. Your people are safe now."

Abhaya nodded, her gaze still locked with his. "All those deaths, Krishna. The burden still…"

"The burden of death," Krishna said, his gaze moving across the room to halt at the window before he looked back at her, "isn't in our hands, Dhaarmaseni. But we can repay their sacrifice by the way we live the rest of our lives."

"Is that how we combat guilt?"

"Guilt is when you see yourself as the reason for their deaths. But if you see in yourself what they saw in you as they gave up their lives for you, they become not your burden but your strength..."

Abhaya sighed and nodded. Krishna's eyes fell on the scrolls.

"You must be concerned about the traders," Krishna replied.

Abhaya nodded, reaching out for the scrolls. "I have to think about the terms and conditions that the guild offers my traders."

"I spoke to the traders from Anagha," Krishna said.

She looked up, surprised. "You spoke to them? When?"

"This evening. I heard out the terms they decided on and told them to consult you. Then they sought my opinion, which I gave."

"No!" Abhaya protested, the sudden hiss in her voice startling Krishna. "I cannot be a mute approver, Krishna. It is my duty to ensure that they are treated with fairness."

"When did royalty start deciding the terms between two trade guilds, Dhaarmaseni? Aren't they supposed to have the freedom to decide on a mutually agreeable ground?"

Abhaya sighed at the obvious. "I meant, I should have been the one to speak to my traders, not you, Vaasudeva. Did they approach you or..."

Krishna nodded, his lips curved in amusement as he saw the disappointment in her eyes.

"Krishna, is this just the beginning of the consequences of admitting to my people that we, the rulers of Anagha, could not protect them? They trust you over me now. No, I am not jealous. Everyone knows that it was you who saved us from the midnight massacre. But is it my gender that made them approach you instead of me?"

"Relax, they only came to me because they felt you needed your time to recover before they bothered you with their queries. Besides, we cannot deny biases." Krishna smiled, knowing where the conversation would wander to. "But have you pondered the cause behind the bias, as narrow as that sounds?"

"It is a lethargy of intellect," Abhaya said, in a quiet voice. "It is the unwillingness to think beyond what they've always seen and been told that makes them assume that women don't make as good counsellors or rulers or warriors as men do."

"Intellect is never asleep, Dhaarmaseni. But it does get clouded."

"By fear?" Abhaya asked.

Krishna's smile told her that he concurred. "I was expecting you to say masculine arrogance, a chauvinist mindset, patriarchy and other things, Abhaya."

"My intellect isn't yet clouded enough to mistake the effect for the cause." Abhaya found herself chuckling.

"We face the weakness of people behind these facades of rigidity. Can we combat fear with faith?"

Abhaya nodded. "Maybe, yes. I want to believe we can. That is a thought I would like to reserve for later. But for now," she paused, taking the scrolls back, "if they continue to dissociate themselves from me and subsequently their home city, should I stand as a mute spectator? What do I exist for?"

"Mute spectator," Krishna repeated and said, "Aren't you writing yourself off too soon, Dhaarmaseni? And as far as your existence is concerned..." Krishna's eyes toured the room and met hers again, "it is a question everyone needs to introspect on, to find his or her answers. Even the seers and philosophers struggle in that quest."

"Philosophy and metaphysics are not my areas of expertise, Krishna. I only know that one lives to fulfil a purpose. I had always thought that mine was to ensure the well-being of my city."

"If you only cared about the well-being of your city, Dhaarmaseni, you would not have come to me two years ago, pressing me to save Mitravinda from a forced wedding."

"I have faced enough blame for that. Even from ... those dearest to me."

"Blame," Krishna sighed. His smile had vanished and his eyes conveyed a knowing camaraderie. "Blame is the first thing that accosts us when we defy certain constraints, Abhaya. And it is a long-term companion when we continue on the path of that defiance. It is easier if we make peace with it, or even start liking it."

"Start liking blame? Stop joking." Abhaya shot him an annoyed glance. He winked. She turned away, fighting an unexplainable girlish urge to giggle. "For someone with four wives, and Mahakala knows how many more in waiting, you are the one who needs to accept blame as an eternal spouse, not me."

Chapter Twenty-Six

Gomantaka

From his mountain abode, the lord of the Garudas looked at the expanse of land running to the western shores. The sight of the setting sun seen from the Gomantaka mountain had been a treat to his eyes since his boyhood days and, to this day, he retained that same awe for the setting red ball that bathed the skies in an orange hue that gradually gave way to the greyish blue of the night. It would be some time before he could watch this again, Vainateya knew, filling his lungs with the mountain air as he turned back to face the Garuda settlement. The place was in a hustle, as people hurried in and out of their homes with last-minute chores. They were getting ready for a long journey—a journey to the north with their beloved king and leader.

"Bhrata!" Shyeni walked up to him, carrying a newly woven cape of feathers that was a feature of the Garuda attire. Vainateya smiled his gratitude as he held the cape, then handed it back to her so she could pin it to his shoulders.

"I must say the cape makes you look more regal! And more Garuda, when you visit other lands," Shyeni chuckled, stepping back to give him an appraising look. The feathers fluttered in a sudden whiff of wind but her weaving kept them in place. The cape was much lighter than it looked, given the layers of multicoloured feathers. It made Vainateya's already broad shoulders look even broader and then tapered gradually down his torso, thinning down to a single large feather at his knees.

"How about our meal, Shyeni?" Vainateya asked, removing the cape from his shoulders after her scrutiny. Shyeni nodded and walked towards their home, a home that did not boast of any extra grandeur over other Garuda homes except for the higher pedestal from which Vainateya would publicly address his people. The Garudas liked to eat, drink and make merry in the open courtyards of their houses where stone seats were installed for that very purpose.

Shyeni picked up a bowl of locally grown millets cooked in broth and handed it over to her brother. Vainateya promptly scooped out a ball of the paste and brought it to her mouth. To his surprise, Shyeni refused the offering, helping herself to a smaller bowl, and sat down beside him.

"What is the matter, Bhagini?"

Shyeni shook her head and swallowed the broth in her bowl at one go, as though it were a bitter medicine, not her favourite broth.

Vainateya tried to take her hand but she turned away. "Why should you go, Bhrata?" she demanded.

"Our friend might need us, Shyeni."

"Did he send for you, asking for help?"

Vainateya shook his head. "He did not yet ask for our help, Bhagini. But, knowing him, he will need us sooner or later. We are his friends, not just political allies. What is the point of friendship if we cannot anticipate the needs of our friends before they ask us?

Your brother, Shyeni, does not need to be anyone's political ally. But for friendship, he can give his life."

"Bhrata, I am not against helping a dear friend," Shyeni protested. "But this is the first time you are embarking on this long a journey, leaving our Gomantaka. That too for a conquest for which our help was not formally sought. Besides, this conquest is not even led by our friend, the Yadava leader."

"We have nothing to do with the conquest, Shyeni." The lord of the Garudas smiled, gulping the last mouthful of the broth and reaching out for the pitcher of wine on the table.

"Why else would you want to leave our home then?"

"Our home." Vainateya became solemn. "We owe this home to Krishna Vaasudeva. But for him, our mountain abode would have been destroyed long ago."

"I don't disagree, Bhrata. But..."

Vainateya shook his head. "No, this is not about returning a favour. Favours are done and sought between political allies. This is something which we don't indulge in, unlike those in the plains. This is about us, Shyeni, about how we view the world around us and make ourselves a deserving part of humanity. Every time a friend faces a crisis, we have a choice to either treat his crisis as our own or to turn away, like those ushtra birds that bury their heads in the sand. We worship the divine eagle Suparna and not that lowly desert bird, Shyeni. I want to be there for my dear friend even before he feels my need. I want to be there by his side before my name comes to his mind. I want to hear him exclaim, 'Vainateya, how did you even guess I was just thinking of you!' and reply with pride that our beloved God Suparna did not become the chosen vehicle of the God of gods Narayana for nothing. I want to be able to say 'we, the eagle worshippers, know where we are needed, Krishna'."

Shyeni giggled at her brother's dramatic speech, then turned serious. "So, by being available to those who might need us even before they call out to us, we find a way to fulfilment?"

"Why do you repeat it like it's something new, Shyeni? Wasn't this what we learnt as infants listening to mother's lullabies, as toddlers hearing the stories of our grandparents, as budding members of our tribe undergoing our initiation as eagle worshippers?"

Shyeni shook her head and stared into the horizon. "If there was someone who was dear to me and I chose to let him go alone on his path because..."

"If you let him go, then he was not as dear to you as ... wait, are you talking about that Naga? Manikandhara?"

Shyeni's squeezed her eyes shut and pressed her lips together.

Vainateya sighed. "No Garuda could impress you so much as to be allowed to sit by your side to drink wine but this man is actually making you angry even after he's gone?"

"Why couldn't he stay here with us?" Shyeni blurted out, loud enough to startle Vainateya.

"He was here on a quest, Shyeni. He was searching for his lost mother. He said that his home faced a crisis ... What happened between you two, Bhagini?"

When he heard what had taken place, Vainateya smiled sadly to himself. This was the first time he had seen his sister fuss over a man and already her beliefs were clashing with the priorities of the one she loved. His little sister had been doted upon and pampered by the whole village. It fell to him to place the harsh realities of life before her.

"Shyeni, he had his priorities. Is it fair to expect him to forget what he came for and stay with you? Even if he did that, would you be comfortable with the fact that he could forget his dear ones so easily? Wouldn't you question how he would treat you in the future?"

Shyeni sighed. Vainateya patted her cheek. There were many things he could tell her but this was something she needed to figure out by herself. Knowing Shyeni, he also knew that planting a thought in her mind was enough and she was very capable of deciding her course of action.

"Shyeni, I dearly want you to retain your freedom but a love for freedom is not the same as fear of commitment."

Shyeni nodded as the king of Garudas rose to his feet.

"Suparna protect us, mind, body and spirit!"

"Suparna protect us, mind, body and spirit!"

Shyeni sat on the cliff, perched on her favourite boulder, watching the departing Garuda regiment until they disappeared from view. She stared into the horizon for a long time. Vainateya's decision to stand by his friend made her proud. It also made her thoughtful. Vikrama had not left her thoughts ever since he had parted from her.

"Why couldn't he tell me he could use my help? I could have gone with him to search for his mother too. I could have helped him find that lost girl." Talking aloud made her feel less lonely.

Did I fail my Garuda spirit?

Vikrama's shocked eyes haunted her. His shock at that time had been beyond her comprehension but now she understood.

Was I scared of commitment as bhrata implied?

The very thought of a new home, new relationships and a strange environment had made her reject any thought of their marriage outrightly. But why could she not take him off her mind? Darkness had set in but Shyeni still could not find the will to return home. She felt that Vainateya had wanted to advise her about what she should do next but he had desisted from doing so. He had always let her make her own decisions.

Will Vikrama nurse a bitter feeling about Garudas in general? Will he think that we are a tribe of betrayers?

The thought made her more uncomfortable than ever. She owed it to her tribe to set things right. Not because the world's opinion mattered to her but because a good man had had to leave the land of Garudas with a broken heart.

No, it is not even that! It is much more than the reputation of my tribe!

The moon appeared from behind the clouds and she smiled to herself. She had made her decision.

Chapter Twenty-Seven

Indraprastha

"Ten years of trade operations at Indraprastha!" Abhaya was in the hall where the traders' meeting was to be held that morning, some days after having settled into the city. She had arrived early to confer with Srinayana Sreshti, who had been her father's confidante in matters of trade. The two were alone in the hall at the moment. She frowned, reading the scroll again.

"Srinayana Sreshti, while it is admirable of the trade guild of Indraprastha to invest in our traders, are you sure that this condition is agreeable to us? Why did you not voice any concern about it earlier?"

"How is that a concern, Devi?" the trader replied with the indulgence of one who had known her since her infancy. "They are investing their wealth in us. They want us close."

"But for ten years?"

"At a practical level, it is negotiable based on the nature of each trade, Devi. But this is the least they expect to invest in us."

"What if we choose to leave for Anagha?" Abhaya asked, flipping through the scrolls in her hand to find the one that dealt with violations and termination of the arrangement.

"Then we would have to liquidate the trade and they would have the greater share of the resulting wealth.

Their share reduces with each year. At the end of ten years, it comes to half," Sreshti explained.

Abhaya stared at him. "So if we leave, say, after a year, we leave with practically nothing?"

"It would be unwise to leave after a year, Devi. Two years is the minimum the traders will need to stabilise in the new place. Four years is a realistic period for most trades to become profitable. Some may take longer."

"But that means that you cannot return to Anagha for the next five years even if the gods favour your trade!" Abhaya spoke more to herself than him.

"This is a trade agreement, Devi," he smiled. "It is not an irrefutable decree of an emperor. There are negotiations at every stage and terms can be changed as we build a stronger case for ourselves with time."

"But even then, we don't see a possibility to wind up and return before a minimum of five years!" Abhaya protested. "Why, Sreshti? Why this servitude to their conditions? We are not their slaves."

"Nobody thinks we are their slaves, Devi," Srinayana responded. He opened his mouth to continue but stopped, seeing Abhaya's disappointment. After an uncomfortable pause, he said, "Devi, allow me to speak frankly. Returning to Anagha in the near future is not high in our list of current priorities."

"Sreshti!"

"I know this is hard on you, Vatse," the trader interrupted, resorting to the endearing term, invoking his age and experience. "Call us ungrateful but for us, traders, our loyalty lies with the trade and the king who rules the place where we trade. Not with..."

"Not with the failed royalty who fled a war-torn motherland. Not with the motherland."

"Vatse, please don't think that the city of Anagha means nothing to us. But considering our present condition, patriotism cannot be the basis on which we can negotiate terms. Livelihood for our people is what matters the most."

Abhaya glared at the trader as reason and ideals clashed on the battlefield of her mind.

"Is that the opinion of the other traders too?"

The trader nodded, not meeting her eyes.

Without flexing a single muscle of her jaw, she flipped the scroll. "Fine, so, is there something in here that does bother you and the other traders?"

The rest of the discussion dwelt upon minor specifics of how a middle ground had been reached. Abhaya mostly concurred with Srinayana Sreshti's opinions, given his three decades of experience in a variety of trades. Casting her final seal, Abhaya rose to her feet and moved towards the door of the hall.

"Devi, the traders of Indraprastha will be here shortly. Are you not presiding over the meeting?"

"Will my presence make a difference when both sides owe their loyalty to the king of Indraprastha?"

"Vatse!"

"Don't bother consoling me with symbolic positions of nominal authority, Sreshti. I trust your experience shall ensure fair treatment to our traders. Please feel free to reach out to me when you think my presence can make a difference."

Abhaya returned to her quarters and remained there, consciously avoiding meeting anyone as she feared she would further debase herself with an inappropriate emotional outburst. She sat on a seat close to the window and looked out at the skies. Sunset was still more than an hour away. Her mind could not help dwelling on the way things were spiralling out of control, leading inexorably to the dreaded possibility that her city would become a mere relic of the past.

"Devi!" A male voice at the door drew her attention. "I apologise for the intrusion but is the lord here?"

"Which lord?"

"Er … your husband Vaasudeva?"

"Pardon me, Dwarapala, I never knew I was married."

The guard brought his hand to his head in confusion and fumbled for words.

"Are you drunk in the middle of the day?" Mrinalini's harsh voice came from the corridor. She walked in, nodding at Abhaya. "Lord Vasudeva is staying at the emperor's palace, not here. But who let you into the antahpura in the first place? Get out! Beware of using that damned tongue of yours here again!"

"Pardon me, the emperor wanted to see him and I was in a hurry…" He hurried out with a bow.

Abhaya was annoyed by the guard's impertinent assumption but she also felt Mrinalini had been needlessly harsh. Mrinalini took out one of the lighter shawls from the closet and draped it on Abhaya's shoulders, replacing the shawl she had worn for the meeting "Don't mind him, Devi. He has been a bit lost ever since his wife ran away with some sadhus."

"I wish people would take the time to think before they spoke," Abhaya replied, reaching out for the scrolls on the smaller table by her seat. Then, she paused. "Did you say his wife ran away?"

"Yes, Devi. I knew her well. She was working here until a month before you came. But there were these sadhus who caught her fantasy. And one fine day she just disappeared."

"What kind of sadhus were they?" Abhaya rose to her feet.

Mrinalini halted in the middle of cleaning the huge bronze lamps that hung from the ceiling. She looked at Abhaya in surprise. "I don't know but why are you so disturbed? Devi, is something wrong?"

"What was her name?"

"Nilambari. We used to call her Nila. She was close even to Devi Subhadra."

"Can I meet Subhadra right now?"

Before Mrinalini could answer, Abhaya was already on her way to Subhadra's quarters. It was the first time she was visiting her friend in her private chamber. The female guards knew her and allowed her in with a bow. Abhaya saw Subhadra sitting on the steps of an elevated dais and toying with a collection of wooden toys arrayed in war formation. Sensing a presence, Subhadra turned and smiled when she saw Abhaya. "How was your meeting with the traders?"

"Not as I had expected. But..."

"Why? Is the guild being difficult? I shall personally request Jyeshta bhrata Yudhishtira to intervene if you are dissatisfied."

"No, no, I don't seek anyone's intervention. I have no complaints," Abhaya said. "But Subhadra ... what is this?" she interrupted herself and pointed to the miniature wooden replicas of elephants, horses, chariots and foot soldiers.

"The Chakravyuha—the wheel formation," Subhadra answered. "A puzzle that Arjuna keeps me busy with. The red ones are those defending the formation. The yellow ones have to break the formation. He wants me to figure out a way in and out. It is a sort of training on war strategy. I did manage to find a way in but…" Subhadra put her hand on her belly and leaned back against a pillar for support.

"Interesting…" Abhaya studied the formation. On any other occasion, she would have liked to sit with Subhadra and solve the puzzle together. But there was something else on her mind. "Subhadra, I wanted to ask you something. About your former maid Nila."

"Nilambari? Who told you about her? Is Mrinalini bothering you with unsolicited tales?" Subhadra commented, rising slowly to her feet, supporting her pregnant belly. Abhaya stepped forward to help and Subhadra led her to two chairs on the balcony of her room that looked over River Yamuna.

"No, it's just that I heard she went away with some sadhus. Who were they?"

"I have no clue. She did tell me that their ways of worship were different and even brought me some meat delicacy that they prepared in a ritual, saying it would be auspicious for my child. But the taste made me nauseous."

"Were they Shaktas? Who else cooks meat for a ritual these days? We gave it up quite a while back, didn't we?"

"Could be. Yes, it is hard for those who are used to it to forego meat. But at least it stopped being a part of our rituals, except for some big ones, I guess. Abhaya, what is the matter?" Subhadra frowned, knowing that Abhaya's interest in this went beyond palace gossip.

Abhaya did not speak for some time and looked up only when Subhadra shook her by the arm. "Subhadra, did this Nila know any crucial information about you? Or about your family? I mean, information which would be valuable to your enemies, or would make your family vulnerable?"

Subhadra stared at her and then smiled. "No. Nila was hardly a spy. The poor woman was just unhappy in her marriage. Her husband is a guard at the emperor's place. I think she just wanted to leave him."

"I saw him. He came to my quarters just now, without seeking the permission of the female guard, I'm afraid. And referred to your brother as my husband."

"What!"

"The great assumption culture of Indraprastha, I believe," Abhaya retorted, then bit her tongue.

"Well, now you know why Nila left him," Subhadra laughed. "So don't worry about her."

"Well, I was more worried about whom Nila left with. They could be harmful. Do you know that my fortress fell in a night because a Shakta group whisked away the daughter of my family priest? She knew about a secret tunnel and that information was used by the prince of Avanti. I only wanted to warn you."

Abhaya paused as a maid brought two bronze goblets of a fruit drink and placed them on the low table before them.

Subhadra took Abhaya's hand in hers. "Thank you, Bhagini. But be rest assured. I am sure she does not know any such crucial secrets about us. She might at worst know some gossip and rumours that would be of no use to any enemy."

Abhaya sighed and nodded, taking one of the goblets into her hands.

"Speaking of Avanti," Subhadra continued, "Our conquest has reached its gates. You shall soon hear the news of your enemy's defeat."

Abhaya's nostrils flared and she nodded. "My soldiers could have joined if…"

"Does it make a difference?" Subhadra asked. She cupped her palm under Abhaya's chin. "Abhaya, I am partly responsible for your miseries. I stopped Bhrata Krishna from telling you about the Rajasuya campaign. He wanted to warn you well in advance."

"I got all the clues that day when you visited us, Subhadra. It is just that we never anticipated Avanti to act in this underhanded manner." Abhaya stopped as Subhadra caught her arm.

"Abhaya, all of Anagha's monetary loss will be recovered from Avanti. But how can anyone get you back what you lost? No, you will need to tell me how the citizens of Anagha can be compensated."

"Anagha's loss cannot be compensated. My traders are not willing to return home, Subhadra."

Subhadra nodded, guessing what had happened in the trade meeting. She sighed. "Traders are not loyal to the soil, Abhaya. They are loyal to their trade."

"I know," Abhaya nodded, turning away. "And I know that new traders will be ready to come and settle when I rebuild my city. The legacy of my great-grandfather cannot be doomed to dust and ruin. I will start again. From scratch, if I must."

"And you will not be alone," Subhadra said. "Abhaya, I know what it is to abandon one's home and move to new shores. I was a girl of twelve when we left Mathura in fear of a vengeful king who invaded it several times. I know how it feels to bear the blame. But nothing lasts forever, Abhaya. Who knows? This empire of the Pandavas is on the rise now but the day may come when this too falls into a rival's hand."

Abhaya gripped Subhadra's shoulder. "Mahakala forbid such a thing should ever happen! Do you think the possibility of your miseries will make me feel any better?"

"No, Abhaya, that isn't what I meant to say at all. All I'm trying to say is nothing lasts forever. Faith in ourselves is what will see us through the highs and lows. And faith is what I can give you as a friend." Abhaya smiled at these words and turned to leave. Subhadra caught her hand. "Another team of spies has gone in search of your brother. I know you would have wanted to join them. But, Abhaya, I do not want you to leave Indraprastha, at least not until the southern conquest concludes."

It was hard to disagree.

Abhaya sighed, praying that Vikrama was alive and well.

Chapter Twenty-Eight

"Avanti is defeated?" Abhaya asked. Her grip on the sword and the shield tightened.

"Yes, Devi," the messenger said.

"Is Anuvinda here? Was he sent here?" she asked. Her jaw throbbed as she threw a glance at the trainer who had engaged her in sword practice in the last two months that she had been at Indraprastha.

The messenger nodded. His face fell, realising the same time that Abhaya did, that her attire for sword practice carried no jewel that could make for a ready reward. The left end of her lips curved.

"Meet me tomorrow."

The messenger grinned and left with a deep bow.

The trainer chuckled. "There goes your practice into the Yamuna, now that your enemy is already defeated even before you donned the armour! No, I was just joking. The skill of sword fighting is much more than seeking revenge. It is, more than anything, related to a battle. You know that, don't you?"

"I know someone who used to think so," Abhaya replied, placing the weapons back and collecting her long tresses into a loose bun.

"Congratulations, Devi," the trainer bowed, averting his eyes from her lithe figure as she did her hair. "Let me know when you would like the next session."

Abhaya bowed in return and exited the quadrangle, conscious of the emotions that threatened to break the walls within which she had carefully imprisoned them in her heart.

She insisted on meeting Anuvinda alone despite Subhadra's offer to accompany her or send her with an escort.

Mrinalini had insisted that this was the occasion to deck up and show Anuvinda who the victor was. Abhaya refused but finally consented to wear a pearl string with a metallic signet medallion of Indraprastha. She did not respond to Mrinalini's suggestion to pile her hair into a bun on her head and the maid took the liberty to implement her idea.

"This will make you appear taller," she explained. Abhaya nodded absently. When she stepped out of her room, she saw women and men carrying in plates and vessels filled with coins of all sizes. Some carried jewellery, weapons studded with precious stones and other objects of value.

"Your rightful due from the conquest of Avanti," the maid leading the group said with a bow. Abhaya took a step back, repulsed at the sight of the riches.

"I … I'll look into that," Mrinalini offered, noticing Abhaya's clenched fists. Abhaya strode towards the guest house alone, past the guards who exchanged confused looks, unsure if they were meant to follow her into her meeting with Anuvinda or not.

Entering the guest house, which could not be called modest by any standards even if it was housing a rival defeated in war, Abhaya saw Anuvinda seated on the carved master seat.

His eyes fixed on her as she walked in and he rose to his feet. Anuvinda was too proud to bow and Abhaya knew that even the act of rising was a wound to his pride. Her right brow arched up and her lips curved into a measured smile.

"Welcome, Yuvaraja." Abhaya took the seat opposite his. "As the daughter of someone who considered Avanti his ally, it doesn't please me to see you in this state, a defeated prisoner."

"And it doesn't please me to see you as a refugee when you could have ascended the throne of Avanti."

"A friend in distress may be a refugee to you, Anuvinda, but thankfully Indraprastha thinks differently. I see the battle has done little to change you."

Anuvinda shrugged. "Not that it matters now but I regret letting you fall into the crocodile moat that day. It did not have to come to that."

"I could have believed you if you hadn't killed our soldiers after that."

"Your pride stops you from realising the truth, Dhaarmaseni. You could have saved them, your father and many more had you consented to come with me."

Abhaya's fingers curled as she lifted her left hand to her lips. "This method of making the woman feel guilty for the actions of men is fast becoming stale, Yuvaraja. Even a child could guess that your motive was control over trade routes and highways of Saurashtra. I was just a means to conquer Anagha without risking your army, wasn't I?"

"You could have seen yourself as the future queen too, Dhaarmaseni. But then, I was right about your pride."

"Future queen? Or the bride of a defeated prince?" Abhaya's brows arched higher.

"It might upset you but, despite the defeat, I am still the soon-to-become king now that I have pledged my allegiance to Indraprastha."

If Abhaya was disappointed, she did not show it. It was also a war code of those times to reinstate the defeated king once he accepts the overlordship of the victor. Anuvinda saw her chuckle instead. "Chivalrous enemies are an asset, aren't they? I wish I had been as lucky with enemies as you, Anuvinda."

The silence that followed was heavy. Abhaya had hoped to see his conceit destroyed. But his lack of remorse challenged her faith. Abhaya knew that she was no longer feeling vengeful but something inside her seemed to shatter. They glared at each other until finally Anuvinda blinked and looked away.

"Dhaarmaseni, there can be new beginnings. I shall compensate your loss." He raised his hand to stop her contemptuous words. "Now, I think you can do better than asking dramatic questions like, 'Will you help me get back my father?'. Both of us know I didn't kill him either."

She remained unimpressed. "At least you realise that lost lives can't be brought back." She leaned against the backrest of her seat. "Perhaps it is too much to ask you to think about innocent commoners who died because of you or your soldiers. And I suppose no one told you about a nineteen-year-old who was raped and killed by your soldiers that night."

She saw Anuvinda's eyes close for a moment. "I shall punish those soldiers myself if you can identify them. I hope you don't think I am capable of stooping to such levels as to order the rape of women."

"If a prince approves of the covert raiding of forts of his ancestral friend and the capture of his daughter as ransom, what can one expect from his soldiers, Anuvinda?"

"Boys will be boys, Abhaya."

Abhaya rose to her feet in fury. At that moment, they heard a metal plate fall in the adjoining room. The clang startled her as much as Anuvinda's words did. A maid emerged from the room. She begged their pardon and hurried away.

Abhaya sat back and stared back at Anuvinda. *How can one expect a change across Bharatavarsha if the likes of Anuvinda continued to wield power?* Her disappointment now directed itself at the Pandavas who had pardoned and reinstated Anuvinda. Reasoning with him about the brutal insensitivity in his words was pointless. Her hand gripped the side of the seat tight enough for her veins to show.

"Identify them for me. I shall see that they are punished," Anuvinda repeated. "I am prepared to go the distance for the new beginning, Abhaya. Can we put the past behind us?"

Abhaya's response was a hostile silence. She did not need anything from him, especially when he made it look like he was doing her a favour.

"I was given an estimate of the losses Anagha suffered. You should have, by now, received treasures valued at double the estimate. Still, this offer is from me. Let me know of anything more needed to rebuild the city."

Abhaya's nod was a formality. Only she was conscious of the urge she fought back in the later part of the conversation. Walking back towards Subhadra's mansion, she felt like she was swimming against a current. Determination built up within her but it lacked direction.

The female guard at the door of Subhadra's mansion heaved a visible sigh of relief as she entered. She had received an earful from Subhadra for not accompanying Abhaya.

When Abhaya passed through the door of Subhadra's room, she heard a voice that instantly made her smile. She entered the room and then halted just inside the threshold.

"It's good that Anuvinda was spared. His killing would not have helped our cause."

"I am only worried about how Abhaya will take it." Subhadra's words showed concern.

"We will have to convince her, Subhadra."

"Why don't you first go and check if she is safe? She went to meet Anuvinda alone."

Laughter met Subhadra's words. "Is Indraprastha that unsafe that a prisoner, sorry, *guest*, can harm your friend?"

In the silence that followed, Abhaya could see that Subhadra was annoyed. She chose not to interrupt the conversation between the siblings and turned to leave.

"Why don't you marry her?"

"What?"

"You have to move quickly, or I shall start extolling the virtues of my brother-in-law, Sahadeva, in her presence."

Abhaya froze at the threshold. The silence that followed Subhadra's taunt made her throat go dry.

It was Subhadra who broke the silence again. "Why can't I? Sahadeva knows swordplay well enough to beat the best of swordsmen across Bharatavarsha. He conquered Avanti and defeated Anuvinda. Don't you think he is a good match for her?"

"If you wish, I will speak to her about Sahadeva myself," came the cheerful response.

Abhaya's nostrils flared. She bit her lip to keep the retort that came to her mind from escaping. "Just go away! You aren't worth a woman's love!" Subhadra spoke the very words she wanted to say. Without a sound, she strode out, instructing the maid to inform Subhadra about her return.

Chapter Twenty-Nine

The usual song of the visiting milkmaid did little to cheer Abhaya at sunset. Despite multiple attempts by Mrinalini to find out what transpired between her and Anuvinda, Abhay remained inscrutable. She looked blankly at the pile of jewels, gems and coins made of different precious metals. The estimates of the riches that lay before her had been recorded in the scrolls that were presented to her that morning.

Then, to Mrinalini's surprise, she began to examine each of the jewels.

"Why are you surprised, Mrinalini? Is it a crime to try these jewels?" In her smile, the maid sensed something wrong.

Age and experience had taught Mrinalini to gauge minds. "Why would it be a crime to wear what belongs to you, Devi? But when you evince an unusual interest in things that you spurned till now, I think it would certainly be a reason for surprise."

Abhaya sighed. She had grown to like the maid. And, to Mrinalini's credit, Abhaya did benefit from her unsolicited advice. "Do you want to know what is wrong with me all of a sudden?"

Mrinalini cleared her throat and was about to say something when a shadow at the door made her pause.

"Girls will be girls! What is wrong with that?"

Abhaya's eyes closed at the voice. She had to swallow hard to keep her emotions in check. She gestured to Mrinalini to leave.

"Those giving me refuge will want me to look presentable when they talk about my wedding, won't they?"

"Dhaarmaseni."

Abhaya expected to hear a quip but the ensuing silence made her look up. "Why, Vaasudeva?"

"That is just Subhadra grabbing the first opportunity to play the big sister. You can fight her off, can't you?"

"It is not Subhadra that I am disappointed with." Abhaya's brows knitted and she threw a glance at the treasures piled before them.

"How did the meeting with your dear friend go?"

"You know already. Your spies were there, eavesdropping." There were no traces of accusation in her tone but her eyes betrayed annoyance.

Krishna's lips curved. His remark about girls as he entered, he knew, had clued her into his spying. He sighed and settled down on a seat. "The conquest did little to change him, didn't it?"

"It did nothing! But why would it change him? Did your dear relatives throw him out of power after he lost? His is not the sort of arrogance that melts at chivalry. And..."

"His lack of remorse is a concern not just for you, Abhaya. It is a concern for the whole of Bharatavarsha."

Abhaya met his gaze defiantly. "What was the inspiration behind the Rajasuya, Krishna? Wasn't it to usher a change from the oppressive rules emerging from power-thirsty kings who seek to command their smaller neighbours by hook or crook, from the quasi-marital alliances that look upon women only as a means to consolidate power, from the attitudes that consider the lives of others as lesser than their own?" Abhaya had to pause to catch her breath. "My problems are not those of the whole of Bharatavarsha, but..."

"They are," Krishna retorted. "No kingdom can be called prosperous till every kingdom is so. No woman can be considered safe unless every woman is."

"How is that possible if people like him get to rule even after a crushing defeat, Krishna?"

"The change we talk about, Abhaya, if it can be brought about overnight simply by changing rulers, how much time do you think it will take for things to revert to the present rot?"

"Do you still believe that he will change?"

The nod that came in response spoke more of a vision than of faith. "Dhaarmaseni, it is easy to rebel and call for a revolution. What is difficult is to inspire evolution. That happens with transforming hearts, not by condemning people. That happens with challenging their thought and not by provoking their egos."

"What will challenge and transform the 'thought' of the likes of Anuvinda? I know the answer. Nothing. But probably some like me need to die at his hands for you to get rid of blind faith and realise the bitter truth."

Krishna gripped her wrists instinctively but his words were measured. "Never hope to make death an example, Abhaya. Make your life one instead. You must prevail, not perish, during the transformation." He saw the spark of curiosity in her face and smiled inwardly. It was this curiosity that had endeared her to him years ago and, in his heart, Krishna acknowledged the bond that had developed between them ever since. He released her wrists and noticed the impressions his fingers had left on her skin. It was a compelling moment but he knew they had to wait.

He leaned back and arched a brow. "Think about what makes Anuvinda's arrogance prevail over this defeat. He hopes that the conquest will not succeed. He may be right. The northern and eastern conquests will not prove easy."

"So, you feel if the conquest continues to succeed, he would eventually change his outlook?" Abhaya queried. But the possibility of Anuvinda being neutralised by a power much larger than him, she had to admit, was not non-existent. "And how long would it take for you to say the same thing with greater confidence?"

"This is a hypothesis. A year more to prove its possibility and another year to ensure it. It is not faith that makes me say this, Abhaya; it is the study of his mental construct. Transformation of his kind is possible when we can defeat his methods. When what he believes in fails, when he sees those concurring with his line of thought fail, one after the other, he will be compelled to change. This is the reason why we should aim to persist and prevail."

Abhaya avoided his eyes. She realised that what he spoke of was a well-thought-out plan to teach Anuvinda a lesson. But it was a long-term one that required a lot of things to come together. Strategy, ideology, execution and fate needed to unite. It was beyond the personal rivalries and limited scopes of rights and wrongs. She dearly wanted it to succeed with all her heart. But what would she do until then?

"Are you planning to return to Anagha?"

The question made her look up. Her instinct was to say an unequivocal yes but Abhaya shook her head. "The soldiers are now joining the ranks of Indraprastha, the traders are settling here. Other citizens too are settling into a safer life after that traumatic exit from Anagha. I cannot put their lives into that uncertainty again by foolishly asking them to prove their loyalty. But..."

"Indraprastha gives you no peace, does it?"

"Emperor Yudhishtira, his brothers, Empress Draupadi, Subhadra and every other member I have met has been more than warm and welcoming. Call me egoistic but I feel unable to return the warmth and settle here for so long, Krishna." Abhaya let her frustration speak. "I have to do something, find my purpose. I don't know what it is. I want to explore further and I don't think that is possible being at Indraprastha."

"You don't like it here, do you?"

"I just feel suffocated."

"Is there anything at all that can hold you back?"

"Captivity. Imprisonment will, at least, give me the satisfaction of being physically helpless, but..." Abhaya stopped, as Krishna's finger pressed against her lips.

"Careful what you wish for," he said, his eyes twinkling.

"So, you would bind me and hold me prisoner?" Abhaya returned, with a smile.

"A tempting idea," Krishna said before growing serious. "By all means, explore and seek your purpose, Dhaarmaseni. But I want you to promise me something. Will you reach out to me if things go out of your control?"

"I shall. We both have few choices."

"In situations forcing you to choose between life and death, will you choose life over death, instead of sacrificing yourself in the name of bravery?"

"That makes it two promises."

"Stay here until Subhadra's child arrives. She might need your help after that too."

"She will need my help amidst scores of women who know what it is to give birth to a child ... that sounds very believable. Why don't you admit that you are trying to put off my departure?"

Krishna raised his hands in admission. "Trying isn't a crime, is it?"

"Listen to me, Vaasudeva. I shall not disappoint you or her. But you need to trust me."

With a smile, Krishna rose and turned to leave. Abhaya was taken aback at the abrupt departure.

"Wait," she exclaimed but, when he turned back, she realised, to her embarrassment, that she had nothing to say.

She rose as well in a bid to buy time. "Tell my new 'elder sister' not to talk of my wedding," she said in mock anger. "If she cares about me, shouldn't she try to find out if I like someone in the first place?"

Abhaya avoided his eyes and gazed down at the floor. She could picture his faint smile and the arch of his brows, and it made her heart race.

"And will you not tell me who it is?"

Abhaya tried to slow her breathing. "Not now. Later."

"Let me try and guess." Krishna stepped closer, his brows coming together. "What's new in you? You've started to practise sword fighting and you are learning about battle formations from Subhadra. Is it safe to guess that you are trying to lure a warrior?"

"How intelligent! If I had taken to reading in my boredom, would you guess that I was trying to lure a rishi instead?"

"I think I know who it is!" Krishna exclaimed, dismissing her taunt. "His name is..."

"No!" Abhaya shouted, her finger sealing his lips. "It'll kill me if you say the wrong name!"

"Pardon me!" Krishna laughed, his fingers squeezing his earlobes. "I shan't guess if you don't want me to."

"You will know but only when the time is ripe."

"That's my line!"

"Well, do get used to hearing it from others then." Abhaya's eyes pleaded with him. "I want to tell you, Krishna. I cannot lie to you and insult our friendship. But I need time to brace myself. Let me be prepared to face the consequences of speaking the truth. I mean, no offence, but I would hate to threaten suicide if I were to be rejected. That is not love."

"Mahadeva forbid, if he has the nerve to reject you, do you mean to say you want him to live in peace after that?"

His attempts to lighten the conversation did not bring a smile to her lips. She nodded in complete sincerity. The smile that bloomed on his lips filled her heart.

"Go now," she said.

Krishna bowed his head to hide the lump in his throat. He walked out to the corridor. Walking back to his quarters, he could see her sinking into the seat. He could see her fight her tears and swallow hard. He could still see her tossing in her bed as sleep evaded her.

In his mind, he heard the voice of the formless woman who always kept him company in the solitary depths of his soul.

How could you come away like that?

Krishna smiled to himself. *Time, my love, is not yet ripe.*

"You are hopeless; it is high time I stepped in."

"I never regret your stepping in."

"This time, it might be a long pursuit."

"I can only follow your lead!"

Chapter Thirty

Near Gomantaka

It was a week since Vikrama had left the mountain settlement of Gomantaka. Shyeni's casual rejection clawed at his heart, making him wander aimlessly for the first couple of days. The clues about the Shakta settlement that he had gotten from the Garudas had proved only partly useful. When he reached the location, he found it deserted. There was a pile of half-burnt firewood and a thatched hut in which he found a bed and some pots. Whoever had left the place, Vikrama felt, had done so in a hurry. He wondered why.

There was a stain on the wooden cot. *Blood*. Upon examining it closely, he estimated it to be not more than a day old. *Which means they were here as late as this morning*. Walking out, something caught his eye—a metallic medallion that lay on the ground.

The Avanti signet! What has this got to do with the Shaktas?

Vikrama saw the marks of horse hooves. They made a trail out of the settlement. Mounting his steed, he followed it, all kinds of questions and new suspicions arising in his mind. He rode for a good couple of hours deeper into the wilderness, further away from the shore. The howl of a wild animal was audible at a distance. Wherever the trail was leading him to, he concluded, it was not towards any janapada, but away from civilisation.

At long last, he was rewarded with the sound of the neighing of what seemed to be two horses.

That makes it just two soldiers of Avanti. Dismounting, he tied his horse to a tree and walked towards the sounds. He heard a sudden shout and sprinted in the direction, drawing his sword.

He reached a hill and followed its perimeter to the entrance of a cave where he saw a soldier of Avanti drive his spear towards a rustic youth. Instinct took over and Vikrama attacked the soldier, saving the stranger from certain death in the nick of time.

"What is going on here?"

Everything happened in a flash. Men and women armed with crude weapons swooped down from the trees and surrounded them. Undaunted, Vikrama fended off three attackers with his sword, one wielding a pitchfork and the other two, axes. His attackers could not figure out that he was using their brute strength against them with his calculated dodging. Another joined the cumulative attack. From the corner of his eye, he saw three more of them disarm one of the soldiers of Avanti. Vikrama stood against a large boulder, holding his sword in a deadlock against two of the forest warriors wielding axes.

A scream escaped an Avanti soldier just before his head was severed. Vikrama pushed against his opponents with superhuman effort and freed himself. A javelin pierced the other soldier's heart and emerged out of his back. His agonised cry rent the air as he fell. Vikrama's eyes met those of the soldier's killers.

Shaktas!

The woman in her early fifties gazed at him, frowning as she pulled out her javelin from the dead soldier's body. The group closed in on him.

Then, the boy he had saved, shouted, "This one saved me!"

Vikrama looked at him and frowned. He looked familiar. The next moment, Vikrama grabbed the nearest opponent, tripping him over the other two holding him back and, in a trice, he caught the youth. "Weren't you one of those who whisked our Pingala out of Anagha?!"

He held his sword at the Shakta's neck and ordered the others back.

The Shakta trembled in his grip. "Spare me! I did not kill her."

"She was killed?!"

"By these Avanti people! Not by me. I swear in the name of the Goddess!"

"Leave him!" the woman ordered.

"Leave this despicable creature who lures away innocent girls and can't save them?" Vikrama sneered, rage rendering his tone unusually coarse.

Another Shakta tried to attack him from his blind side. But Vikrama whirled around and kicked him in the belly.

"If not for the promise I made to my father, I would have killed every last one of you!"

The spear in the woman's hand lowered when she caught sight of the serpent tattoo on his hand. She looked at him intently and walked up to him.

"It is you?"

Vikrama's grip tightened on the hilt of his sword till it cut into his palm. Then, he let the weapon clatter to the ground.

The Shaktas watched in surprise as the lone intruder dropped to his knees.

"Manikandhara!"

For the first time in many years, they saw Kadambari, her eyes moist as she stood in front of her son.

"He adopted you? As his son? Are you a prince now?" Kadambari brushed Vikrama's hair. They had moved back to the original settlement by the next morning, sensing that the threat from the soldiers of Avanti had ended.

Vikrama's hand rose to shake hers away but stopped midway and clenched itself into a fist.

"Such anger, Vatsa? All because I chose to pursue a life of my choice?" Kadambari's tone turned bitter.

"You had all the right to throw me away. But did you have to resort to luring innocent girls away, Amba?"

"I know whom you are talking about. I did not lure that poor girl, Manikandhara. It was that idiot student of mine who made that terrible mistake," she paused before asking, "Vatsa, who is Abhaya?"

"Don't even dare to take her name! You will have to pass through me to get your hands on her!"

"Enough!" Kadambari snapped, startling Vikrama. "You can blame me for abandoning you, Manikandhara, but don't you dare accuse me of underhanded designs!" The growl in her tone made him step back.

"Abhaya is my sister."

"And the secret tunnel, Anagheshwari..."

"How do you know that?!" Vikrama caught her by both arms. "That was a secret known only to my father, my sister, myself and our priest Katyayana."

"That girl, Pingala, knew it too." Kadambari sat on the wooden log that served as her seat, thinking. "And I gather that she was tortured to the point of death by these soldiers of Avanti for this information."

"What!" Vikrama's eyes widened. The horror was palpable in his voice. "That could be the end of ... Amba, why did your students have to help the soldiers of Avanti?"

Kadambari fell into thought, not letting Vikrama's accusation affect her. In her mind, the pieces came together to form an image that made her shudder. "Listen to me, Manikandhara, something is being planned. I can tell you what I know and you should also listen to what I have deduced from all that I have heard."

She continued, "Regrettably, it was one of my group that lured this Pingala. Some months ago, another group of Shaktas visited us. They requested us to accompany them to Ujjayini where they wanted to worship Goddess Mahakali. I could not go but sent some of my students along. The boys did not come back for a long time. I assumed they had decided not to return. But about a fortnight ago, one of them brought this injured girl in a stolen horse cart. I came to know that she was lured from her home by him and the members of the other group to Ujjayini, from where soldiers took her away. This boy suspected foul play and broke into their quarters. He saw them torturing the poor girl for information. What child of fifteen can withstand such pain, Manikandhara?"

Vikrama bent his head in sorrow. If only they had managed to stop Pingala from leaving Anagha. "Amba, I want to speak to that boy too."

Kadambari nodded. "Just remember that he is as horrified as you and me. He learnt his lesson to not mingle with soldiers at a high cost. But before you leave, Manikandhara, I must warn you there are evil ones among your janapada folks, among their kings, who don't think twice about kidnapping and torturing innocent defenceless girls. There are those among the Shaktas who are no less evil. They want to disrupt civilisation and enslave people in the name of religion. These two forces, I fear, have come together, Manikandhara. If you can, Vatsa, do something to stop them. Both are enemies of what we know as humanity. They don't mean well."

"Is there something more, Amba?" Vikrama prodded in a gentler voice. He could not say if Kadambari was merely speculating or if she knew something that had led her to make this prophecy.

"I am trying to piece it all together now, Manikandhara. It was a couple of years after I left you at Anagha. I had practised the rituals of Shakta order and taken the religion to my heart. Meeting my guru, Vamanatha, was the best thing that could have happened to me. It was an idyllic, blissful life of spiritual elevation until he received an invitation from this place called Kamarupa. Kamarupa is in the kingdom of…" Kadambari pointed towards the east.

"Pragjyotisha. Did you go there? And come back?" Vikrama asked, awed at the long journey she had undertaken.

"What I took for a temple of Shakti worship turned out to be something else, Vatsa. It was…"

Vikrama was listening intently and he moved closer to her and sat on the floor at her feet.

"We went there and met other Shakta practitioners too. The first half of the day was a joyful experience, meeting so many of our kind. I even contemplated staying there forever. It wasn't until I heard the lord of Kamarupa, Bhauma, address our gathering that I began to feel uncomfortable."

"How is that related to Pingala's death?" Vikrama protested, glancing outside. Every moment of delay increased the probability of Anagha's walls being breached.

"You can make up for the lost time in the course of your journey. I am not whiling away time in pointless tales!" Kadambari hissed. She then resumed. "Bhauma went ahead to declare some woman as the mahayogini or mahadevi of Kamarupa who was supposedly the medium of the Supreme Goddess. He also went on to denounce other gods and deities worshipped across this land. That, Manikandhara, is not what Shakta philosophy and religion stand for. My guru and I were distressed and had planned to leave the place when Bhauma killed him! Hiding behind a pillar, I saw that power-hungry monster strangling Guru Vamanatha!"

Vikrama made a move to rise to his feet. Kadambari pressed his shoulder, her sharp gaze puzzling him.

His lips parted to say something and then he shook his head.

"That Bhauma is up to something sinister. He was instigating the Shakta cult to turn against the ways of Aryas across Bharatavarsha. Manikandhara, he was using and subverting the religion to control people."

"And you continue to stick to this cult of barbarians, monsters and murderers!" Vikrama snapped. "Your cursed religion, Amba, has destroyed my family. It now threatens to destroy those who opened their hearts to your unfortunate son." He rose to his feet and strode out of the hut. Saving Anagha was his priority, not theories about what had happened in an obscure temple years before. At the threshold, he paused. "Amba, were you harmed at Kamarupa?"

"I am alive, Manikandhara," came the cold answer. "Even in this 'cult of barbarians and murderers', there exist some true men, like they do in your world of Aryas." A vague memory of her confrontation with Mura came back to her. Kadambari could not help feeling grateful to the senapati of Kamarupa who had helped her escape despite his loyalties.

Vikrama swallowed hard and turned around, feeling guilty that his insensitivity had hurt Kadambari. "Amba, come back with me. Give your home another chance. That man who abused you is no more and you have nothing to fear there." After a pause, he added, "My father, the king of Anagha, considers you his sister. He would be delighted to welcome you home."

"Those were his words you were speaking then," Kadambari sighed.

Vikrama stepped back into the hut, a genuine regret showing in his eyes. Kadambari raised her hand.

"Go now, Vikramasena, your father and sister need you now." Kadambari's voice betrayed no trace of emotion. "I shall come when you need me."

Chapter Thirty-One

Indraprastha

"He left? When?" Abhaya sighed, toying with the dagger Subhadra had given her.

"At dawn," Subhadra sighed. "The news reached us in the middle of the night." She settled on the couch with a maid's help. The maids, Abhaya noticed, had been staying close to Subhadra all week. She was never left alone. Visits from other family members had increased too. The birth of her child was expected any day. Abhaya bit her lip, reminding herself to not say anything that would agitate the soon-to-be mother.

"It's just that it's all very sudden," Abhaya said. "He remembered to leave this for me." She held the dagger up and examined it in the light. The rays of the sun glinted off its razor edge. "And yet, he never stopped to tell me that Dwaraka has been attacked by that king of Chedi!"

She swallowed hard to ease the constriction in her throat and asked, "When did this happen? *What* happened? Krishna brought most of the Yadava army with him here. Most of your family are still there at Dwaraka. Are they alright? How about your sisters-in-law?" She was seized with worry about Mitravinda.

Subhadra shook her head. "I don't know. But this isn't new, Abhaya. Hopefully, they left by the sea route and have met our armies on the western front.

Krishna was confident about their escape. We should get to know more in about a fortnight."

Abhaya sighed and leaned back, her face expressionless. At last, she said, "He dared to elicit promises from me that I would ask for his help if I ever got into trouble but did not consider me worth sharing any of his!"

"Abhaya!" Subhadra leaned forward to gently grip her shoulder. For a moment, Abhaya's eyes shut tight, her jaw clenched and her lips quivered. Then, with an effort, she schooled her face into a stoic mask. Subhadra shook her head. "I have seen Mitravinda despair in this way at times."

"What?"

"If it makes you feel any better, my sisters-in-law have gone through the same emotions you're feeling now."

"I can empathise!" Abhaya burst out. "You just can't tell where you stand with him! What do I mean to him, Subhadra? What does he think of me? There are times when ... but now, he just goes off and..."

Subhadra gave her a long look. "Abhaya, can you be honest about what he means to you?"

"Like you don't know!"

"Don't dodge the question, Abhaya. You shall find the answer to what you mean to him if you can be honest with yourself about what he means to you."

His is the first name that comes to my mind during every crisis. He is the one I think of in every moment of joy. Dare I say what he means to me? If I do, will I have the courage to find out what I mean to him?

"Subhadra..."

"You hate to be his burden, Abhaya. I know you hate being anyone's burden, for that matter. But you did reach out to him when you needed him and you feel you have a right to the crises that he faces too. Don't you?"

"He is just heartless!"

"Stop being so predictable! At least be different from the rest of his wives!"

"By Mahakala, stop throwing his wives in my face!" Abhaya slammed her fist on the handrest of her seat.

"I fail to find a difference," Subhadra said, quietly.

"Do I look like someone who shows up with a suicide letter because she is helpless against this world and needs refuge at his feet?"

"No, you just look like someone helpless against herself."

Abhaya met her eye. Then she smiled. "Alright, I will admit he is skilled in—for lack of a better expression—lingering in one's heart."

Subhadra rose to her feet. "Abhaya, as a woman, I urge you. Break every constraint that holds you back. Face the truth. Embrace it without any baggage of assumptions to burden you. That truth, free of preconceptions, will define your path ahead. Claim it, Sakhi. Claim what is rightfully yours."

Abhaya watched her leave, then turned her attention back to the dagger.

What could this signify? The other dagger Krishna had given her had been lost in her fight with the crocodiles at Anagha. This dagger seemed more than a casual gift. She stretched out on the wide seat, drawing aimless lines on its wooden frame with the tip of the dagger.

What does he mean to me?

You love him.

The voice inside could not have been clearer. It was not this she was worried about but the possible consequences of admitting it. In her present state as a dependent of Indraprastha, such an admission would only make her look more helpless. As much as she appreciated the respect and honour with which Subhadra's family had treated her, Abhaya knew that her status here was not more than that of a supplicant.

Claim what is rightfully yours, Subhadra had said.

What is rightfully mine? She turned to her side, continuing to etch with the dagger.

The city that was mine is now just a dilapidated ruin. My citizens are unwilling to return. My father is no more. My brother has not returned. What is left that is mine? Who is mine?

If you love him, acknowledge all that is his as yours.

Abhaya shook her head. *That doesn't make sense. How can his city become mine? How can his people be mine?*

Which is his city? Who are his people? What is his?

From what she knew about Krishna, Abhaya knew this question had many answers.

The highway robbers he absorbed into mainstream life and reformed—were they his people? The village of cowherds that he left to save it from a tyrant—didn't he love it and its people? The city that he convinced his tribe to abandon—was it not his? The city that he helped build on unknown shores in a strange land, was it his? The other kingdoms including Anagha that he stood by, were they his?

Abhaya let the dagger drop from her fingers.

You belong to none of these, Krishna. But you take charge of everything around you, including my life, as though it belongs to you. You claimed my crises as your own. What is rightfully yours, Krishna, and what is rightfully mine?

Why did you have to leave so suddenly, Krishna? Why aren't you here when I want to talk to you?

She drifted into a fitful sleep in which various voices debated in her mind. Some voices died, some prevailed. She did not resist them. She let the clash of opinions continue in her mind. But she was undisturbed by them now. Every voice, she realised, was her own, though she heard it from the mouths of Subhadra, her father and her brother, Katyayana, Vajrabahu and everyone she had known and met. With them came strange images of people she had neither seen nor heard of. But their voices, too, were a mere image of what she felt herself. She made her peace with the voices, with the strangers who did not seem unfamiliar. As she drifted into a nap, only one thought remained.

I shall claim what is mine.

Chapter Thirty-Two

Abhaya awoke, refreshed. It was close to midday. Her eyes fell upon the dagger and she smiled, picking it up and tucking it into her inner garments.

The excited voices of maids from the direction of Subhadra's chambers caught her attention. The clouds covered the sun and the room went dim. A hand on her shoulder startled Abhaya.

The woman had a face that practically glowed. Abhaya did not remember seeing her before but guessed from her finery that she belonged to the Pandava family. She had not met all the wives of the Pandavas and, except for Empress Draupadi, she did not remember the faces and names of the others. She felt compelled to rise to her feet.

"Subhadra has gone into labour," the woman told her. Her smile seemed strangely familiar.

Abhaya rose to go to Subhadra but the woman held her hand. "The labour room is not for unmarried girls like you."

"Why not? How is Subhadra?"

"Fine, by the grace of Gauri."

"Is she in pain?"

"It is her first time," the woman responded.

"I'd like to be with her." Abhaya tried to leave only to be stopped by the woman's iron grip.

"Do us a favour, Dhaarmaseni," she said, couching a command in a request with the grace of royalty. "Could you ride towards Vrindavan and offer our prayers at the temple of Katyayani? By the grace of the Goddess Katyayani, may celebrations welcome you on your return."

Abhaya found herself nodding mutely. The woman exited. Abhaya collected her sword and got ready for the ride. She could not help wondering who the woman was who had that irresistible authority to ask her to ride down to Vrindavan. It was not as if she would have refused such a request. Still, there had been something almost overpowering about this stranger.

"Who was that woman who came in just now?" she asked the female guard who stood at the other end of the corridor.

"Who, Devi?"

"The one who came up to my room now," Abhaya frowned at the guard's absent-mindedness.

"Forgive me, I came here only a moment ago. And every important woman of the royal household is in Devi Subhadra's room now."

Abhaya shrugged and walked down the corridor, wondering what had made her give in so meekly to the woman. The courtyard by now was crowded with many more members of the family and she had no inclination to be amongst them. The clouds parted, revealing the bright day, and a ride along the banks of Yamuna, she thought, was rather tempting. Perhaps she would meet Sunanda, the friendly gopika, at Vrindavan.

The breeze wafting in from the Yamuna was pleasant on Abhaya's limbs. The horse that the stable boy had prepared for her did not need much goading and the ride was easy. She was glad she had refused an escort—it was liberating to ride alone on this bright spring day.

Just what I needed.

She kept the horse at a brisk canter along the path strewn with spring blossoms. Two hours later, she reached the village of Vrindavan. Though the women who were filling their pitchers at the river did not recognise her, they could guess that a visitor from that direction could only come from the imperial city of Indraprastha. When they found she was a friend of Queen Subhadra's, they were warmly welcoming. As more people gathered, Abhaya dismounted from the horse and politely accepted their offer of buttermilk. Then she asked for directions to the temple of Katyayani.

Sunanda pushed through the crowds and greeted her enthusiastically.

"I'll take you," she offered. The streets of Vrindavan looked festive; every home, regardless of size, was brightly painted and covered with wall art and doorways were adorned with strings of colourful blossoms. The gopika called out to her friends in the cowsheds behind and introduced Abhaya and more freshly churned buttermilk was forced upon her.

"The priest is away!" Sunanda exclaimed, seeing the closed gates of the Katyayani temple. "I shall send the children to look out for him. You can wait at my house." She tugged at Abhaya's hand. "This is a small village. It does not take much time to find people," she added reassuringly.

"Mine was a small city too. Everyone knew each other, like the people in this village," Abhaya said with a tinge of nostalgia. Sunanda nodded sympathetically; she had heard of what had happened at Anagha. They arrived at a cottage. Abhaya tethered her horse under the shade of a tree and settled on a stone bench along with the milkmaid.

"Would you sing for me?" She smiled as Sunanda blushed.

"My daughter is a better singer. Let me call her. She will sing to you while you have the midday meal."

Abhaya was about to protest about the meal when she saw two other gopikas rushing towards them. One look at their worried faces and her hand went instinctively to her sword.

"Our Viraja!" one of the women screamed as they drew nearer. "They have taken her away!" The women sprang to their feet.

"Poor girl! Who and where?"

"Those sadhus who had come to Vrindavan some days back! I saw them taking the girl by force when she was playing near the river."

Sunanda dashed into the hut and emerged with a sickle in hand.

"Are they Shaktas?" Abhaya asked as she mounted the horse.

The women nodded vigorously.

"Where did you see them?" They pointed in the direction of the temple.

"They crossed the river. They had a horse cart waiting for them on the other side. We shouted at them to stop but they just placed her onto the cart and set off!" the second woman said.

"Our men are away grazing the cows. They will be back only by the evening. That poor motherless child!" The first milkmaid wrung her hands in dismay.

"Don't despair like weaklings! What are we here for if we can't protect a daughter of this village?" Sunanda thundered, hurrying in the direction in which the women had pointed.

"Wait." Abhaya raised her hand. "This is a serious matter."

"Of course, it is!!" Sunanda shouted. "I am not holding this sickle for nothing!"

"I mean to say, I shall follow them on the horseback. You alert your men and send word to the soldiers at Indraprastha too," Abhaya persisted. The finality in her tone convinced the two gopikas. Abhaya turned to Sunanda. "Please, Bhagini. Rush to Indraprastha now. I know these sadhus who take away girls. I shall follow them and bring back Viraja. But we shall need the soldiers too."

The women held back the angry gopika and Abhaya set her horse to a gallop. Anger enveloped her with the memory of what had happened to her city came rushing back. It was the Shaktas who had taken Pingala away and extracted information about the secret passage from her. They were no mendicants; they had worked for Anuvinda.

These Shaktas mean no good! I shall get to the bottom of this!

Chapter Thirty-Three

Anagha

"Is *this* Vikrama's city? This graveyard?"

Shyeni exclaimed turning to Kadambari who seemed equally shocked at the sight before them. The gates of Anagha lay open and deserted. Skeletons lay strewn on the streets. The bloodstained walls seemed to wail soundlessly of what they had seen. Kadambari, who had last seen the city in times of peace and prosperity, was too stunned for words. Bats flew from the broken ceilings of abandoned houses. Vultures fed on a carcass of a larger animal. The sight sickened her heart. Rodents ran over the stone seat that had served as Dharmasena's public throne. Kadambari rushed towards the throne, driving the animals away with her staff. The walls of the empty city added eerie echoes to every sound, making her close her ears for the moment. "This can't be. This can't be! By Amba, this can't be Anagha!"

Her instincts warned of a lurking shadow and Kadambari froze for a moment before her hand went towards the scimitar that was tied to her back. A howl that seemed to come from nearby greeted her ears before the animal leapt into the air.

Kadambari's scimitar was out of its jute scabbard, positioned to take on the wolf when Shyeni leapt from behind her and drove her dagger into the animal. Both landed on the ground. Shyeni rolled over and cut the animal's neck, sustaining an injury on her shoulder.

Another slash from Kadambari's scimitar saw the wolf finally succumb.

"Are you alright?" Kadambari pulled Shyeni to her feet, looking around, expecting more attacks.

For someone who had taken on the predator with lighting instinct, Shyeni's eyes betrayed fear uncharacteristic of her. She caught Kadambari's hands. "Where is Vikrama?!" Her voice rose in distress.

Kadambari turned to calm the younger woman.

"Didn't we follow him barely three days after he left my home?"

Shyeni nodded, her eyes widening in relief and realisation. "Whatever happened to this city took place long before he could have reached here!"

"If I remember correctly ... the older Naga settlement..." Kadambari words petered out as she tied back her grey tresses into a knot and turned towards their horses. "Let us ride out."

Shyeni followed, her pace now fuelled with renewed hope of seeing Vikrama alive.

"We must check my old village, the Naga settlement. If Manikandhara found the city in ruins, that's where he would have gone."

They found the Naga village reassuringly undisturbed, though it had undergone glaring transformations, mostly due to the increased prosperity of the interim years. The people, though, did not have the usual cheer in their eyes. It was understandable, for the lives of the Nagas were tightly coupled with the activity in Anagha. Kadambari did not see familiar faces amongst the youngsters they met—most had probably been born after she had left.

They collected around the two riders, some coming forward to offer clay goblets filled with water.

Kadambari mutely pointed to the serpent tattooed on her wrist. It was barely visible in the dark of the night but the young Nagas knew what it meant.

"The old chief's sister?" they exclaimed at her introduction. The older Naga women from the nearby huts rushed out to meet the long-lost daughter.

"Our Manikandhara's mother!" someone exclaimed.

"Where is my son?" she asked them.

They pointed towards the house of the current village chief, conspicuous at the dead end of the prominent street.

A man in his late thirties opened the door, hearing the excited chatter outside and his eyes widened as the light from the lamp he carried fell on Kadambari's face, which had not aged much. Her body still had a youthful vigour and her distinct demeanour was one of those memories that he had retained of his long-lost aunt.

"Maatulaa! It can't be! Is it really you? By the God of gods, Pashupati, am I dreaming?"

She recognised him as the son of her brother. "Where is Manikandhara?" she asked, brushing aside pleasantries.

"The king is dead. The princess went away with the rest of the city dwellers to..." he paused, trying to remember the name of the city Abhaya had gone to.

Kadambari's shoulders slumped in disappointment.

"But, did Manikandhara come this way?" Shyeni persisted.

The man stepped out of the mud house and pointed his lamp towards the hill that stood a furlong away.

In the moonlight, they saw the distant figure of Vikrama. They mounted their horses and headed in his direction. When they reached the foot of the hill, Kadambari halted.

"You go first, Garuda girl," she said, unsmiling.

She followed Shyeni's progress up the hill with disapproval. The girl had not bothered to respond to her gesture with even a word of gratitude and was now sprinting up the hill, yelling Vikrama's name in a tone loud enough to wake the whole Naga settlement.

Not an ounce of subtlety in the girl, she reflected. *What in the name of Amba did my boy see in her?*

The thought had troubled her ever since Shyeni had barged into her residence, demanding to see Vikrama. Initially, Kadambari had been charmed at Shyeni's innocent straightforwardness and unabashed admissions. She had agreed to go with Shyeni to Anagha, hope rising in her heart. But the journey had been a bit of a disappointment. Shyeni turned out to be an obstinate girl who questioned every single thing.

Goddess save my son!

"It is me! Shyeni, your Kalabhashini!" Shyeni shouted.

Vikrama's eyes carried the same emptiness that she had seen the night they had parted at Gomantaka. Shyeni ran to him. When she felt the lack of strength in his grip, she threw her arms around him even tighter.

"I heard what happened to your family, Vikrama. We shall find your sister. I shall help you find her." Shyeni's words were more frantic than soothing. Her heart skipped a beat when she saw tears stream down his face. She tried to cup her hands around his face when he suddenly resisted and pushed her away.

"Go away, princess of the Garudas. You are better off without me. I was of no use to my family. You will not fare well with me either."

"Why?" Shyeni exclaimed partly in anger, clutching at his arms. "I have come all this way for you. I followed your trail till your mother's settlement. You had left by then. I did not even go back to Gomantaka to inform anyone. I just rode all the way here!" Vikrama's jaw dropped and Shyeni saw a spark of hope rising in his eyes. Then she shook her head, seeing it surrender to the melancholy that had engulfed him.

"To raise my hopes and then dash them again?"

"How can you say that?! Aren't you my Vikrama?" Shyeni lost her cool and punched him in the chest.

"He can't help being a man," Kadambari's voice answered from behind her.

Vikrama's eyes widened as "Amba" escaped soundlessly from his lips.

"We came together for you, Manikandhara. I stayed back to give you both a moment of privacy and then realised that, between you both, you are capable of spoiling it. I was not wrong."

"Look at the way he talks to me!" Shyeni turned to her, fighting back tears.

"Men," Kadambari said to her. "This is the way they react to misery and that is why we are the better ones to handle tough situations."

She passed her hand through Vikrama's hair in blessing as he knelt at her feet and bade him rise.

"I did not bring your lover to you so you could turn her away in false pride, Prince Vikramasena."

"Amba, I am not angry with Shyeni. Do you even know what happ…?"

"This is not how I expect my son to treat the woman who left her home for the first time in her life and travelled this far only for him. Manikandhara, the ways of your upbringing have defined your expectations, and so has Shyeni's. Can't you see beyond that mismatch and realise that she loves you?"

"She will only leave me again. And I don't and can't blame her for that, Amba."

"I shall not leave you until we find your sister and rebuild your home." Shyeni clutched at Vikrama's arm and, this time, he saw her bewilderment at the way he had spurned her.

Kadambari sighed internally. *Women. Always the first ones to give in.*

"What do you intend to do about the princess of Anagha?"

"I shall go to Indraprastha and bring her back, Amba."

"*We* shall all go to Indraprastha and bring her back. We shall start soon after Shyeni and I get some rest. We just had a long journey."

The finality in Kadambari's voice brooked no dissent. She turned to go downhill. "I shall sleep at my brother's place. You children decide where you want to..."

Shyeni turned to follow suit but Vikrama caught her hand. She looked back at him, and, in the meeting of their eyes, they felt all their differences melt away.

"Aren't you mad at me?"

"For?"

"All those angry words I said just now."

"Why did you say those things?" In Shyeni's question, he saw nothing but plain curiosity. He so wished that she would return the anger, forcing him to pacify her and demand endearments that she rightfully deserved. But Shyeni's eyes and words were a perfect reflection of her heart. Vikrama started to wonder if he deserved her in the first place.

"I ... I was just being selfish. In my fear that you would leave me again, I just neglected the fact that you came for me." Vikrama replied, realising that baring his heart to her was the only way he could do justice to their relationship.

"Was I too selfish then?" Shyeni asked, mentally gazing into the past, exploring her thoughts.

Vikrama's arms went around her and, this time, with all the warmth that had filled his heart.

"It was hard for me after you left," Shyeni confessed with no hesitation. "I could not sleep or eat. It was like I forgot how to smile. I just wanted to meet you. I could not rest until I saw you, Vikrama."

Each word melted Vikrama all over again and he made Shyeni sit on a low boulder and descended to his knees, resting his head in her lap. "I am glad you came. You came when I needed you, Shyeni. That's more than I ever expected or thought would happen."

"Tell me all. What happened to your father?"

The response was an anguished sob.

"It was me. I failed him! I failed my sister!" He could not speak further.

Shyeni brushed his curls, realising he had too much to share and his bloodshot eyes told her that he was too exhausted to recount the details of who had wrought such destruction in Anagha. His hands wrapped around her waist. She bent over him and the moon slipped behind the clouds, leaving the world shrouded in darkness and peace for a much-hoped-for reunion of two lovers.

Chapter Thirty-Four

Varanasi

Drops of water splashed on Abhaya's face, bringing her back to consciousness. Her eyes opened to the sight of the eastern sky in the saffron hue of sunrise.

"She is conscious!"

She heard a voice and turned in its direction.

A woman who seemed to be in her thirties came up to her, relief evident on her face.

"Where am I?"

"This is a gurukula of students pursuing the study of medicine." The woman helped her to a sitting position and brought a small pitcher of water to her lips. "We are near Kashi. You seem to have travelled from a great distance."

Abhaya looked around. She was indeed in a gurukula. A student entered the room with food and a bowl of medicine, which she accepted with a slight bow of gratitude.

It was close to ten days since she had left Indraprastha, pursuing the Shaktas who had taken the young gopika from Vrindavan. She had crossed the Yamuna and pursued their trail for two days. The abductors had taken care to avoid routes frequented by people and patrolling soldiers and it was only by the end of the third day that a famished Abhaya and her tired mount had found a humble hutment that served as a wayside inn. The elderly couple who took her in for the night had tried to persuade her to give up the chase and let the royal authorities pursue the abductors. Logic too dictated that she wait until the soldiers from Indraprastha found her instead of going after the Shaktas alone. But then they risked losing the trail of the group. She, therefore, chose to continue her pursuit. Abhaya's experience after she had crossed the borders of the Kuru provinces was mixed. The encounter she had with a lone soldier at the borders of Kampilya two days later was far from pleasant. He had seen an opportunity in a maiden travelling alone, something she understood was not very common on the eastern side of Yamuna, and she had to fight him off. The commotion awoke his peers who restrained and reprimanded him. Her identity as a royal guest of Indraprastha had ensured their patient hearing when she explained the purpose of her journey. The leader of the patrol team also advised her to turn back. But seeing she would not be deterred, he had informed her that the way she had taken was headed towards Varanasi and promised to guide the soldiers from Indraprastha who she told them would be following in her path. Keeping close to the Yamuna, she reached the borders of the kingdom of Vatsa, where a moment of carelessness led her horse, who was as weary as her, to sustain a leg injury. This had made her waver in her determination to carry on for the first time since she had started her pursuit. She left the steed in the care of the innkeeper at the borders of Vatsa. The golden chain around her neck, the lone jewel she had worn, managed to secure her a place in a caravan that carried her to the borders of Kashi.

Overcome with fatigue, she had been finding her way to the banks of the Ganga and that was the last thing she remembered. She realised she must have collapsed from exhaustion and the residents of the ashrama had taken her in.

She looked at the woman with gratitude but said nothing about the purpose of her journey.

"I am Atulyaprabha," the woman smiled, sensing Abhaya's discomfort. "Get some more rest, Bhagini. I shall return by noon to check on you."

Abhaya lay down, feeling her fatigue subside. A melodious voice sang at the gates of the ashrama.

Ruler of every heart O Hari
The one in the peaks of piety
The one content in impiety

She saw a student give the mendicant singer something in a clay bowl, presumably food. The singer continued to sing, strumming his stringed wooden instrument. Abhaya rose and went to the door. Her faith in the gods above had suffered a serious setback and devotional singing no longer appealed to her. Yet, there was something in this singer's voice that was extremely soothing.

The one praying in anxiety
The one lost in ambiguity
Dweller in every heart, O Hari
Ruler of every heart O Hari

She felt his gaze on her as she stood at the door. The smile that greeted her was that of someone familiar, though she could not recollect ever having met him. After a lingering look, the singer walked away.

Atulyaprabha returned by noon as promised and was delighted to see Abhaya recovered. Abhaya took the opportunity to explore the streets of Varanasi and visit the famed temple of Vishvanatha. She prayed to find the lost girl and for strength to find out the sinister reasons behind this disappearance. She was almost sure that the Shakta group had days of lead on her. A thought suddenly struck her and dots joined themselves in her mind. The kingdoms of Magadha, Avanti and Kashi were all allies in the past, before the Rajasuya. Perhaps Kashi had something covert going on! Abhaya pursed her lips, excited at the possibility. There was a bright chance of finding them around Varanasi itself.

Searching for the Shaktas in the huge crowds, she realised, was not going to be easy. Reason also suggested that they would keep to themselves, away from the crowds, wanting to draw as little attention as they could. She followed Atulyaprabha to the lesser crowded of the ghats. She watched as the woman pulled out a cart from under a temporary shelter close to the ghat. Atulyaprabha continued to banter as she worked on removing the weeds and dirt that had collected on the steps of the ghat.

"This is now my daily routine," Atulyaprabha smiled seeing Abhaya stare at her.

Abhaya's attention, however, was caught by something different.

"Are you a rishika?" she asked Atulyaprabha. "You wear a sacred thread, Bhagini."

Atulya nodded. "And I was taught the shrutis and the shastras. I know what you will ask next." She chuckled. "You are not the first to be surprised by the work I do."

"Don't you want to build an ashrama and teach students of your own?" Abhaya asked, feeling compelled to lend a hand.

"I do," Atulyaprabha replied. "It's just that I would like all my students to realise the importance of the work I immerse myself in and participate in the same. The essence of all learning, Bhagini, is in realising the need to explore the spirit that drives this universe. When one pursues that spirit, he or she needs to give up attachment to notions of high and low, clean and unclean, sacred and sinful. Someone who considers the activity of teaching or a religious pursuit as something higher than cleaning the ghats of Mother Ganga cannot realise the nature of the universal spirit, the Para Brahma."

"But aren't there people employed to keep the ghats clean?"

"There are but the crowds at Varanasi are enough to overwhelm them. Besides, one needs more than mere pay to do this work with sincerity."

"But what drove you to take up this daunting task? Given the crowds that throng Kashi, your work will never end."

"I know," Atulya said. "It was a choice I made a couple of years ago and a choice that makes my life worth living."

She smiled at the curiosity that she saw in Abhaya's eyes.

"When we graduated from our gurukula close to the Naimisha forest, five of us came to Kashi to explore the city. We wanted to work with the teachers here and teach them what we had learnt. The night after we had visited the temple, we were still too excited to sleep and decided to stroll along the ghats. The light of the thousands of lamps would have made the heavens look pale compared to Kashi. Then the lamps went off one by one and we came face to face with the reality. People defecate on the ghats of the very river they worship. They cast their garbage onto the steps. The filth reaches River Ganga. The mother who washes our 'sins' has to carry our filth too."

Abhaya's eyes closed, not at the reality but the sensitivity that Atulyaprabha expressed towards the river.

Atulyaprabha sighed. "Three of my friends were depressed beyond measure. They shouted at every other person who came to defecate or abandon a corpse on these ghats. As the night passed, the stench of the filth became unbearable. My friends had by then lost their faith in humanity. They lost their interest to pursue anything in the land of Kashi. They started to hate the pilgrims and one of them even went so far as to deride Lord Vishvanatha. I watched them despair and leave. I refused to leave with them. After all the efforts of my gurus, I could not let my education come to this. I had two choices—ignoring and despairing or taking the corrective action."

Atulya paused and then added, "The purpose of our life often beckons to us in the guise of a challenge or a hopeless situation. We define our worth based on whether we choose to ignore it or face the challenge. Ganga is our mother. The very thought is enough for me to realise that it is my dharma to help my mother in washing away the 'sins' of the pilgrims who come to visit her."

Abhaya was moved beyond measure by this daughter of Ganga. She hastened to help Atulyaprabha with the cart she used to carry away the filth, dried flowers, weeds and other things that dirtied the steps of the ghat.

"Wait!" Atulyaprabha cried suddenly, sprinting down the steps into the river. Abhaya's jaw dropped when she saw her dragging a half-burnt corpse out of the river. "This can help my brothers at the ashrama."

"What? The corpse?"

"The study of medicine goes beyond grinding herbs and leaves," Atulyaprabha laughed. "The students of the ashrama use these half-burnt corpses to understand and study human anatomy."

Abhaya nodded, seeing Atulya in a new light. She saw the futility of the usual definitions of "clean" and "unclean" before the higher cause that drove Atulya's work.

"The constraints of tradition cannot limit those taking up the cause that seeks the welfare of the universe. Ganga Mata needs more children like you, Bhagini."

"No, we need her more than she needs us. I wish the pilgrims understood that too." Atulyaprabha smiled and resumed working. When they decided to end the work for the day and took a dip in the Ganga, the sun had set and Varanasi glowed in a new light, the light of the thousands of lamps that were lit as part of the ritual Ganga Aarati. In the light of those lamps, across the river where the crowd was lesser, Abhaya caught sight of a lone camp. Her lips parted as she saw what the people outside the camp were up to. She turned to Atulyaprabha.

"Bhagini, there is a reason that brought me here. I need your help."

Chapter Thirty-Five

Kamarupa

The gates of Kamarupa opened for a stipulated time every day. Those couple of hours saw the guards at the outer fortress on their most alert state. Every pilgrim needed to be scrutinised before being granted entry into the hill town of the Goddess of the universe. At times, guards were also known to take advantage of the pilgrims' desperation and demand bribes. When complaints of such occurrences reached Senapati Mura, he ensured that he was present at the gates himself all the time, keeping an eye on every entrant and guard at the gate.

The towering figure of the senapati was an invisible whip that cracked amidst the guards who were now reconciled to doing their work with honesty.

He signalled to the guards to halt the entrance of seven carriages, each with ten to twelve people, and several palanquins escorted by the trusted guards of Kamarupa who had earlier gone to the foothills to receive something important for Lord Bhauma.

"These came willingly," the head guard reported to Mura. Mura's face showed no expression, except for a nod which meant that the doors of the inner fortress could be opened.

"These," the guard pointed to the palanquins that followed, "were willing in the beginning but later changed their minds. They needed some amount of coaxing." Mura swallowed at the audible groans coming from the covered palanquins. "But it was fine by the time the group reached Pragjyotisha," the guard continued his report, his face betraying no emotion.

"You know where to take them," Mura spoke, ignoring the lump in his throat. "The lord might want to speak to them personally."

The guard nodded. Then his face darkened as the last palanquin entered, surrounded by a heavier guard than usual. "This one gave a good bit of trouble, Senapati." He motioned the palanquin to come to a halt before them and signalled for the gates to close.

The palanquin was placed on the ground and Mura could see the relief erupt on the faces of the bearers. Another guard unlocked the door of the palanquin and pulled out a woman who seemed to be in a faint. Her hands were bound behind her back and her feet were tied together. Mura's eyes narrowed when he noticed the welts on her waist and shoulders. In the sudden light, she blinked and opened her eyes.

"What was the need to bring her if she resisted that much?" Mura's voice rose in anger, drawing the attention of other guards. The woman, now cast on the ground, lifted her head and looked at him.

"Senapati, this woman joined the group faking acceptance. At Varanasi, she instigated five women into escaping and, at Pundra, another six or seven left our group while this one was distracting the guard."

"Girls, not women! Girls, all under the age of fifteen!" the woman spat out. She looked barely nineteen herself.

"You should have sent her away!" rebuked Mura, not able to tear his gaze from her.

"Senapati!" the head guard protested tugging at Mura's arm to take him out of earshot. He lowered his tone. "It could also mean that someone down in the plains is watching us. We need to know who they are."

"Don't strain that pea-sized brain of yours, you imbecile!" Mura thundered. He threw a glance at the woman who was struggling her bonds, despite her clothes tearing and skin chafing from her efforts.

"They were too young to even be aware of your barbaric practices, you monsters!" she shouted, breathless from her struggles.

"I don't need to remind you that no woman leaves the city without the knowledge of Lord Bhauma ... Prabho," the guard persisted. The "Prabho" was uttered almost as an afterthought, and his eyes showed contempt.

Mura looked at the girl, thinking fast. "I shall take her to the Mahadevi," he declared, throwing his shawl over the woman's shoulders and lifting her easily into his arms. He paid no heed to the guard's visible consternation and carried her through the inner gate as he announced to the guards, "Get back to your positions and don't act smart unless you want to be kicked off the cliff where even the vultures cannot reach you!"

"Quiet, Yuvati," he whispered to the woman. "You shall not be harmed."

He entered the last door of the inner fort of the temple town that granted access to the apartments of the mahadevi. His eyes looked around in a frantic search for his daughter. But his pace did not slow down until he reached the doors to Dhatri's chambers and pushed them open.

"Remember this, Yuvati," Mura's words fell into the woman's ear. When she looked at him, he shook his head and shifted his attention when another voice greeted him.

"I did not think you would defy the orders and come in, Mura." Dhatri appeared at the door, escorted by two other women.

Mura's eyes clouded. He placed the woman down gently on a seat and bowed.

"By Kamaksha, what have you done to her? Why do I have to see an injured woman in your arms every time?"

"Not he," the woman replied, rising and settling on the stone.

Dhatri glanced at the woman, then turned back to Mura. "Leave." Her voice was just louder than a whisper but the authority in it was audible.

Mura opened his mouth but she waved away his explanation.

"Leave," she repeated.

Mura had no choice but to comply.

Dhatri sat on the other stone seat and gestured to her escorts. "Untie her."

The blood rushing back into her limbs made the woman cringe in pain. A female guard entered, requesting a quick word with Dhatri. As she left, Dhatri turned again. "So, you instigated other women to rebel against our group in Varanasi and made them leave?"

"You have some good storytellers for guards!"

Dhatri frowned. Rebellious women were not new to her and she knew exactly how to make them accept the ways of Kamarupa. She did not believe in coercion and most women submitted, some to her kindness, some to her authority and others to her patience. Looking at the defiance in the new woman's eyes, Dhatri was already thinking of which path to adopt.

"When did you last eat, Yuvati?"

The woman remained silent and looked away.

"Wouldn't you like to bathe and eat first before you tell me your side of the story?"

When the woman returned her gaze to Dhatri, her eyes were spitting fire.

Dhatri moved to her side. "Treat me like a mother, Vatse. It pains me if you starve. Trust me, I shall not harm you and you shall be safe."

"Your group, Devi, was luring and kidnapping innocent girls, barely into their teens. Those who resisted were drugged or starved and even beaten into submission!" She glared at Dhatri. "I only helped them escape so they could return to their homes."

Dhatri stared at her without batting an eyelid. She took a deep breath and rose to her feet, unsmiling. "The ones who harmed those girls shall be punished." She put her hand on her head. "Vatse, your courage has won me over. Bathe, eat and braid this lustrous hair of yours. Rest for today. And trust me to watch over you. What do they call you, Yuvati?"

The woman looked up at her defiantly, suspicion still visible in her eyes.

"Abhaya ... Dhaarmaseni."

"Fearless one," Dhatri smiled. "An apt name for one such as you. You shall dine with me at noon. Mother Kamaksha tells me that you are an invaluable child of hers."

Dhatri looked at the female guards, a different light flashing in her eyes. Coming out of Abhaya's earshot, she ordered, "Tell Lord Bhauma that I want to see him."

The female guard faltered in surprise at the abrupt change in Dhatri's manner, then hurried towards Bhauma's mansion.

Abhaya looked after her as Dhatri went inside. All the physical pain she had had to suffer on the way had finally borne fruit. She had reached the epicentre of the Shakta religion.

Kamarupa.

One of the escorts held out a hand to help her up.

If only I can make this woman who is revered here see the consequences of what they have done. If only I can know more about these people and plan my next move.

Abhaya took a deep breath, waved away the outstretched hand and rose to her feet.

Chapter Thirty-Six

The altitude and cold wind blowing against her face were something Abhaya was not used to. It added to the lingering fatigue from the rough journey she had had. The sentry at the gate of the innermost walls cast an unsure glance when she asked him the whereabouts of Senapati Mura, then complied with a shrug. Following Dhatri's new decree to not limit women's movements within the walls of Kamarupa, there was not much he could do.

When she stepped into the courtyard of what she was told were Mura's quarters, Abhaya felt the simplicity of the house striking. In contrast to the glitter and conspicuous prosperity of the inner township, the senapati's quarters were practically monastic. The most aesthetic aspect of the courtyard was a painting on the wall, of the face of the Supreme Goddess Shakti. Abhaya remembered noticing a similar wall painting on a couple of other houses, including that of Dhatri's.

Mura came out to the courtyard dressed in his official attire—leather armour, a lower garment in red and a thick cape pinned to his shoulders. Two swords hung at his waist and Abhaya saw him holding a blunt club menacing enough to make anyone think twice before rubbing him the wrong way. He looked surprised to see her.

"You..."

Abhaya held out his shawl. "I came to return this ... Senapati Mura." Mura nodded in acknowledgement.

His face remained stern but Abhaya saw kindness in his eyes. "I am indebted to you for your generosity, in the wake of your people's boorish behaviour."

Mura took the shawl, studying her closely. "Have you rested well?" he enquired with a courteous smile.

Abhaya gave him a sarcastic smile and brought her palms together before turning to leave. Mura saw defiance in her eyes and his chest constricted. Before he could stop himself, he blurted, "Wait, Vatse..."

She froze, then turned slowly, with genuine surprise in her eyes. Mura shook his head and turned away. Abhaya saw his inner struggle in the way he clenched his fists.

"Could you..." Mura left the sentence incomplete and, signalling her to wait, disappeared into the house. He reappeared carrying a wooden toy, a model of a cart painted red and bearing a similar impression of the face of Shakti in white. Mura handed it to Abhaya, who examined it in surprise.

"If you spot an eight-year-old child who is under the care of the mahadevi ... her name is Kamakanthika. She also responds to Mauri."

"I shall give it to her," Abhaya affirmed, touched.

Mura nodded his gratitude. He hesitated, then added, "The mahadevi might not approve of your coming here like this."

"Senapati, I am no slave of your mahadevi."

"A little discretion won't hurt, Vatse, especially in hostile lands," Mura muttered.

Abhaya considered his last words on her way back to the inner township. The weight of her mission still sat heavily on her shoulders. She knew she needed allies and Mura held promise. Abhaya studied the toy in her hand. There remained the matter of this child.

His daughter? The name Mauri suggests so.

Late morning was a quiet time in the circular yard behind the sanctum. When Abhaya entered the yard, she saw two children playing. The elder one, about eight years of age, was arranging pebbles according to some shape in her mind and the younger girl, about six years of age, was bent upon altering the shape.

"I know more than you, Nandini!" the elder girl shouted in exasperation.

"You are wrong, Mauri!" the younger one retorted.

"Nandini, this is how the fort is built. We shall ask mahadevi and she will tell you that I am right," Mauri said.

But Nandini continued rearranging the pebbles her way.

"Listen to me!" Mauri snapped, pushing the pebbles away.

Nandini broke into tears.

"Now, now! Children, don't fight." Abhaya stepped between them and drew Nandini closer. "Mauri, I thought your father said you are a good girl. Nice girls don't yell at smaller children."

"They don't!" Nandini affirmed through her tears.

"So, I shall not give Mauri the toy her father sent for her," Abhaya said, winking at Nandini.

"My father has gone far away. How did you meet him?" Mauri asked, brushing Abhaya's sermon aside.

"Your father…" Abhaya stared at her, then nodded with effort, "has gone far away."

"Far … far ... away," Mauri stretched her right arm to indicate the western horizon. "Did you meet him?"

Abhaya was shocked at what the child had been told when Mura was just outside the gates. She smiled at the girl and held up the wooden cart Mura had given her. "What did he tell you before he left?"

"He never told me anything. I was asleep. He left in the night. Mahadevi told me he will return when I grow as big as you. Give that to me." Mauri reached out for the toy but Abhaya lifted it out of her reach.

"First promise me you shall not yell at Nandini."

"But she is wrong!" Mauri shouted. "There are no steps at the back door. They are broken. Father showed me a long time ago."

"How can there be a door without steps?" Nandini appealed to Abhaya. "This Mauri refuses to take me there so I cannot prove her wrong."

"Which door are you girls talking about?" Abhaya calmed them. "I shall see and decide which one of you is right."

"But the door is locked. We cannot go there," Mauri explained, pointing in the direction. "Give me the toy."

Abhaya smiled and held out the toy cart.

"Nothing for me?" Nandini asked, scratching her head.

Abhaya patted her head. "I will bring another one for you, too."

"You can play with this till then," Mauri offered.

The girls forgot their pebbles and pranced away to play with their new toy.

"You have a way with children. A natural maternal instinct."

Abhaya turned, recognising the voice. She considered the approaching woman with raised eyebrows.

"The poor girl is being told an untruth!" she said. Her palms came together in salutation, but she did not bow. "...Mahadevi."

"That is an affair I would rather not see you involved in," Dhatri said. For someone who was only a religious head, Dhatri, Abhaya felt, had too much authority. "Were you always a stubborn upstart or...?"

"Where would my world of Aryas encourage girls to be stubborn or bold? I had a magical transformation the moment I set my foot in this holy place. The Goddess entered me and made me realise I don't need to regard anyone with undue reverence—be it the Goddess herself or her stooges."

"Yuvati!" Dhatri cautioned, gritting her teeth. "A day might come when the Goddess will suck every ounce of arrogance out of you, a day the entire world, including that of your Aryas, falls at her feet in supplication."

"Why do you tolerate this one so much, Mahadevi?" The female guard behind Dhatri came forward but halted when Dhatri raised her arm.

Dhatri caught Abhaya by her arm and led her towards the mansion beside the temple. Abhaya shrugged off the grip but followed Dhatri. She wanted to explore the place and find out everything she could.

These people lie to a child about her father. A man as strong as Mura is helpless. The girl seems to be held a prisoner without her knowledge. Mahadevi's words are the law of the land. What kind of place is this?

For all her suspicions, though, Abhaya could not find a single trace of malice in Dhatri. Who, then, was responsible?

She did not have to wait long to find an answer as she followed Dhatri into a huge hallway. Two burly guards bowed low at the sight of Dhatri and held a door open. Dhatri led Abhaya inside. The door closed behind them. Abhaya instinctively felt for her dagger, then remembered with a pang of disappointment that she had lost it in Varanasi.

Seated on a carved metal jhoola, Bhauma watched the women enter his room. He rose as they approached and greeted Dhatri, who returned his salutation with a wave. "Hear this girl out, Bhauma. She is a princess from the far western provinces and has something disturbing to share."

Bhauma turned and greeted Abhaya. When their gazes met, Abhaya felt instinctively wary. His grey hair suggested he was in his late fifties or even older. But his arms and shoulders boasted the strength of a much younger man. She returned his salutation and sat on the seat he indicated, before the huge swing. The chains that bore the swing creaked as Bhauma's immense bulk descended on it. Dhatri moved to Bhauma's side and took her place.

"Tell me everything, Devi," Bhauma said, looking first at Dhatri and then at Abhaya.

"Arya Bhauma," Abhaya began but he stopped her with a raised finger.

"I don't go by the name of Arya. I am only a devotee of the Goddess, Devi."

His tone suggested a hatred for the word more than his devotion to the Goddess.

"Address him as prabho. He is the lord of this place," Dhatri said.

Abhaya gripped the hand rest, glaring at both of them. "May I remind you that I am no slave? This gentleman is not my lord, nor are you my mistress, Mahadevi."

Bhauma raised an eyebrow in displeasure. But he spoke in a measured tone. "We can do away with formalities. You can call me Bhauma."

"Your men, Lord of Kamarupa, abducted innocent adolescent girls from the villages of Bharatavarsha. The defenceless girls were bound against their will and even starved and coerced into obedience. When I helped them escape, your people held me prisoner and injured me."

Bhauma's eyes closed and his hands covered his ears as though her words were too difficult to bear. "May the Goddess forgive our sins. This is unfortunate."

Abhaya sighed at the response. Dhatri spoke, "Identify the soldiers and we shall punish and chastise them."

"What about the women still held by you against their will?" Abhaya demanded, alternating her gaze between Bhauma and Dhatri. She noticed Bhauma looking at Dhatri before either of them spoke anything.

"We have not kept anyone against their will. All the women with whom you came—we will inform them of our faith and our ways. The introduction shall not take more than a week. After that…"

"It is up to the will of the Supreme Goddess," Bhauma interjected with a smile.

Abhaya caught the momentary frown that appeared on Dhatri's forehead but then she smiled in response.

"From what I hear, the women here do not have a choice or the freedom to leave. They are prisoners here." She sneered.

Bhauma rose, startling even Dhatri in his abruptness. "Devi! How dare anyone insult our treatment of women?" Dhatri caught his arm from behind. She could not see what Abhaya saw—the flash of anger on Bhauma's face at her interruption, which he quickly brought under control. When he turned towards Dhatri, his eyes carried the same reverence she always saw.

"Let me handle this, Bhauma," she told him.

Bhauma bowed. Turning towards Abhaya, he said, "Disrespect towards the mahayogini, Devi, is beyond my tolerance. I hope you shall not take undue advantage of her limitless compassion and provoke the rage of the Supreme Goddess!"

"Bhauma," Dhatri protested again. She lowered her tone and gave him a meaningful look that Abhaya could not read. "Leave now. I shall take care of the rest. I had called on you only to ensure that the soldiers who harmed the women are punished."

With another slight nod, Bhauma turned, casting another long glance at Abhaya before taking his leave. Abhaya looked after him. Bhauma made her feel uncomfortable. In the course of the conversation, she had felt him, despite his advanced years, look at her with desire. She had resisted the urge to pull her shawl tighter around herself and glared back at him instead. With Dhatri, Abhaya had to admit, she felt coerced with all the talk of the Shakta cult but never threatened.

"You may retire now, Yuvati. Join the other women in the quarters allotted in the middle ring of the town. We shall talk tomorrow."

"A request, Devi," Abhaya said. Dhatri raised her brows. "Let me have a weapon to defend myself."

"You need not fear anyone here," Dhatri responded. But she seemed to reconsider and held out a scimitar, which Abhaya thought looked more like a slaughter knife than a battle sword. "It will be taken back if I come to know that you caused trouble with it," she warned.

"I do not seek trouble, Mahadevi, and I hope I will not find it," Abhaya said, taking the weapon.

Dhatri rose. A female guard showed Abhaya the way out of the innermost fortress towards the rooms that Dhatri had indicated. Alone at last, for the first time since she began her quest, Abhaya felt foolish about her decision to pursue the Shaktas alone. The idealistic voice that had prodded her all along faded away. She felt like she had been released from the hold of an unseen power that had controlled her all this time. The feeling sat bitterly on her tongue. But she knew this was not the time for regrets. The probability of anyone in Indraprastha tracking her to this end of Bharatavarsha was bleak. She remembered her promises to Krishna and her eyes misted over with tears. She would not be able to keep even one of them. She swallowed hard, convincing herself to play along and rely on her resources to fight back the Shakta powers. That seemed to be the only way ahead.

Chapter Thirty-Seven

The temple of Kamaksha had all the splendour worthy of the high seat of the ancient Shakta order. The sculptures and art on the walls spoke of the ancient tales and legends behind its establishment. The stories were not new to anyone from Bharatavarsha but Abhaya observed that the tone and message of the very same stories underwent a significant change in Kamarupa.

The temple city was closed to pilgrims on this particular day, which was reserved for orientation—when Dhatri took it upon herself to introduce the order of Shaktas to the maidens who came to Kamarupa from various corners of Bharatavarsha. Abhaya threw glances at the other women around her. While a few betrayed their reluctance at being there, some dwelt sincerely upon the legends that were being expounded. Still others bore an inscrutable expression that she found difficult to interpret.

"The legends you are familiar with … we take them with a pinch of salt. Unfortunately, these are the stories that came back to us from the plains after the men of religion corrupted the stories to suit their ends," Dhatri said, addressing the gathering from the dais. "Take, for example, the episode of Daksha Yajna. The story speaks about Daksha Prajapati's Yajna from which he excluded Mahadeva, the husband of his daughter Dakshayani. Who will tell me what happens next?" Dhatri looked at the women and then at Abhaya.

Abhaya looked away, ignoring Dhatri's bid to make her speak. Another voice among the women answered. "Dakshayani—Sati is her other name—goes to find out why her father failed to invite her husband, much against the wishes of Mahadeva. She goes to the yajna only to be further insulted by her father. Unable to hear the insults heaped on Mahadeva, she leaps into the fire. When Mahadeva comes to know of it, he summons the personification of his rage, Veerabhadra, who destroys everyone responsible for the death of Dakshayani, and..." The woman had to pause for breath and Dhatri raised her hand at that moment.

"Wouldn't Sati have gone back to her loving husband after she realises that her father is beyond reason? What made her so helpless as to end her life?"

The women looked at each other and then at Dhatri. Abhaya pressed her lips together. This was not exactly one of her favourite stories.

Dhatri cleared her throat. "This is how the chauvinists in the plains want to rule over women. They make goddesses out of women whose lives somehow become meaningless just because someone insults their husbands. Their stories place an unseen leash over women, who feel compelled to stand up to these false standards."

For the first time, Abhaya felt herself partly agreeing with Dhatri's words. The chauvinistic interpretation of Puranic legends was not new in the plains. *But did it make a difference to strong-willed women? Did it even make a difference to morally upright men? Those who ill-treated women were consistently on the wrong side of history.*

She remembered the words of Katyayana, swallowing a lump in her throat.

The poets, the bards, the rishis, all of them have the heart of a woman. Rather, those who cannot see the feminine side of the universe never get to become a kavi or a rishi. And the one who takes women for granted will never win them over to his side.

It was a light-hearted remark that Katyayana had made in one of the storytelling sessions she had loved as a child. Abhaya's thoughts came to a halt when she heard Dhatri silence another murmur among the women.

"Uma Haimavati is a much more inspiring Goddess. We take inspiration from her. She showed the reclusive Mahadeva that abstinence was of no avail. He was complete because she chose to disrupt his stubborn abstinence. The whole of creation came about from the basic instinct to seek union. Call it the union with pleasures, with tastes, with the mind, with those of the opposite gender. Shying away from union leaves one incomplete, unfulfilled and stale. The state of Shiva is nothing but the union with Shakti. Man needs the grace of Shakti to transcend his limits."

Abhaya had to concede, albeit grudgingly, the fascinating magnetism of Dhatri's words. In Dhatri's eyes, she saw the pinnacle of belief, something she could not bring herself to mock.

"We, the Shaktas, abhor abstinence. Abstinence is another way of denying the boons given by the Goddess. Everything given by Her is sacred. Let yourself free, Yuvate. Own indulgence, shun abstinence and strive to reach the pinnacle of pleasure. That is where you will find the ultimate state, the state of Shiva transcending from the state of shava, the corpse. Shakti, the unleashed femininity, is what makes a Shiva out of a shava. You are that Shakti, you who can grant the ultimate state to those who worship you through the ritual of maithuna. It makes you the yogini—the embodiment of the 'union'."

The words carried a compelling energy that Abhaya could not ignore. She saw Dhatri rise to her feet and move towards a wall that had some sculpted figurines depicting the rituals that were upheld by the Vamachara Shakta tradition.

"Madira, maamsa, mudra, matsya and maithuna. Each of them breaks your inner barriers and helps you transcend the myth of abstinence. Think about that for today."

The women fell into awed silence as the session ended. Abhaya looked at Dhatri, whose smile betrayed a sense of superiority. A voice within her told Abhaya to stay calm. This sense of superiority could be the undoing of the Shaktas.

Back in the room that had housed five other women besides herself, Abhaya chose to keep silent and hear the other women out. She guessed she was the youngest among them. They carried the knowledge of the masses with them, which gave her new insights. The women were speaking about the initial reactions of their families when they heard about their decision to explore the Shakta religion.

"What prompted you all to take to this?" she asked, taking care to show no disgust in her voice. What she had seen and heard in Kamarupa had largely eliminated her disgust towards maithuna and maamsa which she had earlier considered as crude rituals. She realised that it was not the rituals or the religion which was the cause of the problem but something else, some underlying factor that was making everything seem wrong. Abhaya acknowledged this missing piece in the jigsaw she was trying to put together.

"I was just fed up of being treated secondary to men," a woman replied. She took Abhaya's arm and examined a scar her wound had left. "Did you come against your will? Did someone force you?"

"Never mind," Abhaya smiled and introduced herself.

"Kanakangi," the other woman replied. "Call me Kanaka."

"Why did you have to accept the secondary status of women back at home? Wouldn't they listen to you or respect your views?" Abhaya asked.

"I am one among eleven children," Kanakangi replied with a sigh. "Neither the eldest who commands obedience nor the youngest who gets pampered but someone in the middle who is supposed to obey my eldest brother and sacrifice for my youngest sister. How will my state be of any importance?" Kanakangi said.

The mention of ten siblings made Abhaya slightly envious. She thought of Vikrama, her lone brother, now seemingly lost to her. "Your siblings don't love you back?" she asked Kanakangi.

The reply was a melancholic sigh. "We never had enough to love each other. It is a fight for survival every day. For food, for clothes, for gifts, for work. We were always at the mercy of the eldest. He got to decide almost everything. Even mother would side with him when I objected—even when it came to matters related to my marriage." Kanakangi's voice broke in the end.

Abhaya listened in silence. There was a man she had liked, Kanakangi said. She would have liked to marry him but he had disappeared from her village one day.

"And there was this old man who offered a high bride price for me," Kanakangi added after a pause. "Maybe things would have been a bit different if we had not been this poor but…"

She did not need to say any more. Abhaya fell into thought. The tales of the other girls differed only in nature and place but the pain was similar.

Can oppression happen within a family?

Abhaya was aware of fraternal rivalries within royal families. But that was a function of a thirst for power, combined with poor upbringing. The fraternal bonding among the common families was something she had taken for granted and had also envied until now.

Is it poverty or gender bias or both? Aren't the rulers responsible for such disintegration within the families? Or should citizens think before they give birth to more children than they can bring up with adequate care? Bharatavarsha is rotting and the rot is deeper than I had ever imagined!

They lay down on the stone cots over which rugs had been spread. Abhaya could not sleep as conflicting thoughts overtook her mind.

The aggression of the Shaktas is not without reason. The reason is the falling apart of Aryan society. We are diverging from the very aspects that held us together. Whose fault is it? Whoever is at fault, though, the responsibility to pull society back to its feet lies with everyone who cares for human civilisation.

Abhaya's eyes closed. She yearned for someone who would have had ready answers for her doubts.

"Krishna."

Chapter Thirty-Eight

It was a week since Abhaya had reached Kamarupa. The days were spent in Dhatri's sessions of initiation on Shakta worship. The discourse that had started with the supremacy of Shakti had somehow taken a turn towards vilifying Aryan society and its dynamics, which, Dhatri said, were betraying the primal deity, the Supreme Goddess. The evils of oppression that plagued the society, she claimed, could be overcome only when the order of Shakti took over Bharatavarsha.

"Aren't you painting a conveniently homogenous picture of a civilisation that has a hundred sides and flavours to it?" Abhaya questioned.

"This is the truth, Yuvati, even if the truth is bitter to face."

"Truth is not bitter, Mahadevi Dhatri. Truth is truth. For those who strive to work towards it, it is the light. For those who revel in predictions of doom, it is darkness," Abhaya laughed. "Truth does not carry the stench of hatred or anger. But your hatred for the Aryas betrays the truth, Mahadevi."

Dhatri smiled through her visible annoyance "Attachment blurs your vision, Yuvati."

"If this attachment is what makes me resist the untrue portrayal of my world, then so be it, Mahadevi," Abhaya declared. "I would prefer to go back to my land and take on the rot rather than betray it in the name of religion. This hatred in the garb of faith can only harm." Abhaya thought of the destruction Anagha had suffered because of the deliberate or unknowing actions of the Shaktas.

In Abhaya's presence, Dhatri found her philosophy being constantly challenged. Yet, she couldn't help but marvel at the girl's spirit and clear-headed arguments.

"If I can influence her, the spread of our faith will be faster," she had declared to Bhauma once. "I am willing to wait." Despite Bhauma's doubts, Dhatri continued to work on Abhaya. The week had come to an end and she had informed the women that they would get one more week to make their decisions.

Most of the girls agreed to be initiated into the Shakta order more out of the fatigue from their journey than out of genuine willingness. Two maidens in Abhaya's group had shown a lot of inclination to initiate themselves into the ways of Vamachara. But, for some reason, their initial enthusiasm had petered out by the end of the week. Abhaya felt thankful for the added strength in numbers and did not prod for reasons behind their abrupt change of mind.

"That makes it six of us," she said aloud to herself.

"Does that mean we can make our way out and flee from here?" Kanakangi's voice made Abhaya raise her eyes from the flame of the lamp.

"What makes you so restless to leave now, Kanaka?" Abhaya asked with a smile, massaging her eyes to relieve the strain of staring at the flames. "Didn't you say just days ago that you wanted to stay forever?"

"I don't anymore," Kanakangi replied, turning away. "But what if, on some pretext or the other, this mahayogini imprisons us here forever? You saw how determined she looked today."

"I think it is not the mahayogini we need to worry about," Abhaya spoke softly, glancing at the four other women who were asleep. "I think it is someone else who is behind this and he means no good."

Kanakangi cocked her ears and inched closer to Abhaya. "Really? But the mahadevi is no better. After coming here, I have realised, she is the biggest fraud I ever saw."

"Is there something you want to tell me, Kanaka?"

"Shh," Kanakangi whispered, leaning close to her. "The miracles that this lady performs on the occasional deformed person are all fraudulent!" Abhaya's eyes narrowed. "I came across a woman yesterday when you had gone to talk to the little girls in the evening. The others were still inside the temple. I just felt like taking a stroll to the outer circle and I overheard something." Kanakangi paused for breath. "I heard a woman shout at someone. It was outside the fortress. She was saying if people came to know that the person cured yesterday was not a blind boy, then people would tear down the temple."

Abhaya pursed her lips and took a deep breath. "It is not that I ever believed her magic show. But..." She fell into thought.

"Abhaya, I know that something is not right. As the woman's voice became louder, a guard came up to me and ordered me back into the inner fortress. He almost dragged me in himself. I don't want to leave our fate in the hands of this fake yogini. We must escape."

Abhaya nodded. "Escaping is not impossible, Kanaka. But give me some time. Just lay low for now. If she does not let us leave this place after this week, don't revolt or do anything like that. Don't do anything that would make them suspect our meekness." She leaned close to Kanakangi. "I have figured out a way to escape. Through the broken stairs from the doorway behind the temple. We just need to get the key to the passage gate. I will get it. Trust me."

Kanakangi stared at Abhaya. "How will you do this?"

"I have friends," Abhaya said with a smile. "Don't ask me who they are. That will be my secret."

Kanakangi nodded and retired to her bed.

Abhaya sat staring into the flame, mulling over what she had done over the week in Kamarupa. *Poor Senapati Mura.* Mauri was living in a delusion that her father was in a faraway place while Mura was overcome with fear about what would befall his daughter if he rebelled.

Early the next morning, she found herself in front of Mura's home. It had taken Abhaya some amount of effort to convince the guard at the second fortress to allow her to the outer ring. But, with some amount of reason and intimidation, Abhaya had succeeded in getting there, though the experience only highlighted the futility of trying to escape the outer fortress.

"I can't keep telling tales to your daughter, Senapati," she said abruptly to a startled Mura.

Mura shook his head and stalked back inside; undeterred, Abhaya followed him in. "She has to know the truth sometime."

"Quiet, Yuvati!" he hissed, not hiding his annoyance. "Even you don't know the truth."

"Which is why I came to ask you. Else, I would have told her by now."

"Is it your habit to meddle in affairs that don't concern you? If not someone else's, don't you value your own life at least?" Mura showed her the door. His harsh expression mellowed a moment later when he regretted his own words.

"Which means that something is happening here, meddling with which is a life-threatening danger." Abhaya stood her ground. She averted her eyes from Mura's steely gaze and her eyes fell on a large bunch of keys.

"Spare me this pointless talk..." Mura was about to hold her arm when she backed away.

"Why should I stay here like a prisoner when I don't accept your ways?"

"Forgive me. I wish I had the power to free you but I don't."

"Forgive me, I wish I knew the truth to tell your daughter but now I shall tell her what I heard about you."

Mura blocked her way, finding himself at a loss for words. "You would not have come to my door in the wee hours if you believed what you heard about me."

Abhaya turned away unsmiling. "When she grows older, it would kill her to know that she has been your weakness, Senapati."

Mura sighed and spoke nothing. Abhaya turned to face him. "I think I know a way out."

Mura seemed unsure. He then motioned her to sit on a stone seat. At the end of their conversation, he still shook his head. After a while, though, he gave a small nod. "So, the next full moon it is."

Abhaya smiled and walked towards the exit.

"Will you be alright?" Mura asked.

Abhaya nodded, unsure about why Mura asked the question. She then considered something else. "If I can somehow get your daughter out, will you also make use of the opportunity, Senapati? What is the point in serving a fraudulent temple and a fake mahadevi?"

"Neither is this temple of the Mother Goddess fraudulent nor is the mahayogini a fake!" Mura whispered fiercely. "Yuvati, even the mahayogini does not know that her 'powers' are fake. She is as much a prisoner in this fortress as you are, as I am, as my child is." Abhaya turned to face him. He continued, "I have seen this for too long now, Devi. I am taking the risk of helping you escape now. But a day will come when Dhatri will come to know of Bhauma's deceit. She will not be able to bear that. I want to be by her side then."

Abhaya felt her eyes grow moist at his admission. "You love her, Senapati?"

Mura turned away and took up his weapons. "It is time you went back inside."

Abhaya fell into deep thought as she walked back.

"This is the last time!" the guard at the gates of the second fortress said gruffly.

Abhaya took no notice of him. For the rest of the day, she was lost in thought. A lot of things fell into place now after her conversation with Mura. Bhauma's plans were far larger than controlling a cult through fraudulent means. He sought to brainwash innocent people into believing the miraculous powers of the Goddess. He brainwashed innocent women, including Dhatri herself, into believing in Shakta supremacy.

He then sought to send his network of brainwashed Shaktas to influence the rest of Bharatavarsha.

Control in the name of the Goddess! In the name of religion!

At the end of the day, Abhaya walked into the room and collapsed onto the stone cot. Sleep certainly would not come to her tonight. Bhauma had to have a partner within Bharatavarsha to help him spread his network of Shakta spies.

Who was it? Krishna, you should know about this! The person, whoever it is, can destabilise any empire if the network of these religious Shaktas gets any stronger.

Chapter Thirty-Nine

Indraprastha

"Disappeared?" Krishna looked at Subhadra as he cradled his infant nephew, Abhimanyu, in his arms.

"Yes," Subhadra sighed. "It has been more than a month now since she went alone to rescue that gopika child who was carried away by some unidentified Shaktas."

"Shaktas," Krishna repeated, shaking his head. "That would have been enough for her to set off alone."

"She told the stable boy that some woman from our family asked her to go to the Katyayani temple in Vrindavan. And I came to know that none of our family even remember seeing her. It is fishy, though unrelated."

Krishna's brows came together and then he leaned back, thoughtful. "None of the women in the family are that timid to deny what happened. Could it be..." His sentence petered out. Subhadra sighed as he shook his head.

"Soldiers did go in their pursuit, Bhrata. But they could only trace her trail till Kashi. No one knows where she went from there."

Did she mean to not return? Or is she in danger?

Krishna pondered, "Did the gopika return?"

Subhadra shook her head. "Vrindavan is such an idyllic and peaceful village. I have gone there scores of times all alone and returned safely. Bhrata?" She saw that Krishna was lost in a different stream of thought. "What do you think?"

"Let every Shakta in the city be brought to our presence," Krishna spoke, his brows coming together in a dark frown.

"Do you think I haven't done that already?" Subhadra said, extending her arms to take Abhimanyu back. "I asked every Shakta practitioner myself. There weren't many, to begin with. Some of them came from the south of the Vindhyas, some from the north. Some from the easternmost corners of Bharatavarsha. None of them could cast any light on the incident. Most seemed genuinely shocked."

"Then we should start our search from Kashi, where the soldiers' search ended. She might have left some clues for us. Something happened at Kashi."

"Bhrata ... I promised you that I would keep her safe. I have failed you." Krishna shook his head reassuringly but Subhadra could not contain her distress. "Katyayani Gauri has mocked us with this. If we cannot protect our dear friend within the limits of our province, what can we promise to the unified Bharatavarsha?"

"Maybe she is not someone who needs protection Subhadra; maybe she has undertaken a task that she believes she must do on her own. What did our friends at Avanti reveal? Were they interrogated?"

"I questioned them too," Subhadra said. "The leader of Avanti's spy network was sent to my presence upon jyeshta bhrata Yudhishthira's orders. He did reveal something. But..." Subhadra glanced at Abhimanyu, who had now drifted to sleep on her shoulder. Placing the infant on the bed, she continued, "He revealed that the Shakta spies were sent by the erstwhile emperor of Magadha, Jarasandha."

"Who is no more," Krishna said, piecing together the bits of information. "Shaktas come as spies from Magadha and help the prince of Avanti, as Avanti and Magadha were allies. But after the death of the Magadhan emperor, we should not have heard any more of them."

"I thought so, too," Subhadra responded. "Jarasandha was not a follower of the Shakta path. Was someone helping him?" She looked at Krishna. "If so, this unknown enemy is still out there. That is not safe, Bhrata."

"Abhaya's trail could be traced till Kashi. Kashi and Magadha are not very far apart. Subhadra, you are right. Jarasandha was not a Shakta. The king of Kashi … no, he isn't, either."

"I was thinking of sending a messenger to the present king of Magadha. He is our ally now, isn't he?" Subhadra suggested.

Krishna shook his head. "We cannot wait until then. I shall start for Kashi shortly."

"But the eastern conquest is yet to start. We are waiting for our forces to return from the south and the west!" Subhadra protested.

Krishna raised a hand. "This is not just about her, Subhadra. This might be about the safety of women across Bharatavarsha. Something big is going on. It might concern the very social stability across the land." After a pause, his lips curved to reassure her. "I shall go in disguise."

"That is evident, Bhrata, but what if you need help? Who knows what would unfold?"

"I shall go with a force, Subhadra." Krishna halted at the door and turned. He then added with a wink, "A force need not necessarily be big to win. And it shall go in disguise."

"There is something you should know," Subhadra added, now rising to her feet. "She loves you, Bhrata. But you..."

"But I..."

"What can I say? If only you had been here when she talked to me about you."

"What did she tell you, Subhadra?"

"The last time I saw her, she was very disturbed you did not tell her about the attack on Dwaraka."

"She was already disturbed about how we handled the Avanti conquest, Subhadra, and fairly so."

"She could have come with you to Dwaraka and helped you out, Krishna. At the very least you could have told her. Of all men, you should know what a woman goes through when the man she loves considers her only as someone to be protected and not a partner. Don't the scriptures say that the bride is also the sahadharmacharini?"

"Bride? Subhadra, you really cannot assume things without Abhaya telling you herself."

Subhadra sighed. "I expected better from you, Bhrata. Did you think she would tell you herself, the kind of self-respecting woman that she is?"

"You know me to have been a disappointment more than once," Krishna chuckled, "And yet you expect me to do better every time."

"And you know me to understand you better than you want me to," Subhadra protested. "And yet expect me to fall into that verbal trap every time."

"Alright, we'll bring the princess of Anagha back and let her clarify your doubts herself." Krishna smiled. "And as your guest room is not occupied right now, I expect I shall not be encroaching on your guest's space if I sleep there tonight."

Subhadra shrugged and nodded.

Krishna turned away. He walked up the stairs to the room where Abhaya had stayed before she left Indraprastha.

As he entered the room, the window blew in a soothing breeze off the Yamuna. A maid followed him and lit the lamp, making as little noise as she could. Like the one in a trance, Krishna walked up to the window. Hours passed and he stood by the window, not resisting the flood of memories and the emotions that overcame him. A nostalgic smile played on his lips before it gave way to a sigh.

The Yamuna soothed his heart, bringing back reminiscences that drenched his weary soul and his eyes had the same twinkle that had danced in them years before. Sensing the presence and hearing the city bell that indicated how much of the night was left, Krishna walked towards the bed and reclined.

He heard the laughter in the depths of his inner self.

Did you tell her to go behind the Shaktas? he found himself asking.

I warned you I would have to intervene. The faceless formless voice spoke in a musical rhythm, betraying indulgent mischief.

You beat me this time.

Relax, Krishna. Would I let harm befall your love?

Where is she now?

You shall know when the time is ripe.

His eyes opened and he rose, brushing the locks out of his eyes. The lamp was still burning. His eyes fell upon the wooden frame that served as the backrest for the bed. With its intricate carvings, the frame was visible in the light of the lamp. On the plain part of the frame, Krishna found writing etched in the wood. The etching was fresh but carelessly done, as though someone had done it subconsciously while lost in thought. He peered at it.

"Krishna ... Abh." The syllables were left incomplete.

His fist closed at the constriction in his heart and the nails dug into the skin of his palm. "I'm coming, Abhaya, have faith."

Chapter Forty

Indraprastha

The intricately carved stone archway of Indraprastha was a symbol of its rulers' patronage of the arts and looked like it was an entrance to a different world, perhaps the realm of Indra, the king of gods, after whom the city was named. Art and aestheticism, though, was the last thing on the minds of the three weary travellers who entered the gates. Vikrama, for one, could think of nothing beyond seeking Abhaya's forgiveness for deserting her and their father in their time of need. Shyeni and Kadambari had tried to convince him that none of what had happened could be helped. But the image of the deserted city of Anagha continued to haunt him, as did the disappointed face he imagined of Dharmasena.

"Why should I have to lose a family always to gain a family?" His words had even hurt Kadambari, who knew he resented her for abandoning him.

"She left you in the care of a man who commands so much love from you today. What is her mistake?" Shyeni had tried to reason with him.

Vikrama did not have the words to disagree with her but the anger persisted.

"Where do we look for your sister?" Kadambari asked, dismounting. The words "your sister" were not uttered without some bitterness but Vikrama chose to ignore that.

"We should ask someone from the royal household. I think we should ask for Krishna Vaasudeva. Everyone will know him. I shall make the enquiries. Can you both attend to the horses and find us a resting place for the time being?"

The women found that Indraprastha was generous with hospitality, though Kadambari noticed an occasional pair of brows rise at the sight of two women leading three horses. Guest houses too were lavish by the standards of what Kadambari had seen.

The first person Vikrama asked could not help him with Krishna's whereabouts but led him to where the traders of Anagha had settled. He hurried there without asking further questions. As he entered the street, his eyes fell upon a woman whom he knew as erstwhile Senapati Vajrabahu's wife, Meenakshi.

"Maatulaa!" he cried. The woman recognised him and opened the door of her home, a room in a building that housed many from Anagha. He looked around, not daring to ask about anyone as he was not sure who was alive and who was not. The Nagas near Anagha had only known about the king's demise and the exodus led by Abhaya.

Meenakshi sighed at the pain in his eyes. Handing him a pitcher of water, she proceeded to light the fire to cook food. "The battle claimed my brothers—they were all who were left in my family. My husband, you know, died long before…" She paused and placed a large vessel over the fire. Vikrama stared at her, at a loss for words. Looking at him, Meenakshi swallowed hard and said, "There is something you should know, Yuvaraja. Your sister, she is not here. She went riding to some nearby village and never returned."

"Never returned?"

"It happened on the day that queen with whom she used to stay went into labour. People said she went to rescue a milkmaid's daughter who had been abducted by some Shaktas."

Vikrama rose to his feet. "Was anything done to find her?"

"That Yadava leader, Vaasudeva, your friend ... he too was not here then. He came to us about four days ago and assured us that he would bring her back. He left for Kashi."

"Kashi?"

"That's where she was last seen. I heard she left messages with the patrol guard along the highway up to that place. But there is no trace of her after Kashi."

Vikrama felt his mind go blank. "Why this now?"

His question, Meenakshi knew, was not directed at her. She sat in silence, numb with her pain and his.

Vikrama nodded to himself and sighed. "Maatulaa, I shall go after her. I dare to ask you this despite all that befell your family. After I bring Abhaya back safely, Mahakala willing, would you return home with us? I ask you as a son."

"Bring her back, Vikrama," Meenakshi replied. "I don't like it here either. Let us all go back home."

Vikrama made his way to Subhadra's mansion after quite a bit of deliberation and was promptly ushered in. Subhadra confirmed all that he had heard from Meenakshi.

"Forgive our lapse, Bhrata, I promise..."

"Who am I to forgive, Maharani? Pray, let me know where she was last seen. I shall pursue her myself."

Subhadra tried to convince him about the efforts she and Krishna were making to find Abhaya.

"Can't you stay in the city until you can talk to the king?"

"I shall seek his pardon for not meeting him when I return, hopefully in happier circumstances." Vikrama rose to his feet, hands folded in a final salutation.

"Take some of our reserve forces with you. I am sure…"

"With the bulk of your armies fighting the campaign, the reserve forces better stay back here, Maharani," Vikrama politely declined. "I may find a way to send a message if there is a need. Thank you, my queen. But three swift horses would help."

Subhadra nodded and arranged for the same. Vikrama's steadfastness made her feel happy for Abhaya. But it was her commitment towards a friend and the pride of Indraprastha that was at stake. She dearly hoped Krishna would reach Abhaya before Vikrama did.

"Krishna's horses are among the fastest. I expect him to reach Kashi in a day or two. I hope that comforts you in some small way," she said.

With a bow, Vikrama took her leave. He was filled with foreboding. If the worst had befallen Abhaya, he would have little in the world to live for. *But what can I do with this mad girl from Gomantaka, who has trusted me to this extent? Do I even deserve her?*

Vikrama reached the guest house and Shyeni ran up to him. The excitement he saw in her eyes made him forget his woe for the moment.

"The Garudas were here days ago!" Shyeni chirped to him. "They left for Kashi. We missed them by mere days. Where is your sister?"

When she heard about Abhaya's disappearance, Shyeni pointed out that Krishna had left with the Garudas to Kashi.

"We shall not be alone in searching for her, Vikrama! Let us ride and catch up with them. We can do it if we ride fast enough."

Kadambari, who had been a mute listener to Vikrama's tale, clutched his arm. "She has pursued those Shaktas to Kamarupa. Manikandhara, this isn't a small matter concerning one person. We should alert the king here."

"Kamarupa?"

"Yes," Kadambari said with emphasis. "I can't think of any other place beyond Kashi to where a Shakta group can carry away women. If Abhaya had left a trail of messages with the respective patrol guards, it would have continued after Kashi too. But something seems to have happened at Kashi."

"Amba," Vikrama interrupted her, not wanting to let her speculate the worst. "If she is at Kamarupa and is in trouble, can we go and rescue her?"

"We should then catch up with Vaasudeva and Vainateya at Kashi and let them know!" Shyeni protested. "We are talking about a new place which none of us except Kadambari has ever visited."

"I am done taking their help," Vikrama declared. The women perceived a sense of disillusionment more than anger in him. "Some friendships cost us dearly. Let us rescue her before we feel more indebted to him."

"We'll debate it on the way," Kadambari concluded.

At dawn the next day, they set out in the eastern direction and crossed the bridge across the Yamuna and rode across the expanse of the countryside. On the way, they paused by the side of River Yamuna when Kadambari explained in detail what she had encountered at Kamarupa years before.

"It is a temple town on the hill of Nilachala, with three layers of fortification," she explained. "If we are planning to go by ourselves with no help, we will need to be aware of the topography."

"Fortification of a temple town? That too three layers!" Shyeni exclaimed.

Kadambari nodded and continued. "The outer fortress, the middle fortress and the inner fortress. The inner fortress is where the temple is situated along with the residences of the lord of Kamarupa, Bhauma and possibly that of the woman who was declared mahadevi then, or the current one if she has been replaced."

Shyeni drew a map in the sand as Kadambari described the place from memory. "There is, however, a passage behind the temple in the middle ring. The hilly structure does not allow for complete fortification there. But the climb is steep and the path is broken in places. From the outside, it is camouflaged by undergrowth and rocks. When my guru Vamanatha was killed, I ran into the senapati of Kamarupa. By the grace of the Goddess, he helped me escape through that exit though he refused to believe me." Kadambari shook her head, brushing aside the memory, and continued to explain the geography of Kamarupa. "The outer ring houses the soldiers and the guards mostly. Some of the practitioners stay there too. The middle ring houses the yoginis and the sadhakas. This is where we should look for the princess."

She saw Vikrama's fingers curl into a tight fist. Kadambari worried that his emotions would get the better of him at an inopportune time. Later, when they halted for the night, she decided to take Shyeni into confidence.

Chapter Forty-One

Kamarupa

"Now!" Kanakangi whispered as she peered into the corridor. The guard who usually patrolled the circular corridor of the middle ring had just passed by their room. They would not encounter him for another hour or so.

"Cover as much distance as you can while it is dark," Abhaya told the five women as they crept out of their room, keeping to the shadows.

Kanakangi hesitated, looking at Abhaya imploringly but Abhaya nudged her towards the passage. "Stop by Varanasi on your way back. I shall pray for your safety."

"Come back soon..." Abhaya stopped midway as she instinctively spoke the traditional parting message. "Why in the name of Mahakala am I telling you to come back!' Abhaya laughed at her foolishness and quickly added, "Now hurry up and leave!"

Kanaka's lips parted. "Abhaya, are you sure?" When a silent nod was the response, she shook her head vigorously. "We might feel better if you came with us."

"No Kanaka, we have talked this over. I must stay back."

"They might harm you if they found out!" a woman called Mandakini protested.

"Don't worry about me. Your disappearance will make it easier for me to achieve what I want to." Abhaya assured them, showing the way towards the gate. "Hurry now, I beg of you before it is too late."

Abhaya unlocked the door that led to the passage and saw the girls descend to the hidden stairway which was thought to be broken. The moonlight, she hoped, could help the girls find their way down safely. She placed the key behind a marked stone as instructed by Mura, who planned to take it back when he went on his pre-dawn rounds.

Mura would be surprised to find that she had not gone herself and had instead helped the other five women escape. Walking back to her room, Abhaya fought the urge to turn back and follow the other girls. She had to stay back. She had to make Dhatri realise the wrong that was happening in the name of religion. The details that Mura had shared about Dhatri churned in her mind. She could not bring herself to leave Kamarupa without convincing Dhatri to give up her hatred of the Aryas, fuelled by Bhauma's manipulative ambition. There were moments in the long night where she felt deserted by her confidence and she could not come up with a further course of action. Given her irreverent behaviour from the day she had arrived at Kamarupa, Abhaya knew she would naturally be suspected of having played a part in her roommates' disappearance. But, in her heart, she felt a strange sense of determination overcome her restlessness. Then, all of a sudden, she felt a presence hover around her. She could see or hear nothing. But as an unusual breeze brushed over her, she felt the tug from within her heart. It felt like some invisible force had reached out to soothe her. Her eyes closed and a form manifested in her consciousness, though in a blur. Her lips curved into a beatific smile.

"Should I believe that you had nothing to do with their disappearance?" Dhatri's eyes pierced hers. The sun's rays from the eastern windows bathed her face in a crimson hue. Though her face showed no emotion and her voice remained placid, the light had the effect of making her look as though she were anger personified.

Abhaya smiled, refusing to raise herself to a sitting position. Stretching herself and fighting a yawn, she chuckled. "You should perhaps believe that it was the will of the Supreme Goddess … Mahayogini." She added a deliberate pause to irk Dhatri.

"Yuvati," Dhatri cautioned with no apparent change in her tone. "I tolerate your irreverence only because I find your frankness endearing. If you only knew what you have just done by helping those women go." Dhatri walked up the cot and Abhaya felt compelled to get up but she remained seated holding on to the edge of her stone cot. "Tell me who helped them. It could not have happened without your knowledge."

"Would you believe that I would let go of an opportunity to leave?" Abhaya replied, looking directly into Dhatri's eye. A lump formed in her throat as she remembered Mura's words. She estimated that Kanakangi and the other girls would have crossed over to the settlements of Pragjyotisha by now. If fate favoured them, the news of the abductions and the fact that Bhauma of Kamarupa was behind them would start reaching the rulers of their respective kingdoms in a few days. It was then bound to reach Indraprastha and Krishna. Abhaya took a deep breath and rose to her feet. "If my frankness has indeed endeared me to you, Devi, then take my frank advice. Stop these attempts to abduct women from the plains. Stop the brainwashing going on here in the name of some Supreme Goddess whose existence is questionable. Stop giving in to greed for power in the name of religion."

"Reason is apparently not the language you understand, Yuvati. Tell me at once where the women are headed to!" Dhatri admonished. "Let me not resort to using..."

"...force." Abhaya completed the sentence. "Dhatri, do you think threats would make me change my mind? Listen to me, Devi. What is being done here is a heinous fraud in the name of that rock you call the Supreme Goddess. You, Dhatri, are not the chosen medium of any Goddess nor can you cure anyone's illness at will. The women discovered your fraud and left. Yes, I stayed back only to convince you to stop this adharma. Stop being a puppet in the hands of that Bhauma. Let every woman here return to her rightful home in the plains of Bharata. Devi, you return to yours, too. Go back home."

Abhaya stopped as a shadow fell across the room. Her hand went to the scimitar she had placed by her bedside when she saw the figure standing in the doorway.

"Didn't I tell you to not tolerate this one anymore? Leave her to me, Mahadevi," Bhauma said, glaring at Abhaya.

"Yes, leave me to him. And I shall teach him a lesson or two about how women should be treated. Let this end today, Bhauma—the fraud, the murders and who knows what else in the name of this Supreme Goddess? Rapes? I shall end it today!"

Bhauma did not need any more provocation to step forward. He was about to unsheathe his sword when Dhatri turned and stopped him by the arm.

For the first time in many years, Bhauma saw a forbidding glare on Dhatri's face. She rarely wielded authority over him.

"Force is what she would like us to use, Bhauma," she spoke, her lips curving at the end. "She provokes us to resort to force because that would destroy our steadfastness to the order of the Shaktas." In the moment of silence that followed, Bhauma saw the tinge of rebuke that flashed in her eyes at his disregarding the obvious. Dhatri then turned to Abhaya whose smile continued to defy her. "Enjoy the last days of your delusion, Yuvati. What you did shall come back to haunt you."

The words slipped from Dhatri's lips with emphasised pauses. An unearthly resolve flashed in her eyes. Abhaya threw her head high, refusing to give in. But in her heart of hearts, something about Dhatri's words unsettled her.

Dhatri turned around and stormed out, briefly halting for Bhauma to join her. To her dismay, she heard Bhauma lock the door from outside. That would mean that he would be able to enter the room whenever he wanted. Abhaya's lips parted in protest. Then, to her relief, through the window, she saw Dhatri hold out her hand. Bhauma reluctantly put the key in her palm. Dhatri threw back the key to Abhaya through the carve hold in the door. Her parting glance warned Abhaya of something to come.

The knocking at the door made Abhaya look up. Her solitary confinement in the past couple of weeks had done little to break her will. Dhatri had, in the initial week, tried to ask her about the details of where the women lived. Abhaya chose to remain tight-lipped and sought to reason with Dhatri to give up the idea of pursuing the women. She could see Dhatri seething with an unknown rage at something Abhaya could not guess at.

"You shall reach a state where you cannot forgive yourself!" Dhatri had thundered before she left and she had not returned after that.

With her repeated calls to reason with Dhatri going unheeded, Abhaya's confidence had started to weaken. When she saw Dhatri at the door after more than a fortnight, relief washed over her.

Dhatri gripped her hand in an iron grip. The cold stare in the older woman's eyes quelled any defiance that Abhaya could muster. Before she could wonder why, Abhaya found herself shoved to the front section of the passage that surrounded the inner fortress.

"Kanakangi!" Abhaya gasped at what remained of the girl from Pundra. The purple-hued body lay motionless on the floor.

"Poison," Dhatri muttered and looked at the guard.

"Her family had put her in solitary confinement. A week before, they discarded her in this state."

"Why did you let us out at all?" What started as a shout petered to a whisper.

Abhaya whirled to stare at one of the women who had escaped along with Kanakangi.

"She is the only one left alive of the five girls whom you so graciously helped 'escape' the week before," Dhatri said. "The rest were given a 'glorious farewell' to their afterlife by your esteemed civilisation ... forgive me ... what was it you had said? The civilisation that believes in universal wellness."

Abhaya felt something crumble within her as the truth dawned on her. Her legs seemed to desert her and she fell to her knees. The heart seemed to have come to a standstill.

"I knew this would happen. Had you told us what you knew about their homes and where they came from, our soldiers could have tracked them and saved them before this." Dhatri's hoarse voice pierced her ears.

"Who helped you in letting them escape?"

Abhaya sensed Mura's presence and consciously avoided looking in his direction. She said nothing.

Bhauma pulled her up with a violent jerk and she put up no defence. Dhatri's hand restrained him and she ordered her to be locked back in the room.

Three days later, Dhatri's concerns increased when the female guards told her about the untouched food in Abhaya's room. When she went to convince Abhaya to not give up food, she saw a different Abhaya from what she had expected. In the darkness of her room, Abhaya's eyes flashed with renewed determination. Dhatri had expected that the death of the women would break her resolve but Abhaya continued to maintain a stoic defiance.

"I think we should let her go back home," Dhatri confided in Bhauma after another unsuccessful conversation with Abhaya. "She is not prepared to accept our ways. Neither is she willing to forgive herself for what happened. If she dies of starvation, it would not bode well for Kamarupa."

"No!" Bhauma exclaimed. "The conditions in the plains have changed a lot, Mahayogini. Our patron king of Magadha was treacherously killed. His enemies are consolidating power. If this girl is set free and she tells them about our efforts to spread Shaktism, it would be the end of Kamarupa! They may come after all these women. An excuse is all they want to tear down this place. We can't let that happen!"

"What happened to your faith in the Supreme Goddess, Bhauma?"

"It is stronger than ever," Bhauma muttered, his lips barely parting. "The plains below are witnessing the churn. Our Shaktas should be able to accrue more power in this period. We shall emerge stronger."

Dhatri shook her head. "It was unwise to engage anymore in that spy strategy. I don't think we ever had the approval of Goddess Kamaksha."

"Dhatri?" Bhauma stared at her.

"No, Bhauma, you were the one who was inclined to go ahead. Your words played in my mind. It was never the signal from the Goddess. I don't know if she ever spoke to me or through me or I kept fantasising and deceiving myself and you."

Bhauma's further arguments were of no avail. He had to be content with Dhatri agreeing to not let Abhaya leave Kamarupa. Bhauma felt sure that her escape would alert some king or the other. The traditional methods of impressing gullible Arya women had failed with Abhaya. Her continued defiance could spell doom for Kamarupa. Bhauma now hated the very sight of the girl. Her very presence seemed to drive a wedge between him and Dhatri, a relationship he had carefully nurtured for years. He could not let everything he had planned come to nothing just because of one girl from the plains.

Chapter Forty-Two

When the door closed behind her, Abhaya did not even move to take the key that was thrown back to her. Safety was not something that mattered to her anymore. Her faith in everything she had learnt since childhood had crumbled into pieces. Kanakangi's face haunted her. Dhatri's sneer pierced her soul.

"Is this what the civilisation of the Aryas has come to? What is left to save of Bharatavarsha when the lives of innocents are no longer valued?" she sobbed out.

The death of the four women was a brutal betrayal of everything Abhaya believed in. The pain rent her soul apart. Rage, helplessness and despair danced in furious unison in her mind.

"Does this world merit sustenance any longer?!"

Her fist struck the stone wall. The physical pain was no match for the turmoil within her. The three days of self-imposed starvation was telling on her strength but food failed to interest her.

Dhatri's softened stance and entreaties were of no avail. The mahayogini had misjudged Abhaya's state of mind for guilt. Abhaya was far from feeling guilty. Her conscience was clear. She had done no wrong in helping the girls. It was Kamarupa and the families of the women who had to bear the burden of guilt. As for civilisation, everything she had learned was an ironic myth fit only to be mocked at by reality. Every destructive event in history, she felt, was to be applauded, for mankind deserved only destruction.

"What is stopping Mahakala from ending this undeserving world?!" In the quiet that greeted her screams, Abhaya could see apparitions of every wronged soul she knew and many she did not know. "Why should I bother? Mahakala does not exist, nor does any deity that preserves the universe. There are no gods. If they existed, this would not happen!"

Sleep came at irregular intervals. Dreams alternated between visions of her dear ones trying to console her and others condemning her for her actions.

"Did you teach me untrue folklores in the name of history?" she blurted out as she saw Dharmasena smiling down at her.

"History had its glorious side and a horrendous one, too. The present also has them. Which side are you on, Vatse?"

"Where is the glorious side? It is just a mirage!"

"How is one sure of something being a mirage unless they believe in life-sustaining water, Vatse? The glorious side exists but perhaps not where you are looking for it."

"Janaka!" The face faded away when she extended her hand to touch it. Abhaya's eyes opened. It was dark. "Where am I looking for the 'water'?"

Breaking the odd silence of the night, Abhaya heard someone sing.

Dweller of every heart, O Hari
Ruler of every heart, O Hari

Abhaya reached out for a jug filled with water and splashed some on her face. This was not a dream. The voice of the singer came closer.

The one in the peaks of piety
The one content in impiety
The one praying in anxiety
The one lost in ambiguity
Ruler of every heart, O Hari
Dweller in every heart, O Hari

The song was familiar. Abhaya rushed towards the door. The door gave way. *The guards forgot to lock the door?* She stepped out into the passage and found herself face to face with the singer.

"Aren't you from Kashi?' she exclaimed, remembering him from the ashrama at Kashi.

"I am from nowhere," he replied. The moon came out of the cloud cover. Abhaya saw his smile. As in Kashi, he was attired in the same faded lower garment and carried the same musical instrument. "Kashi is as much mine as is Kamarupa. I wander everywhere."

"Are you a mirage too?"

"A mirage is a function of fantasy, Devi. Truth, on the other hand, never disappoints." He looked at her. "If one can accept it."

"The truth I learnt disappointed me, Arya," Abhaya protested. "What I had believed as truth has become a mirage, a fantasy, today. The truth is the brutality of this world and the apathy of gods if they even exist."

The singer raised his brows. He stepped towards the room. "Why is the world brutal?"

"That is its nature, probably." Abhaya's jaw tightened as she led him inside.

"Are you brutal?" he laughed.

"Now, I certainly have the mind to be!"

"Now. You say 'now', which means you think you were not brutal till now." He smiled. Silvery moonlight flooded into the room and Abhaya saw his locks flutter in the breeze that blew into the room. She opened her mouth to speak and then shut it wordlessly. "You have the mind to become brutal because of something. Else, you would choose not to be so."

"Because of the killings of innocents, Arya. Just because they chose to explore a faith that is not acceptable to the world of Aryas."

"How can someone kill an innocent and still remain an Arya, Devi?"

"The definition of being Arya is only debated by a few like you. The reality is different. The meaning of the word Arya seems to be plummeting to a depth where life carries no value."

"What would you do, Abhaya?"

His use of her name startled her for a moment. But then she reasoned it was not an impossibility that he had found out from Atulyaprabha at Kashi.

"What are the choices that you and I have to change all this? Do we want to change it at all or do we let peril take over the world?"

In her anger, Abhaya would have agreed to let peril take over but something tugged at her heart. Visions of the past flashed before her.

In situations forcing you to choose between life and death, will you choose life over death…?

Krishna!

She remembered her promise. She also remembered the promise to reach out to him.

"Arya! Do me a favour! Carry my message to someone who could be our only choice!"

His head tilted and a smile bloomed on his lips. "Carrying messages. That makes me feel as important as … never mind, tell me."

Krishna Vaasudeva

I side with life over death, with hope over despair. I see hope in you. The temple of Kamaksha, the high seat of Shakti, is now the house of a wayward religion. This religion believes not in the union of the human spirit with the Supreme but in uprooting the basis of what we consider eternal. Women are being abducted and brainwashed to spread this religion, spy on kingdoms and entrench this wayward cult. The social foundation of the Aryas is in danger.

How I wish I could defend the Aryas! How I wish the world of Aryas did not give in to this onslaught! But wishes remain wishes, Krishna. We are headed towards an internal peril if not the one posed by the Shaktas. If Aryas kill, abandon and castigate their women only for exploring a different religion, how do we defend our world? I promised to reach out to you when things get out of my hands. I am reaching out to you. Not one, but two challenges await us.

We have the choice to act and the choice to ignore. I know what you would choose and you know what I would. Come Vaasudeva, your cause awaits you. Dhaarmaseni awaits you, in hope, in faith.

Her head leaned against the stone bed and her eyes closed in fatigue. When she opened them again, Abhaya did not find the messenger.

"Another dream," she sighed. "It did remind me of my promise to Krishna, though. I cannot fast till I die like this. I cannot be content with inaction. I cannot make the choice of ignoring or abandoning my dharma. The Shaktas and Aryas might lose their way. I cannot lose mine. There has to be a way."

Chapter Forty-Three

Varanasi

The sight of the placid river offered a welcome respite to those braving the hustle of the crowds of pilgrims on the ghats of Varanasi. The Ganga was known by many names and epithets. But commoners of the day knew her as the "Mother who washes away one's sins". On the banks of the river, Atulyaprabha laboured alone through the day, collecting the waste on the ghats into her basket, piling it into a cart and wheeling it away from the banks only to reappear again in a while with the empty cart to repeat the whole procedure.

As the sun reached the western horizon, Atulyaprabha sensed that she was not alone on the ghat which was almost deserted owing to broken steps and weeds. She expected the man to go for a dip, as a pilgrim would. He did not look like an everyday pilgrim, though, who had come to Kashi with the hope of fulfilling a desire. As she neared him, she saw the placid waters of the mother of rivers reflect in his eyes with the multitude of pilgrims. The eyes contained the very image of Kashi, a phenomenon which she thought was impossible to see from the distance where she stood. As she blinked, wondering if it was a hallucination, she saw the magnified vision of his eyes disappear like it never existed.

"Are you waiting for the sight of the harati lights, Arya?"

The words broke his contemplative gaze and he turned towards her with a smile that widened when he took in her basket. He shook his head.

"Nobody comes to the lap of Ganga without a quest, a desire or a bid to 'wash away' his sins. Though I must say that you don't look like one who has sinned." She found herself smiling when a whiff of wind blew his upper garment off his left shoulder, revealing a part of his frame that spoke of restrained strength, adorned with a sacred thread and a lone string of beads.

"Who does not have a quest, Devi? What sets our quest apart is its scope, backed by our will and endeavour. I must say, what you have been doing has aroused my curiosity."

"Mother Ganga is believed to take away the sins of her children, Arya. I am trying to share a minuscule portion of her burden." She smiled, emptying her basket into the cart.

"One pair of hands against the perennial flow of 'sinners'?" he asked, pointing to the crowds collecting on the other ghats.

"Didn't you say that the endeavour is something that sets one apart from the others?" She smiled, descending the steps back to the river. "As for this lone pair of hands, they will multiply when the Mother wills. That is not my worry as long as mine are immersed in what they are doing right now."

She was pleasantly surprised as the man extended his hands to take the basket and then emptied it into the cart as she stood on the steps, partly submerged in the water.

"Do you get to observe many of these pilgrim groups, Devi?" She nodded, taking the basket back.

"And among them, ascetic groups which have women, who are, perhaps, not looking too happy?"

Her brows came together in a flash of memory. "I have not but a while back, a young maiden had come in search of a similar group." She turned in the direction of a distant ghat and paused before resuming, "And the same day, I found a girl who swam this way as per the maiden's directions, and..."

A broken but melodious voice interrupted her words and she turned in its direction, pointing to the distant figure sitting on a stone bench singing. "She is the one."

Did you see him, the dark-hued one?
Did you see him, the lotus-eyed one?
The one from whom grace and beauty flow;
The one on whom the plumes of peacock glow.

The man turned abruptly and sprinted in the direction of the singing girl. Atulyaprabha followed, wondering about the sudden change in him. Seeing him, the girl's voice shook at the next line but the rest followed in a flow of melody as she got up from the boulder and walked towards him.

Smile bewitching never leaves his face;
To his call of flute, our hearts race
Creepers of the Vrinda Grove, Speak well;
Is that one hiding among you? Do tell.

"Viraja!" he called out.

The girl broke down, wrapping her arms around his waist. He enveloped her in his arms, trying to soothe her sobs.

"My mother used to believe that you would come when I sing this perfectly. Take me home, Dark God Govinda!"

When she was comforted, he lifted her chin up, wiping away the last of her tears.

"How did you come this far, Vatse?"

Before she could reply, he noticed the bracelet that looked too big for her wrist and held up her hand. "Where is the one who gave you this?"

Viraja gave him a troubled look. "More than two months ago, those bad people lifted me from the temple of Katyayani in Vrindavan and they brought me here. I thought they were taking me away to kill me and I would never reach home." Fresh tears sprung into her eyes and he wiped them away. "There were many girls who were not scared. Some were, but they were fed sleeping medicine. Then, she came." Viraja pointed to the bracelet. "She came and sat among us like she had no fear. She told us not to be afraid. The night before the demons planned to take us away from here, she crept up to five of us and cut the rope that bound our hands and legs. She told us to escape and to swim here. We made our way into the river. But one demon saw us!" Viraja stopped for breath and felt his grip on her arms tighten.

"Viraja, where is she?"

"She could not come with us, Govinda. We jumped into Ganga and I saw her fight the demon, shouting at us to escape. We swam here. She did not come with us. She wanted to help the other girls who were given the sleeping medicine. But the demons have taken her away." Viraja unclasped the bracelet and held it out to him. "She told me you gave her this."

The bracelet shone against the setting sun, bringing back the memories of Avanti and, with them, a smile to his lips.

Where are you, Dhaarmaseni?

As the older woman approached, Viraja cheered up a little. "This bhagini is Atulya. Atulyaprabha. She feeds me every day. I sleep in her gurukula."

Atulyaprabha, who had chosen to stay quiet as Viraja completed her story, broke her silence.

"All the five girls swam to where I was cleaning the ghats..." she said, pausing to consider how the address the man, "Arya, about two months ago, a woman had come to Kashi on a quest she would not reveal everything about and sought my help. She requested me to stay on the ghats that night. I was sceptical but something in her demeanour made me trust her. That night, these girls swam across the river and came to me. The woman never came back. I could ensure that the other four girls were sent back to their families as all of them were visiting Kashi then. But this one had come from a faraway land. I could not entrust her to strangers and was waiting to meet a caravan from the lands known to her."

"He is no stranger, Bhagini!" Viraja chirped, now in a complete state of cheer. "He is our friend, our Dark God, Our Krishna, Govinda."

Atulyaprabha's eyes held new light as she remembered the tales that Viraja had told her about him. Her hands came together in a salutation. "Krishna! I have heard about you. And I knew you would come here."

Krishna's brows came together as his lips curved slightly. Atulya wondered if it was curiosity or amusement at her sudden revelation. "I shall take you to the one who told me that you would come. Come with me, Lord."

Krishna followed Atulyaprabha further up the ghat. The path got wider after it reached a clearing surrounded by thick vegetation. Atulya observed as Viraja hopped by his side with renewed excitement, having established a carefree intimacy with the one about whom her village told endless legends. She did break into a song now and then and he hummed along. Engrossed in each other, they did not observe Atulyaprabha disappearing through the vegetation, her footsteps making no more noise than the wind that blew from the river. Krishna's hand tightened over Viraja's shoulder instinctively, and the very next moment they heard a woman scream for help from behind the cover of bushes.

Krishna darted through the bushes, keeping the young gopika close. Within moments, they reached the woman who was screaming in terror as a man in his sixties towered over her, holding a lit torch and a pot of oil.

The man was about to splash the oil over her when he found his hand restrained. He turned in annoyance to meet the fiery glare of Krishna.

For someone of his age, the man possessed a surprising level of strength. He shoved Krishna back and the impact threatened to upset Krishna's balance but he remained steady on his feet and succeeded in making the older man back a pace or two, taking advantage of the opportunity to wrench the pot of oil from his hand and shatter it on the ground.

"Why in the name of..." The sentence had to be abandoned as Krishna ducked away from the blazing torch that the man wielded as though it were a mace. Krishna was careful to keep himself between the man and the cowering woman.

"She is my daughter and I have the right to end her life too!" the man thundered as his torch cut the air menacingly close to Krishna.

"No!" The woman's cry distracted Krishna long enough for the man to be able to draw out his long sword.

"Quite a father you are, bent up on taking the life of his daughter!" Krishna said, his lips curving into a sarcastic smile. "Do you realise that even animals desist from such an ignoble act?" Krishna drew his sword. "You are welcome to demonstrate that humans are completely capable of besting all other species in the race to barbarism but I cannot let an innocent woman die so that her father can show the demon in him to this world."

"Demons are those who don't follow dharma. Mine goes beyond my familial ties! If you come in my way, be prepared to face Yama!"

"Dharma is that which values life over frenzied beliefs," Krishna said in the same measured tone. "Dharma balances and ensures sustenance; that which strengthens from within against fears and weaknesses. You are only weak and fearful."

The man jeered in response. "You claim to defend dharma. What will you do with the girl you protect? She will face ridicule and take her life on her own one day."

"She shall not do so. Nor shall I let her."

"The world will not let her live in peace."

Krishna responded with an amused chuckle. "Didn't I say you were fearful? The world's ridicule matters only to the fearful. The wise would teach the world to make peace."

"What makes you this arrogant, or should I say confident?" The hue of the man's face had assumed a mysterious shade. The angry barbarian had faded into a stern interrogator.

Krishna looked at him and then at the woman whose sudden calm roused his suspicion. He turned to the man in new realisation. "What makes you test me like this?"

The stranger considered him for a long moment. "Did you mean everything you just said, Vaasudeva?"

"You seem to know me better than I have imagined," Krishna replied, sheathing his sword.

"Forgive my theatrics, Vaasudeva. Call it my mischief but I find it fun to test everyone's patience and even bring them to the point of raising weapons. They call me Narada for that very reason."

Narada held Krishna's hands that had come together in salutation.

"No, Vaasudeva. I was only curious to see what someone who commands so much trust and love is made of."

Krishna looked around for the woman who was nowhere to be seen.

Narada smiled. "Actors don't linger on the stage after their act is done, Krishna."

"Does that imply that my 'act' is still on?"

Narada's eyes showed instant admiration. His eyes remained fixed on Krishna's and turned solemn. "I have a message for you."

He conveyed the message that Abhaya had given him at Kamarupa and saw Krishna's eyes close.

"What awaits you is not minor, Krishna. This isn't just about overcoming an enemy. It is about overcoming the rigid fundamentalism that ails our world. Can you save civilisation from decay, Krishna?"

"That is for this civilisation to decide, Mahatma. We individuals can only choose between the options we have."

"And what is your choice, Vaasudeva?"

"Mine is to dwell on strengths while accepting weaknesses, to stay with faith while acknowledging fear, to side with reason over rigidity without abandoning those who are rigid. The result, the evolution we dream of, will come with time as a function of our choices, Mahatma."

Narada held Krishna's arms, finding in those words answers to the innumerable questions that had arisen in his mind. His hands then came together in a realisation of the universal acceptance he saw in Krishna's eyes.

"Vaasudeva?" Atulyaprabha said. "What made you stop?"

Krishna smiled at her. When he turned, Narada was gone. "Were you completely unaware of the 'play' that was enacted, Devi?"

"I might have a confession here. Varanasi has much more to offer than what meets the eye, Vaasudeva. And my 'act' in your quest comes to an end here."

"But not the action and inspiration that drives us on our respective paths." Krishna waved and turned to leave, Viraja following. The smile on his lips was that of a warrior at the sight of a battlefield.

Atulyaprabha walked back to the ghat. There, to her complete amazement, she was met by the sight of sparkling clean steps, free of every trace of weeds, silt and filth.

Chapter Forty-Four

Pundra

The infant opened her eyes. The toothless smile could captivate any heart but not that of the one who held it.

"It is a girl child!" the man thundered. "Where is the boy?"

The infant only giggled at his theatrical outburst.

"Where is the boy?!"

The giggling got louder and it echoed around the room, making him clench his jaw. The infant continued to giggle, blissfully unaware of what lay in store for her. He lifted her with his left hand and, in one smooth motion, slammed her head against the wall.

"Don't!" Krishna opened his eyes and found himself staring at the ceiling of the temporary encampment he had set up with the Garudas on their way to Kamarupa. His exclamation was not loud but his sudden movement made Vainateya stir too.

"Same dream?"

"Yes," Krishna sighed and fell back on the bed. From the holes that served as a window, he could see the moon in descent. Dawn was not a long way away. "I have lost count of the times I dream of her."

"It's not your fault, Krishna. You were just a day old." The Garuda lord stretched himself. "Why do you burden yourself?"

"A burden is different from a cause, Vainateya. We look forward to getting rid of what we feel is a burden.

But when it turns into a cause, it becomes the very energy we need to bear. Then, we can neither escape it nor shun it. We are no longer helpless bearers but become willing champions of the cause."

"So, you don't believe what your parents said about the girl—that she transformed into a fearful being, a goddess, who warned your tyrant uncle Kamsa about your existence?"

The response was silence, which spoke of a million possibilities.

Krishna's enigmatic silence, though, did not surprise Vainateya. He was used to the ways of his friend. With another stretch that flexed his sculpted shoulders, Vainateya rose into a sitting position. This had been the longest he had stayed away from the sea and the farthest he had come away from the shores. He had seen the rivers of the northern plains and observed the subtle changes, both social and climactic, as they continued to proceed eastwards. Days seemed to get shorter. They were a group of around a hundred, most of whom were Garudas except for Krishna and his friends who accompanied him. The hospitality that they received from the villages they passed was mixed after crossing Kashi.

"We should move faster. It gets colder every day and..." Krishna left the sentence unfinished, leaving Vainateya, as usual, to wonder what he would have said.

"Tell me about it! I am more used to the humid sea winds than these cold plains," Vainateya chuckled. "But something else disappointed me more. What is it with the women here?"

"Not the kind of debate I would want to start the first thing in the morning," Krishna said, laughing. As he rose to his feet, his smile faded. "Maybe the answer lies in what we can do at Kamarupa, and, most importantly, after that."

"What we do at Kamarupa is important as well!" Vainateya exclaimed as Krishna buckled his sword to his belt. "Unless, of course, you are expecting them to welcome us with full honours and hand over all the women to you."

"I was hoping to leave that to you, king of Garudas!" Krishna quipped.

"At last, you have come around to seeing the benefits of my method of brute force," the Garuda said with a triumphant smile.

"Not entirely. We shall need a team inside too. That is, if a couple of us can get inside and achieve something which might not need brute force."

"Yes, I know your theory behind aiming for a minimum loss of life." Vainateya went to the door and signalled to his people that they would leave shortly. Turning back, he found Krishna bundling his weapons. His deftness within minutes of waking up was something Vainateya could not help but admire. "Besides, we have to ensure that the neighbouring kingdoms who might be friends of this Bhauma don't come to his aid. But who can get inside without arousing suspicion, Krishna?"

"Is brute strength your only method, Vainateya?" Krishna winked. "I thought you were just a loving king of a simple mountain tribe. It turns out that you are as heartless as the warmongers of the plains. As for who can risk going inside the fort, let us detail and discuss that with the others. Who knows? We might find someone who could achieve what we want them to and more!"

Not long after, the line of horse carts was back on the highway that connected the kingdom of Pundra to Pragjyotisha, whose king, Bhagadatta, was related to Bhauma. The kingdom of Pragjyotisha treated Bhauma like a saint who had renounced the throne to devote his life to the Supreme Goddess. The chances of securing Bhagadatta's support were bleak. Krishna and Vainateya concluded that it had to be a covert operation.

"Unless Bhagadatta is informed about the Rajasuya campaign that would follow soon and be convinced to stay away from this," Krishna observed. "It is a good possibility. The king of Pragjyotisha might not support an aggression against a widely regarded temple town in his own country, however autonomous it may be. But he would not want a rivalry with greater powers."

"Let me do the job of terrifying him to a sufficient level," Vainateya said. He only got a nod in response. He considered Krishna's other proposal of sending a spy to the fortress of Kamarupa. There was little conversation until midday and an occasional word with Krishna told him that he was in deep thought too. It was past midday when the group came upon a lake and decided to rest the horses. When Vainateya was returning from watering his horse, he saw someone approaching. His jaw dropped in surprise.

"Bhrata!"

"Shyeni! And Vikrama! How, by the divine eagle…"

"I knew that we both were on the same pursuit, Bhrata," Shyeni said, running ahead of Vikrama and Kadambari. "We were on your trail for a long time. At last, we have caught up with you. You are going to find Vikrama's sister at Kamarupa, aren't you? It was not an easy task convincing him to talk to you. Where is Vaasudeva?"

Vainateya nodded at Vikrama and pointed towards the lakeside where Krishna was personally tending to his horses and Vikrama immediately hurried in the direction. "He is not exactly in a frame of mind to exchange pleasantries!" Shyeni shrugged but her brother did not seem to mind.

"I expected that. But my issue is that..." Vainateya looked at him sceptically and pulled Shyeni out of earshot. "Are you sure you like this one? He is so lanky that you can practically lift him off the ground!"

"He has his strengths," Shyeni retorted defensively.

Her wrathful glare almost made him laugh. They followed Vikrama to where Krishna stood, feeding his horses.

When he met Krishna's gaze, Vikrama felt like the tumultuous flow of questions in his mind had encountered a dam.

A warm smile appeared on Krishna's lips as he put the bag of feed down and approached Vikrama. He stopped Vikrama's hands from coming together and clasped the latter's elbows. "Abhaya will be glad to see you safe."

"Why, Vaasudeva?" Vikrama said, accusation in his eyes. "How could you let this happen? Abhaya trusted you more than she did our father and me. How was she left defenceless against those Shaktas? Or ... is it not my place to ask you this?"

"Not your place? How could you think so, Vikrama? And defenceless? Isn't that a demeaning word to use for a warrior who braves all odds to protect an innocent girl? Vikrama, weren't you the one who trained her in sword fighting? You should be proud of her."

"Proud of her … Krishna, I *am* proud of her!" Vikrama replied looking straight into Krishna's eyes. "I am also envious of you. It was you who were there when I was needed by her side and by my father's…" The lump in his throat prevented him from going on. He swallowed hard, trying to keep his mind focused on the current situation. "What now?"

"Vikrama, I need your help."

Krishna explained his plans.

"We can do that," Kadambari spoke up. She stepped up near Krishna. "I have heard a lot about you, Vaasudeva." Something about him filled her with hope and resolve. "I know Kamarupa and what happens there."

"Amba, I have heard about you too." Krishna smiled his gratitude. "Please tell us everything you know about Kamarupa, about its ruler and about what happens there."

"What happens there is fraud, Vaasudeva; fraud in the name of the Supreme Shakti. Shaktas do seek out women to join them in their sadhana but only with their consent. What Bhauma desires can bring doom to both the Shakta and Arya ways of life. He seeks to spread his crony Shaktas across Bharatavarsha. They, in turn, influence gullible people to hate the tenets that define the Aryan code. Those who are not knowledgeable about the rational side of both streams of thought fall for this rhetoric. These wayward Shaktas start by targeting the oppressed and wronged people among the remote janapadas of Bharatavarsha. In their next step, they influence the small-time warlords and headmen of tribes who are sympathetic to them. They also align themselves with certain kingdoms as spies and make their mark on the political front. But the kind of Shaktism they evangelise is against the very spirit of Supreme Shakti. The universal Mother has suddenly been given the form of an angry and vengeful goddess who demands total subjugation. The vulnerable folk who give in to these claims become their pawns in fuelling mutual hatred."

Kadambari paused and cast a glance at the others who had joined in to listen to her and resumed, "If Bhauma is allowed to carry out his mission, the Bharaṭavarsha we all know shall soon be history. The common folk would see rulers and rishis as oppressive. The fault lines and aberrations would be magnified to show Aryas in a bad light, worthy of the Goddess' scorn. Soon, it might come to a state where those who don't subscribe to this new Shaktism will be scorned on and even harmed. History would be rewritten and children would grow up learning an untrue story of their ancestors."

Krishna closed his eyes and he drew a deep breath. "How can we prevent it, Amba? As much as it seems the only way out, I am against attacking a city that is the temple of the universal Mother. As much as some of the Shaktas scorn us and paint her as an angry goddess, she is still the very Mother who *is* the very vitality that sustains you, me and the rest of this universe. Is there a way we can put an end to this Bhauma without offending the very spirit that defines us?"

Kadambari did not bat an eyelid as he spoke. His words, she noticed, put her mind in a state that made her feel secure as well as alert and conscious, inspired to act, as well as detached from the implications of the action. Like one possessed, she locked her gaze with his and replied.

"The Supreme Shakti would laud you if you put him to death, Krishna. To the one who slayed the demons that tormented this earth, his blood would be but a worthy offering. Don't you worry about the propriety of attacking a place of pilgrimage, Krishna. I, from my years of sadhana, feel this in my every cell. My guru, who taught me the secrets of the Shakta religion, would have approved of this. The Goddess calls out to you, me and everyone who can hear Her. It is as you said, She is the vitality that fills us with life. She is the supreme realisation that elevates our consciousness to a state of eternal joy. She is the energy in our limbs engaged in action. She is the action and she is the fruit of action, too. She is you. She is me. Honour Her call and put him to death, Krishna. Free Kamarupa from narrow-minded religious overlords."

Kadambari's sight blurred and she reached out to Vikrama who rushed to her side, preventing her from collapsing. Krishna leaned forward, stretching his arms to support hers. Kadambari steadied herself and smilingly said, "No, I was not possessed. I uttered every word completely conscious of what I was saying, Krishna. Tell me how my son and I can help you in this."

In her eyes, Krishna found the sparkle that he saw in the eye of every woman he knew. The sparkle that had been the source of his never-ending hope and faith. It made him smile. He looked at Vikrama and Kadambari and started to chart out his plan.

Chapter Forty-Five

Kamarupa

"That is the hill of Nilachala. The home of Goddess Kamaksha!" Three pairs of eyes looked at the distant hill capped by clouds. Kadambari smiled to herself. "It feels like it was yesterday that I escaped from there."

"Will they allow us inside if we say we are pilgrims?" Shyeni asked, stroking the mane of her mule absently, pondering their next move. Kadambari nodded, showing some caution. Instinctively, both the women turned to Vikrama who had become rather quiet since their meeting with Krishna and the Garudas. He nodded.

"We are not just pilgrims. We shall go as practitioners. I hope I am not recognised at the gates."

"How about we go separately?" Shyeni suggested. "Even if Kadambari is recognised, nobody knows me or Vikrama yet."

"We shall be together. Amba is good at weaving tales that are convincing even if someone suspects her," Vikrama remarked in a bland tone and rode ahead.

"What is it now?" Shyeni demanded, catching up with him.

Vikrama shook his head. "Just a thought, Kalabhashini." The reference of the name made Shyeni relax as Vikrama always referred to her voice when he was in a more relaxed mood. "I realised I was just being possessive about Abhaya. I was not ready to accept that anyone else could help her or befriend her to the extent that she calls out to him in her need and not to me. Well, she could not have known where I was then, but…" He paused to turn and check on Kadambari. The older woman, all through their journey together, had kept her distance when Shyeni attempted to converse with him. "My mother wouldn't approve of this protective attitude but then she never knew what my sister means to me." Shyeni nodded, not fully understanding what he meant to convey but she did feel the note of pain in his tone whenever he spoke of Abhaya. Vikrama shook his head again. "It stuns me, Kalabhashini. How could your brother let you go with me just like that? I mean, I was expecting some resistance and thinking of how to counter it. But then he just let you go!"

"He trusts me," Shyeni replied, shrugging. She was surprised at the sudden shift in topic, then her brows came together as she understood. "Do you mean to say if you were in his place and Abhaya in mine, you would not have let her go with her lover?"

Vikrama's lips parted and then closed. "I admit I would have resisted the idea. Not because I don't trust my sister, but…"

"You feel only you have the right over her and not anyone else, no matter what her feelings are in the matter. Am I right?" Shyeni said, knowing fully that Vikrama could not deny it. "Did you ever wonder what made me turn you away when you first wanted to wed me, Vikrama? It was this gap between what each of us feels about this right over the other. The commitment you promised at that moment came with an overwhelming demand that I give up my roots to come and live with you. It felt like a huge punishment for the sin of loving you. I realise I overreacted. But you did, too."

"I am trying not to think about what we will do after all this is over."

"By the time all this is over, both of us would have grown up enough to understand each other better and stand by each other. That is what matters about love, doesn't it, Vikrama?"

"What makes you so confident, Shyeni?"

"Don't you realise that by the time this is all over, we would have travelled the breadth of Bharatavarsha twice over? Travelling improves one's ability to understand multiple perspectives. I am so glad I decided to come, Vikrama. I have realised how big the world is and how different people are from each other. I learnt how you are unique among them."

"No, false praise is not what I need now," Vikrama said with a smile.

"Wait, it is not all praise that I have for you. I mean, it is for our good that we realise it. Love is not just about trusting each other's loyalty or respecting each other's freedom. It is also about trusting ourselves about what the other person means to us. Trust yourself, Vikrama; you will be able to trust me or Abhaya better then."

"Trust myself," Vikrama repeated and smiled to himself. "It will need some practice, I'm afraid. I shudder to think what Abhaya feels about my not being by her side in all the difficulties she has had to face. After all this, can I trust myself, Shyeni?"

"I agree, it isn't easy. But you will learn. My heart tells me that your sister will not be angry at you. From what you have told me about her, she doesn't sound like someone who would blame you for something that was not in your control, Vikrama. But, didn't we go off on a tangent?"

"That happens when Kalabhashini converses," Vikrama quipped. "For the moment, Krishna and Vainateya intrigue me. Can I ever be a Vainateya to Abhaya and a Krishna to you?"

"Just be yourself, Vikrama. That is enough for me. Learning from the world means that you become a better you, not change yourself into someone else."

They had reached the foot of Nilachala, and they reined in their mounts to let Kadambari take the lead.

"Dismount," she said, halting her mule. "And remember the story we have to weave."

The climb was steep and it was past sunset when they reached the fortress gates. Kadambari pointed at the great bell at the entrance, which Vikrama rang and a small window in the enormous gates of the fortress opened.

"We are Shaktas from the south of the Vindhyas! We need refuge!" Kadambari shouted. "Those in the plains have made our lives miserable. I seek shelter at the feet of the Supreme Goddess Kamaksha."

The window closed. The hinges creaked as the gates opened.

"I have come with my son and his yogini," Kadambari said, stepping inside. The guard raised his brows and let Vikrama and Shyeni inside.

"Wait here until the morning. You can speak to the lord then." The guard led them to a porch where they could spend the night.

"What now?" Shyeni looked at Vikrama. He shrugged, casting a glance at Kadambari. He attempted to stroll by the circular corridor inside the fort but was pushed back by another guard.

"Don't move from here until the lord hears you out in the morning." The voice was gruff and Shyeni had a good mind to give him a piece of her mind but was stopped by Kadambari's restraining hand.

"See what they have brought the temple of the Supreme Goddess to. It feels like She is their prisoner and not the Goddess that rules the universe!" she whispered out of the guard's earshot.

"I suppose Abhaya will be in the next circle within these walls?" Vikrama asked, looking at the dark curved corridor lit by flaming torches.

"It depends," Kadambari whispered. "I just hope she had the wisdom not to ally herself with those who openly challenge Bhauma."

Vikrama did not have the courage to ask what she meant. "She is diplomatic when the situation demands it, at least, more so than I am." He leaned against the wall, his heart racing.

"Tomorrow, I shall ask Bhauma to make you a soldier in his army. You will have better access to places where she is likely to be kept."

"Likely to be kept? You mean she is a prisoner?"

"They wouldn't exactly be giving her state honours for letting girls escape from their clutches at Kashi,"

Kadambari replied. She brought her finger to her lips as a guard passed by them. "Not much you can do tonight with these guards around."

Vikrama sighed and leaned back. Shyeni stared at him for a while and then at Kadambari, whose eyes were half-closed. They fully opened seeing the sudden resolve on Shyeni's face. Before Kadambari could react, Shyeni got up and walked to the guard. "Can you please let us inside? We are very cold here. We can sleep in the temple tonight."

Kadambari hit her forehead with her hand. "This one is going to land us in trouble!" Vikrama clutched his sword and rose to his feet, gauging the guard's response.

Kadambari whispered urgently, "That is Senapati Mura! He knows me. What shall I do now?"

Mura walked up to them, led by Shyeni. Recognition dawned in his eyes when he saw Kadambari. But his tone, when he spoke, was measured. "What brought you back here?" he asked, his expression unreadable.

Kadambari was at a loss for words, remembering the vehemence with which she had spoken against the temple town and about Bhauma before leaving Kamarupa years before.

"We had to come here," Vikrama stepped in. "We are fleeing the plains. Life has become difficult for Shaktas there."

Mura considered him and Kadambari for a couple of moments. Vikrama saw his brows come together. He looked like he wanted to say something but, when he finally spoke, all he said was, "You will have to wait for the lord's decision tomorrow."

"I thought he would be angry to see me back after what I told him that day about his 'lord'," Kadambari commented as they settled back at the porch. "Something has changed. I wish I knew more."

"Hmm…" Bhauma said, nodding in sympathy as Kadambari dished out the tale she had woven with a few calculated additions. "But why did you leave Kamarupa then? You said you were here the day when the mahayogini was chosen by Devi Kamaksha herself."

"I had left my son behind," Kadambari replied. "But even when I was away, we practised the Shakta ways."

"I don't trust them, Prabho!" Mura interjected and Kadambari looked at him in dismay. Mura avoided her eyes. "They could be spies."

"Of whom?" Vikrama demanded. He then lowered his tone and addressed Bhauma humbly, "Prabho, the Shaktas are being hounded by the soldiers across Bharatavarsha. There is also a campaign going on in the continent now. There is this new king from some northern province who wants to declare himself as the emperor of all of the land. If you doubt your own, there will soon be nothing left of the Shakta order."

Bhauma leaned back in his seat.

"I can't take all of that on face value, whoever you are," Mura said. "As the senapati, I cannot allow them in here, Prabho. I have my doubts."

"Quiet!" Bhauma snapped. He cast a lingering look upon Shyeni, which made Vikrama clench his fists behind his back.

"My son can be a good soldier. We shall not be a burden on Kamarupa, Prabho!" Kadambari knelt before Bhauma.

"Soldier? What next? The position of the senapati himself probably!" Mura sneered.

Bhauma looked at Vikrama and then back at Shyeni, who smiled at him and his lips pursed in response. "What a way to treat another Shakta in this temple of Shakti, Senapati!" Bhauma said. "Where has your compassion gone?" He sneered at the contempt in Mura's eyes.

"I am duty-bound to ensure the safety of Kamarupa," Mura replied. "Prabho, compassion is your forte, isn't it?" Mura's eyes carried the contempt that only Bhauma could comprehend.

"It's good that you remember your place," Bhauma replied, meeting his eye. "Yes, you are duty-bound. You may go now."

Mura left, discreetly meeting Kadambari's gaze who saw no hostility in them. Her brows rose in surprise.

"What a hard-hearted man!" Shyeni chirped after Mura left. "You will have pity on us I hope, Prabho!"

"Who can be that hard-hearted with a woman?" Bhauma commented, smiling down at her.

"Why is the woman kneeling?" The voice behind him made Bhauma turn and he motioned for Kadambari to rise to her feet.

He stood. "Mahayogini Dhatri, the chosen one by Goddess Kamaksha," he announced as he bowed low to Dhatri. Kadambari did the same. Vikrama's hands came together though his head stayed high. "These are Shaktas from the south of the Vindhyas, seeking refuge at the feet of the Supreme Goddess."

"Welcome," Dhatri smiled.

Vikrama was surprised by the warmth in her smile.

Bhauma continued, "Their lives, they say, are rendered miserable by the Arya lords. Not a new story, is it Mahadevi? Pray, take pity on them."

Dhatri looked at Kadambari. "There is no need for a Shakta woman to kneel before a man," she remarked. "How much do you know of the Shakta ways?"

"My mother has practised it for the last seventeen years. I was initiated recently," Vikrama replied. "So was my wife . . . uh ... yogini," he corrected, looking at Shyeni.

Dhatri nodded and beckoned them towards the temple. "The Supreme Goddess shall see that no harm befall you. Are you willing to dedicate your lives to Her?"

Kadambari nodded and walked towards the temple, followed by Vikrama and Shyeni.

Dhatri continued to speak, "Would you then help me in training the uninitiated girls here ... you are..."

"Kadambari. Yes, I would be glad to impart what is true Shaktism to anyone."

"I would love to welcome a senior teacher like you to Kamarupa. Something tells me that the Supreme Goddess sent you here."

Kadambari nodded. "Supreme Goddess." She paused, smiling to herself, "Her ways are indeed strange."

Shyeni and Vikrama followed them at a distance and observed the temple. The sanctum, Vikrama hoped, carried the power that would put down the likes of Bhauma soon and show his sister. After the darshan, they reached Dhatri's residence when she turned to stop him. "This home is for women, Vikrama. You can rest for today in one of the rooms in the outer corridor."

Chapter Forty-Six

"Who wins and who loses today? A total of eighty coins at stake!" a guard quipped, throwing up a small pouch of coins and catching it midair.

"This gets more unpredictable each day!" another laughed.

Vikrama, who had been sharpening his javelin, looked up at the banter. It was six days since he had arrived at Kamarupa and he was yet to find Abhaya. Kadambari had confirmed that she was not in the inner circle. It was not possible for either of them to search for her in the central ring of Kamarupa without causing suspicion.

"She has eaten yesterday. Greater odds that she will not today."

"Well, it is not like she eats on alternate days only. People have lost betting on that."

"I can bet only two coins today. I haven't been really lucky with predicting the moods of the 'younger mahadevi'."

"Who is this younger mahadevi?" Vikrama enquired.

"That's just what we call this troublesome girl who is unduly favoured by the mahadevi."

"Mahadevi has been gracious to feed and lodge that obstinate girl," the other guard added.

"Do you want to place your bets too about whether this girl eats her meal today or not?"

"Don't!" the other guard warned. "You'll lose your hard-earned wealth! The girl is unpredictable."

"Why should someone go without her meal?"

"We thought she was atoning for the sin of deceiving the Supreme Goddess and driving some other yoginis away from Kamarupa. The Goddess indeed was outraged. All the girls died."

"One survived," one of the guards corrected.

The narrator nodded. "But it turns out that she is just obstinate and likes to test Mahadevi's patience and compassion."

"It is only a matter of time before Lord Bhauma loses his patience and punishes her as she deserves to be."

Vikrama's heart beat faster. He resumed sharpening the tip of his javelin.

Could it be her?

The knock on the door signalled the arrival of her evening meal, which was delivered by the female guard. Abhaya threw the key out of the window and the door opened. She turned away and heard a sigh from the woman, presumably at the untouched food. Though she had given up the idea of fasting, food was now only a means to survive. Her solitary condition devoid of any physical activity had killed her appetite and Abhaya's food habits had become erratic.

The sound of the door locking made Abhaya turn, instinctively alert. The food was placed in a large earthen bowl in the usual place. Yet, something was amiss.

"The key!" the guard had not thrown it back.

Abhaya rushed towards the locked door to call the woman back. None responded to her call. She wondered if Dhatri had changed her mind or if Bhauma had taken things into his hands. The scimitar that Dhatri had let her keep, she realised, would be of little use in case of a fight.

The hours following sunset increased her restlessness. She had to struggle to fight sleep and stay alert. The night seemed never-ending and she found it increasingly difficult to keep her eyes open. From the gap in the door, she strained to track the movement of the moon. At dawn, she would call out to Dhatri about the key.

Suddenly, there was the sound of a key turning in the lock. She stiffened. She moved towards the door, still wondering how she could take on an opponent with her primitive weapon. *It has to be Bhauma*, she thought. The presence outside the door, Abhaya felt, was not of a woman.

She crouched in the shadows as moonlight flooded the room. Abhaya considered making a dive towards the door but he was quick to close the door. She held her breath as he came closer. The room was thankfully dark and Abhaya hoped that when he didn't find her in bed, he would panic and rush to raise an alarm, leaving the door open long enough for her to slip out. She inched her way towards the other corner, guessing the direction he would take. As he moved away, she rose to her feet. But, before she could move, his hand wound around her frame from behind and his other hand closed around her mouth. The touch, she realised, was familiar and she froze in her attempts to resist.

"Is it you?"

"*Bhrata*!" Abhaya turned and wound her hands around his neck. "By Mahakala, tell me this isn't a dream!"

They held each other close. Their silence spoke more eloquently than words, letting each know the joy, sorrow and pain of the other.

"How did you get into Kamarupa? And how did you manage to find the key?"

"My mother. She managed to get us inside and also got this key, offering to 'counsel' you tomorrow."

"So, you found her!?"

"It's a long story," Vikrama whispered, glancing at the door. "I found her and also found out what happened to Pingala and the more sinister Shakta plots. But … I failed you and father. What did he say about me? Was I fortunate enough to be at least cursed by him or was…"

Abhaya's hand on his cheek made him stop. "Don't you know him, Bhrata?"

Another spell of silence followed, Vikrama realising his folly in fearing Abhaya's anger. Each tried to talk and then gave up knowing time was a luxury. The details of their story since Vikrama had left Anagha in search of his mother would have to wait.

Finally, Abhaya found her voice. "What now?"

"It will all be over soon, Abhaya. We shall leave this all behind," Vikrama said, still holding her close. "Your Vaasudeva is coming for you. His Garuda friends are not far from Kamarupa."

"So the messenger was for real!" Abhaya exclaimed softly.

Vikrama looked at her questioningly but there was no time to make deeper enquiries.

"Following Krishna's plan, I came in here posing as a Shakta, with my mother and … Shyeni. I'll tell you about her later. One of us needs to escape soon with information about the defences and weaponry here. If possible, Krishna wants to secure inside help to avert a violent skirmish."

"To avert a skirmish," Abhaya repeated and fell into a thoughtful silence before she said, "Only Dhatri can do that. Senapati Mura gave me a way to escape but I let five other women go instead and..."

"I heard of that." Vikrama's hands again went around her, sensing her distress doubling at the memory.

"Dhatri needs to realise Bhauma's a fraud! Mura too could help us if he is not still outraged about what I did. But nothing much is possible without Dhatri getting to know the truth of Bhauma." She clutched his arm suddenly. "You would never approve of this. But it is our only way. Just hear me out fully first."

Vikrama paled hearing what she had to say. It took him a couple of moments to digest her plan. He was caught between anxiety at her scheme and admiration for her ability to strategise even in her present dire condition. "Does it need to come to that?"

Abhaya's stoic silence made him steel his heart. He swallowed and focused his thoughts on the plan. "Can you keep him off until Shyeni can get to Krishna and they attack Kamarupa? It could take a good couple of days."

"Let me see," Abhaya said, her grip on Vikrama's hand tightening for a moment.

"Abhaya," Vikrama said in a sudden burst of finality. "Leave this. You know of an escape route. Let us all go out this very moment. I shall break that lock of the passage and take care of the guards who might come in. Let the armies of Indraprastha tear down this place in the course of their conquest. We've done more than enough by alerting them about the heinous fraud here. Let us head back home." He tried to rise but stopped as Abhaya showed no inclination to follow.

"Which home, Bhrata?"

"The home where your brother was not by your side when you needed him. He will give his everything to rebuild it."

"No. Making you feel guilty wasn't my point, Bhrata. But our home isn't just Anagha. Our home is anywhere that civilisation stands by dharma. Our home is the whole of Bharatavarsha. I know it sounds unrealistic and idealistic. But if I only wanted to escape, I would have done it long before. We cannot choose to run away now. I want to wait for Krishna. I want to give this whole thing the closure it deserves. This isn't about Bhauma's wayward religion, Bhrata. This is about what we learnt and believed and about what sustained the spirit of our ancestors ever since the beginning of time. This is about our Bharatavarsha. Let us stay till the end."

"Wait, am I hearing right?" Bhauma snapped. "You say you have changed your mind and are ready to accept the ways of Vamachara?"

Abhaya smiled, drawing patterns on the ground with the scimitar. "On a condition."

"I heard that. Know this, Yuvati—you are delusional if you think I would give up on the mahadevi for your stupidity."

Abhaya sighed and leaned back against the wall. "It's your loss, Prabho, if you think of forethought as stupidity. For your grand vision, a younger and more capable partner would suit you better than an old complacent idealist like her."

Bhauma stepped forward and gripped her neck. "You know nothing about what you're playing with!"

"And you know nothing about how many more decades you will need to wait before your plan fructifies!" Abhaya managed to spit out, fighting the suffocation.

Bhauma shoved her against the wall. Abhaya's upper garment fell from her shoulder. She made no attempt to set it right.

"The mahadevi will resist every move of yours with double the caution now. Things are no easier in the plains. I am a princess who knows the political dynamics of the plains well. Would you still prefer her over me, Bhauma?"

Bhauma's brow furrowed. "What do you know about the politics of the plains?"

"What do you seek to know?" Abhaya smiled and sighed. "Besides, you will do better with a mahadevi who knows your heart than with one whose heart is with that stone in the temple." Abhaya put on a practised smile, cautiously placing a hand on his chest.

Bhauma's breathing became heavier. He caught Abhaya by both shoulders, pinning her against the wall.

"You need some wine," Abhaya smiled. "And a night of contemplation. I am not running away anywhere."

Bhauma dug his fingers into her heaped hair and the loose bun gave way, her long tresses falling over her shoulders. His struggle against his impulses was visible. "I am past the phase of falling for youthful charms, Yuvati," he chuckled.

"You should give my intellect an opportunity. Trust me, Bhauma, I shall..." Abhaya consciously modulated her tone, "raise the religion of Shakti to a pedestal you haven't seen in the past."

Bhauma's gaze lingered over her frame. He took a step back and raised a finger. "Don't try to get smart with me. You will regret it."

She laughed.

Bhauma left the room without a word, showing her the key to the lock which he did not intend to throw back to her.

Abhaya sank to the floor. This effectively made her his prisoner. She swallowed, steeling herself.

If my attempt can derail Bhauma, it is worth dying for!

Dhatri took in the view from her western window. The sight of crimson skies during the time of sunset usually had a soothing effect on her. But today, the skies were covered with clouds from all directions.

"Looks like it might pour anytime. Are the children indoors?" she asked a guard who promptly left to check. The guards knew Dhatri's affection towards Mauri and Nandini. When the guard did not return for some time, Dhatri walked out of her chambers. Not finding the girls in the courtyard or the temple premises, she entered Bhauma's residence and found him seated on his regal swing.

"Welcome, Mahadevi. I was about to come to you."

"Have you seen the children?" Dhatri asked him.

"It is not yet their mealtime," Bhauma said with a smile.

"I haven't seen them or heard them in a while. Did Mura, by any chance…?"

"Mahadevi, you worry too much. They are safe. I have seen them safe." Bhauma laughed, opening his arms. Dhatri smiled in relief and stepped closer into his embrace. "At times, I wonder if I have robbed you of your peace by thrusting the heavy burden of being the mahayogini on to you."

Dhatri's eyes closed for a while and she sighed. "How is the service to the Supreme Goddess a burden, Bhauma?"

"Maybe you have done enough," Bhauma replied, his arms tightening while leading her into the adjoining room. "I think you should appoint a successor soon."

Dhatri looked up at the sudden suggestion. He had never mentioned a successor before. "Isn't that the choice of the Goddess? How can I choose the next mahadevi? Bhauma, what do you… "

Dhatri's words came to a halt as she stepped into the room where she saw Abhaya, dressed in saffron, seated cross-legged on the wooden pedestal that used to be her seat. Abhaya smiled and rose to her feet. Dhatri saw Bhauma exchange a glance with Abhaya.

"You have the successor ready in front of you, Dhatri." Bhauma extended his hand and Abhaya stepped forward.

In her shock, Dhatri did not notice Abhaya's jaw clench as Bhauma's hand rested on her bare shoulder.

"How can you or I choose her, Bhauma? The decision is neither yours nor mine to make. And she, of all people?" Dhatri protested, brushing aside the uncomfortable thoughts that crept into her mind.

"You are the Goddess, aren't you? You can make the decision," Bhauma replied, his eyes narrowing as he gripped Dhatri's arm, jerking her closer. Dhatri's eyes turned wrathful. But the worst was yet to come. "The children will be kept safe if you do!"

Abhaya cast a glance at Bhauma when he mentioned Mauri and Nandini. Dhatri turned to her, narrowing her eyes in contempt.

"So, this is the grandiose civilisation you were talking of!"

"Looks like she is going to give us trouble, Prabho," Abhaya remarked, turning to Bhauma, trying to sound as bland as she could.

"Don't you worry," Bhauma said.

Without a change in expression, he shoved Dhatri against the wall and reached out to a lever. The impact made Abhaya realise that the portion of the floor where Dhatri stood at the moment was actually made of wood. As Bhauma turned the lever, the wood below Dhatri slanted, casting her into a hidden underground cellar.

"You have until morning to make up your mind," Bhauma said with the same dispassion and turned back the lever. The wooden floor fell neatly back into place, leaving practically no trace in the floor pattern of the cellar below.

Dhatri was not yet out of shock even after she landed on the floor of an underground cellar.

What kind of a nightmare is this? By the Goddess Kamaksha! Did he just threaten me about harming those children if I didn't appoint that obstinate girl as the mahadevi?

She sat in a daze for a long time. When she recovered, she was seething with rage.

"Curse you, Bhauma! Curse you!" Her voice echoed against the walls of the dark chamber.

A groan caught her attention as she realised that she wasn't alone in the cellar. As her eyes adjusted to the darkness, she looked keenly in the direction of the sound.

"Who is that?"

The groan, which seemed to come from a woman, wounded again and Dhatri made her way through the darkness and stumbled upon a couple of steps. What she saw there froze her in her steps.

Chapter Forty-Seven

Krishna saw the clouds gathering in the skies. "We should scale the mountains before it gets too slippery to climb," he said to himself but loud enough for Vainateya to hear.

"The group of thirty Garudas who shall breach the fort from the rear passage will leave immediately," Vainateya replied. "Shyeni will go with them."

"Hope Vikrama and Kadambari can cover for Shyeni's absence there. She seems to possess an energy that we can only hope to have," Krishna said with a smile. "Or is the source of her energy currently at Kamarupa?"

"Can I say the same applies to you too?" Vainateya chuckled and then added seriously, "We are ready, Krishna. We can march now despite the darkness."

"We should. The rains might start anytime. But we should be able to shelter ourselves and the horses at the foothills. Can we scale the hill against the slippery rains?"

"You are talking to the lord of a mountain tribe, my friend," Vainateya laughed. "How dare you doubt the ability of my Garudas in scaling this hill?"

"I am talking about facing a three-hundred-strong guard with barely a hundred Garudas, Vainateya. Now, of course, you will say one Garuda is equal to ten men."

"And rightly so, Krishna. Now before you get into your minimum loss of life theory, give us the nod to march ahead."

"Very soon," Krishna replied.

A peculiar shift in his tone made Vainateya look at him. Lightning flashed in the skies in that instant and what he saw in Krishna's eyes made Vainateya's heart skip a beat.

The king of Garudas hesitated for a moment, then laid a hand on Krishna's shoulder. "I shall call them all to be ready."

Bhauma leaned forward as he poured wine into the bronze goblet and frowned as he emptied it down his throat.

"I hope you are convinced now," he said.

Abhaya smiled, gripping the chains that fastened the wooden plank of the swing to the high ceiling of the hallway.

"Nobody has ever dared to put forth conditions to Bhauma. You did, and not just any condition. You demanded to become the mahayogini. Dhatri has never questioned me until now."

"Well, I am not Dhatri." Abhaya's words were sharp. "For the ambition you have, I already told you that you need someone younger and wiser to run this show, Bhauma." Her lips curved as Bhauma looked up. "You will anyway insist that I address you by name. I might as well start doing that right now."

"There is something about your irreverence..." Bhauma said, his eyes narrowing. "But now that you are convinced…"

"Not yet." Abhaya caught his hand that reached around her waist. "I mean, there are questions in my mind. About whom I can trust and whom I can't. The senapati, for instance."

"He won't dream of harming us as long as his daughter is with us," Bhauma replied and moved closer, clutching her arms.

It took her some effort to keep the smile on her face. "Now listen to my two pieces of information, lord of Kamarupa. You will need a better strategy to control the world now. The method of sending waves of brainwashed practitioners to exploit the dissent among the 'oppressed', I am afraid, might not work for long."

Bhauma knitted his brows. "And why do you think so?"

"The powers of Arya dharma are consolidating, Bhauma," Abhaya replied. "The fault lines that your network of Shaktas exploited all these days might not exist in a couple of years from today. It will become more and more difficult to convince people they are being victimised." Abhaya continued to smile at his frown. "The codes defining trade and governance will be made uniform across Bharatavarsha. Regaining and retaining social equity, while ushering in a new wave of prosperity, will be the aim of the new empire. The matter of balancing religion with rationality too will enter public discourse. Do you think it will be easy to pay some imbecile to act crippled and then fake a miracle? In other words, how will you convince the aspirational citizen of Bharatavarsha that he is a victim?"

"Governance. Social equity. Prosperity. Aspirations," Bhauma laughed. "It will be a long time before they are all achieved, Abhaya. We have a lot of ways to derail this new empire. The Supreme Goddess Kamaksha shall show us the way." His brows rose upon seeing Abhaya's frown. "Errr … that, I spoke out of habit with Dhatri," he laughed and resumed. "Until now we were only sending those who preach the benevolence of Shaktism against the civilisation of the Aryas. But now we can take a different route. I know how to influence the places where the children of these Aryas go to get their education. We shall start there. We shall influence the way the younger Aryas see their ancestors. Their current faith in their civilisation is based on their glorious history where the unjust and unrighteous are always defeated. What if that premise were to be questioned?"

"You'll need to explain what you mean, Bhauma."

Bhauma brought a finger to her cheek, tracing her jawline with a fingernail. "Education, Abhaya. You will see apologetic Aryas themselves handing the land to us on a platter. You are smart enough to understand."

"Education. The gurukulas." It dawned on Abhaya what Bhauma was aiming to achieve. The thought left her too dazed to stop Bhauma from undoing the knot of her heaped hair. Her tresses fell over her shoulders, jerking her into consciousness.

"I wanted to ask you, Abhaya. What made you change your mind all of a sudden?"

Abhaya sighed at the sudden question. "What do you think, Bhauma? I had figured it out when you had left me alone in confinement. It helped to be away from that annoying preaching by Dhatri." Abhaya wanted to tie her hair back, but with Bhauma dangerously close to her, she only pushed her long tresses over her shoulders. "I think it is almost dawn."

"How does that make a difference?" Bhauma chuckled. "Even the sun does not dare disturb the lord of Kamarupa in his private moments."

Abhaya held the edges of the plank as his arms caught her frame again. She considered taking out her weapon when footsteps caught their attention. To Bhauma's surprise, Mura entered, followed by two uncertain guards.

"How, in the name of the Goddess, have you dared to defy my orders about not entering the inner circle!"

It was Mura's turn to be shocked when he saw Abhaya by Bhauma's side. But her relieved expression at his entry spoke more than he needed to know. He thrust a scroll at Bhauma. "Kamarupa is under attack, Prabho." Abhaya thanked all the gods and goddesses above.

Bhauma opened the scroll and his frown became more intense. "Krishna Vaasudeva? That trickster who was behind the death of Jarasandha of Magadha!"

"It may be possible that he knows your designs, Prabho. It is evident from what he demands. And grant me leave from your services!"

Bhauma glowered at the jibe. He told the two guards to summon all the soldiers and archers in the inner fortress.

"I shall wait in the mahayogini's chambers." Abhaya rose to her feet, only to be pulled back by Bhauma.

"You, Mura, will not let anyone enter the fortress if you value the lives of your daughter and Dhatri."

"Dhatri, too?" The horror in Mura's eyes increased as he turned to Abhaya who gave him an almost imperceptible nod.

"Yes, my dear Mura, so, your daughter has been starving with no food and water for a whole day. If you want me to feed her, go and kill that invader."

Abhaya could barely conceal her horror.

Mura advanced upon Bhauma and caught him by the throat. "Bhauma! Let them go."

Bhauma shoved him away and reached for his sword. "Even if you kill me, Mura, you will not find where they are concealed. Who knows what can happen to the children by the time you reach them. They can die of thirst or fear of darkness or suffocation." Mura stepped back, still in shock. "My dearest friend, I can release them, and you too. But I will do so only if you can thwart this enemy. This invader should not escape alive! Kill him and your daughter will be free. I mean it."

Abhaya's blood ran cold seeing helplessness replace the rage in Mura's eyes. She had never seen Mura in action but his frame and gait were that of a hardened warrior. Her heart dreaded to think about the result if he duelled with Krishna to save his only daughter. Mura stepped back, sheathing his sword. He shook a warning finger at Bhauma and cast a glare in her direction. She could save the situation if only she got to know where Bhauma had kept Mauri and her companion Nandini. After Mura exited, she forced a smile onto her lips and turned to Bhauma.

"Will he not turn and deceive you, Bhauma?"

In response, she saw Bhauma's lips twitch as he chuckled. "It is not he that I am worried about."

"But are you sure that girl is out of his reach?"

Before he could respond, guards poured in and Bhauma called the archers to step forward. "Stand by the high-rise platforms on both sides of the inner gates. Shoot at whomever enters."

Among the guards, Abhaya sighted Vikrama and gave him a discreet signal, indicating the archers. Her dishevelled hair made his heart miss a beat. But Vikrama steadied himself, trusting her poised demeanour. Between him and Kadambari, who he knew was experienced with the sword, they had quite a bit of work to do if they had to take care of the archers as Abhaya indicated.

As the guards left, Bhauma turned to her, the smile returning to his face. "You wanted to know where Mauri is. Come with me." Abhaya followed Bhauma as he unlocked an inconspicuous door, camouflaged by the art painted on it with dark colours. The door did not creak as he opened it and showed her in. It was a small chamber that had nothing except for a trapdoor in the floor.

Abhaya sighed. "So that is where they are."

In the dim light, she could see Bhauma nod but his expression was not clear to her. When she turned back to exit the chamber, his hand wound around her waist, hauling her back into the room.

"You really thought you could fool me, didn't you?"

"What? What are you talking about?" Abhaya protested only to be shoved towards the wall.

Bhauma laughed, closing the door behind him. "Let me first thank you for ridding me of Dhatri's burden. You were right—she was slowing my plans down." His eyes narrowed. "Your abrupt change of mind, your driving that wedge between Dhatri and me and this attack now. Do you take me for a fool?"

Abhaya was not unprepared for this. Something in his manner had kept her defences up. She breathed in and responded with an aimed kick at his groin. Bhauma, though, was prepared for resistance and caught her leg midway. Her fists landed on his side and he stepped back. Abhaya too took a few steps to stay out of his reach and took out her scimitar. She saw him move towards the door and sneer. "Keep the kids engaged."

The very moment she realised that she was on the trapdoor, it gave way!

Chapter Forty-Eight

Krishna looked up at the fortress wall and the towering figure of the commander of Kamarupa.

"A temple town with three layers of fortification and an army too. I wonder how the kings of neighbouring kingdoms did not smell foul play."

Vainateya nodded but his attention was elsewhere. He was estimating the gap between what looked like niches on the wall. Formed because of an occasional brick or a stone falling due to a natural impact, they were irregular.

"Unless the neighbouring kings of Pundra, Pragjyotisha and Shonita also see a benefit in letting this Bhauma carry on with his activities," Krishna concluded. "Vainateya, do you see what I see?"

The king of Garudas caught Krishna's shoulder, pointing to a bushy growth from the gaps in the walls of the fortress. "If we can get there ... but the gap between the lower niche and the growth is way too..." When Krishna turned to him nodding, he saw Vainateya's face clear. "Krishna, didn't you adopt the symbol of our divine eagle Suparna as your war banner? For that mark of friendship, you will have the privilege of riding on an 'eagle' too today." He dug his hands into the sack that hung from his shoulder and took out two metallic claws. The claws were a Garuda invention, driven by their passion for mountaineering.

Krishna gave the signal to those on his right and at the wave of his hand, huge balls of an inflammable mixture were lighted with flaming torches and hurled at the gates. The guards of Kamarupa rallied in two lines, one behind Mura on the fortress wall, pointing their javelins at the advancing Garudas, and the other behind the outer wall, steady with their shields. About twenty Garudas advanced with clubs, roaring, braving the javelins and the impact was felt on the gates of Kamarupa. The inflammable balls burnt and gave them a smoky cover, blinding the defending guards above. Vainateya and Krishna sprinted towards the left side of the fortress, followed by ten more Garudas. Judging the momentum, Vainateya lifted Krishna by his waist and let him balance his knees over his shoulders before he placed his foot over the first niche. The metallic claws helped him find a grip over the next niche even as his frame shook under Krishna's weight.

"For Suparna! For Mahavishnu! For the sustenance of the universe!" Vainateya shouted the Garuda slogan and lifted himself over the niches.

"Higher, Vainateya!" Krishna shouted, rising and balancing his feet over Vainateya's shoulders. Vainateya obliged and shouted back that he had come to the last niche he could spot. Krishna hauled himself to the thick bushy growth. He saw the relieved Garuda king claw into another gap, vigorously carving a new niche. Krishna's foot balanced over the shrub and his right hand reached up to the edge of the bastion wall. He held his sword in his teeth to hold the edge with his left hand as well. A foot stamped on his right hand. Krishna's jaw clenched at the pain. A javelin then cut into his hand. He looked up and met Mura's piercing gaze.

Mura saw Krishna gasp as he twisted the javelin that had pierced his right hand. But, instead of pain, he saw defiance that glared back through Krishna's eyes even as blood oozed out of his hands. Even with the sword clenched between his teeth, Krishna's lips curved in a smile that tugged at Mura's conscience and, before he knew what he was doing, Mura had pulled him up over the fort wall. "Who do you seek here? Flee from here if you value your life ... Vaasudeva, is that your name?"

"What if I do not?" Krishna replied, taking the sword in his right hand. "What if the value of my life is based on how I respond to the cry I hear out of this fortress?"

"That smile of yours can lure any other girl into your arms. Why would you be foolish enough to walk to your death for someone here?"

"So that I can retain that smile," Krishna quipped. "Now that you are engaging me in a dialogue, why do you defend the peddlers of untruth, Senapati? You look too honourable for that."

"None of your business!" Mura snapped. "I spared your life hoping to make you see the foolishness in challenging the seat of the Supreme Goddess!"

"I am not challenging the seat of the Supreme Goddess. I only want to knock some sense into those siding with untruth in her name. If you are one doing so, it is perfectly my business, Senapati." The blood dripped from Krishna's hand and Mura saw his unaffected smile. "Leave the side of untruth and dishonest religiosity, and come over to my side, Senapati."

"All that Senapati Mura can give you, given your refusal to leave, is an honourable death." Mura gritted his teeth and pointed his javelin at Krishna.

Krishna placed his sword in its way and winked. "Let us see which one of us has the smile to lure the maiden of death." His sword rose, shining against the rising sun and Krishna launched his attack. Mura's javelin locked the sword as Krishna grinned. "And who among us can convince her to return some other day."

Mura drove his javelin towards Krishna's neck. Krishna ducked, arching his back and, catching the weapon midway with his left hand, he drove his blade towards Mura's side. Mura drew back the javelin to defend the move. The impact was harder than he had expected and the weapon broke, hit by the sharper edge of the sword.

Five guards came to Mura's aid. From the corner of his eye, Krishna saw Vainateya climb up the fortress wall and engage Mura. Two more Garudas followed Vainateya and three more guards came to Mura's defence. In the fight that followed, the Garudas, though outnumbered, managed to get the upper hand. Another guard launched himself at Krishna, driving his javelin into his shoulder. Withstanding the excruciating pain, Krishna kicked at the guard, simultaneously driving his sword into the guard's belly. Two more guards charged at him as he rose to his feet and pinned him against the wall. Krishna ducked in a swift move, cutting through a guard's leg and pulled the other guard to the ground.

Mura charged at one of the Garudas with renewed fury, pushing him off the fortress and turned towards Krishna. "Call off the fight, Vaasudeva, if you don't want to see more of your men fall." Before Krishna could reply, Vainateya smashed a guard's head with the club he had snatched from him and roared, hitting another guard fatally on the back. The gates then gave in with a crash, catching everyone's attention.

Mura sneered in response. "A bare fifty against two hundred. What do you hope to achieve other than give us some scavenging trouble and a feast for vultures?"

"Six to one!" Vainateya shouted in response, slamming the third guard's head against a wall.

"Scavenge your conscience instead, Mura," Krishna responded, his eyes gathering a fury that made Mura step back. Conscience was not one of the things he could afford on this day, despite his heart not being in the fight. But the words landed on his ears as hard as the blows of a club.

"Enough!" Mura shouted, looking at Krishna and then at the Garudas. "This will be a fight to the death just between the both of us!"

Krishna exchanged a glance with Vainateya and turned to Mura. "So be it."

Throwing away the broken javelin, Mura drew out his double-edged sword, the same length as Krishna's but wider. The metal of their swords clashed in rapid succession, each attack parried or met by the other. The sun rose in the eastern sky and the intensity of the duel grew. Blood dripped from the wounds of both and neither showed signs of fatigue. Mura withdrew his blade and charged again, this time aiming directly for Krishna's chest. Krishna nimbly turned aside and the weapon grazed the skin of his arm. Krishna aimed the next blow at Mura's sword in a swift move, partially upsetting the latter's grip. Mura caught Krishna's sword with his bare left hand and, with sheer brute strength, parried the blow while retrieving his weapon from the ground. While holding back Krishna's sword, he cut his weapon across Krishna's legs, making him jump to escape the blow. Krishna landed on the ground, dangerously close to the edge of the fortress wall.

Another blow by Mura was aimed at his neck. Krishna's sword came in between, giving him the edge to arch over his side and, in the deadlock, Mura kicked hard at his side, succeeding in disturbing Krishna's balance. He rolled over to the safer side, escaping another attack and drove his sword towards Mura's side, injuring him. Roaring in pain, Mura pulled out Krishna's sword, fighting the resistance and charged again.

Abhaya's eyes opened as she heard a voice. The impact of the fall had stunned her and she could not tell how long she had been unconscious. Mauri's cry jolted her into consciousness and she saw the child almost in a faint in the dark cellar while Nandini lay motionless by her side.

"Mauri! Nandini!" Abhaya gasped, shaking Nandini. Mauri was the first to respond.

"Take me to my father! Bhauma will kill us!" The child burst into sobs and threw her arms around Abhaya who embraced her back, glancing at Nandini.

"I shall not let anyone harm you, Vatse. We'll escape from here!" Unable to revive Nandini, she lifted the younger child over her shoulders and looked around. Bhauma's mansion had too many mysterious, hidden chambers. A thought struck her when she saw a broken piece of what could have been a table by a corner. Placing Nandini back on the ground, she dragged the table towards the opening and climbed on the broken top. The trapdoor could be opened only from outside and she could not find a way to pull it down. Abhaya then took out her scimitar and drove the edge against the wood, which started to give way. The splinters flew, one hitting her close to the eye. Undeterred, Abhaya continued to chip at the wood, wishing she had a sharper weapon. She drove the scimitar into the newly formed wedge, hoping to pull the trapdoor open.

At the very instant, the remnant of the already broken table collapsed under her weight, landing her back on the floor with a thud. Abhaya kicked at the leg of the broken table in frustration, sending it to crash into the wall. The sound made her start. The wall also seemed to be of wood! Pulling herself up, Abhaya felt the wall, hitting it at various places. It seemed like a partition made of wood dividing a large cellar into two.

"Stand back, and pull Nandini back too!" Abhaya told Mauri, picking up a large piece of the broken table and summoning all her strength to slam it against the wooden partition. The impact was in vain, however, and she knelt on the ground, catching her breath before hitting it again. As she prepared her next blow, she heard a sound. Someone was hitting the partition from the other side. *Dhatri!* The blows then repeated in succession and portions of the partitions weakened gradually. Abhaya persisted despite her fatigue. Another blow was heard from the other side and, suddenly, the wood splintered. She collapsed onto her knees again and saw the partition give away under one more blow.

Dhatri stood on the other side, having demolished the partition. Mauri ran to her crying and Abhaya lifted the still-unconscious Nandini.

"I wanted you to see Bhauma's truth, Dhatri. I never wanted to be any mahayogini," she pleaded but the cold fury in Dhatri's eyes didn't abate. The older woman pulled her by the arm into the other part of the chamber where Abhaya found women bound to pillars or chained to rings on the wall. In the dim light, Abhaya could see a woman's mauled body lying by a wall. She gently placed Nandini aside and rushed to the woman to feel her pulse.

She stared mutely in horror. Dhatri, she could see, was equally disturbed.

"These were the women who had insisted on returning to their homes in past," Dhatri said, her voice full of pain and anger. "Bhauma had me believe they were sent away!"

"They are alive!" Abhaya gasped. She gathered herself and then turned to the older woman. "Dhatri, Bhauma's days are numbered. Kamarupa is under attack. But you can stop the battle and save the innocent guards of Kamarupa and the soldiers on the other side." Dhatri stared at her, unmoved. "Dhatri, your people look upon you as the mahayogini who is the medium of the Supreme Goddess! You can pronounce Bhauma guilty. The soldiers would listen to you."

Dhatri seemed to consider though the anger in her eyes remained unchanged. She then shook her head. "The position of mahayogini is all fake! I am no medium of any Goddess!"

"The soldiers still think so! Other practitioners at Kamarupa still consider you as the supreme authority!"

Abhaya exclaimed. "Dhatri, the one attacking Bhauma is none other than my dearest friend Krishna Vaasudeva. Bhauma compelled Mura to fight him holding Mauri as ransom. Mura is innocent. He has not done a single thing he's been accused of. You can stop that duel and punish Bhauma instead!"

Krishna stared at Mura as the senapati continued to charge against him. He had mounted his attack in his characteristic gradual style, being on the defensive and waiting for Mura to tire. But Mura seemed to be possessed by some unknown desperation to fight on despite being almost incoherent with fatigue. It was midday but the commander of Kamarupa through his exhaustion continued to put up the fight, rejecting multiple moves by the guards to assist him. Krishna too had called for the Garudas to stay back. Blood oozed out freely from the wounds on his forehead, palms, shoulder, chest, right arm and foot. Mura wondered what kept Krishna going without any sign of fatigue despite the pain and loss of blood.

"It is me or you!" Mura growled. Others had lost count of how many times he had said that in the course of the duel. He charged at Krishna again and Krishna ducked, this time, not needing much of an effort.

Mura crashed against the wall, not able to stop the momentum of his bulk. Krishna hit him on the shoulder and then his wrist, weakening his grip. Mura tried to hit back but Krishna's next move locked his weapon but, in the deadlock, he managed to push Krishna against the wall.

"The cause you defend is not worth your blood, Mura," Krishna said as his sword held Mura's from cutting into his neck.

"My cause is worth it," Mura smiled and hit back with his fist. Krishna caught his fist midway and pushed him around, and, gaining the advantage, swirled his sword, sending Mura's weapon flying into the air. Mura collapsed to his knees, howling more at the defeat than at the pain. "Give me that honourable death!" he demanded.

"Don't fall for those myths around death. Opt for an honourable life instead, Mura." Krishna extended his hand. Mura pushed it back and instead caught Krishna's other hand that held the sword and stabbed himself. Vainateya hurried to his side as Krishna drew out the sword, shaking his head. Mura's form fell prostrate at his feet.

"Take him to your lord and tell him to correct his wrongs," Krishna told the dazed guards of Kamarupa.

Mura tugged at his leg, making Krishna kneel by his side. "Dhatri," he spoke out as Krishna bent low trying to hear. "Tell Dhatri I am innocent. My daughter ... Mauri..." The sentence was left incomplete. Krishna gently closed the bloodshot eyes that seemed to speak to him even in death.

"Take him inside. Tell Bhauma that he will have to surrender by sunset or he shall not see the sun rise again!"

Chapter Forty-Nine

"Imbecile!" Bhauma clenched his fists. "Who told him to ask for a one-on-one duel? Is this the temple of the Supreme Goddess that he fought for or his playground?" The guards stared at him as they stood around Mura's body, which was placed on a platform in front of the temple of Kamaksha. "Finish them off now and don't return until they are all dead!" Bhauma thundered and entered the temple.

As the soldiers dispersed, Vikrama took the opportunity to slip into Bhauma's mansion. He searched room after room with no luck in finding Abhaya or Dhatri, who he knew had entered Bhauma's chambers the previous night. He had to find them before Bhauma finished his midday ritual.

"Mahakala forbid, even if he has killed them, there has to be some sign somewhere!"

Despair and hope alternated as he wondered how he could find Abhaya. With Mura's death, it would not take Krishna much time to break into the inner fortress.

Is there an exit route from here that she could have taken?

Then, out of the blue, he was rewarded with a sound. It seemed to come from the southern side of the mansion. He rushed in the direction of the sound through a dimly lit passage that ended with a locked door. He put his ear to the door but could hear nothing. Had he imagined it? Then, there it was again—a loud thudding sound from the opposite side which also stopped as soon as he reached the wall.

That is someone trapped on a side of the house I am not able to enter!

Retreating to the hallway, he leaned against a pillar, calming his heart. The entry to the other side had to be from somewhere here.

A trapdoor? Yes, a trapdoor!

At that moment, he heard a sound coming from the western corner of the very hallway and he hurried to respond to the sound. Whoever was knocking should at the very least know of a presence on the other side. He tapped on the wall with the hilt of his sword and realised that the wall was made of wood!

The next moment, he slammed his shoulder against the camouflaged wooden wall and heard a similar sound from the other side. Continuing his tapping, he felt for the gap that separated the wooden portion of the stone wall. The dim light and the dark colours of the artworks that adorned the wall made for very good camouflage. As he reached the corner, he sensed a gap. A pillar-like structure stood beside him in the corner, which, at first glance, appeared to be built for aesthetic balance, but an inconspicuous difference at the edge. Vikrama's heart gave a leap as he found what he thought was a lever. He turned it, opening the trapdoor.

"Dhatri!" he exclaimed.

Dhatri wordlessly handed him the unconscious Nandini before turning back to extend a hand to pull out Mauri, followed by Abhaya.

"The child needs to be revived!" Dhatri said.

"We shall do it. You inform Mura that his daughter is safe and he does not have to fight for Bhauma."

Abhaya patted Nandini's cheeks as the child lay motionless in Vikrama's arms.

"Mura is … no more," he said quietly in a voice audible only to the two women. "The outer fort has been breached."

Dhatri's eyes narrowed on noticing Abhaya who could not help the relief shining from her eyes at Krishna's safety. "How?" she asked, her voice going hoarse, "Who killed him?"

"They say that he invited Vaasudeva for a duel unto death," Vikrama said alternating his gaze between her and Abhaya.

"Your dearest friend killed Mura then."

"What else is one supposed to do in a duel to the death?" he retorted before Abhaya could come up with a pacifying response.

"And you are?"

"My brother," Abhaya interjected, noting changes in Dhatri that she had never seen before.

"A fake Shakta, aren't you?" Dhatri's eyes flashed.

"I don't see anything wrong in what he did!" Abhaya protested seeing where the argument was going. "Dhatri, hear me out! Please stop the war and denounce Bhauma. That is the only way we can stop more deaths."

Dhatri shoved her out of the way and snatched Nandini from Vikrama's arms. She then pulled the bewildered Mauri along with her and stormed out of the mansion.

"I cannot say how relieved I am!" Vikrama whispered. "Abhaya, are you alright? What's that blood?"

"I am fine, just some splinters." Abhaya waved off his concern, brushing the drops of blood off her forehead.

"I just walked through a maze of an underground chamber, a hell on earth!" she replied, still watching the corridor down which Dhatri had stormed off.

"What happened with Bhauma?"

"Nothing to fear," Abhaya sighed, "except that he figured out that the attack by Krishna coming at the same time as my proposition could not be just a coincidence and trapped me in that dungeon."

"Bhauma refused to surrender and has thrown all his might behind defending the fortress," Vikrama told her. "Shyeni is expected to come any time now with the Garuda contingent. Ready?"

She nodded. They made their way out of the mansion. Turning a corner, they found a guard blocking their way.

"He is mine!" Abhaya leapt forward. An aimed stab to the belly, a kick in his groins and a slash across his chest and the guard lay motionless on the ground, blood trickling from his wounds.

Abhaya had injured opponents in the past, but realising that someone died in her hands sent a shiver down her spine.

"First kill, isn't it?" Vikrama asked, looking at her dazed expression. Seeing another guard approach, he pulled her behind him and slammed his shoulder into the guard. He stopped the javelin driven towards his belly midway and banged the guard's head against the wall.

"Snap out of it. You can't afford to be in a daze now!"

Abhaya nodded. Vikrama, as a teacher and a warrior, had always evoked respect in her and, in the face of his valour, her spirits rose.

She sprinted towards a third guard and ducked in the nick of time, successfully tripping him. "Now!"

Vikrama's sword had done its job even as she uttered the word. "The one knocking at the doors of Kamarupa has called for a minimum loss of life. Just informing you."

"Just like him to make things more complicated," she shot back. They reached the entrance of the mansion and stared down the stairs.

"Now how do we get past these?" he asked, pointing at the ten guards who blocked their way and a sneering Bhauma behind them.

"Your parents did not seem to have told you two about the hazards of snooping."

Vikrama caught Abhaya by the shoulder as the ten javelins closed in on them. Abhaya looked around and her heart sank as she found no signs of Dhatri. *Was she captured again?*

"Neither did yours teach you about building a foolproof fortress!" A voice was heard.

"Shyeni!" Vikrama exclaimed as he saw a figure blocking the sun. "And the Garudas!"

The guards turned in the direction, perplexed at being outnumbered by the fifty strong Garuda contingent.

"Where did the coward go?" Abhaya asked. Bhauma was nowhere to be seen. He was the kind who would leave his people to face the peril and save himself and she felt he deserved to meet death before anyone else died for him.

A resounding sound was heard from the gates of the fortress.

"Drop your weapons and you shall not be harmed!" Vikrama declared as the Garudas surrounded the guards.

Shyeni hurried to Vikrama's side as he said, "Open the doors and offer no resistance!"

"Not so fast!" Bhauma was back and behind him stood about fifty more guards.

"The reserve force!" one of the guards exulted.

Shyeni shouted a two-syllable instruction that Vikrama and Abhaya could not comprehend. The Garudas immediately rallied around them.

The crash on the gates was heard again. The second ring of the fortification had been decisively breached too! The archers of Kamarupa took positions.

"Can you both distract them?" Vikrama whispered, referring to the guards. Abhaya nodded and made her way towards Dhatri's residence. Shyeni blocked the first guard who tried to follow her and hurried behind Abhaya. Vikrama backed away and sprinted towards the fort wall, spear in hand. He aimed at the archer standing closest to the gates. The spear found its target. But it alerted the neighbouring archer who shifted his attention to the advancing Vikrama.

"To the gates!" Shyeni shouted at the pair of Garuda soldiers to back Vikrama.

But it was not easy. Outnumbered two to one, the thirty strong Garuda force did their best to hold back the guards. Abhaya ducked a guard and drove her weapon into his side, keeping her distance from Bhauma and hurried towards Dhatri's residence to see if she was there.

Shyeni handed Abhaya the second sword she had with her. She wanted to stay by Abhaya's side but Vikrama needed help. She turned towards where Vikrama stood, battling three archers all by himself and sprinted towards the gates. Another guard who accosted her only ended up surrendering his javelin to her which found its mark in his chest. Pulling out the weapon, Shyeni aimed it at another guard approaching her.

The banging sound was louder this time. But the gates still had not given in. Shyeni rushed towards the gates. A piercing pain erupted within her just as her hand reached the heavy rod that barred the gates from within.

"Shyeni!" It was Vikrama's voice.

Arching her back and reaching out behind her, she removed the knife that was stuck there, fighting down the scream and pushing the stopper rod with her left hand. A couple more Garuda soldiers managed to reach her and pushed the stopper further. The gates gave in. Shyeni backed away and collapsed onto her knees, unmindful of the Garuda force that rushed in. A pair of hands held her by shoulders and raised her; she gasped unable to hold back tears.

"Krishna!"

He could not give her a longer acknowledgement except for the glance that seemed to comprehend and experience her pain but the moment made Shyeni's pain fade away. She only felt it again when Vainateya and Vikrama caught her and rushed her towards cover.

Abhaya's heart leapt as the gates opened. Kadambari rushed out of Dhatri's home at that very moment and pointed at the line of five archers hidden behind the temple pillars.

"They are another backup that Vikrama is not aware of. Stop them or blow their cover, quick!"

Abhaya wanted to ask about Dhatri as she was the one person who could stop the guards from more bloodshed. But when the archers nocked the arrows to their bowstrings, Abhaya waited no longer. Rushing up the steps of the temple, she screamed to draw their attention, her sword reaching out to cut the steel string of the first archer. The second archer missed his aim and she caught the third, pushing him to the fourth. The first archer caught her with his broken bow and another kicked her in the stomach. The fifth was out of her reach. She let out a warning cry seeing Krishna advancing. He saw her the very instant the arrow of the fifth archer left the bow, finding its mark on Krishna's right shoulder.

Bhauma's laugh broke the tense silence that followed. Krishna pulled out the arrow as though it was a mere thorn. The Garudas rallied around him. He considered the tall figure of Bhauma. The lord of Kamarupa stood upon the topmost stair of the temple, flanked by his personal guard. He looked at least fifteen years younger than his age, which, Krishna guessed, would be way past sixty. He signalled the Garudas to step back and came forward.

"Take this last opportunity to make amends, Bhauma. Let the fraud end today, along with the bloodshed."

"Doom has lured you here, you maggot! Your blood shall wash the feet of the Supreme Goddess! Bhauma, Her worshipper, shall not forgive your sins!"

"Worshipper!" Krishna laughed. Blood dripped from his shoulder. The wounds he had sustained during his duel with Mura were enough to make one faint. But his gaze as he stared down Bhauma showed no pain, no weakness and no fatigue. "No more lives shall be lost to your lust and whims, Bhauma. Fight me!"

"Cut him to pieces!" Bhauma thundered.

Four burly guards stepped forward from the reserve force, wielding menacing swords of varying lengths. Krishna turned to the Garudas, forbidding them from stepping in. Vainateya opened his mouth to protest but Krishna's sharp glance left him wordless.

Two of the Kamarupa guards lunged forward and Krishna took measured steps, his pace quickening at a calculated speed. His double-edged sword clashed against the blades. He stood against the cumulative bulk, drawing out his short knife to stop the third sword only a finger length away from his neck.

Abhaya gasped and kicked hard against the four archers who had by then caught her by the arms. A fourth guard rushed at Krishna, aiming at his stomach. That very moment, Krishna's knee knocked the third guard, upsetting the balance of the first two. Ducking sideways, he slashed against the neck of the approaching guard. One of the earlier guards charged at him, brandishing the sword menacingly low, joined by the other two approaching from his sides. The pincer seemed formidable. Krishna stopped the progress of the advancing sword and waited for the other two to get closer. The moment before they closed in, he lunged forward and arched his back, diving almost parallel to the ground and piercing the belly of the guard in the middle. Two swords crossed above him as he fell. He rolled sideways, upsetting the balance of one of the remaining guards and beheading him. The blood splashed on the last guard's face, making him back away.

Krishna's smaller frame seemed to camouflage the hidden strength that manifested at his will.

Abhaya sighed and collapsed onto her knees. Bhauma gritted his teeth.

"Not anymore, Bhauma!" Krishna warned before he sprinted up the stairs, his sword raised towards Bhauma. Bhauma pulled two long swords out of his garment and crossed them to stop Krishna's advancing sword. Bhauma had the advantage of height as he stood at the top of the stairs. Holding Krishna back with his blades, he thundered, kicking at Krishna's chest. Abhaya saw Krishna back down by three steps in an attempt to retain his balance. She took the opportunity to kick at the archer who stood to her left and ducked her head to bang against the groin of the other. But the two from behind pulled her back, one by the hair and another by her arm. She did not see Bhauma exchange a glance with the fifth archer. The archer nodded and nocked an arrow to his bowstring. The twang as it left the bow jolted Abhaya.

"Watch out, Krishna!"

The arrow again pierced his back. Words and voice failed her seeing him fall to the ground, blood still flowing freely from all his wounds. Bhauma advanced upon his still body and lifted his sword.

"Krishna!" she screamed. The blood in Abhaya's veins seemed to have frozen.

Many things happened at the moment. Vainateya charged with a blood-curdling cry but he was too far away. The tip of Bhauma's sword touched Krishna's chest but stopped and a painful cry escaped his lips. Abhaya looked up. Bhauma's eyes were wide and his limbs had frozen. His frame shook as he stumbled back and then to his side.

Dhatri stood at the top of the steps, the trident of Goddess Kamaksha in her hand. Abhaya felt the grip on her arm loosen and rushed to Krishna, shaking his frame. Warm drops of tears made Krishna's eyes open. His hand reached out to pat Abhaya's cheek. His lips curved into his characteristic smile, unaffected by the wounds and pain. His gaze then rested on Dhatri, holding Bhauma at a distance pointing the trident at him.

"It is you who has sinned all this while, Bhauma!"

"You ungrateful wretch!" Bhauma spat, much to the shock of the guards.

Dhatri only drove the trident towards his chest in response. "You deserve to die for what you did to those women chained in your dungeons! For Mura!"

Bhauma shook the weapon through his pain and pulled it out, despite Dhatri's grip. With a violent shove, he drove her to the ground. "Whore!" he cried as he lifted the sword. Abhaya tried to rise but Krishna's frame leaned against her for support. She saw Krishna pull out a rounded weapon, sharpened around its edges.

"Chakra?"

Abhaya had thought the ancient weapon only existed in the sculptural depictions of gods. The discus spiralled through the air and severed Bhauma's head, which fell at the feet of an uninjured Dhatri. The headless body rolled down the stairs.

Abhaya turned back to Krishna, throwing her arms around him.

"It is over, Krishna!"

His arm caught her waist as he rose to a sitting position.

"It's over, love!"

Krishna's lips curved again. "No, love, it is hardly over."

Abhaya could not comprehend what he meant. His brows rose. Before she could say anything, she saw a trident point towards his neck. Her jaw dropped as she looked up.

"Dhatri! No!"

Dhatri looked like the one possessed, pointing the trident to Krishna's neck. "Tell each one of them to leave the fortress," she whispered with no emotion, her eyes icy. Abhaya caught hold of the trident. Dhatri twisted the weapon sideways, hitting Abhaya's shoulder with the blunt edge. The stunning pain made Abhaya double over and, at that moment, Dhatri pulled Krishna away from her. "Tell them all to leave, if they want him alive!" she hissed to Abhaya.

Abhaya looked around, finding Vainateya rooted to the spot, just a few paces away from Krishna. Shock, helplessness and despair met her gaze.

"Dhatri, what has come over you?"

"Leave, Vainateya," Krishna said, unaffected by the looming death that stood only a hairbreadth away from his neck.

Vainateya backed away, his muscular frame shaking with helplessness. Abhaya moved closer only to back away when she realised that the tip of the trident was piercing Krishna's neck. Dhatri's cold stare rested on her as the Garudas backed away, out of the fortress.

"Dhatri!" Abhaya's tone broke into a sob. "Don't tell me to leave!" Dhatri was about to shake her head when

Abhaya's hands came together as she crumpled to the ground, forehead almost touching Dhatri's feet. "Take my life instead."

"Relax, Abhaya, she will not take a life she saved moments ago," Krishna said, his lips still curved in a smile that seemed to suggest that everything that was happening was but a play.

"How are you so sure?" Dhatri growled in an unearthly voice.

"Don't say things to provoke her further!" Abhaya screamed at Krishna. She saw his eyes close. "Dhatri! Don't do this! This serves no purpose!"

Dhatri signalled to the guards who moved to close the gates and stopped as Vainateya and Vikrama still stood at the gates, stupefied.

"Those two don't want your lover to live," Dhatri's words were just more than a whisper.

"I beg you both, just leave!" Abhaya screamed at them. She saw Vainateya dragging Vikrama out of the fortress. The gates closed after them. "Dhatri, he is wounded beyond measure. Let me attend to him. I beg you!" All she got in response was a cold stare. "Dhatri, I'll do anything. Anything you wish. Just..." she swallowed a sob, "...anything."

"Kadambari!" Dhatri cried. "Take him inside," she ordered the guards, still holding the trident to Krishna's neck. Kadambari, who had been keeping Mauri and Nandini safe, rushed out.

"Amba!" Abhaya screamed at Kadambari, pointing to the guards who lifted Krishna's limp form. "Tell her to allow me to soothe his wounds."

"No! You aren't moving from here!"

"Dhatri!" Kadambari exclaimed at what she thought was a cold personification of rage. "Is she the target of all your rage? Fraudulent as it was, you are the mahadevi by your conscience. Are these the tenets of Shaktism you practised?"

"You tend to him," Dhatri ordered Kadambari, ignoring her words. "But the guards will stay. If this one moves from here, they will kill him."

"No, I shall not move from here," Abhaya said. "Amba!" Kadambari knelt by Abhaya's side. "Amba! His wounds need tending. A lot depends on him. Many would curse me for calling him here if anything were to happen to him. Look after him. I shall serve you the rest of my life!"

Kadambari saw the earnestness and truth in the younger woman's eyes. It reminded her of the late King Dharmasena. In the past, Vikrama's steadfastness to Dharmasena and his daughter had made her envy them. But Abhaya, she felt, was worthy of his devotion. She nodded, gripping Abhaya's folded hands, unable to see her pleading anymore and rose to join the guards as they carried Krishna into Dhatri's chambers.

Dhatri strode towards Bhauma's chambers. Abhaya did not dare to move, despite the sight of the five corpses right in front of her, including Bhauma's. She closed her eyes in sheer fatigue. When they opened, it was dark. A cold wind blew against her frame. Her eyes fixed upon the entrance of Bhauma's house, unmindful of the shiver that shook her frame. She sensed another presence when a rug fell around her shoulders.

"Dhatri?"

"You did not move from here!"

"How is Krishna? Has he recovered? Is he conscious?"

"How should I know?" Dhatri's lips turned down in the corners. "I was rescuing those women in those dungeons. It is freezing out here! How were you able to stay this way?" Her hand gently passed through Abhaya's hair.

"Do you think the cold would matter to me at this time? Or is this a new way to torture me?" Abhaya sighed, turning to look towards Bhauma's home.

Her heart leapt when she saw Kadambari hurrying towards them. "Amba! Is he conscious?"

Kadambari saw the hope in her eyes and did not know how to answer. "He hasn't opened his eyes. But he is alive," she managed to say. "His body feels like a fire is burning inside him. He has Shivajvara!"

"Shivajvara?"

"Shivajvara?" Dhatri repeated. "I think I have the herbs that can tend to it. Someone left it with me a long time ago. He had told me that they stay effective for decades." She considered Abhaya and Kadambari staring at her, hope rising in their eyes. "But why should I give those? Why should I save him?"

"Right, why don't you kill us all instead?" Kadambari retorted, squeezing Abhaya's arm, knowing what she was undergoing.

"Do that, Dhatri. Spare me this hell of seeing him succumb."

Dhatri gazed at her, a smile playing on her lips, contrasting the redness in her eyes. "You want to save him?"

"What do you want me to do to please you?"

"What can you give up for him, Abhaya?"

"Anything, I already promised you I shall do anything to save him," Abhaya replied.

"Can you give up even your civilisation and your Arya dharma? Show me your readiness to accept the Shakta ways?" Dhatri asked in a calm voice, little more than a whisper.

"Dhatri, no!" Kadambari stepped forward but she was restrained by Abhaya.

"I shall. Tell me what you want me to do."

"Agree to indulge in maithuna. I shall give him all the herbs that I have. You will see him cured by dawn."

"No!" Kadambari exclaimed. "This is worse than what Bhauma did! You are just being heartless!"

"Amba, let it be." Abhaya held her arm. "She does not know the burden she bears. His life is worth it. No, it is much more than all my beliefs. I am giving up nothing."

Kadambari looked at Dhatri. "You have taken Shaktism to an unbelievable low, Dhatri! I can't let you do this. Coercion of a vulnerable woman! By the Supreme Shakti, do you even see what you are..."

"No, Amba. Reasoning with her is something we don't have time for," Abhaya said. "If Krishna dies, it would be the end of any hope for civilisation. The angry armies from the plains will tear down this place but the rot in society will continue to wreak havoc. Humanity shall descend to a display of brutality of which even animals are incapable. Let us do whatever we can to stop that."

Kadambari stared at her in horror. She did not even dare to guess the horror Vikrama would feel if he heard of this. She was not sure if it was maternal instinct she felt towards Abhaya but she wanted to do everything she could to protect the girl.

But Abhaya smiled away her fears. "Dhatri, I am ready. Give him the medicine."

"Bathe, plait these long tresses … I don't want the sadhaka to be terrified by his yogini," Dhatri smiled. Abhaya nodded and walked towards the temple bath.

Kadambari stood rooted to the spot. For the first time, her faith in the Supreme Goddess was shaken.

Chapter Fifty

The hand brushed across Krishna's face. The warmth of her lap soothed his skin "How long will you carry my burden, Krishna?"

"What made you think you were one?"

"What else am I?"

"You are..." It was Krishna's turn to smile as he attempted to catch the elusive hand. Giving up the attempt, his hand rested on his chest "...me."

"I am you?"

"Do you doubt it?"

The response was a smile. "Is that how you console your conscience?"

"Why would I need consolation?"

"The dream that haunts you."

Krishna's lips remained curved. Mist covered his eyes. "I did pass through a phase when it used to haunt me. Not anymore." Her brows rose. "I do admit that you were a burden as long as you remained that infant who was kept in my place to face the death meant for me."

"After that, you got used to the burden."

"I only felt you alive."

"You hallucinated."

"I realised."

"What?"

"You are much more than a defenceless infant put to the sword. You are hope. Hope never dies as long as there is life. Life is not over as long as there is hope. You are life so how could you die? You are hope so how can you be a burden?"

"Flatterer! I am only an illusion."

"You may be an illusion, Maya, to those who shun life. I celebrate life. You are my Shakti."

"So, I am your tool in achieving your aims now."

"You are the aim, the tool and the act of achieving. Didn't you instigate Abhaya to go to the temple of Katyayani in the first place?"

"I thought that had surprised you!"

Krishna smiled. "Didn't I tell you that you are my own self?"

"So, are you ready to face what follows next?"

"Your wish, my command."

"Why this dualism when you say I am you, Krishna?"

"Isn't it fun?"

"Work awaits you and you think of lying down and having fun."

"With this Shivajvara burning within me, I can only have fun."

"Why don't you invoke Vishnujvara?"

"As you wish."

They laughed.

Her hand stroked his forehead. She bent low and he closed his eyes. "It is time," she whispered.

His eyes opened to the light of a lamp placed before him. Krishna rose to his feet. His eyes fell upon a painting on the wall.

Shiva, the Mahadeva, sat in deep meditation. His third eye spat flames, burning someone with a bow. The art had faded there.

"Kama . . . desire? But what is life without kama? Did Mahadeva really need Uma Haimavati to show him that?"

"Krishna?" Dhatri entered the room. Krishna turned and met her gaze. "Are you cured?"

"Does that disappoint you?"

Dhatri felt compelled to smile. "Why would you think so? Maybe someone has staked a lot in convincing me to give you my precious medication, the cure to Shivajvara." Dhatri stepped forward as she spoke and placed a hand on his forehead. "You don't look like you ever had it!"

Her gaze passed from his hair to toe before rising to meet his gaze.

"Maybe it was the grace of Goddess Kamaksha," Krishna winked.

"How do your wounds feel? Can you walk?"

Krishna gestured at his feet, his smile pointing out the obvious. "Could you, Devi, kindly let my friends outside the fortress know I am well? I am sure they would have spent a sleepless night."

Dhatri nodded, her intent gaze still on Krishna and sighed. "Years ago, an insecure emperor in the plains, Jarasandha, wanted to re-establish his control and sought Bhauma's help in providing him with a spy network in the garb of Shakta practitioners. The Shaktas are frowned upon by the men of religion in your plains. But it is easy to win over the country folk."

"So, Bhauma trained Shaktas to work as spies for the kings who were against me," Krishna nodded. "In the process, he did go quite a distance in spreading his reach across Bharatavarsha. But, the Shakta order lost."

"I wish I could deny that. But the fault lines in your society of Aryas were lying right there to be exploited,

Krishna. Oppression was rampant. If not Bhauma, someone else could have taken advantage of it."

"I can only hope the order of those who claim to worship Adi Shakti will not play on the weaknesses of others. Does the Supreme Shakti need an army to spread her influence?"

Dhatri gave him a long look, then averted her gaze. She sat on the stone seat, motioning to Krishna to sit. "Will you not ask me why I had to hold you captive, Krishna?"

"I shall wait for you to tell me, Dhatri."

"It comes across as the most heinous act to do, capturing the very man who saved my life. But I have a burden on me, Krishna. You cannot leave without ensuring that Kamarupa will not be torn down by angry plains folk."

"They are Aryas, not demons to tear down a temple," Krishna laughed before turning serious. He leaned forward and said, "If someone does that, he would do so at the risk of angering the new emperor of Bharatavarsha. You have my promise."

Dhatri nodded. "Come with me, Krishna." Krishna followed her into the passage that opened into the hallway. The sight that greeted him made him stop in horror. Women lay on the floor, some writhing in pain, some injured and some barely conscious. "They were those who were brought to Kamarupa either by force or coaxing. They refused to become yoginis. Bhauma did this to them."

"...to his peril," Krishna concluded, seeing a woman in her twenties struggle to reach out to the jug of water placed by her side. He knelt to support her to rise and held the jug for her. Her incoherent blank look of misery greeted his eyes. He wiped the tears from her eyes and she buried her head into his chest.

"Can I die?" He heard the words, lower than a whisper.

"No!"

"I am yet to count how many of them are hidden. Bhauma has an underground dungeon in the hidden caves below Kamarupa," Dhatri added as Krishna rose. "They cannot return. They fear ridicule, torture and death."

At the moment, she saw Krishna's brows come together as he shook his head. "They, the willing, shall return."

"And be put to death or left to rot by their own people? I saw that happen, Krishna."

"They shall come with me to live a life of dignity that is due to them."

In the statement, Dhatri saw resolve manifest in his eyes that answered many of her questions without her needing to ask. About the security, status and safety of the women, Dhatri felt reassured. Then, she said, "Krishna, what if . . . what if they were violated against their will? I fear most of them are."

"The burden is not theirs to bear."

"How can I be sure of this, Krishna?"

"What can I do to assure you?"

Dhatri stared into the dark passage behind Krishna. "If you accept your lover who has already indulged in maithuna, who, by the standards of your world, is not 'pure' anymore, I can know that you will feel their pain too."

She saw Krishna step forward. "Where is Abhaya?"

"Probably getting ready for the ritual of maithuna with a sadhaka who approaches her. She swore on you that she would do that if I could give you the medicine for Shivajvara. I hope you know about the ritual worship offered to Kamaksha that involves maithuna."

The lamp succumbed to the sudden whiff of breeze that blew in and Dhatri could not see Krishna's expression. But when she saw him shielding the dying flame, she knew that the flame had not been put out. The wind stopped and the lamp burned brighter.

Krishna turned back to face her and she saw his solemnity fade into a pointed smile. "Dhatri, I seek to worship Goddess Kamaksha in the ritual ways of Shaktism."

Dhatri stared at him. She then shook her head. "Is that your idea to save her honour?"

"No, it is my idea to save you from guilt once you realise what you've done. Dhatri, her honour is intact. No, it has grown manifold."

"You cannot comprehend what I am going through, Krishna! Do you think I would ask a woman to consent to a sexual union without her will for my pleasure?"

"If protecting Kamarupa and the women were your only concerns Dhatri, you would not have done that." Krishna's voice had become cold. His words remained measured but hit their target precisely. "What do you want to punish her for, Dhatri?"

"Do you think I hate her?" Dhatri exclaimed. "I want her to realise the truth. The world of Aryas will have no place for her either way. You will realise that, too, if you give up your Arya dharma and perform these rituals."

"Give up Arya dharma … Dhatri, my Arya dharma shall not give me up that easily, neither will hers." The wink was amicable and the smile that accompanied it was free of concern. Krishna's eyes, though, did hold a mysterious mix of pity and reproach that made Dhatri's soul shrink within herself.

Her eyes welled up for the first time in years. And when she recalled Abhaya's stoic acceptance and her pleas to save Krishna rent her heart. "I ... what have I done!"

"It shall not be held against you."

Before she could reply, she found Krishna heading towards the temple. She sank to the ground, staring at the shadows. It would take quite some time before she came to terms with her conscience.

Chapter Fifty-One

The wind blew hard that moonless night. The lamps in front of the shrine of Kamaksha flickered. The cold was sufficient to bite into her skin but Abhaya took little notice of her shivering frame as she stood facing the sanctum. The fire that burned in her heart made the cold pale in comparison.

Maithuna! Abhaya's lips curved in contempt and her eyes narrowed. Coercion was the only way that could have broken her resolve to not bow down to Shakta ways. But Dhatri had finally achieved what she had resolved to.

It is an irony that sacrificing my Aryatva is the only way to ensure the ushering in of true Arya Dharma! The defeat is not mine to feel ashamed about! It is yours, Kamaksha, or whoever you are!

Loudly, she proclaimed, "Gauri! How ironic that the maidens across Bharatavarsha worship you to be united with the spouse of their choice. But you seek to feast on my virginity to save the one I love! You cannot be the love that reined in the rage of Rudra. You are only a tool of Dhatri's hatred towards Aryas!"

Who am I talking to? To something that is just a figment of everyone's imagination? If she truly existed, wouldn't she have saved the lives of Katyayana and Kamalakshi?

"How does it benefit Dhatri even if I consent to maithuna? When she knows that my heart is not aligned with the ways of Vamachara, why does she yearn to only break me?" she thought aloud, bewildered and hurt.

The idea of what was to come left a bitter taste in Abhaya's mouth as she stood mindless of the wind that blew over her. *Is it only my token submission Dhatri wants and not my true belief?* Abhaya wanted to laugh at the lameness of the thought. For all the anger she had against Dhatri, the mahayogini of Kamarupa was not dumb to demand the superfluous adoption of Shakta ways.

I pity that sadhaka who is going to seek my union today. The ritual of maithuna with a yogini who is a manifestation of Shakti is supposed to result in the state of Shivatva But far from attaining that, his faith would only break to know what made me a Shakta yogini.

A presence behind her made her tilt her head slightly. *The sadhaka.* Her fists clenched with steely resolve. She knew what the approaching person would say. And she, like an actor playing a scripted role, would parrot the response that Dhatri wanted her to give. *Who is betraying whom?*

"A hilarious puzzle that you can try answering, Krishna" The words slipped out of her lips.

"What puzzle? And how in the name of Mah … er … Kamaksha did you know it was me?" The voice rang in her ears like the wake-up call that drags one caught in the maze of nightmares to consciousness.

Abhaya gasped and turned. "Krishna! You … you … recovered!" Her hand went up to Krishna's forehead, checking for fever. "Just hours ago, you were burning with that cursed Shivajvara! How did this happen?"

"Vishnujvara came and drove the Shivajvara away!" Krishna responded, mimicking the wonder he saw in her eyes. "You should have seen the fight. It was spectacular!" He saw a momentary smile appear on

Abhaya's lips and then fade. "It was like the ice-cold hand of Uma Haimavati, the daughter of the snow mountains, taming the third eye of Mahadeva that burnt Kamadeva to ashes."

"Enough! Who let you come out here? Aren't you supposed to be resting?" Abhaya snapped, resisting the momentary flutter that shook her frame.

"I only came to worship the very Goddess Uma Haimavati here, the way it is done in this place," Krishna said. "You apparently have been here for a while and might know how it's to be done. Guide me, Abhaya."

The words took a moment to sink in and she pulled away from him, glaring. "What? Don't even think about it!"

Krishna tilted his head to a side, his brows coming together. "Why do you react like a mother who refuses to let the child eat more of a sweet? I only wanted to worship the Goddess."

Abhaya stared at him and mist covered her eyes. "Dhatri told you what she asked of me?" She got her answer in the smile that she saw. "And you come up with this juvenile plan to 'save my honour'."

"Dhatri also told me that you promised to do anything for me! And you refuse now…?"

Abhaya shook her head. "Will you let me carry the burden of destroying your Arya dharma only to guard my … is the physical body this important to you too, Krishna?"

Krishna's lips parted as he sighed and said, "One thing a time. Destroying my Arya dharma, Abhaya? Really?" Abhaya's eyes dropped and she attempted to turn away, expecting him to hold her arm. But he did not.

"Dhaarmaseni, what makes you and me Arya? Surely not just the rituals we follow in the plains."

"Not just the rituals. Not the race as far as some stupid claims go. Faith, Krishna. Faith that keeps us together and keeps the world together." When she heard no response, she turned to face him. "And courage to see ourselves in others, when they ridicule us, when they praise us, when they open up to us when they close us out…" Abhaya halted.

"So, you agree that observing Shakta rituals does not make us any less Arya."

"That might be for just you and me, Krishna. How can I not consider the fact that a lot depends on you back in the plains of Bharatavarsha?"

"And a lot on you too, Abhaya. Starting with forgiving Dhatri. Behind her rage and hatred was fear."

"She hates us, Krishna," Abhaya stated, remembering the steely apparition that Dhatri had become that evening.

"She only generalised the limitations she saw in others into the whole of the populace bound by the Arya dharma. When you stood by it, her pent up rage was directed towards you." Krishna came closer, his finger holding up her chin. "But you have the courage to see yourself in others. Abhaya, the fearless one who took on this hazardous pursuit to save an innocent gopika, can you see yourself in the Shaktas? Rituals and beliefs apart, are they so different?" Abhaya frowned and shook her head in a bid to protest. "No, Dhaarmaseni, you need to think beyond the malicious intentions of Bhauma and the anger of Dhatri."

The moment of silence was more of a wordless conversation as their eyes met. Behind the anger that Dhatri nurtured, Abhaya realised, lay deep-rooted fear. "Can we assuage Dhatri's fears?" The recognition of fear, Abhaya felt, was liberating. "Krishna, was that fear too—those heinous killings of those girls that our own people committed?"

"Fear and more fear." Krishna's wry smile made the tears that glazed her eyes spill down her cheeks.

"Can we combat the fear with faith? Can we keep our faith undeterred when the last traces of hope melt away? Can we receive blame and adulation, accept them and yet not give in to them?" Krishna said and held her gaze even as tears continued to fall from her eyes.

"May history forget my name. May the world call me anything that satisfies its limited ego. But, with a smile, let me cross fears, limitations and every emotion that attaches my spirit to all that is perishable..." She paused and extended her arms. "I questioned the existence of the gods and goddesses above and did so rightly. But the limitless spirit within us that commands our existence is to be realised by us. I know that you, Vaasudeva, are one with it. You are *that*, the Parameshwara, let me realise that I am *that too*. I am you!"

The wind had come to a halt and Abhaya's words echoed around the walls of the sanctum. The lamps glowed brighter than ever in the moonless night. Abhaya continued to hold out her hands to him. The curve of Krishna's lips widened as he held her right hand and went down onto his knee.

"Will you, the personification of Shakti, grace your worshipper with the union of your spirit?"

As she nodded, Abhaya's hand went up to the knot that held the garment around her frame. The wall behind her hosted their shadows in the glow of the lamps. Seated in the sanctum, the Supreme Goddess Kamaksha witnessed, in the light of the hundred lamps, the two shadows merging into one.

EPILOGUE

"May we take your leave, Mahadevi?"

"What should I take that as, Krishna?" Dhatri turned from the lamps that she had been arranging at the sanctum of Kamaksha.

"Take it as it seems, a leave-taking from the Goddess personified."

"You decided everything, Vaasudeva. About the safety of Kamarupa, about taking the women back to the plains of Bharatavarsha. You don't need my leave. And I am no personification of the Goddess," Dhatri smiled. "If I were one, I would have stopped you from leaving Kamarupa."

"How I wish you had done that!" Krishna chuckled sitting on the stairs of the sanctum. "Life in the plains of Bharatavarsha will not be as kind as the respite that Kamarupa has given me."

"Then why don't you stay back, Krishna?"

"I belong here as much as I do in the rest of Bharatavarsha, Dhatri."

"You have too much faith, Krishna," Dhatri remarked, lighting the first lamp in the sanctum.

"Faith is what keeps fear at bay. If fear is quelled, change is possible, isn't it Dhatri?"

"I hope you succeed," Dhatri said, looking into his eyes. "Else, it might not take much time for another

Bhauma to attack your people." Her gaze pierced Krishna's. He smiled at her, unfazed by her warning. "It is not easy, Krishna. You underestimate the ridicule you have invited onto yourself by taking on the rigid beliefs of your world."

"Rigidity too is a function of fear, Dhatri. Like the lights of these lamps would overcome the darkness of the moonless night, faith shall infuse courage to overcome that fear."

Dhatri could not help smiling back. "You compel me to pray for your success. Where is Abhaya? I should admit something to her."

Krishna pointed in the direction of a smaller dais near the stairs of the temple where Abhaya was speaking to a large group of women. He motioned to Dhatri to come with him as he joined Abhaya.

"I appeal to you to come back home," Abhaya was saying. "That home where your rightful place is waiting for you."

"There is no place for us in the plains," a woman said.

"No, Bhagini, it is there for us to claim," Abhaya reasoned.

"They, our people, shall never accept us back," another woman rued.

"The home is ours to return to," Abhaya persisted. "They who reject you are not your people. They are just victims of their fears and insecurities. I can only pity them. But there are those with their hearts open. I strive to rebuild my city Anagha, the city of the sinless. I welcome you all to claim your new home there."

"Will we be safe there?"

"I can only promise to stand between you and any danger," Abhaya replied. The sincerity and valour in her tone had a visible effect on the women. "I shall stand by you until my death. And so will my people." Her gaze passed to the far end of the inner circle, where Vikrama was engaged in a conversation with Kadambari, Shyeni and Vainateya. Abhaya could read joy and relief in their faces. Vikrama had succeeded in convincing her to rule the newly rebuilt city, promising to stand by her in building the army. She turned back to the women. "My family too is with you. And I promise you the assurances of the soon-to-be emperor of Bharatavarsha. I promise you a life of opportunities to build prosperity, driven by our endeavours and industry."

The women listened in silence. Abhaya smiled. "I shall not give you a false picture of a cosy life without hindrances. We are going to face ridicule and scorn and perhaps even violence. But we shall face it, not with anger, but with a detached commitment to ourselves, striving for the evolution of humanity, paving the strengthening of true Arya dharma, beyond the fetters of fears and oppression. If I can promise you anything more..." Abhaya paused, sensing a presence by her side. Her smile became more pronounced and her eyes misted over. She extended her hand into Krishna's outstretched palm and continued, "It is hope."

Her eyes met Dhatri's wordless gaze, conveying genuine reconciliation. Abhaya nodded her salutation and turned back to the women.

Krishna's hand gently squeezed hers and the moment filled her with the surge of inspiration to face the future, as uncertain as it looked with so many questions as yet unanswered. Abhaya knew she had what it would take to face whatever awaited her. She smiled and added, "Add your faith to mine, my sisters. Let us go back home!"

GLOSSARY OF SANSKRIT AND INDIC TERMS

Relationships and Addresses

ACHARYA Teacher
AMBA Mother
ARYA Noble one
BHAGINI Sister
BHRATA Brother
JANAKA Father
MAATULA Uncle
MAATULAA Aunt
MAHATMA Great One
PRABHO Lord/Master/King
SENAPATI Commander of an army
VATSA Son/Child
VATSE Daughter/Child
YUVARAJA Prince
YUVATI Maiden

Other Terms

CHUDAMANI A gem-studded regal hair jewel worn by royal brides
HAALAHALA Poison that emerged during the Puranic episode of the samudra mathana or the ocean churning and was consumed by Shiva to save the world

JAYATU Victory be to (Jayatu Anagheshwari means "glory be to Anagheshwari")

MAHADEVA Great God (used to evoke Shiva)

PRASAD Food distributed to worshippers/devotees/visitors after being offered to a deity in worship

SHAKTA Practitioner of a religion worshipping Shakti

SHAKTI/ADI SHAKTI Primeval energy regarded as the female aspect of the Supreme Being

SWAYAMVARA A ceremony where a bride marries the groom of her choice among the suitors

VAMACHARA The "left" path of worship, usually considered unorthodox as against the Dakshinachara or the "right" path, which encompasses the orthodox ways

VRATA A ritual worship aiming to achieve a deity's blessing for a certain purpose

REFERENCES AND WORKS THAT INSPIRED *ABHAYA*

2003. *Sri Lalita Sahasranama* (trans. in English by Swami Tapasyananda.) Chennai: Sri Ramakrishna Math.

Chatterjee, Bankim Chandra. 2008. *Krishna Charitra* (trans. by Alo Shome). New Delhi: V&S Publishers.

Barua, B.K. and H.V. Sreenivasa Murthy. 1965. *Legends and Temples of Assam*. Mumbai: Bharatiya Vidya Bhavan.

Das, Bhagavan. 1962. *Krishna—A Study in the Theory of Avatars*. Mumbai: Bharatiya Vidya Bhavan.

Magee, Michael. 2011. *Shri Yoni Tantra: Unveiling a Key Tantric Sexual Ritual*. UK, Australia, India: MetaPlume Corporation.

Misra, V.S. 2007. *Ancient Indian Dynasties*. Mumbai: Bharatiya Vidya Bhavan.

Munshi, K.M. 1963. *Krishnavatara Series Volume 2: The Wrath of the Emperor*. Mumbai: Bharatiya Vidya Bhavan.

Osho. 1991. *Krishna, the Man and his Philosophy*. Mumbai: Jaico Publishing House.

Pothana, Bammera Sri. 2010. *Andhra Mahabhagavatamu*. Tirupati: Tirumala Tirupati Devasthanams Publications.

Vartak, P.V. "Brahmaputra Culture Is At Least 15,000 Years Old". Available at https://www.scribd.com/document/206418233/ARTICLE-Narakasura-Brahmaputra-Culture-is-at-Least-15000-Years-Old

ACKNOWLEDGEMENTS

Conceiving a story, its characters and our world is beyond the single-handed capabilities of an author, if not for the world that comes together in supporting him or her. The journey of writing *Abhaya* showed me a wonderful side of the world that opened its supportive arms to me.

The dynamic editorial team from Bloomsbury—Praveen Tiwari, Nitin Valecha and Shreya Chakraborti—and the freelance editor, Gauri Kelkar, deserve all my applause for their proactive efforts due to which the book reappeared in this new form.

The foundations of Hindu epics, legends and philosophies were laid for me by my parents. My mother, Usha Krishna Swamy, ushered me into the ageless world of the Ramayana, the Mahabharata and the Bhagavata Purana with her regular reciting sessions, compelling insights, bedtime stories and much more. My father, Krishna Swamy Kumar, cemented my love for Indian history through his unique way of combining current affairs with scriptural knowledge from Indian itihasas.

My husband, Arvind Iyer, is my single pillar of support. He saw to it that I get past multiple writer's blocks and pessimistic urges to give up my attempts to write. His love and companionship—not to mention the many occasions where he treated me to a dinner or a gift upon the completion of every small milestone of my manuscript—are things I shall cherish for life and beyond. I am thankful for the support of my in-laws. Trust me, it is tough to bear with a family member whose mind is forever captured in 2000 BCE all the time and they did it!

My extended family, my grandparents, uncles and aunts, who were there for me to support my crucial necessities as well as my wildest ideas; my cousins who used to humour me by listening to my endless stories—this was possible because you all had a huge role to play in encouraging the storyteller in me.

The journey of writing *Abhaya* started in my late teens when it was only a collection of disconnected wild fantasies about Lord Krishna, written in stray sheets, which I tore away later, laughing at myself. I am thankful that the characters succeeded in capturing my attention this long and chose me to be the medium—despite my multiple attempts to give up—to weave their story.

Expressing any amount of gratitude would fall short when I take the name of Sri Hari Kiran Vadlamani, founder of Indic Academy, who made countless milestones happen all along my career. I pray that he, his family and his team are blessed with a long life of health, prosperity and happiness. My humble words of gratitude to Sri Amish Tripathi, bestselling author and director, Nehru Centre, and Sangeeta Bahadur, a wonderful author. Both of them supported me with their kind words of praise, along with insights and encouragement that boosted my confidence just when I needed it.

I would also like to mention the team that was behind the self-published edition—Vrinda Baliga, Anoop Ravindran, Ritesh Kala, Emily Tippets. I could not have done it without you. The very first step of my literary career could take off because of you all.

Critical feedback from different angles is a priceless treasure an author can hope to find. Authors—Nilanjan Chaudhuri, Krishna Udayasankar, Nandini Vijayaraghagavan and Venkatesh Ramakrishnan—had a lot to teach me through their timely advice, insights and their own writings too. Mahesh Mohan, Jijith N. Ravi, Sindhuja Ramasubramanian, Suraj Sharma, Mrinalini Krothapalli, Ramaa Prabha, Shashank Davanagere, Uma Shankar Das and K. Chandrashekhar come to mind. Without their inputs, right from character suggestions and structural elements to linguistic improvements, the novel would not have come this far.

Finally, I would like to thank my friends and batch mates—it is a long list and, though I wonder why these wonderful people chose to believe in me, I'm nevertheless grateful that they did: Jyothi Gonuguntla, Pavan Kunchapudi, Aditya Kumar, Nandhita V.M., Anjali Vipparthy, Bhavna Baral, Shambhavi Satya, Hitesh Jogiya, Rakesh Nath, Ramesh Badiger and many others chose to believe in the very first draft and were generous with feedback and lots of unconditional support.

My memory could be failing me and I am sure I am forgetting many more names. Technology and social media have indeed made the world a lot smaller and closer and, yes, many lent me a kind word or two when I needed it the most.

A big shout-out to all the early readers who read the online version and validated my digital-first approach with their reviews and also promoted *Abhaya* on their social networks. And, finally, a big thank you to you, the readers, who chose to believe in an unknown name and bought the book. I pray that Krishna Vaasudeva manifests to each of you in his way to delight you eternally.

ABOUT THE AUTHOR

An alumnus of IIT Kharagpur and an investment professional turned satisfied writer, Saiswaroopa Iyer is the bestselling author of five novels, all based on legendary female protagonists from ancient Indian literature. Her second novel, *Avishi*, based on a Rig Vedic hymn, has been acquired for screen adaptation by a major studio. She also curated an anthology of short stories based on the Kurukshetra battle of the Mahabharata, published by Bloomsbury India. Saiswaroopa is passionate about ancient Indian history, philosophy and literature. She is a curator at Indic Academy and holds a certificate in the Puranas from Oxford Centre for Hindu Studies.

As a trained Carnatic classical singer, she has also been awarded a gold medal by Tirumala Tirupati Devasthanams (TTD), a trust that provides comprehensive information about temples in Tirumala and Tirupati. In her spare time, she likes to search for her next inspiration in books, pravachanas and historical temples. She lives in Bengaluru.

If you enjoyed reading the books and would like to stay updated with the author's forthcoming projects, you can follow her on social media:

Twitter:
@Sai_swaroopa
Facebook:
https://www.facebook.com/AuthorSaiswaroopa/
Instagram:
@AuthorSaiswaroopa

BY THE SAME AUTHOR

Avishi

Long before the times of
Draupadi and Sita
Immortalised in the hymns of
Rig Veda
But forgotten to the memory
of India
Was the warrior queen with
an iron leg, Vishpala.

Brought up in the pristine forest school of Naimisha, Avishi reaches the republic of Ashtagani in search of her destiny. When Khela, the oppressive king of the neighbouring Vrishabhavati, begins to overwhelm and invade Ashtagani, Avishi rises to protect her settlement but at a high cost.

Separated from her love, her settlement broken, with a brutal injury needing an amputation of her leg, what can Avishi do to save herself?

Will her disability let her continue to be the warrior that she was?

Can she fight Khela and save everything dear to her?

Separated from her love, her settlement broken and handicapped by a brutal injury, can Avishi overcome Khela?

If stories about ancient India, especially those with strong women characters, interest you, then *Avishi* is a story you must read!

Mauri

She wants to kill the man whom others call God. However, love unwittingly becomes an obstacle in her sworn path.

With her father's death shattering her world, Mauri is torn away from everything she had once loved. Anger has replaced every emotion within her, and she seeks only one thing. To kill her father's killer. Even if the man is none other than Krishna Vaasudeva, the man whom people worship as God!

Someone is standing in the way though, reining in her bitterness when she is least prepared for it—the Rakshasa prince, Ghatotkacha! But, by the time love sprouts within her, Mauri has gone too far in her thirst for vengeance and has endangered Kamarupa, the high seat of the Supreme Goddess.

Does Ghatotkacha realise the true intentions of his lover?

Can Mauri fight her own monsters and defend the temple?

Can Mauri save herself and Ghatotkacha before both their worlds are destroyed?